The Surratt Revelation

Don Moore

PublishAmerica
Baltimore

ISBN: 1-4241-3549-4
PUBLISHED BY PUBLISHAMERICA, LLLP
www.publishamerica.com
Baltimore

Printed in the United States of America

The writing of *The Surratt Revelation* has been a happy adventure. I want to thank my wife, Pamela, for her unflinching support and her genius as my proofreader and guide. Our sons, Kayle and Kent, and their families have been there every step of the way—thanks guys. My manuscript typist and coordinator, Kim Vidito, has been always ready with suggestions and guidance—thanks Kim. Without these great people, *The Surratt Revelation* would never have been written.

Chapter 1

"Pat, another round of drinks over here!" the oldest of the three priests called to the bartender from the corner of the pub. "We haven't had a round for ten minutes. You're supposed to be looking after us." They sat around the little corner table, which was filled with empty ale bottles.

The youngest priest, Father Sean, was feeling relaxed and mellow. They were here for two hours. This was their custom twice a year and they drank the hours away. Father Gerry O'Flynn, a White Fathers Priest, was back from his six-month study leave at Notre Dame. He was reliving the experience day by day. Father John McFlynn, who was getting to his feet to roar for more ale, was a failed Jesuit and still bitter over the experience. Since leaving the order twenty years ago, he was the priest in a small parish in Cork, here in Ireland. He worked on research in his spare time.

Their semiannual visits to the pub in Dublin were becoming legendary, over the past decade. Many times, Father McFlynn spent his holidays at the American Seminary and the Jesuit Library in Rome. He regarded himself as a frustrated scholar who resigned himself to his present fate. He continued his latest tirade against the Jesuit Order.

"It's the same old story. They tinker around in politics until they come to a soft place and then they probe. When push comes to shove, they're rarely in the wrong place at the wrong time!"

"Oh, there you go again on the same old track. How often have we heard it, what's so special this time!" muttered Sean pushing his chair back to get more leg room. "I suppose you can give me an example or two to back up your claim!" he continued.

"Yes. As a matter of fact I can! When I was in the Jesuit Library last month, I was reading some old reports one afternoon when I met an American priest doing some research on the order's activity in America in the mid-1860s. He had heard there was a small Matthew Brady photo collection in their library. Brady was the great American photographer of the Civil War!"

"Yah, I've seen examples of his work when I was at Notre Dame," replied

Gerry. "Actually he was a damned good photographer; I'd recognize his work anywhere."

"Well," John continued, "there on a table was a great pile of the photos of the period. The father was doing work on the Civil War and he had all the pertinent ones out. There in a row was a number of pictures taken a few days before Lincoln's death and apparently related to the conspiracy to kill him. He was trying to identify two people in a picture. I don't know the reason he wanted to know and I didn't dare tell him. After that afternoon I never saw him again!"

There was a thump on the table as the bartender set down another three large steins of ale and muttered, "I think you good fathers have had enough don't you think?" He was a large overweight man with a protruding pot and dirty clothes.

Father Sean looked up with an Irish smile and replied, "Andy, you're starting to behave like a stupid Englishman! Move your Irish arse back behind the bar before I help you." The man walked away muttering to himself. The three priests roared in laughter.

"So, John, what was so earth shaking about some old pictures, specially if the Yank didn't know what any of the material meant?"

"That's the point! There were two men seated in the back row of a small picture who were Jesuits!" John snapped.

"So, what's the deal?" Gerry answered. "There are thousands of Jesuits all over the earth at any time doing a thousand and one things!"

"That's true, but they're members of the closest inner Order of Jesuits and the most secret one. This is the one you never hear about and which sometimes stays dormant for years at a time. They're the Jesuits' mafia!"

"I've heard a few rumours every few years about such an organization that gets involved in politics and assassinations and the like, but never paid much attention to it!" Sean mused.

"Well, believe it!" snapped John. "Those two priests in the picture were from this special order which is called the Order of the Red Rose. I recognized the little lapel pin that each of these priests wore in the picture. What I can't understand is why they allowed themselves be photographed! I've learned of a number of cases where public attention has been drawn to them and they go to any length to eliminate the source. I tell you, several cases would make the Mafia proud!"

"Jesus Mother of Our Lord," Gerry commented, "I've heard of letting the end justify the means, but this is ridiculous! I think we'd best be out of here and no more talk about this business! Besides I find the whole thing too farfetched to even bother discussing. Come on down to the mother house, I've got a bottle of good Irish stuff there and a pack of cards as well!" The other two priests grunted their ale-ridden agreement. As they started to rise, a small thin priest came up to their table and paused before speaking. He was a man emaciated in appearance and in his early forties.

"I'm looking for a Father McFlynn! Would you gentlemen know him or where I might reach him?

"I'm Father McFlynn!" he said. "What can I do for you, Father?" As he finished speaking his eyes darted to a tiny rose in his lapel pin. His face went ashen as he got to his feet.

"Would you please remain seated, Father, I'm afraid you'll be going nowhere. I work for the good and glory of our Mother the Church. I'm afraid you three know things that are best not known."

"What do you mean?" stammered Gerry, his face as pale as a new sheet.

"I mean simply for the good of the Church, your lives are about to end!" The other two priests sat straight up in the midst of their overindulgence. As they did the thin priest drew out a small but deadly Smith and Wesson with a large silencer attached.

"What the shit..." muttered Sean as the gun faced him for a moment before coughing. The small bullet caught him to the left of the breastbone throwing him back against the wall. He clawed at his chest in disbelief before falling in a heap. The other two priests were hit in the chest in rapid succession. Gerry collapsed in a heap, dead before his body hit the floor face first. John was struck higher up in the chest in a non-killing shot. He rose to his feet and tried to grasp the thinner man. He never had a chance. The gun coughed twice and the two bullets passed through his heart at point-blank range. He collapsed onto the table, his eyes in an open stare, and then rolled in a heap on the floor. The thin priest carefully turned each man over with his foot. Only Father Sean was still breathing. Two quick shots in the chest and he was dead. Standing over the bodies, the thin priest laid a small red rose across each man's dead face with the words:

AD MAJOREM DEI GLORIAM

He turned and to put his gun away when the large bartender arrived on the death scene. As he looked, his chin dropped and he gasped, "Mary, Mother of the Angels, what's been happening here?" he turned to the priest as he saw the gun rise to meet him. He raised his hands as if to protect him. The gun grunted once and a small red hole appeared in the man's forehead over his right eye.

He remained standing for an eternity and took a step back. Then a glaze came over his eyes and he fell lifeless backward bouncing off the bar onto the floor.

The priest quickly put the gun away in an inner pocket and stepped out into the dank humid air of a Dublin afternoon in March. As he did he muttered to himself, "To the greater glory of God!"

Chapter 2

The air-cooled engine on Tony's old Porsche roared in protest against the heat and altitude. Keeping one eye on the heat gauge he noticed the needle creeping into the danger zone. April, sitting at his side, glanced over. "What's the matter? The old engine overheating?"

"Yah! I'm probably driving it too hard! Besides at this altitude, it's not getting enough oxygen! But no matter, we'll be at the summer home in a few minutes."

"I love these hills. Look at the view of the ocean and the cliffs, they must be several hundred feet high!" she exclaimed excitedly.

"That's what I've been telling you about this Big Star country. I've travelled all over and I'll take this area ahead of anything else. I only wish I had the money to buy a place up here," Tony added.

"Who owns this place? You keep raving about it, so it must be quite a summer retreat," April commented. As she did, Tony glanced in her direction and pointed to the top of the hills, which they were approaching. She was a girl of average height and dark brown hair. She wore a pale beige summer dress that complemented her thin figure. Tony wore the standard California cutoffs and sleeveless T-shirt. His hair was short and blond.

"Gord's father is a vice president of the world division of Standard Oil and money is no object. It's around the next corner." In a few minutes, they turned a sweeping corner and drove into a large parking area. The summerhouse was palatial and overpowering in appearance. It stood at the back of a long-running slope with sculptured lawns, covering fifty acres. To one side of the house, which was built entirely of red adobe brick, was a large tennis court adjacent to a huge swimming pool. This, in turn, wrapped around the back of the house. When Tony parked the Porsche, April quickly got out and stood gaping at the house and grounds.

"It's the most beautiful place I've ever seen! It's unbelievable! Look at the pool and the grounds, it must cost a small fortune to keep up."

"That's no big deal, April, the Hasketts have a permanent man living here year around. He has a small apartment in the basement." April rolled her eyes in response. They pulled their two small overnight cases from the back seat and walked toward the rambling front door. As they did, he noticed five other cars in the yard with various plates.

A familiar voice with an Irish accent called out, "How y'are doing there, Tony lad, begora it's great to see you!"

Before he saw him, Tony replied, "Father Jim, it's been years, where the hell are you?"

"Right here behind you, you young dimwit!" the laughing voice continued. They turned and there was the cherub-like figure of Father Jim McGuire. He and Tony threw their arms about each other in a tight hug. The Jesuit priest was the image of a young Barry Fitzgerald, even to the steel-rimmed glasses he wore. Tony used to wonder if he actually tried to cultivate the image. He had known the man for over ten years since he sat in his classes in moral philosophy at Fordham University in St. Louis.

"And who might this gorgeous creature be?" he asked Tony as he looked April over from head to toe.

"You must be Father Jim McGuire. I'm April Savitz and I work with Tony in the history department at Cal Tech." As the priest spoke she blushed a deep crimson, her strong Catholic conscience coming quickly to the fore.

"Come on, I'll show you two to your rooms! Gord had to go down to the valley and get some more supplies for the weekend but will be back in time for dinner. Why don't you two get settled and come down for a swim!" He turned and walked down the long sweeping white staircase that dominated the central foyer of the house.

Tony threw the small overnight bag he had brought with him on the bed and put his shaving kit in the large bathroom. He was rummaging through his bag looking for the old swimsuit he thought he had put in back in LA. There was a knock at the door. He called out, "Come in, it's open!" and finally pulled out his old cutoffs he used for swimming and for his passion of surfing. He turned as April's voice came up behind him.

"I can't get over this house! Look at your bed, it's a king size, the same as mine. Boy, wait 'til Art hears what he's been missing. You ready to go swimming?"

"Give me a minute to change and I'll be with you!" he said as he went into the washroom. He was surprised to find it was equipped with a full four-person spa. Shrugging his shoulders, he pulled up his trunks, threw a large towel over his shoulders and returned to the bedroom.

"Boy, you've got a great tan, you must spend a lot of time on the beach.

Look at me, I'm as pale as a ghost!" April blurted and pulled up the knee-length robe she was wearing, exposing her right leg to the thigh.

"Well, let's get to the pool and do something about it," he replied.

Wandering through the huge houses they found the back entrance and stepped out onto the pool deck.

"Tony Cassell, for God's sakes how are you!" Bev Hanyk called out from the pool's edge. She was a short, slightly pudgy girl and wore a simple one-piece yellow swimsuit. She came running over to Tony and gave him a great hug.

"It's so good to see you! It must be over two years! Have you heard the news about Gord and I, we've set the date!" The words literally danced on her lips as she spoke. Tony was pleased. She and Gord had been two of his closest friends when he was in grad school and had helped him through several rough spots in his own life.

"Bev, this is April Savitz, my assistant at Cal Tech. She's here to help Gord and I with that problem that has cropped up in our research." The two girls shook hands and smiled warmly at each other.

"Why don't you both have a swim and I'll get you both a beer. It's been a hot day even up here in the hills. By the way that's Susan Quintesse, over there on the cot. She's a good friend." An attractive blond-haired girl in a flowered bikini lay stretched out on her tummy. Looking up she waved and lay back down. Her bare back glistened with sunscreen as she soaked up its rays.

Tony jogged over to the pool's edge, felt the water and dove in. Surfacing, he swam over to the edge where April had seated herself and dangled her legs in the warm water.

"What's the problem? The water's beautiful, so why don't you jump in?"

"Well, I'm not sure if I should with this suit! Art doesn't like me to wear my bikini, he says it's disgraceful. But, I know he's rather conservative. I think I'll go back to my room," she spoke, a note of disappointment in her voice.

"Oh, for Christ's sake, April, everyone wears them down here. Art's a stick, so don't pay any attention to him!"

Reaching out he set a hand on her warm thigh. She looked at him for a moment and then undid the robe and tossed it aside. Her suit was white and fairly skimpy. Hanging on to his hand, she held her nose and jumped into the warm water. A few minutes later he heard the familiar Irish voice from the pool's edge.

"Hey, Tony lad, come on out and have an Irish with me, we've got to talk." Looking up he saw the short scrawny figure of Father Jim. He knew there were probably some good reasons for his original request to see Tony. Especially here in the relative isolation of the Big Sur Hills.

Later, after several drinks over a table in the corner of the huge pool deck, the priest asked Tony, "How's the research into the Lincoln thing going? You were pretty excited the last time I talked to you."

"Everything is progressing as fast as we can push it. I brought April along as she knows more about the details than anyone around. We're having some difficulty getting to the various diaries and it's going to take time. The area we haven't done a thing in so far is a new examination of all the pictures taken at the time and the event. I shudder how long that is going to take!"

"You're saying you haven't done anything there?" the priest asked with a curious tone in his voice.

"That's right...and probably won't for some time!" He was about to mention he knew a gal who worked for Kodak and who was completing an exhaustive study of the Brady Collection, but was cut off by McGuire.

"Tony lad, sometimes there are those things in history which are best left alone! They become a waste of time and taxpayers' money. Those pictures have been looked at so often, there couldn't be anything new." For the first time in all the years he knew and loved the good father, he felt a funny feeling in the pit of his stomach over the whole matter.

"Listen, Tony lad. I'm going up and have a speck of sleep. I'll see you for supper. You go ahead and have a good time for me!" With these words he rose and walked into the house.

Tony meanwhile walked over to where April had stretched out on one of the lounge chairs. She was sprawled out on her tummy with the strap of her halter undone letting the sun get to her entire back. Her skin was pale and smooth. As he approached, she rolled over holding her top in place with her arms.

"How did it go with the good father?" she asked. "I was going to come over but the two of you seemed so intent. I thought different about it."

"As I mentioned before, the father and I go back to my student days at Fordham. He's a great guy, but there was something in his words I'm having trouble with. I've never felt it with him before. For the first time I felt I was talking with a priest."

"Tony, I remember talking with a young researcher at the office one day and she was talking about the resistance she encountered when she contacted the Stanton family over the missing pages of the Booth diary. So I wouldn't be at all surprised at the good father. Besides, I'm a Catholic and my dad once said, 'Once a priest always a priest.'"

"I hear what you're saying, but I'm still disappointed!" Tony replied.

"Would you rub some of that sunscreen on my back? That sexpot, Susan, is on the way over here and she's making eyes for you!" April said caustically as she rolled over on her tummy on the nearest lounger.

"Hi, Tony. Want to come for a swim? I'll beat you to the pool!" Susan said as she placed a warm hand suggestively on his shoulders ignoring April as she talked. She leaned over him and whispered in his ear, her full breasts almost falling out of her halter.

"Not right now. I want to put this screen on April," Tony replied coolly.

"Well, suit yourself, you'll be in the pool later all by yourself!" she snorted.

"I don't know about that!" April snapped as she rolled over and glared at Susan. "I think I can more than look after any of Tony's needs." Susan turned on her heels and walked back to the pool.

"What did that tramp whisper in your ear?" April asked with anger in her eyes.

"You don't want to know," he answered.

"Yes, I do, tell me!"

"Alright, she wanted me to come to her room tonight and she'd make it worthwhile!" he replied in embarrassment.

"Like I told you, she's a tramp!"

Chapter 3

"My research is going nowhere," Gordon Haskett muttered as he leaned forward to make his point. "We're no further ahead than those people who have been speculating on the Lincoln assassination for years."

"I thought you were making headway, especially with the Stanton family," Tony commented.

"That's what we all thought on my staff. Then, the doors were slammed shut. We still have hopes of getting those missing eighteen pages from the Stanton archives. This was especially true when we finally got access to the George Sultan papers," he added.

"I'm sorry, but I'm not familiar with those," Tony added in a note of surprise.

"They're the diary accounts that substantiate the fact the Booth diary was intact when it was first delivered to Secretary of War Stanton," Gordon Haskett continued.

"Holy shit. If you can establish that for a fact, what does it do to the character of Stanton?"

"That's where we've had to do a little bargaining to see the pages. Their authorities will let us see the missing pages as long as we agree to print nothing derogatory about Stanton himself," Gord said in a concluding tone. As he finished talking, April arrived at their table.

Gord immediately got to his feet. "April, I haven't had a chance to talk to you since you arrived. Tony told me about the work you've been doing on the Lincoln project."

April wore a simple cocktail dress of a white shiny material with an off-shoulder style. She pulled out a chair on the other side of the table and sat down. She listened to the train of conversation between the two men. Gordon turned to her and asked, "April, have you been able to bring anything to light over the past three months from your work?"

"If you are asking me that question about my work from all the existing material, then my answer is a quick no! But if you are referring to some newer material we have brought to light, then I have trouble giving you a definite answer."

As she talked, she crossed her pale legs that had picked up a fair dose of sun around the pool.

"I don't follow you," Gord said.

"I don't know how to say this except there has been some pressure to back off from a hitherto uninvolved source. It was a veiled threat of the most subtle nature."

"You have no idea where the threat is coming from?" asked Gord.

"That's right, not a clue as well as a reason why. If it were a family worried about the reputation of their ancestors, I can understand it. This is the case of the Stantons. I have no quarrel with that and would probably feel the same way."

"You're saying you think this other source is a new one but you haven't any idea where it comes from?" Gordon added.

"That's right, and further, I can find no reason behind it. All we can say is it is a real one," April said in a cryptic tone.

"We'll have to talk more tomorrow. Meanwhile if you'll excuse me, but I have other guests coming." Gordon rose from the table and walked back into his house.

"Tony, have you been introduced to this Susan Quintesse or whatever her name is? What a royal pain in the ass!" April asked as she looked at Tony.

"Not formally, aside from the little whisper in the ear this afternoon. All I know is she is the private secretary to this senator from Iowa who has been making such a fuss over the Lincoln conspiracy. I'm convinced he's onto something that will give him national prominence. Speak of the devil, look out, here she comes, bikini and all!"

"I knew you'd notice that!" April said sarcastically.

"Tony, darling, when are you going to come over and have a drink with me? You must be tired of having no one with any brains to talk to," she said acidly not looking in April's direction.

April stood up immediately. "Tony, I think I'll be going over there, the air about here has suddenly taken a rotten odour."

"Who's your scrawny friend, Tony? I saw her by the pool this afternoon but didn't recognize the body off the street."

April ignored the crudity and walked over to the pool area and sat down by the bar.

"Miss Quintesse, I don't know why you're here, but I would appreciate more of my own company if that were possible!" The girl's nose went into the air as she turned on her heels and strode into the house.

About half an hour later, Father McGuire found Tony sitting by the pool's edge talking to April. They got to their feet as he stopped and greeted them. He was dressed in a short-sleeve shirt and shorts. It was the first time Tony had ever seen him without a black clerical shirt.

"May I join you two? Or would I be disturbing you?" he asked.

"Of course not, Father. You're very much a part of my life and April here knows all about you."

"Would you join me in a beer?" he asked as he looked from one to the other. They nodded and he went into the kitchen to get them.

"Tony, are you going to ask him about his comments to you this afternoon? I think it's worth looking into. I'm disturbed by what I hear, especially from Gordon. I've talked to Bev in private and she's terrified about the whole business. She wants him to drop the whole matter!"

Tony looked at April in amazement as she talked. "You're right, I was thinking of asking him, which is good as here he comes with our beer!"

After fifteen minutes of engaging in small talk, Tony finally broached the subject.

"Father Jim, you made several comments this afternoon that have me concerned. You suggested in strong language we should stop these searches into the Lincoln conspiracy. What did you mean and what compelled bring you to bring it up?"

The priest looked at the younger man for a long time before answering.

"I know there has been an off-again, on-again interest in the story leading up to the Lincoln killing. I know for some the jury is still out. I'm convinced there are things in history that should be left alone. This is one of them!" he answered.

"But that goes against everything I believe in and you taught me!" Tony said with great feeling.

"That's true and I appreciate your position, but because of certain past experiences, I am sticking with my advice!"

"Father," April asked, "you may resent me asking this question, but I'm getting the feeling you've stumbled on some facts through your experience that are behind your advice!"

Tony squirmed as she had asked the question he had wanted to ask but hadn't out of his respect for the priest. Again the priest paused a long time before answering. Finally he spoke, "Young lady, I see you're one of those people who comes directly to the point. The answer to your question is yes! There was an incident in Dublin last week that brought this whole matter back to light! Three good friends of mine—all priests, and one of whom was a Jesuit like me—were brutally assassinated while they shared some drinks together!"

"What were they sharing that was so serious they were killed, especially in a small city like Dublin?" April asked.

"The word I used before was assassinated. They were killed in a systematic and professional manner. It had to be a part of some sort of elimination process. What they were involved in I don't know, but that was part of the reason for their semiannual get-together. They were close friends of mine and I'm going to miss them."

Tony looked aver at April. She was pale as she listened to the story as the details came out.

"Father, are you trying to tell us we're digging into this Lincoln thing too deeply?" Tony asked.

"On the contrary, it's a fascinating story that needs to be told and I wish you luck." With these words he got to his feet and said, "I want to bid you both a good night. I'm not as young as I used to be." With those words and a tight smile he left.

April and Tony sat and looked at each other. Finally April commented, "I still think he's trying to tell us something. I felt that from the first comments he made to you and I still do."

"From who, where and for what reasons, April?" Tony asked again.

"I don't know any more than you, but I think the good father knows a lot more then he lets on and he is running scared," April said as she got up and walked over to the pool in the twilight.

Chapter 4

The crowd roared its approval to the senior senator's keynote speech. The packed high school gym gave him a standing ovation. His twenty-five years in Washington gave him a feel for Iowa and its people. He was honoured when asked by the campaign manager for John Beecham, the junior senator, to give the keynote address.

As John Beecham sat on the podium he turned to Gloria. "Don't you think our campaign is off to a good start, dear?" His dark good looks and flashing smile brightened the platform.

She smiled and nodded towards the platform as the crowd chanted his name over and over again, "BEECHAM, BEECHAM, BEECHAM, BEECHAM, BEECHAM."

The roar of the stuffy gym charged him as nothing else. When his campaign manager suggested they open the campaign in Cedar Rapids, he was dubious. He was raised and practice law in Sioux City, on the other side of the state. Yet he learned early to trust advice. The state, east and south of Cedar Rapids, was a weak point in his first election six years ago, and he was soft there. Getting the senior senator on side was major coup and he was milking it for all it was worth. He stood up and strode to the bank of mikes for his acceptance speech. He crafted it well with the help of his writers, but insisted on his own personal theme. John Beecham was not only a Republican, but an unabashed conservative one! He fought in Vietnam and was decorated three times. Six months in the vet's hospital recovering matured him and given him a passion for his home state. That bitter period forged a steel-ribbed code deep in him. His was the calling to restore the glory of the American past. He saw it as a sacred duty of every patriotic American. His speeches were bathed in this heady brew. His overriding hero was without doubt, Abraham Lincoln. Even in his college days, he was caught up in the questioning of the conspiracy ideas of the assassination. He arrived at the conviction the Kennedy killing was the work of those wanting to upset the stability of the government as with Lincoln. He saw them as facts to be cleaned up, which took much of the aura from these figures in people's minds. He used this theme as a pillar of his speeches over the last two months. As he strode to the podium amidst the lights and noises he was to propose, if reelected, a reopening of both the Kennedy and Lincoln killings.

For the next thirty minutes, the eloquent ringing oratory of John Nathaniel Beecham mesmerized the twelve hundred people in the muggy gym, that fourth of April, 1986. It was be a night to remember. When he finished what many considered the finest speech of his career, the crowd went wild, chanting his name over and over. There were a few chants extolling his name for president in 2000. It would be a long time before Cedar Rapids forgot the evening.

At the end of the speech, a slim man in his early forties stood up and slowly wound his way out the main door. He looked like nobody and vanished into the night. A few minutes later a small Chevy Cavalier started up and drove down the main street.

There was bedlam around the front of the gym as great numbers of the news media crowded about the young senator and his wife as they emerged from the school. Again there were cries of Beecham for president. His wife, Gloria, looked resplendent in a knee-length black sheath dress and brown hair flowing to her shoulders. She was born in Des Moines but raised in Washington. She grew up knowing every nuance of the city. Later she worked for the State Department before meeting the senator. Many were extolling her as a breath of fresh air in Washington, much akin to Jackie Kennedy in 1960. An hour later, they were sitting in their limo outside the mayor's office preparing to drive to Dubuque. They waved their goodbyes and were preparing to drive off into the night when a stranger approached on the driver's side.

"Senator, would it be possible to talk to you for a few moments? It's very important!" he said.

"Look, sir," the senator responded holding his finger to his lips as he looked at Gloria. " We've got a important meeting in Dubuque in several hours and must get going! I hope you'll understand!"

"Yes, I think I understand only too well! Your political machine is busy on its way and you've no time for us little guys!" the stranger muttered. He had a thin pocked face shadowed with seedy unwashed brown hair. Gloria Beecham shifted impatiently in her seat. The driver was looking back from behind the wheel.

Suddenly a deadly-looking revolver and silencer appeared in his hand.

"Oh my God!" muttered Gloria Beecham as the gun coughed twice, catching her high in the chest and slamming her back against the car seat. Before he could shoot the senator, he was grabbed by the driver. He quickly clubbed him to the ground, catching him point blank in the face with one shot. Then in an action the senator could hardly remember he was on the ground wrestling with the gunman. In the confusion for the gun the trigger was squeezed and the weapon fired. The bullet passed through the gunman's head, blowing out the back of his skull and scattering brain and bone tissue on the pavement in a pool of blood.

A crowd quickly gathered and found the senator cradling his wife's bloody body in his arms. Tears were streaming down his face as he looked about him and asked, "Someone call the police, I need an ambulance?" A few feet away on the ground beside the dead gunman, was a bloody piece of paper with a few partially blurred words:

AD MAJOREM DEI GLORIAM.

Chapter 5

The Eternal City rang with the sound of the bells. The Holy Father had returned. Their crystalline notes echoed through the streets. The city seemed to take on its eternal purpose again. Since assuming his pontificate in 1559, Giovanni Angelo Medici was determined to turn the Church to the future. He prepared to conclude the Council of Trent, which had been on since 1545. His Holiness Pius IV, as he was officially known, was as loved a Pope as had ever sat on the throne of St. Peter. He left his diocese in Reguso in Sicily with great heartache and regret. But as he was fond of saying, he was serving a larger diocese.

Pius was concerned with the welfare of the Church. He was determined the erosion of the Reformation would never happen again. With that in mind, he set out to tighten the papal controls and inject a warning system so such an upheaval could never reoccur.

He remembered the blessing his predecessor gave to Ignatius Loyola and his new Order of Jesuits. He sent a message to the new head of the Jesuits, Fr. Luigi Giuseppi Pacelli, to meet him in his offices later this morning.

The air in the papal apartments was sticky and tepid. The Holy Father's private secretary, Father Achille Sarto, was an impatient and protective man. He came from Taranto in Sicily by birth and education. Entering the Pontiff's apartments at ten, he was surprised to find His Holiness reading the Greek New Testament. Again he was reminded of his mentor's agility in languages. As he turned to leave, the pope spoke. "Father Sarto, when Father Pacelli and his aids come please usher them in even if they are late. If possible we would like to finish early. We wish to go down to the poor areas of the city and do some parish work. There is a great need here!"

"But your Holiness, I don't see where there is time in your schedule!" Father Sarto replied with sincerity.

"Father Sarto, you know us well!" the Pontiff replied from his posh chair. "Over the years we have learned to keep contact with God's least, if at all possible. Years after we are gone, these other things won't matter, but these are the people our Master came to help. Set it up, Father!"

"Yes, your Holiness, immediately," he replied and left the Pontiff's study.

Twenty minutes later Father Sarto walked softly back to the pope's apartment and spoke, "Your Holiness, Father Pacelli and his people are here!"

"Do you want me to send them in?" he asked in a quiet respectful voice.

"Yes, immediately."

Several minutes later, three men dressed in austere black cassocks, which had become characteristic of the newly formed Jesuit Order, arrived in the papal offices.

The Pontiff, dressed in a resplendent white cassock, rose to greet his visitors. His presence and the opulence of the apartment were overpowering. Each man immediately knelt before the pope and kissed the extended papal ring.

"Father Pacelli, it is indeed a pleasure to meet you again. You may not remember but you visited our parish in Reguso several years before we became the Holy Father. Please be seated." Father Pacelli was a tall thin man and dedicated even in appearance.

"Your Holiness, you have summoned us and we are honoured to be here. How can we serve the Church?"

"How is the state of your new order? We are concerned with the health of the church!" the Holy Father intoned.

"Your Holiness, the Church is weak in northern Europe and elsewhere. The damage caused by Luther and his movement is still coming to the surface. I am proud to say we have been able to stem the erosion throughout southern Europe. Our order is already established in over fifty countries. How can our order be of help?"

"Father, do you think what we have done in the Church is enough to prevent this from happening again?" the pope asked.

"No, I can't say that it will prevent it," Father Pacelli replied.

"I thought so! Too many people have tried to convince me otherwise."

"Your Holiness, I fail to see where that involves our order," Father Pacelli answered.

"That's right! There's nothing more you could have done up to this point. Now I want to take us down a new track. First of all I want you to send out your two aids. This will be an entirely confidential conversation."

Father Pacelli turned and waved the others out. They hesitated. He waved again, this time with anger in his motion.

"When you Fathers are leaving please tell my assistant to stop the lunch from coming until we send for it." The two men quickly left the room.

"Father Pacelli, it is our thought we must set up a structure that will prevent such circumstances which caused Luther and his followers to rise—it must be nipped in the bud. The Church might not survive it! Do you follow us, Father?" the pope asked.

"No, your Holiness, I'm not sure I understand what you mean," the Jesuit replied.

"Father Pacelli, I want you to set up in your order a structure that will protect our Mother the Church. In this case, to quote St. Thomas, the end is the existence of the Church. You would be permitted to use whatever means you or this group would deem necessary. The Church must be preserved at all costs! Do I make myself clear, Father?"

Father Pacelli remained deadly quiet for a long time. The Pontiff spoke again.

"I can see we've caught you off guard! Let me put it another way. As Pope I will not tolerate even the possibility of this sort of event ever again. We will not be a Pope who presides over the breakup of the Holy Church. Father, remember God may be your Father, but the Church is still your Mother. We have to protect her with even more diligence we would be prepared to use to protect our earthly mothers!"

"Your Holiness, it is my deep regret that our sacred founder, Father Ignatius Loyola, wasn't here to hear your words. We will proceed immediately to set up such a small but effective group of people to promote and, most of all, to protect our Holy Church," Father Pacelli finished with tears of great emotion and passion in his eyes and on his face.

"I want to emphasize great care and secrecy be observed at all times! No one on my staff will ever know about this and we want the same in your order. You will be responsible only to me and my successors! Do I make myself clear, Father?" the Pontiff whispered in a voice that penetrated the bricks of the old apartment.

"Father Pacelli, I remind you of your order's motto, 'Ad Majorem Dei Gloriam.' If we forget this, the Church will die! Do we make ourselves understood!" the Pontiff snapped as he stood up. As he did Father Pacelli immediately kneeled and kissed the ring of St. Peter.

"Yes, your Holiness, I understand clearly. Rest assured we will not fail you!" The pope raised him by the elbows as he only did for those he required help from. The gesture wasn't lost on the other man. He walked quickly from the papal residence.

Chapter 6

The Cedar Rapids Police Station was in total confusion. The attempt on Senator Beecham's life turned the tranquil city of 100,000 upside down. Violence, that curse of American politics, had struck. It was before noon the morning after the killings. The constable on the front desk called through the intercom.

"The medical examiner is here to see the chief."

"This is the chief, Constable. Send the good doctor in!"

"Yes, sir," answered the constable's pleasant voice. In a few moments the young coroner rapped on the chief's door.

"Come on in, Bob, it's open," a voice called out.

He turned the knob and entered the chief's office. It was an oak-panelled room with two large windows overlooking the main square of this peaceful Plains city. Behind the big desk, piled high with papers and reports, sat the middle-aged figure of Chief Paternick. Looking up he signalled to a chair. After a few minutes silence the chief shoved his chair back and said, "Thanks for being so prompt on this one, Bob. It's going to be big and nasty. What have you got for me?"

"Well, on one point there's no problem. All three are dead from extreme trauma caused from gunshot wounds. In each case, death was probably instantaneous. Two of the victims, Mrs. Beecham and the driver, have been identified. The third is a problem. We don't know who the hell he is!"

"What do you mean, Bob? I'm having problems following you. Everyone leaves a hundred and one trails behind them in today's world," the chief replied.

"Well, from your men who examined the body, I know there wasn't a scrap of identification on him. We've taken pictures and got the artist to do a mockup. He did and we sent it out all over the country."

The chief was getting anxious. "And?" he asked.

"Nothing! Not a goddamned thing. It's as if no one has ever seen or heard tell of the man!" The chief sat with his mouth open. The doctor continued,

"But listen to this. There are no fingerprints. Not even any toe prints for that matter."

The chief stood up as he responded in an explosive burst. "How the hell can there be no prints? Everyone person in this goddamned country has prints. You've got to do better than that!" He paced the big office in a state of fury and continued to speak, "Bob, do you realize the effect of this? If we came up with a corpse that no one can finger, we're going to be the laughing stock of police departments everywhere!"

"Look, Chuck, don't take all your frustrations out on me. How the shit do you think I feel, especially with a body that seems to have come out of nowhere!"

The chief turned and pointed his large right forefinger at the doctor and muttered in anger, "What the fuck am I supposed to tell John Beecham? That some unknown stiff tried to kill him and zapped his wife instead? Besides, John Beecham's a national figure on top of it all! The FBI and all the news media are going to be over all of us like maggots on a fresh corpse. If you did your job, perhaps you'd have some better info for me."

"You know, Chuck, as a friend of mine on the city council said the other day, you're a nice guy to a point, after that you're a horse's arse. I've never realized how big a one until now! If you want any more information, you go ask him yourself. You've got yourself set up there so close to Jesus Christ, you can probably bring the stiff back from the dead. There's the rest of my report. You can take it and this job and shove it up your fucking ass!" With these words he turned and stormed from the office.

As he left, the chief roared behind him, "Show your fuckin' nose around here again and I'll have you in irons!" His voice echoed through the office. There was a silence throughout the office. The chief's door slammed with a rattle.

Twenty minutes later, there was a knock at the door. He didn't acknowledge. The knock came again. Still he refused to answer. Finally it opened and two men in conservative grey suits entered. The tall older man spoke, "Chief Paternick, I presume?"

"Yah, yah, that's me! And who the Christ are you, barging in here? Dr. Livingston, I suppose!" he snarled.

"I'm Agent Nyburg and this is Agent Sitzer of the FBI. I would remind you we knocked several times before entering your office. May we be seated?"

Chief Paternick threw up his hands and muttered, "The next thing I know, the governor himself will be coming through my door! Alright, what can I do for you?" He leaned back in his chair with a great sigh.

"Chief Paternick, we're from the Des Moines office of the bureau and are officially taking over this case. There are national ramifications and I think this will take some of the pressure off your shoulders. We've briefed the coroner before you talked to him and think his findings make our action even more pertinent." He stopped and watched the chief.

The man had calmed down and responded, "You're probably right! If what Doc says was true then there are facts here beyond our capacity to deal with! How the hell could anyone not have finger or toe prints? What did he have, some kind of surgery? My daughter had some nose work done last year and you should have seen the difference!"

"We're not at liberty to say, but we would appreciate your cooperation with us throughout our investigation. By the way, have you seen anything like this before?" He extended a blood-spattered piece of paper across the chief's desk. The chief picked it up and looked up at the agent.

"Is this supposed to mean something? It's just a familiar Latin phrase, what's the big deal?"

"Can you read the words?" the agent asked.

"Yes, of course, there are still lots of people who can read Latin," he growled, his impatience growing by the second.

"What does it say, if you please?" Agent Nyburg asked.

The chief picked it up again and looked it over for another moment. "Simply it says, 'To the greater Glory of God.' It's the motto of one of the larger Roman Catholic orders but I can't remember which."

"How can you remember these things, may I ask?"

"Because I'm a Catholic, you nitwit! Jesus Murphy, don't they teach you morons anything? Now it's my turn to ask you geniuses two questions. First, are those spots on that paper blood from last night? And do you think the shooting might be part of a greater conspiracy?" He sat smugly at his desk with his chin resting in his big hands.

"Chief Paternick, I'll try to answer each question," the agent muttered.

"Sure, Father Poulton down at St. Pats is a nun too!"

"Yes, Chief Paternick, the blood is from the gunman and we have reason to think there may be a larger connection to these killings. We'll keep in touch with you on these matters and hope you'll show us the same courtesy." As he finished, they opened the door and strode from the office.

Paternick muttered under his breath, "Assholes!"

Chapter 7

The rolling thunder of artillery echoed through the Belgian hills. There was new hope despite the overpowering presence of many Allied soldiers. Marshall Michel Ney was concerned when the attack came. There would be a linkup with the other French troops in the area. He arrived in Quatre-Bras at six o'clock and ordered his cook to get supper ready. He and his staff hadn't eaten since yesterday. Earlier he had sent his 71,000 men into action against Blucher's 85,000 well-equipped men near the village. After two hours of fighting there was no conclusive outcome and both sides had withdrawn. Ney was furious. He had no further orders to advance from General D'Erlori except to hold at Quatre-Bras for the night. He knew he had no choice but to wait with the fresh Corps until the next day! He believed the emperor would take personal command of the whole army. For the first time in twenty-four hours, there was a general lull in the fighting except for the occasional artillery barrage that sounded as his guns answered the Allied gurus. The testing continued through the night.

Following a substantial supper in his bivouac, the marshall relaxed over a good bottle of Burgundy his valet had smuggled into the camp. As he unwound he wondered about the morrow. What would be the outcome of the battle? He had been an unwavering follower of Napoleon since the Revolution. Even after the emperor's return from Elba, when he was in command of the new government's army, he vacated them to rejoin his former commander. Did Napoleon still have the magic of Friedland and Austerlitz? He remembered the horrors of the march back from Moscow in 1812. Yet what other hope did he have? Stepping outside his tent, he saw the fires of his soldiers by the thousands over the hills and beyond.

He was about to return to his tent when his chief aid stepped over in front of him and saluted.

"Sir, there's a messenger from Rome to see you! He says he's a Nuncio of the Jesuit Order and vital he see you!"

"Lieutenant, you know my orders! When we're in the field, especially

DON MOORE

before a battle, I do not see visitors, especially civilians. I thought I had made myself clear on that matter!"

"Yes, Marshall, you have, but this man's credentials come under the Seal of the Holy Father himself!" he stammered.

"No matter. His Church has no authority in France since the Revolution!" the marshall replied.

"Sir, he says it's a matter of the future of the country!" the young officer continued. "He says he wants thirty minutes of your time!" Ney looked over beyond the nearest fire and saw a portly man dressed in black, carrying a small case. Hesitating, the marshall wondered what was so important that would cause a priest to risk his life coming into the midst of a raging battle.

"Alright, send him to my tent," he muttered.

"Marshall Ney, sir, it is an honour to greet France's bravest soldier! No one has served their country as long and as well as you, sir. I'm Father Angelo Braschi, and represent the head of the Jesuit Order. I wish to talk to you, sir, on a matter of the greatest importance."

"Alright, but realize you were lucky to be alive and in one piece, Father."

"I beg to differ, Marshall, luck had nothing to do with it; it was by the grace of God. Remember, I travel under the Seal of the Holy Father himself." He looked at the imposing figure of Ney, who wore his full dress uniform, and stared him directly in the eye.

"You feel you're here by the grace of God, if I hear you right?" replied the marshall in wonder at the man's devotion to what he believed.

"That's right, sir. Luck had absolutely nothing to do with it. We Jesuits believe we have to work through the existing authorities, government and otherwise."

"But, the Catholic Church no longer has any authority in France. We saw to that in our Revolution when the pope supported the old order," Ney said with a certain tone of satisfaction, in his voice.

"You are correct…sir, and the way the Church behaved towards the French people, that was the way it should have happened. It was a lesson we didn't learn well from the Reformation."

"Father, this discussion is great for a classroom, but I'm a soldier and I have a battle to fight tomorrow! What in hell do you want of me?" Ney asked, the ramblings of the priest starting to grate on his nerves. There was a moment's silence. Ney poured himself and the priest a glass of the burgundy.

"I'll tell what I want from you, sir. You have remained a faithful member of the Catholic Church, have you not?"

"Yes, Father, if you know as much about me as you seem, you already know I've gone on record to credit my faith as the key factor in helping me get through the horrors of the retreat from Moscow. What's your point?"

"My point, sir, is simple. Every so often, the Church requires something from her people. Your faith was your 'rock' in the horrors of that terrible march home from Russia in 1812. Now the Church has a need of what you can do for her."

"I don't follow you, Father," Ney replied, now fascinated by the tight logic of the man.

"Marshall Ney, it's imperative the emperor not be the victor of the great battle tomorrow," the priest intoned. "Your Church requires you to do what you can to ensure Wellington is the victor. You, sir, have that in your power!" Silence hung like a pall in the tent.

"Do you realize what you are asking? This could be my death penalty," Ney snarled.

"If you do your best, and lose the battle, you're a dead man anyway, surely you realize that. Marshall, I risked life and limb to get here, now I'm asking you to risk a little more than you're probably risking already!"

"What if we ignore you and we win tomorrow!" Ney stood feet astride in front of the priest.

"Then, my brave marshall, you will have only the state of your immortal soul to contend with. You will have the knowledge you will have won the day and lost eternity and the link with your Mother the Church. Marshall Ney, the Church has a need of you at this special time! Few have the chance to serve her as you are now being asked!"

The marshall exploded ordering his aid into the tent, "Lieut., get this insolent priest out of my tent. The aid came running, gun drawn. As the priest was about to walk out of the tent in anger, he shoved the aid back. The aid fired one quick shot and the man fell to the ground clutching his chest, which was suddenly red with blood. The Marshall came running from his tent.

"Lieut., what have you done? He was a priest, and you may have killed him. Ney bent down and lifted the wounded man's head onto his lap. He was gasping, trying to talk.

"Marshall,.. Marshall… !" he gasped blood pouring from his mouth, "my mission is complete! The call of the Church has touched you! I have not failed! Don't fail her! The Church needs new hope in, France. You must delay your attack!" The man's voice became weaker. Suddenly he struggled to sit up, "you must not fail the Church! She has not, she has not failed you!" he

29

gasped again, as blood gurgled from his mouth. He fell back, eyes staring nowhere.

The Marshall looked up at several of his aids. He had seen, too many men die not to recognize the moment.

"The man is dead," he whispered. The aids carried the lifeless body to the edge of the camp for a quick soldier's burial.

In, the quietness of his tent Marshall Michel Ney sat and finished off the bottle of burgundy. Suddenly as clear as the sun, would rise, he knew what he had to do. He whispered to himself.

"Forgive me, my Liege, for now the call has come, and I must serve a greater Master!"

Chapter 8

Tony Cassell was frustrated. Every time he tried to have time with Gord to sort out details of the troublesome Lincoln project...Susan Quintesse was close at hand. Even April's rebuffs to her were momentary in their effect. Wherever he went on the property she seemed to be waiting. He returned to his room at nine, in anger. On a hunch, he stepped out and rapped on April's door. There was no immediate answer. He was about to leave, when the door opened. April stood wiping the sleep from her eyes. Her dark hair tousled in all directions.

"April, I'm sorry I woke you, I didn't realize you went to bed this early," he apologized.

"Tony, for heaven's sake, I'm glad you woke me! I was meaning to go for a walk or a swim, but fell asleep on the bed. Come on in., we must talk!" He sat in the large sofa chair by the desk. Her large double bed was messed up where she was sleeping.

"April, am I losing my mind—is this Quintesse dame coming on to me as strong as it seems? I don't know how to deal with her without making a scene. You know me better than most people. How should I handle this broad?" As he talked April had sat on the edge of the bed and rubbed her eyes and hair.

"Well, I admit as usual you come straight to the point," she muttered trying to get her thoughts in line. She wore a brief pair of shorts and sleeveless top and was barefoot.

"Tony, I think you're making a mountain out of a molehill. She looked super in a bikini, but you've got to ignore that if possible. Think of me and you'll get out of the mood real quick!" She seemed intent on putting herself down, a fact that Tony had noticed before.

"April, for Christ's sake, you know that's not true. I don't know what Art is trying to do but I get fed up with it," he said with an edge in his voice.

"Tony, I know you don't like him, but I don't want to lose him. He's there when I need him." Tony sensed a tension in her voice and was sorry he brought it up.

"Tony, I think you and I better have a talk with Gord on the Lincoln project. I've talked at length with Bev and she's terrified about things Gord has been telling her. I don't know what it's all about but I don't like what I hear."

"Listen, April, you're a great friend and I'm sorry if I've put you on the spot over Art. That's none of my business. I only did it because I'm a friend as well as your boss," he said slowly.

"I probably know you better than you know yourself, Tony. I'll try not to come on so strong. About Miss Bikini, stay out of her way and you'll make her madder than anything else." She got to her feet as Tony headed for the door. Stepping past her, she reached up and kissed his cheek and whispered, "That's for being a good friend as well as a super boss!"

He paused a moment and answered, "April, you look much better in your bikini than she ever could. I want to see you in it tomorrow!" As he stepped out, he thought he could see the hint of a smile on her lips. Pausing for a moment, he drew April to him and kissed her firmly. As she pressed against him, he could feel the soft pressure of her breasts against his chest. April stepped back with her hand against her open mouth. She turned and fled into her room.

People often asked him why he wasn't interested in her. He replied there had to be a certain relationship between boss and employee. Besides, she constantly talked about Art and there wasn't a day without a story about him flowing from her lips. Most of all, she didn't seem to be interested in anything from the personal side. As he stepped into his room he heard a noise. Then a voice.

"Well I see why you've ignored me! You've been humping the little brunette. Some guys have enough balls to take what they find. Not you, you're one of those with none, you've got to bring your own along." Looking in the darkness, he saw the pale face of Susan Quinette peering from the room at the end of the short hall.

"Why don't you go to hell, you stupid bitch, you've got yourself and that's the best you'll ever find."

Chapter 9

The emperor was furious. His orders were confused or lost. He called his staff together in the midst of the battle as it raged about them. His return from Elba was a triumph. The first two days of this campaign had gone well. Now it all came down to this one day, this 17th of June, 1815. His staff gathered about him, their uniforms filthy with the grime, dirt and blood of battle.

"Where is General Grouchy?" Napoleon demanded. "He was supposed to cut off Blucher and those damn Prussians! We had them on the run near Ligny! Now we have to stop them on the main field of battle."

"My lord, we have always obeyed your orders. I turned back two days ago on the orders of Marshall Ney!" replied Marshall D'Erlon.

"I never issued such an order nor would I have done so. Where is Marshall Ney?" snapped the emperor.

"We haven't seen him for the last two days, my lord!" responded one of the emperor's many aids.

"I want to know why Marshall Ney failed to attack Wellington yesterday. If he had done that he might have severely weakened Wellington's army and he would not pose the threat we are presently facing."

"My lord, there has been a serious breakdown in communications; which, if we don't rectify could cost us the battle. How do you want us to handle this matter?" Marshall D'Erlon asked. For the first time, Napoleon was silent.

"Gentlemen, we have few choices open to us. We must try to hold Wellington before he starts his assault and try to entrap him. I hope his force isn't too strong. Secondly, we have to make sure Field Marshal Blucher doesn't link up with Wellington. If that happens we're doomed. Gentlemen, this meeting is dismissed! Remember, we fight for the honour of France! Vive La France!" With these words, Napoleon turned and left.

Later, as he stood before his own private tent, Napoleon looked out over part of the rolling field of Waterloo as the battle increased in intensity. He muttered under his breath, "Ney, where are you? You have killed us! You have been faithful all through the best and worst of our campaigns. You even walked back from Moscow like the most common soldier. What greater loyalty can you have than to your Emperor and France? By your treachery you have destroyed France and shamed her honour!" Slapping his hand against his thigh, he walked into his tents a hunched, broken figure.

Many miles away Marshall of France Michel Ney stood and watched as his beloved First Corps charged into the British lines in the distance. He had received word Blucher and his Prussians were linking up with Wellington's forces. Ney knew the die was now cast. Unless there was a miracle, there was no chance for the French army to win the day! As he stood on the small knoll and watched his men charge, his chief aid asked, "Marshall, tell me why you delayed so long before ordering the charge. I fear the day is lost. Why have you done this?"

The marshall looked at the major for only a fleeting moment. "Loyalty, my dear Major, loyalty. Perhaps after I'm gone, you will understand!"

The major was stunned. He turned and looked towards the emperor's tent in the distance. At that moment he knew the army was doomed. On the slope of the next hill, he saw the series of British squares slowly moving toward the French lines. The classic British formation was secure as long as there was no swinging cavalry to sweep over them. The subtle delay of the Imperial Guard gave the British the time they needed. He heard movement at his side. It was his aid, Lieutenant Legere. He was visibly agitated.

"Why would Major Ney do such a thing? He's doomed us all."

"My young friend, it's a simple case of greater loyalty. The marshall had to make a choice and he has done so," the major replied in a tight voice.

"Why, sir, what greater is there in France than to the emperor?" the younger officer said.

"Lieutenant, in France there isn't a greater loyalty than to the emperor's throne. But remember there is always the throne of St. Peter. I've suspected Ney's loyalties for some time," he replied.

"Sir, are you saying Ney's orders are coming from Rome?" Lieutenant Legere asked.

"My young friend, since the Revolution we've known the papacy has looked for the ways and means to bring the emperor down," the major stated.

"How can that be? I've never seen priests in the court or the army?"

"Don't turn your back!" the major snapped.

Chapter 10

It was a hot and steamy day in May. A heat mist hung over the Potomac and the city core. The Jefferson and Lincoln Memorials were barely visible.

Lynn Pollard left the National Archives with her package of old pictures from the Brady Collection. She was in the final weeks of her research for the project and she was relieved. She was nearing the end of her seventh year here in Washington. Following four years teaching at Kent State in Buffalo she went to work at the Kodak Research Lab in Rochester. After two years they sent her to the company office in Washington. She was assigned to Washington to upgrade historic photography in the years following the Civil War. As part of her work she was completing research for Cornell University's Department of Photography and Artistic Design. The material was prodigious and the work tedious. She undertook the project out of a longtime fascination with the development of photography in its early years.

She placed the briefcase in the trunk of her Prelude and drove across the city to her office. It was two-thirty when she arrived at the Kodak office. Walking through the entrances she called out to the receptionist, "Hi, Maggie. How are you this afternoon?"

"Why, Miss Pollard., it's good to see you. I'm fine. How's your project coming?"

"Oh, I'm getting there. I should be back in the office full time in another two weeks. By the way, how's my fill-in doin'?"

"She's getting along pretty good, although I wouldn't be worrying about your job, if I were you!" Maggie replied with a laugh.

In her cramped office, Lynn laid the big file case on her desk and walked to the window. She looked over the city and down the river through her tenth-story window as she removed her green raincoat. She enjoyed her job, but was glad to get out of the office. In the distance the towering Washington Memorial probed skyward like some giant phallic symbol. Shrugging her shoulders she wandered back to her desk. Opening the brown file case, she pulled out file after file of pictures of the 1860s and '70s from the Brady

Collection. Many of these used the old daguerreotype process, which she had studied for years. She felt many of them had sharpness and quality equalling pictures of the present day. Slowly she laid these copies out in order on a large table. Two hours later, bleary eyed and with her back aching, Lynn sat in her large lounger and sighed. The pictures of the Brady Collection all looked alike after a while because of the early stilted posing approach. Taking a break, she walked out to the small staff kitchen to get a cup of coffee. Maggie was there getting ready to go home.

"Well, Miss Pollard, do you want to see any of your messages or shall I keep giving them to your fill-in?" she asked.

"No, no. Maggie, I don't want to see anything until I come back. If I look at one of those, then I'll have to do them all and then I might as well come back full-time. Besides it wouldn't be fair to my replacement," Lynn replied.

Maggie nodded and smiled. "I appreciate your professionalism, Miss Pollard! That makes my job much easier. I'll see you when you come back. Have a good weekend!" Maggie was a pleasant plump woman in her early fifties. Her family was grown and spread all over the country. Her husband died of a massive stroke three years before. She had a rough time but Lynn and the rest of the staff rallied behind her. The office had become her family and she rapidly became a "super receptionist," coming in on weekends and staying late every evening. She waved to Lynn as she walked to the elevator.

Looking at her watch, Lynn wondered about supper. "I'll get something at a fast-food place on the way home," she muttered to herself as she wandered back to her office. In front of the large table, she tackled the varied miles of old photos. She ran her eyes over the myriad of faces. In almost every case the eyes stared out from the snaps, penetrating the conscience of the viewer. Her back was bothering her again as she hunched over the table. She sat at her desk and stared at the rows of pictures littering the shelves. She glanced at the enlarged copy of Lincoln she made a few years ago from his last known picture. It had the quality of gentle strength she remembered in her dad. His untimely death in Vietnam in 1966 still bothered her. He had thrown himself on a Viet Cong grenade to save three other marines. Yet there was a five-hour delay getting him to the nearest MASH unit. Less than three hours after he arrived, he died from acute bleeding. A doctor later said he would have lived if he had arrived several hours earlier. Lynn's mind leaped back to the present with a sudden intensity. For some reason her memory brought up a face she had seen somewhere in the past several hours. Jumping up, she leafed through the piles of pictures. Finally she stopped. There was the picture that been haunting her off and on for several years. She knew she had seen it somewhere before.

Here was an enlarged detailed photocopy of an old daguerreotype taken in a living room in the late 1800s. Picking up the pictures she could see the heavy drapery and ornate picture frames of the period. There were ten people in the photo. It was a picture similar to one directly underneath it. Picking the other up, she recognized it. It was taken in March of 1865 in Washington. The date was written in pencil by some researcher underneath as well as the names of four people. She read through them: Payne, Surratt, Herald, Atzerodt. In the back row there were four faces but only two names, Surratt and Spangler. Lynn wondered why the name Surratt was listed twice, and then she noted the first Surratt in the front row was a woman. Why were two of the faces unnamed? Photography was still in its infancy and if a person was photographed, it was important to get the correct name. Lynn was a concerned about the lack of identity from a historical viewpoint. The second picture was identical to the first except the two unidentified men were missing. Now she was really stumped. She was getting hungry and didn't want to be on the streets alone after dark.

It was five years since her violent assault and rape. Yet it still haunted her as it were yesterday. Again she had wished her dad had been present to help her cope with the problem that grew as the years passed. Shoving the pictures into her slim briefcase and putting on her raincoat, Lynn headed out of the office to her car.

As she wound her way through the heavy suppertime traffic, her mind went back to the picture with the two extra faces. It bothered her because she hadn't seen the picture before and secondly the two new faces weren't identified. Who were they and why was there a picture without their presence?

Chapter 11

Lynn Pollard wandered about her flat for an hour looking through different books she had compiled on American history and the Civil War period. Finally she found the one she wanted, the standard pictorial history of the Civil War. It had the best collection of Brady prints of the period. She found the one she wanted. It was identical to the first picture she brought home from the office. She compared it to the second one. The one in the book had eight people in the picture. It was identical to the one she had from the archives. Where had the second one come from? Who were the two extra faces in the second picture? Had the picture been in the archives all these years and simply been overlooked? The more she looked at the second picture, the more puzzled she became. How could a picture of this importance be overlooked all these years? She had to get some outside advice she could trust.

The only person she could think of was Frank Baird. He was an old friend of her father who remained active in the history department of Harvard long after his retirement age. There was a flap at first but that was over fifteen years ago. Now, he had become an institution. The man still put in fifty hours a week and kept a pace few of the professors half his age could match. His fifty-year area of specialty was of the Civil War period.

Lynn dialled his number but there was no answer. She left a message on his machine.

"Frank, Lynn Pollard here, could you give me a call in the morning after nine. I've come on a problem and I don't know how to tackle it. Thanks. Oh ya, how are you, you old fart?"

Lynn's apartment was on the fourth floor of a modified brownstone fifteen miles outside the city. It was small, but all she could afford on the salary Kodak paid her. There had been a number of opportunities to move up in the company, but the failure of her marriage to Eric had taken the drive out of her. This in combination with the assault and rape two years later almost destroyed her.

She changed to a pair of cutoffs and an old T-shirt, poured herself a cold beer and took a seat out on her small balcony. It was unusually warm this year in the capital and she wished she could afford a spring holiday. She sat for about a half hour before the microwave turned itself on and off with her dinner. Taking her leftovers from the last weekend, which she had frozen and now reheated, she returned to the balcony. She could eat anything she wanted and it had little effect on her slim figure. Only Eric made an issue of her thinness, calling her a bone rack, to the point she was ashamed to go out in public. She was a tall girl, over five feet ten inches in height, with dark brown hair and flashing black eyes to match. The breakup of her marriage took a heavy toll but nothing compared to the assault and rape. Many single men asked her out, but were quickly rebuffed. She in part retreated into the world of extreme feminism. She came face to face with Frank Baird on that issue. She had been lecturing on a part-time basis at Harvard. Two years after the assaults she accused him of not promoting her on the basis he was an aging sexist. His response was simple. She hadn't been promoted for one simple fact. A better-qualified person got the job. She was humiliated but knew the man well enough to know she had brought the issue down on her own head. As she finished her supper, she continued to rehash the past in her own mind. Suddenly the phone rang. Picking it up, she heard the familiar voice of Frank Baird.

"Lynn Pollard, are you there? Thank God. It's Frank Baird here. Hell, it's good to hear your voice! It must be close to a year! Listen, how are you?"

"Frank, I couldn't be better, I've been busier than a wet hen! How about yourself?"

"As usual, Lynn, you're full of bullshit! I want to know how you really are inside. Remember who you're speaking to. At my age, I can't afford to be anything but direct." Lynn felt a sob catching her in the throat as she gulped with the man's insight and directness.

"I never could fool you any more than I could fool Daddy. It's coming, Frank, but I don't know if I'll ever be fully over it. But thanks for asking. Frank, I need to see you some time on Monday afternoon. I've found an old photograph and it has me stumped."

There was silence on the other end of the line.

"What kind of a picture are you talking about, Lynn? Old ones from the latter half on the 1800s are a dime a dozen," he replied.

"What would you say if I were to tell you I have found an original Matthew Brady from the Civil War era? I've never seen it before nor can I find any trace of any one like it," Lynn responded.

There was a distinct tone of interest from Baird that was evident even on the phone.

"If you've got something even close to what you say, I want to see it immediately. What makes you so sure it's a Brady?" he asked.

"Very easy," Lynn replied, "from the general style of the poise and the deportment of the subjects. But mainly because it's identical to another famous Brady, with the exception of two additional people."

Baird was quiet. Then he spoke with tension in his voice, "Look, Lynn, I'm playing on a hunch here, but could we possibly get together tomorrow for lunch? I'd like to see this picture as quickly as possible."

Lynn was taken aback by the sudden response. "Well, I suppose so!" she replied.

"If it's inconvenient or if you've made other plans…?" he asked.

"No nothing, Frank," she responded. "There's a little Italian restaurant near here and we could eat there if that's all right"

"That's great! I'll pick you up at eleven-thirty, is that OK?" he inquired.

"Frank, that'll be fine."

"It'll be good to see you again, Lynn. My daughter Cathy was asking about you recently and I was saying I hadn't seen you in near a year."

"How old is she now, Frank, if you don't mind me asking?"

"Hell no, I'm damned proud of the whole damned crew, all seven of them! Cathy's forty-seven, believe it or not, and best of all she's a grandma three times over."

Lynn started to laugh into the phone.

"I hear you laughing and know what you're thinking! The old man is going to live forever! I'm eighty-one, so there, you don't even have to ask!

"Listen, I'll see you tomorrow and don't forget those pictures. By the way, are you still in the same building?" he asked quickly.

"Yes, no change!"

"Good then, I'll see you just before noon! Sleep well, my dear."

Hanging the phone back in its cradle, Lynn put her dirty dishes in the washer and got ready for bed. Changing to a thin pair of pajamas she settled down for a short read for Tom Clancy's *Without Remorse*.

Finally after reading for an hour, Lynn wandered out on her tiny balcony and gazed out over the rooftops. Her spirits were low these past days and she wondered what she was accomplishing. Maggie suggested she take a holiday South, but it held no interest. She climbed back into bed and drifted off to sleep.

Chapter 12

A strange sound echoed in the room. Tony stirred and went back to sleep. The sound came again. He stirred and sat up. He heard nothing. There it was a rapping on the bedroom door. He stumbled out of his bed and staggered to the door. He opened it and the slim small figure of April Savitz walked in.

"Tony, I'm sorry to wake you but we have to talk!" she whispered as she closed the door behind her.

"What time is it anyway? I was out cold," he muttered as he scratched his head and sat on the side of his bed.

April came over and sat beside him. "Tony, Bev gave me this note before I turned my light out. I was going to leave it 'til the morning but got curious and had a quick look. That's when I got scared and I had to talk to you!"

Looking at his watch Tony saw it was nearly four o'clock. "That's all right, April, I was so fed up with that Quintesse broad, I decided to go to bed. Lets see the paper Bev gave you!"

April handed him a small note that was blank except for some printing:

IF YOU AND YOUR FIANCÉ WANT TO REMAIN HEALTHY, TELL HIM TO LEAVE THE LINCOLN BUSINESS AS IT IS! DIG ANY MORE AND YOU'LL BE DIGGING YOUR GRAVES!

Tony reread it. Finally he looked up at April. She was pale and motionless. "Who gave this to her?"

"That was my first question! Apparently it came in the mail yesterday but she didn't open it until late last evening. Tony, I'm nervous, what's going on?" April said in a low voice.

"We've got to get a list of all the people who might be affected by the research we're doing into the conspiracy. Can you think of anything new we've uncovered that might threaten the descendants of those implicated in the original conspiracy?"

She sat looking out the window into the darkness. She turned and said, "No one to whom we might be a threat. As you've said yourself, our policy from the outset has been to investigate with the full agreement of everyone, now this!"

Tony was half-asleep, but his mind was running over many of the details they had covered the past nine months.

"You know, April, the interesting thing about the note is the reference to the Lincoln conspiracy and nothing about Kennedy. We've spent as much time there. I don't know." As he spoke, he realized he was wearing only a pair of boxer shorts.

"Listen, I'm sorry I've been half dressed. Wait, I'll get some clothes on. Hah! Now you know what I wear in bed," he said with a snort of laughter.

April looked at him shyly. "Tony, I woke you up with my concerns, you don't have to be apologetic. Besides you look great without your shirt. That damn Susan accused me of sleeping with you!"

"Yah, I know, she didn't put it so politely with me! But then, I wasn't polite with her either, so I shouldn't complain," he answered.

April got up and walked to the door.

"Tony, I'm afraid! Do you think we should drop our research?"

Tony picked up her hands as she prepared to leave. "No, that would be yielding to blackmail. I'm concerned who is behind the note. Why would they start with Bev unless as a subtle scare tactic? Listen, April, you've got every reason to be afraid. If you want out, say the word and that'll be fine with me."

She looked at him and replied, "If you can stick it out, then so can I!" As she spoke she kissed him, quickly running her hands over his muscular chest. He caught her and drew her against his chest, slipping his arms about her. He ran his hands under her PJ shirt and caressed the smooth skin of her back. She shuddered and buried her head in his shoulder.

"Tony, we shouldn't," she whispered before his lips pressed hard against hers. His tongue began to probe gently into her mouth and she responded with passion. She sobbed and was losing control of her usually calm demeanor.

"April, I'm not good at this you know." He ran his hands to her front gently rubbing the soft mounds of her surprising firm breasts. As he did he felt her nipples harden with her rising passion. She gasped and stepped back, still holding his arms.

"I'm sorry, April, I've been away out of line, please forgive me. I had no right. I've been such a twit with you," he said, ashamed for taking advantage of her weak moment.

April took both his hands in hers and said, "Tony, don't blame yourself. I think I wanted you to do that as much as you did, perhaps a whole lot more. I'll tell you something, you've stirred more passion in me right now than Art has in three years. He's never touched me," she replied with a sob. She raised her deep brown eyes to his as they swam with tears.

Tony was stunned and muttered angrily, "Well, that's his loss!"

April opened the door and started to leave. He closed it quietly before she stepped through. There was a look of puzzlement in her small face

"Tony, I don't know if we..." He drew her to him and kissed her more passionately than before. As he did, she shuddered and pressed against him hiding her face against his shoulder. There was a look of puzzlement and a slight smile on her face as he started to undo the three buttons of her shirt. He slid it slowly down her arms. Her breasts were not large but high and firm. He caressed them gently. Her nipples became erect as she pressed against his warm chest. He heard her sobbing. He held her tight in his arms as great racking sobs shook her small frame; he held her saying nothing. Finally, she drew back and was about to speak. He put a finger against his lips and shook his head. Again he drew her lips to his. As he kissed her, his tongue began to probe deep into hers. She whimpered and pressed against him again. He kissed the gentle skin down her neck beneath her ear caressing her back as he did. She moaned as she felt a new feeling of warmth and desire surging inside her. He ran the end of his tongue across her chest until her firm nipple was in his mouth. She gasped as her lips hid in his hair. She began responding to his caresses with vigour from deep within her. As she pressed again she was alarmed when she felt his rising erection pressing hard against her loins.

He whispered in her ear, "April, this is right and I think we both want it so much." As he spoke she sobbed again and he cradled her against his firm chest.

He led her over to the window, which looked out into the small balcony. He left the patio window open for air. She stood for a moment in the moonlight. As she did he undid the strap of her PJ bottoms. They fell to the floor with a whisper and she stood naked in the pale blue moonlight. She turned and looked at Tony with a deep smile. Her waist was small and the slim lines of her figure broken only by the dark patch of pubic hair where the fullness of her thighs met. As she stood, he ran his hand down across her abdomen and touched the soft folds between her legs. April moaned and led him by the hand to the bed. There she sat and drew him to her. She shoved his boxers to the floor and giggled as she saw his surging erection. She began to caress him with the tips of her fingers and with her tongue. There was a new sense of peace about the girl. The fear and reluctance were suddenly replaced by an assertive passion. Slowly she drew him toward her mouth and ran her tongue along his manhood. Tony moaned and he began to spin as she caressed him over and over again. Finally she slid him into her open mouth. He felt his control slipping away. This was not the gentle April he had known for three years. She eased him down on his back on the bed and thrust him into her mouth again moaning as she did and rocking back and forth. He seemed to be another person. Suddenly he rolled over and slid between her legs. As he did she gasped loudly, "Hurry, Tony, please hurry, I want everything now." His erection began to caress her deep folds and she writhed as the waves of passion washed over her. April's mouth sought out his as he began to probe gently into her. She writhed and moaned. She locked her legs around his hips. She gasped. She sucked in a great lung full of air as he plunged deep into her. With a deep moan, she arched her back, opened her mouth and moaned loudly. They were gasping in ecstasy. Finally as they reached the peaks of their passion, he sensed the heat of his seed moving deep inside her. She thrashed about on the bed in the peak of her surging passion. Finally speechless and exhausted, they fell in each other's arms and were sound asleep.

Several hours later, Tony awoke to find April gone. He felt bad she had to get herself up and out before the others. Walking to the bathroom he noticed a message stuck to the mirror in her familiar printing:

PLEASE DON'T HAVE ANY REGRETS ABOUT LAST NIGHT! I NEEDED TO BE WITH YOU BUT THERE'S NO WORRY ABOUT ENTANGLEMENT. I'LL NEVER FORGET, YOU'VE DONE MORE FOR ME THAN YOU'LL EVER KNOW! APRIL.

He walked to the shower and stepped into the streaming water.

Chapter 13

Lynn was ready at ten-thirty. She wore a short orange skirt several inches above her knees. She had good legs and liked to show them to the best advantage. She wore a matching orange blouse. She had cut her dark brown hair in a short bob several months ago but left the deep streaks of grey. She would be thirty-six in October, and wanted to look her age.

Her disinterest in men was the subject of morbid conversation at the office and amongst her friends, but she refused to date after her assault. She felt everyone had given up on her or assumed she was gay. As she told her friends, she really didn't care. She regretted not having a family but was content to be an aunt to her sister's brood of six.

The doorbell rang. Opening it she was happy to see the pleasant face of Frank Baird. He smiled widely and threw his arms about her.

"God, it's good to see you, Lynn! You're looking wonderful!" he gushed enthusiastically. He stood back and looked her up and down to the point she started to blush. "I'm glad to see you've put on a little weight too, all in the right places, I might add!"

Lynn could hardly speak. Finally she muttered, "Frank, I can't say how much it means to see you. You get younger every time I see you!" she added with a rare twinkle in her eyes,

"There you go with your blarney again! I figure I'm an old codger who won't quit." He was a man of average height and starting to show his age. He had a great shock of white hair and a complexion with a reddish tinge that gave him a Santa Claus look. When Lynn was a little girl he played the role for her and Tracey and his own kids. For the first time, she noticed a slight tremor in Frank's hands.

"You ready to go or do you have to do anything else to yourself?"

"No, I have to pick up the pictures and I'm all set." She grabbed her large bag and light jacket and closed the door behind them. As they walked to the curb she noticed he still drove the same Caddy. They drove about twenty minutes and Lynn pointed the way to the restaurant.

After a big lunch of pasta and red wine, Frank leaned back in his chair and asked, "Now, where is this picture that has you so wound up? You sounded as if you found the missing link."

Reaching for her bag, Lynn took out the small pile of copies and pictures she brought from the archives. She handed him the first picture with the original six figures. Frank Baird looked at them in silence. After a moment or two, he laid it on the table and commented, "So, what's the big deal? I've see this one a thousand times. You must have access to one hell of a colour copier to give you quality like that!"

"Now, what do you think of this one!" she asked as she set the other picture on the table. He picked it up almost casually. Then he jerked it forward. He sat straight up in the chair. Fishing in his pocket, he pulled out a large magnifying glass. He studied the picture for five minutes. Lynn was beginning to wonder what she had stumbled on. Finally he set the picture down with his usually ruddy face an ashen grey.

"Where the hell did you get this picture?" he asked hoarsely.

"One of the girls over at the National Archives found the original daguerreotype in amongst a pile of old pictures about to be thrown out," she replied.

"Jesus Murphy," he whispered under his breath. "We might have lost what may be the greatest pictorial find of the century. If this picture is what I think it is, we've got some work to do. Lynn, where is the original?" he asked bluntly. "It is important it be kept under lock and key at all times."

"Right now, it's at my apartment. I brought it home by mistake. I'd planned to take it back on Monday. Frank, please tell me what's on your mind. I've never seen you so agitated."

"Lynn, if this picture is authentic, it could be dynamite. I've never seen those two faces before. What's scary is they could be key links for a new inquiry into the reopening of the assassination of Lincoln. You see the original picture was taken in Mary Surratt's living room in late March in 1865. The other is from the same location. Everyone's clothing is the same, but if you look close, the poses aren't identical. That's why I wanted to use my magnification. The picture was taken at the same time, but it isn't a doctored version of the first one!"

"Frank, who are those men?" Lynn asked, a note of anxiety in her voice.

"I don't know. They aren't familiar but there are some details about their clothing that's ringing bells in the back of my mind. That's where I'm stumped," he replied, his voice tight.

"Frank, tell me, what are we looking at? Is it something we should be concerned about?" she asked again.

"I know you're worried and you've every right to be. Let me put it this way, you've stumbled upon the first fresh clue in a mystery that has been running for over a hundred and thirty years. There may well be people who don't want the whole mess opened up again and in addition new and fresh evidence coming into the picture. I think you and I had better be goddamned careful until we see where this thing will go."

"What do you suggest we do?" she asked with a certain feeling of foreboding.

"Keep our mouths shut until we find out if anyone else knows about this picture. You keep everything at home and give me this copy. I want to do some further tests to check out details. Listen, I'm going to have to go, I'm heading back to the office at the university. They've hired a couple of these new geniuses who don't know their asses from their dicks so I have to bail them out. Come on, I'll run you home."

"No, you go right ahead by yourself! I've some shopping to do and Ill take a taxi," she said.

"You're sure, Lynn?" he asked

"Of course...besides, I want more answers on that picture!"

"OK. I'll be in touch by the first of the week."

She waved to him as he walked out of the restaurant after he stopped to pay the bill. Fifteen minutes later Lynn walked into a large mall and a ladies-wear store. As she was approaching the main entrance, she noticed a small girl dart out behind a late-model car backing from its parking slot. Dropping her purse she scooped the child up from the large tires in the nick of time. Her quick movement threw her off balance and she stumbled into the side of the next car and fell in a heap. Dazed for a moment, Lynn struggled to her feet clutching the child tightly.

"Angie, Angie... Oh my Lord," stammered a woman in her late sixties as she rushed to Lynn's side. Catching her breath, Lynn gently let the child to the ground.

A young man came to Lynn's side and said, "Ma'am. Are you all right? That was one hell of a brave thing you did." He held her by the right arm as a crowd gathered.

"Yes, I'm fine! I wasn't sure there for a minute."

The older woman was hysterical as she clutched the little girl to her. As she did Lynn noticed a younger version of the child standing at her side.

Taking the lady by the arms she and the young man escorted the three people to a small bench. Lynn knelt down before the little girl she had saved.

"Angie, don't be afraid of me! I'm the lady who saved you from that big old car. You might have been hurt." The tot lifted her tear-streaked face and threw her arms about Lynn's neck. They sat there for a spell and Lynn comforted her and her sister who had climbed onto her lap as well. Lynn was moved to tears.

Finally the older lady spoke after a great struggle. "I'll never be able to thank you for what you've done for me and my two precious ones. If she'd been hurt, I wouldn't have wanted to live!" As she talked she started to sob again. Finally she said, "These are my grandchildren! I don't see enough of them and I don't know how Angie ever got away from me."

"Grandma," little Angie blurted out, "I had to get my new ball, I couldn't lose it!" She spoke with a wide-eyed innocence. Lynn answered before she realized her growing affection for the child.

"That's all right, sweetheart, we'll get you another one! But you must be careful with these cars; they could hurt you really bad! I want you to promise me that, will you?"

"Yes," she whispered, "I'll try, but…" She stopped and hesitated.

"What's the matter?" Lynn asked.

"I don't know your name!" she asked with great earnestness.

Lynn laughed. "I'm sorry, Angie, I'm so silly. My name is Lynn, Lynn Pollard! And I'm glad to meet you!"

"My name is Angie Fleming and this is my sister Francie and my grandma!" She spoke with grave seriousness, and Lynn and the other lady started to laugh. The tension broke. A small crowd had gathered about them and applauded.

The older lady held out her hand to Lynn and said, "I'm Martha Fleming and I'll be grateful to you for as long as I live."

Chapter 14

Lynn stirred to the ringing of her bedside phone. She rolled over and sat up. She shook her head to clear it; she had slept so soundly.

"Lynn Pollard please," a deep resonant male voice asked.

"This is her speaking."

"Ms. Pollard, my name is Scott Fleming. You don't know me, but you met a number of my family yesterday afternoon."

"Of course, I remember, Mr. Fleming. You have a delightful family," Lynn answered.

"You saved my daughter from serious injury and perhaps worse! You met my mother and she told me the whole story. Would it be possible to meet you? I find it so difficult to say thank you over the phone."

"Mr. Fleming, that's not necessary. I'm glad I was where I was at the time. I shudder to think what might have happened."

"That's why it's important for my family to thank you in a more personal manner. If something had happened to Angie..."

There was a silence on the phone. Lynn was sure she could hear sobs but she said nothing. She answered quietly, "Mr. Fleming, if that is what you'd like, then I'd be meet happy to be a part of it, but please understand, it's not necessary. By the way, please call me Lynn, everyone does!"

"Lynn, you've made me feel much better. Listen, we have a family dinner every Sunday night here at home around six, could you join us?"

"I'd love to. Where do you live? I know the city well but there are parts I don't like to drive through after dark," she asked.

"I couldn't agree more! Listen, I'll have Mother pick you up late tomorrow afternoon—she was raised in the city and is a tiger behind the wheel—then you can leave your car at home. I'll drive you home later myself. I'm in the OR all day at Bethesda and tied up until late in the afternoon. Now if I could have your address. I'll give it to Mother and we'll see you tomorrow," he finished.

"Thanks. I'm looking forward to meeting you in person!" She waited for the mother to come to the phone. When she did she gave her instructions to her apartment house.

Getting out of bed, she walked onto her balcony to be greeted by a blast of the summer air. She could hardly believe she had agreed to visit a stranger's home over the phone. Yet there was something about the whole situation that tugged at her heartstrings. Rubbing her hands through her short brown-grey hair she padded back inside and closed the patio doors. After showering, she changed to a pair of white shorts and tank top. She was a thin girl but with a fuller figure then her clothes suggested. Her legs were slim yet full in her thighs. The thin tank was cool and relaxing yet she was uncomfortable to wear it in public. She had no sooner picked up the folio of pictures when her buzzer from the front lobby of the building.

"Miss Pollard," came the familiar voice of Gus the doorman, "there's a delivery man here with a special package for you! He says you have to sign for it in person with special identification."

"Alright, Gus. Hang on, I'll be right down. Stay with him and I'll be right down!" Slipping into a pair of old running shoes, she grabbed her purse and headed for the elevator. She was partway down before she realized she had forgotten to change. Her breasts were high and full and she hadn't bothered to wear a bra. Her large nipples stood out through the thin material. Her face reddened and she tried to cover herself with her purse.

Lynn had to sign for the large flat package from the UPS man. She felt his eyes looking her over as she produced her ID and signed his large marking pad.

"Warm day out there, miss, but you look cool enough!"

She flushed and turned away. The friendly figure of Gus held the door for the man as he left.

"I tried to save you a trip down but it was no use! I didn't like the look of the guy, he has dirty eyes!" Gus said in a fatherly manner. He was a rotund black man in his late seventies and protective of Lynn in the five years she had lived in the building.

"Tell me about it, Gus. His eyes looked right through these clothes. But I should have changed before coming down," she added bitterly.

Gus took her by the arms. "Miss Pollard, I worry about you a lot. What's the matter with the young bucks around here missing a girl like you?"

She gave him a big hug and said, "You know me, Gus, I'm not much around men. One try was enough."

"Look, girl, I can assure you if I was thirty years younger you'd be getting a lot of attention!" He smiled, showing a mouthful of brilliant white teeth.

Lynn laughed loudly. "You know something, Gus, you wouldn't have to ask twice! You're a rare man, I don't think they make your kind anymore!" She waved as she headed for the elevator.

Late Sunday afternoon Martha Fleming picked Lynn up at four o'clock. She knew the capital like the back of her hand and drove like a maniac. She stopped in front of a huge stone-and-brick house. Lynn turned and asked, "You live here? It looks like an embassy it's so big."

Martha laughed. "Actually it's my home! It's been in the family for generations. The tradition has it Lincoln used to meet my great-great-grandfather here for tea, but who knows? Scott and the girls moved back here three years ago when their mother died and have been here ever since. Lynn, we're a close family and did so to close the break after Pat's death. Come, let's go in. Scott'll put the car away after he comes in."

They were parked under a large ivy trellis which covered the front circular driveway. The house was enormous. A huge spiral staircase with a crystal chandelier dominated the main hallway. Lynn was taking off her light spring coat when she heard a familiar voice.

"Hi! We're so glad you could come for dinner," Angie blurted with a giggle as she stood in front of Lynn. Without thinking, she bent down and drew the child into her arms. The little girl responded by hugging as tight as she could.

"Come now, Angie, let Lynn take her coat off. You'll have lots of time to talk to her."

Martha escorted Lynn into the large library and sitting room. She asked, "Would you like something to drink, Lynn?"

"Not really, I'm not overly fond of alcohol, but I'll have a sherry if you have any," Lynn answered. Martha went over to a large wall unit and poured two large sherrys and came and sat on the other end of the sofa from Lynn. For the next ninety minutes they talked about the girls and the difficulties they had adjusting to their mother's sudden death.

Lynn asked, "Is Scott a doctor, Martha? You have made several medical references and he said yesterday he was at Bethesda all afternoon."

"He's a neurosurgeon at the Washington Presbyterian Hospital but occasionally gets called to Bethesda on the weekends. They've been after him to become the chief resident for several years, but his heart isn't in it as it once was. He's never been the same since his wife's death. If there ever was a love match, theirs was it. It's only the past year I've started to see some of the old Scott."

They were interrupted by Angie, who had come into the library waiting for her grandmother to finish talking. "Grandma, could Lynn come upstairs and see my room?" She came over and was standing by Lynn's right knee.

Lynn responded by picking the child up and said, "I'd love to see your room, Angie, if you'll show me the way." She followed the child up the curving stairway to the door of a large bedroom.

As she was about to enter, she heard a tiny voice, "Aunt Lynn!" She turned to see the small cherub-like figure of Francie standing by the railing. She quickly knelt down and picked the child up. It was the first time she had come close to Lynn. She noticed but said nothing. The child continued, "After you see Angie's room, would you like to see my dolls?" There was a pleading in her hesitant voice.

Lynn carried her tightly as she entered Angie's bedroom and said, "Of course, sweetheart, I'd love to!"

At the bottom of the stairs, Martha Fleming stood in wonder with a mist in her eyes. It was the first the little girl had spoken to anyone besides her father and grandma since her mother's death.

Lynn was sitting curled up on the floor of Francie's bedroom looking at her vast collection of dolls when the girl looked past her. "Hi, Daddy. I'm showing Aunt Lynn all my dollies! Isn't that wonderful!"

Lynn turned, stiff from sitting on the floor. As she did, she looked up into the kindest eyes she had even known.

"Hi, you must be Lynn Pollard. I'm Scott Fleming!"

Chapter 15

The formality of dinner at the Flemings' surprised Lynn Pollard. It reminded her of her own childhood. Scott Fleming was the epitome of graciousness. He sat her at his left side at the table yet maintained an intimate relationship with the rest of his family. Lynn was surprised to find there was a full-time cook and two servants at the home. Graciousness appeared the rule of the day. She found Scott utterly charming. While somewhat older than she expected, he treated her with a kindness and respect she hadn't experienced in a long time. He was of average height, just under six feet. His features were even and he had dark hair that was grey at the temples and along both sides of his head. It was warmth of his eyes and the gentleness of his voice that stopped Lynn in her tracks. As a leading neurosurgeon he wasn't what she expected. She hadn't met a person for whom family life meant so much in a long time.

She felt like an outsider. When she reflected on the warmth transpiring around her, she felt an inner emptiness. Yet she saw the source of Scott's gratefulness for her protection of little Angie at the mall parking lot.

"We are all so thankful to Miss Pollard for her rescue of Angie yesterday afternoon! Lynn, we're a close-knit family and rarely does anyone see inside our innermost feelings. You have been thrust there by fate or whatever you want to call it. We have no quarrel with that! I don't know how to say thank you." Scott Fleming spoke quietly, obviously embarrassed with the situation.

Lynn felt herself warming to the man. She answered, "Dr. Fleming, the hospitality of your family has been overwhelming. I'm thankful I was there when Angie darted in front of that car. I refuse to think what could have happened."

"Scott, Miss Pollard tells me she is the chief research historian for the Kodak Company. I was telling her you're quite a Civil War buff, as some of those friends of yours call themselves," Martha Fleming commented.

Watching Scott, Lynn was surprised to see him become suddenly embarrassed. He added, "Well, it's only something I do in my spare time. It's really not all that important!"

"Listen to him, Miss Pollard, you'd think he never heard of the event, when in reality he's written two historical books in the field!"

Lynn looked up in fascination and said, "Now I remember! You've done a book on Nathan Bedford Forrest! I wish I'd have clicked on that in the beginning! That's one of the best books I've read on the Civil War."

As she finished, Scott Fleming raised both hands upward in a sign of surrender. "Well, I admit, it was a labour of love! Usually when I mention the book, people look at me with the same look when I tell them what I do for a living. How do you tell someone you're a brain surgeon?"

As her son talked, Martha Fleming watched the face of their guest. She saw a deep inner sadness there she hadn't experienced in many people. Yet she sensed a great empathy and depth. She stole a look at her son. He saw him glancing in Lynn's direction. Perhaps there was an interest there for Scott. The wall he had built around himself was one not even she had been able to penetrate. Yet, this stranger appeared to have opened the door. The girls seemed to hold the key.

Throughout the meal the two girls were unnaturally quiet. As they sat on either side of their grandmother, she showed an innate ability to entertain them. Suddenly little Francie asked, "Daddy, can Angie and me call Lynn, Aunt Lynn, please?"

Hers was a tiny request so unexpected that Scott Fleming was dumbfounded. Finally he answered, "Look, sweetheart, I'm sure Lynn has too many children calling her Auntie already!"

Before a moment passed and without thinking about it, Lynn got up from her chair and walked around to where the child was seated. She whispered in a voice barely audible, "Francie, if you want to call me Aunt Lynn, I'd love that! I think that would be wonderful. Yes, I have my sister's five kids calling me that, but please call me Auntie!" With these words, the little girl put her arms about Lynn's neck as she knelt beside her. Everyone at the table was stunned. At that moment, Lynn stood up with tears running down her cheeks. She excused herself and left the dining room in silence. She fled into the softly lit library where she found a small sofa and started to cry and was not sure why. In a few moments, she was aware of Scott Fleming's presence.

"May I come in, please?" he asked quietly. Lynn moved near the end of the sofa but still found it difficult to talk. Scott spoke again, "Miss Pollard, in the few hours our family has known you, you have had a greater impact than some people we've known for years. You're the first person outside this family Francie has spoken to in over three years!"

54

"Dr. Fleming, I'm completely at a loss! I've had little contact with children over the past fifteen years, and that's why I am so overwhelmed! Please forgive me, I normally don't behave in this manner." Suddenly, Lynn was becoming acutely embarrassed.

Scott Fleming continued, "Look, Lynn, please call me Scott, I get enough of fancy titles at the hospital every day! I'm Scott to my friends. I'd like you to be a friend of our family. You already have a special place." As he finished talking he impulsively reached out and took one of her hands and said, "Welcome to our circle of friendship, Lynn Pollard. You've given Angie back to us and opened the door to little Francie! I don't know what else to say!"

Suddenly Angie burst into the library and shouted, "Grandma says if we get ready for bed quick like perhaps Auntie Lynn would tuck us in and kiss our dollies goodnight!"

Nearly an hour later, Lynn returned to the main floor of the huge house finding Martha sitting by a roaring fire in a small family room.

"Martha, I'm overwhelmed by the warmth of your family. I've never experienced this since my childhood. After Daddy died in Vietnam, my mother had to work to raise us girls. We saw little of her and we had to keep each other company. When she was there for us, it was wonderful, but that was rare."

"Lynn, I watched you at our table! I could see the depth of your understanding and something of the sadness in your life, if you'll excuse me for saying!" Martha responded.

Her directness took Lynn aback and she answered, "I didn't know it was that obvious but I suppose that's what happens. Ever since my marriage broke up eight years ago, my life has been very focussed. I've never completely gotten over not having children. Perhaps that is why the warmth of the girls was almost too much!"

"Unfortunately, Lynn, the real victim in our family is not the girls. They'll get over their mother's death when they are adults and then they'll not remember her! My real concern is Scott. Pat has been dead almost four years now and he's still mourning. It tears me apart to see the look in his eyes sometimes!"

Suddenly they were aware of Scott standing at the door of the library.

"Lynn, you asked me to let you know when it was close to ten as you wanted to get back home."

Looking at her watch, Lynn jumped to her feet and said, "Thanks for reminding me. I have to be in the office at eight in the morning so I'd best get going. I feel bad asking you to drive me home but I have a personal rule in the city, I never go out alone after dark for any reason. One bad experience is enough!" As she spoke Martha didn't miss the reference.

Thirty minutes later, Scott parked his BMW outside Lynn's brownstone building and turned to her. "Lynn, I hope you won't take this the wrong way! You've done more for my family than you probably realize. If anything had happened to Angie, I don't think I could have coped. Thank God you were where you were at that moment. But, even more than that, you've given a certain joy back to my girls! I hope you realize that!"

Turning in her seat with her hand on the door, she replied, "Scott, I can't explain any of it, but as I've said I'm so glad that I was in the right place to grab Angie. You're very fortunate to have two such sweet girls. I was never so fortunate and never will be!" She finished on a bitter note.

There was silence in the car as the motor idled. Scott finally spoke, "Lynn, would you come back and see us again? We never did get a chance to talk about our interest in history."

Lynn looked directly at Scott. She knew she wanted his friendship that was all she knew!

"Scott, I'd be happy if you would call me sometime!"

"Would you have dinner with me? It would give both of us a chance to get to know each other without interruption!"

Lynn found herself reaching out and taking Scott's hands in hers and saying, "Please do that, I'd love to have dinner with you! I'm free most evenings!"

Chapter 16

The soft yellow lights winked in the boardinghouse windows. The March days were becoming longer and Washington was starting to come alive in the brightening eventide. He looked about and knew the light from the house came from one of the new Aladdin lamps. Their light was much brighter and even than the older kerosene lamps. As Lewis Payne shuffled along the street he was glad to see the last of the winter snow gone. His shoes were muddy from crossing the streets. He was tense as he climbed the steps to the front door of the boardinghouse. George Atzerodt had sent him a telegram saying come to Mary Surratt's boardinghouse.

Before rapping on the door, he looked out from the veranda and down the street. It seemed unusual to see so much light in the city now that the war was grinding to a close. So many of his friends had rushed to get into Union armies and had been killed. He rapped on the door. In a moment Mary Surratt opened the door.

"Come in, Lewis. The rest of the people are here and we're ready to have our meeting." She stepped aside and closed the door. He walked into the living room where he spent time a month ago. He saw a number of familiar faces. Seated on a brocade-covered sofa in the corner were two strangers. There sat George Atzerodt, Dave Harold and Edward Spangler. He never liked Spangler but bit his tongue because of his contacts in a variety of government circles. He looked for Sam Arnold but he was nowhere to be seen. He nodded to George and took a seat near the door.

Meanwhile, Mary Surratt had taken a seat near the other side of the door. Almost immediately, she looked about the room and spoke in a firm resolute voice, "I want to thank you for coming on such short notice. I haven't been able to reach Sam Arnold, so we'll have to go on without him. Booth may be along later. He wasn't sure if he would be able to make train connections. The last letter I had from him emphasized his feelings that we proceed at full speed even if the war appears to be over!"

"Before we get into any details, I want to know who are these strangers. If we're going to be making serious plans, what are they doing here?" Lewis

Payne asked. As he talked, he stretched his unusually long legs out onto the carpet in the middle of the room.

Mary Surratt responded, "I think the rest of you have met these two gentlemen. Lewis, this is Gilles Verendrye from Paris and William Segregson from London. They're special friends of Booth and he wants them to have their say here at this meeting."

Lewis Payne wasn't totally convinced, but he went along with the meeting only on John Wilkes Booth's recommendation.

"Booth thinks we should go along with the second plan now that it appears the war is about over. He's concerned the present people in government won't be the best prescription for dealing with the Confederacy under reconstruction. So he thinks they should go permanently." Mary Surratt intoned, "Personally, I admit I agree with him. The old kidnapping plan was good as long as the war was raging but now we're looking at a more permanent solution!"

Gilles Verendrye cleared his throat before speaking. "I'm not a native of this country, but I certainly can see you've come through a traumatic war. I suggest that you have a unique opportunity to change the nation's direction in the future. You need new blood at the helm and someone who will not be afraid to form alliances with powers across the oceans. America can't hide from the rest of the world forever. I also think there should be less restriction on some of the religions over here. There is too much Protestant influence!"

"That's bullshit, my friend!" George Atzerodt snapped. "Lincoln himself is a free thinker and not a follower of any church!"

"That's my point!" Verendrye responded. "A man who likes all views is a man of no views. What you need here is a scene where there is far more balance to the overpowering Protestant movement. With Lincoln out of the way, there would be a real opportunity for this to happen. Vice President Johnson is a weak man and that's what you need. This will give these other forces time to marshal their strength."

"Tell me something, sir, what are the real influences you represent?" Mary Surratt asked in an irritated voice. "I have the feeling you're not telling us the whole story."

Before the visitor could answer, the other man, a short portly gentleman in his early forties, spoke up. "One of the things the various nations have learned in Europe is the necessity of getting along with each other. A vital way of doing this is the encouragement of every type of religious group. We don't think this exists in America. This is one of the reasons you've been fighting this bitter Civil War. If the North wins, as it appears it will, some of the old policies that led directly to this conflict will be continued. That's why we believe on such an occasion strong-willed men and women must be ready to take risky actions."

Payne snorted, "Sure, that's brave talk! If we're caught, the chances are we'll be hanged. As soon as the going gets rough for you two gentlemen, you can head back over the ocean under the protection of your governments."

"No, my brash young friend! If we're caught, we're at the mercy of whoever catches us. Our national governments will disavow all knowledge of us or any of our actions!" Verendrye uttered.

Lewis Payne muttered to himself, but made no vocal response. The general discussion rambled on for the next two hours, but there were no new revelations. Finally, George Atzerodt stated, "I think we'll need one more planning meeting at the first of the month, especially when we can get Booth here and hear more of his feelings on this whole matter. I think these two gentlemen have made some valid points and I thank them for their presence and contributions. We owe Mrs. Surratt a debt for bringing them along. I think we basically agree with them and thank them for their moral support."

Gilles Verendrye nodded his head and added, "As long as we are in this country you'll have our full support. I think with certain key people in your government out of the way, your country will develop in the manner it should. I can assure you certain people and influences we represent will be content with that situation!"

"Yes, Father, I'm sure his Holiness would be! By the way, how's the weather in Rome? I see your Revolution is about over!" Lewis Payne snapped under his breath. As he spoke, he looked at Mary Surratt, who sat with her face ashen and her hand over her mouth.

Chapter 17

"Mrs. Surratt, why didn't you tell us a photographer would be present this evening? When we first came to you about our proposal, we emphasized the need for absolute secrecy when we talked to you!" Father Verendrye fumed as he, Father Segregson and Mrs. Surratt sat around the kitchen table in her boardinghouse.

"Gentlemen, I saw no need to inform you ahead of hand! There was only two pictures taken and I'll be keeping both of them. Mr. Brady's associate assures me he will bring the pictures here tomorrow morning. I felt it was an important meeting that should be recorded for our family," Mary Surratt answered.

Father Segregson took Mrs. Surratt by the hand as he talked to her. "My daughter, perhaps you didn't understand the importance of the meeting tonight. It is important that the Holy See increase its influence here in America. At the present time we have had little success in our overall efforts. We in the Jesuit Order are trying to change all this. That was why we approached you in the beginning. You are a new convert to the true Church and have a passion for our position!"

"Why didn't you tell me from the outset? You said you wanted to speak to people who felt it was necessary to make basic changes in our country. That's why I felt you should talk to these people. I can assure you when you talk to Mr. Booth you will see why he feels it is necessary to take drastic actions!" Mary Surratt replied in exasperation.

"Mrs. Surratt, I want you to promise on your oath to your Mother the Church and the security of your eternal soul what you have been witness to this evening both in the other room and here will ever remain a secret. If you ever violate this trust, the Church will deny you are one of the faithful and you will spend eternity in the fires of perdition! Is that what you want?"

She gasped as a fit of panic suddenly came over her.

"No, Father, please forgive me for I have sinned!" she sobbed.

"You have one chance, my daughter! You must keep this secret now and for all eternity. This will be your legacy, the Surratt Legacy!" Mary Surratt covered her face and collapsed into a sobbing heap on the kitchen table.

"Remember, my daughter, now and for all eternity! It's your immortal soul we're talking about!" Father Verendrye's voice cut into her inner self like the razor edge of true Spanish steel. "This will be your personal legacy, Mrs. Surratt! Do I make myself understood?"

Sobbing uncontrollably, she nodded her agreement. With a nod to each other, Father Segregson said as they readied themselves to head out into the night, "Mrs. Surratt, we'll be back tomorrow morning just before noon." With these words, they turned and went out through the back door into the darkness of the night. Mary Surratt continued to sob as she prepared to go to bed. She tossed and turned far into the night as the events of the evening churned over and over in her mind. She knew she had no choice but to turn the two pictures over to the priests when they returned.

Just before noon there was a knock at her front door. Leaving the kitchen where she had been busy with a batch of bread, she was glad to see the Brady photographer standing there.

"Good morning, Mrs. Surratt! May I say you are looking charming this morning? I have your pictures and there will be no charge. It was a pleasure to meet those people last evening. I took the liberty of taking two extra pictures in addition to the originals." Mary Surratt was about to protest for a moment that this was a violation, of their agreement of last evening, but on a hunch she said nothing.

"In addition," the loquacious photographer continued, "there are also two extra pictures I took for you. You'll want to have them to show your grandchildren in years to come! I have a way to take them and no one will ever know it happened." With these words the diminutive man turned and raced downs the steps and across the drying mud of Washington Street.

Mary Surratt watched him go and was thinking to herself. Walking back to the kitchen, she pulled out the stiff photos from the large envelope he had left with her. She left one of each and shoved the other two inside the bodice of her flour-covered dress front. As she did she muttered to herself, "Now, my fine Christian friends, we'll see who'll survive the Surratt Legacy! Maybe my legacy will become one you'll regret declaring."

Chapter 18

Lynn Pollard breezed into her office at eight-thirty on Monday morning. She raced past Maggie with a wave of her free arm. She carried a pile of paper and reports on which she had been working. Maggie followed her with her eyes and shook her head. She hadn't seen Lynn so animated in years. Getting to her feet, she walked into Lynn's office and stood inside the door. Lynn was busy fussing around her desk.

"Alright, what's his name!"

There was a moment's silence, and Lynn looked up with a puzzled look on her small face.

"What are you talking about, Maggie, whose name?" she asked in honest reply.

"Come on, I wasn't born yesterday, I know when a new person has come into your life! You've met someone!" She leaned against the door as she talked.

"I never was any good at fooling you, Maggie! I don't know really if there's anything. I was shopping on Saturday and grabbed a little girl from in front of a car and things fell in place from there!" Maggie waited but Lynn seemed rather reticent to talk. At that moment, Maggie knew something serious had happened to her.

"Lynn, do you mind telling me what happened?"

Lynn looked up and answered, "Maggie, I honestly don't know what to think. Her family was so gracious and kind, I was overwhelmed. Besides, Angie's father wants to take me out to dinner."

"You know what your problem is? You've had a rough experience over the past few years and now you don't trust anyone! You keep this attitude up and you won't have a friend in the world!" Maggie's words cut deep and Lynn paled.

"If that's what you want it's your business! Somehow, I don't think it is, but be careful. Life can be lonely."

"Should I go out with him if he calls me?" Lynn asked in a pondering manner.

"Well, did he ask you already or do you think he might?"

"No, he asked me in the car last evening when he drove me home and I said I'd love to! But Maggie, I swore five years ago after the assault, I'd never go near another man again." Lynn spoke with an agonizing look on her face.

"Well, I've heard it all! You know what your problem is? I think you're glad you were assaulted and raped. It gives you an out from ever associating with a man again. Your problem is a real fear of trust and commitment. You wouldn't know a nice guy if one came along. You know why? You don't want to believe there are any. If I didn't need this job, I'd tell you to shove it right now. Bob was saying the other night, he thinks you hate men! He really pities you" Maggie turned on her heels and marched from the office. Lynn was stunned. All the blood drained from her face. Was she that obvious in her outlook on life? She wondered.

Lynn got to her feet immediately and followed the older woman out to her desk. Maggie turned and faced Lynn. "Lynn, I'm sorry. That was very unfair, I had no right to say those things!" She sounded remorseful.

"No, Maggie, I know you! You were only being honest! Perhaps I really have been hiding behind that reaction to the assault. Maggie, does Bob really feel that way about me?"

"Yes, and the sad thing is he likes you so much. That's why he hasn't come to the office recently to pick me up!"

Lynn sat on the edge of Maggie's desk in silence. She valued Bob's opinions and his reaction cut deep.

"I have to admit Scott Fleming seems a terrific person, and I want to see him again, but simply, Maggie, I'm afraid!" she replied nervously.

"You said his name was Scott Fleming! He wouldn't be a doctor by any chance would he?" Maggie asked slowly.

"Yes, as a matter of fact, he's the head of surgery over at Washington Presbyterian Hospital. Why, do you know him?" Lynn asked.

"Know him, Lynn, he's my doctor! I've had several operations with him! Scott's one of the nicest people I know in the city. He lost his wife about four years ago and became a bit of a recluse after that. If he's asked you out, Lynn, I would consider it… for God's sake, you'll never meet a nicer, more honest person than Scott!"

"He's certainly a gentleman. I've rarely been treated so nicely!"

"That's my point, and what you see is what he is!" Maggie replied. "The only time I've seen him ticked was with another doctor. He's feared in some medical circles because of the high demands he makes upon those who work with him. But if you're his patient, he'll do anything for you!"

"He was beside himself when he saw me after his daughter was almost killed!" Lynn replied.

"Well, that goes with my experiences with the man. You've done something important for his family and he won't forget it!" Maggie added. As she finished talking, there was a buzz on the phone line.

"Lynn, there's a call for you and I think it's your new friend," she called, a lilt in her voice.

"Lynn, it's Scott Fleming, I hope I'm not calling at a bad time? I had a few minutes before I go back to the OR."

"Scott, I'm glad you called. I want to thank you for your kindness last evening. You have a wonderful family," she replied.

"Look, I'm not good at this sort of thing. But would you like to have dinner some time this week? I'm free most evenings, so whatever would be most convenient for you?"

"Scott, you don't have to feel embarrassed around me, I'd love to go out for dinner! How about tomorrow evening. I can be finished around five-thirty or so if that isn't too early?"

"That sounds great! What do you say I pick you up at six? It usually takes me 'til then to finish up my office calls," Scott answered.

"You could pick me up here at work if you like! We're in the commerce block, number H, you may know where that is?"

"It sounds super! Where can I pick you up?"

"The Kodak section is on the eighth floor. I can be at the front lobby if you like; I don't like to wait outside," Lynn answered.

"Yes, I know exactly where you are. As a matter of fact, I was in the building for a meeting a year ago. I'll meet you in the front lobby at six. Goodbye, Lynn, and thanks so much!"

As she hung up, there was a quiet smile on her face. She sat at her desk staring across the room. She was suddenly aware of Maggie at the door with a big smile.

"Go for it, Lynn!"

Chapter 19

The spring sun streamed through the windows of the big house. Tony, in his cutoffs and a sleeveless T-shirt, wandered out on the big deck about the pool. He found Gord and Bev eating their breakfasts.

"Hi, Tony. The cook is making breakfast, go in and help yourself! Come on back and join us! We have to talk anyway."

Tony arrived back at their table with a tray full of bacon, eggs and cereal. Sitting down, he was surprised to find them in a glum mood.

"What's the matter with you folks? You look ready to go to a funeral," he asked.

"Tony, have you had any trouble with this research into the Lincoln business?" Gord asked.

"What do you mean, trouble? I don't follow you," Tony replied.

"You mean you haven't received any threatening notes in the post or in your mail?" Gord continued.

"No. Nothing! I figured we might have trouble with the families of those who were involved, but I've received nothing."

"Strange, we've received several and Bev is terrified. I admit it's giving me the willies. I don't figure it! Who could care what happened a hundred and thirty years ago?" Gord exclaimed.

"I don't blame you for being concerned but I wouldn't hit the panic button. By the way, I did know about the notes you've been getting in the mail. April said she'd been talking to you last evening, and Bev had mentioned how scared you were. She feels we should look into it a bit deeper and if the harassment continues find the source or simply forget the research."

There was some quiet talk between Bev and Gord while Tony went back to the kitchen to bring out the coffee pot.

"Bev and I have talked the matter over while you were in the kitchen and want to stay with the research for the moment. If there are any more of these threats, veiled or not, we'll drop the whole business. One other thing, Tony, we have questions about this Father McGuire. Who is he and how is he tied into the Lincoln business? He's asked far too many questions to be a curious visitor."

"He's an old friend of mine at Fordham and I invited him here to have a free weekend as you've always asked me to do. I'm having the same trouble as you understanding some of his questions. In fact, to quote April, several of them seemed close to veiled threats! I'm going to have it out with him sometime today before we leave. Even the manner he appeared at my office was a bit on the dark side."

"Tony, Bev and I have are concerned with another aspect of our research. Do you think it might be possible we have unwittingly opened a historical hornet's nest? Over the past year since we got the grant from the foundation?" Gord asked in a forthright manner.

Tony thought for a moment. "In all honesty, aside from the risk of stirring up some concern amongst the descendants, no! Now, off the record, I'm not so sure! Right now, I have a gut feeling we may have unearthed something, but I have no proof. Right now, as I've mentioned, my concern is my old friend Father McGuire. The other possibility is a contact I have at the National Archives in Washington!"

"Tony, who else knows about our research outside the members of the foundation?" Bev asked.

"Aside from the three of us, the only person who I've told about the whole purpose is a gal in Washington who has intimate access to the National Archives and the Library of Congress."

"Why the Christ would you tell someone the details of what we're trying to do with the project?" snapped Gord.

"Gord, I've known Lynn Pollard for five years and she has a mouth like a steel trap. She's given me a heap of useful information from the earlier Lincoln years. Besides, she works for Kodak and can't be touched by government pressure. She can be a rough customer and we're safe at that end."

"Well, I hope you're right, Tony. The tone of those notes April mentioned to you was scary," Bev replied.

"Like I said before, Bev, if anything else develops, we'll shut the whole thing down. By the way, have you seen April around this morning?"

"Yes, she was finishing breakfast as I was starting," replied Gord. "She had her bathing suit on and said she was heading down to the beach to soak up some sun. It's over there if you're interested, but be careful, it's a tricky climb to the bottom," Gord warned.

A short time later saw Tony trotting down the last steps of the long descent to the small, protected beach. The blue-green water of the Pacific was rolling in. At first he couldn't see April anywhere. After walking a distance, he found her sprawled on a huge beach towel on her tummy fast asleep. Her back gleamed with sunscreen she had rubbed on to protect herself. She had pulled a large hat over her face and didn't hear him coming.

Finally he spoke, "You're going to burn up there if you're not careful!" As he spoke he sat down on the sand beside her.

April raised her head, her eyes vague. "Oh... hi, Tony! Isn't it beautiful down her?! I felt the need to relax and get some sun. Is there enough screen on my back? I did the best I could do on my own but it's hard."

"Here, I'll rub some more on," Tony replied reaching for the tube lying on the towel. As he began to rub the clear thick liquid, she sighed with pleasure. He moved up and down her back. Finally, she rolled over and sat up holding her top in place. He reached out and ran his hand gently down her smooth cheek.

"April, I hope you're not offended by last night. Things seem to be carried along by themselves. But don't mistake, I have no regrets!" he said softly.

"I have no regrets either, Tony. It was one of those things that happened. We both wanted it and that's what makes it beautiful!" As she talked, she casually removed her top and tossed it on the sand beside her. Her breasts weren't large but still full and round.

"I hope you don't mind me taking off the top! I hate the darned thing. I don't know about you but I'm going for a swim." As she spoke she jumped to her feet and walked into the pounding surf.

"Hold your horses, I'm coming with you!" he called out.

Chapter 20

The April weather was miserable. Now there was a slight improvement with the first week of May. It was unusual for Marseilles this time of year. The glum spring weather was the least of Father Guy Salan's worries. He had done an unusual thing. He called the six world directors of the Order together for the first time since 1919. Some of them arrived by air, others according to their own initiative. That was the basic directive on the last day of the 1919 meeting. A meeting could only be called if there appeared to be a threat to the Order. Everyone was responsible for their own presence. The rare instructions were to be in Marseilles on Thursday, the 2nd day of May, 1998. They were to meet on one of the long finger piers jutting into the harbor. There was no proof of identity aside from the small lapel red rose with the one petal missing. Only the chief of the Order wore the rose with the complete petal structure.

There was a mist in the air as a lone figure sat on the wide bench at the end of the pier. He was a man in his early seventies and his head was covered with a shock of white hair. His black piercing eyes gazed off into the distance looking for something to focus on. Father Salan was a small man with no extra weight. He asked the other five to meet him at nine. Three minutes before the hour, five men of varying sizes and ages materialized out of the mist. One by one they noticed the full rose on the older man's lapel. They seated themselves on the long bench within hearing distance of him.

"Ad Majorem Dei Gloriam," he whispered under his breath loud enough for the others to hear. There was a resounding response from the little group.

"Fathers, I thank you all for coming! Some of you have come at great expense and inconvenience, but the need is urgent. We have a problem in several parts of the world and we must address the problem. I have called you because of two major decisions, and these have to be laid out in detail before you return home. It is now past nine o'clock, this meeting will last an hour. I will then meet with each of you for thirty minutes to explain the changes and perhaps discuss some other problems!" He was silent for a moment. "Does anyone have a comment?"

"I am Father Augustino Mendinez from Italy. We have been encountering some conflict with the more active terrorist groups in our part of the world. Is it Father's belief we should still be adhering to the easiest route approach as a solution?"

There were several heads that nodded up and down. The youngest of the six men raised a finger. "Father Raoul Cortes from Columbia... in our area we have noticed an increased ruthlessness on the part of these peoples as well. Matters would be easier if our hands were not so tightly tied."

"Fathers," replied Father Salan, "that is the main issue we have come here to discuss. Our feeling is we must still adhere to our Prime Rule, the protection and promotion of the Holy Church. Yet there is a desire we become more aggressive. This means you will have permission to be more proactive. If you feel it is to the further glory to our Mother the Church, then do it; we are agreed on that point. But there must be a far more rigid obedience to the rule of silence and isolation. Recently there has been leakage in two areas. One of these has been closed. Father Billy O'Fannon from Dublin took fatally ill last week. I cannot urge enough whom we serve, our Mother the Church. We not only serve her but also protect her with our lives!"

There were some sober faces in the small group as Salan talked. He continued, "The second issue is recruitment and security. Recently we had to eliminate three regular Jesuits in Dublin. We know for a fact that the youngest of these three was a plant for the Mossad. That, gentlemen, we can never tolerate. Any weak links must be closed at once, do I make myself clear? If that does not happen, or if word of any of our activities should ever get beyond us, then our whole movement will be shut down. Moreover, think of the disgrace it will bring upon an unsuspecting Church. We must as always operate with only the praise of our own consciences." He was silent.

"Does that mean we operate entirely on our own from now on?" asked Father Ching Chan from Singapore.

"Yes, Father, that's right, and you must do so with the ruthlessness of a Mafioso Don. It is the way our Mother the Church will move into the twenty-first century. We will be under a far greater scrutiny than ever before. If the cursed Mossad can get as far as it has, then we're going to have to be more vigilant. If you suspect anyone, get rid of them immediately! Gentlemen, I'm now going to give you ninety minutes for questions, then I will see each of you for thirty minutes each."

Following this session, Father Salan met each of the fathers separately down on the beach under the great piles of the pier. When he finished with each priest, they immediately went their separate ways. At two-thirty he met with Father Gustaff Erikson from the United States.

"Father, your presence here is one of the main reasons for this meeting. You have a problem with those people doing the research into the Lincoln assassination. Several of our people in America at the time of Lincoln became more aggressive than was necessary. The two priests had their pictures taken and were involved with a Mrs. Mary Surratt who was later executed for her part in the assassination. Before she died she set up some sort of a public record of these two priests. Father Erikson, it is imperative we plug this gap as soon as possible. If we don't, it could irreparably damage the whole image of the Church in America. Can you imagine what people will think when they find out there were two priests involved in Lincoln's killing?"

"Father Salan, I think we already have made progress in this area. We've made several moves and the issue will be dead before the month is out."

"Father Erikson," Salan responded, "I'm going to say this once. Get the job done and do it quickly and cleanly. If you don't, then we'll have to hire people who will. We've done it before and we can do it again!"

Father Erikson paled at the tone and directness of the older man. "I can assure everything will be cleared up by the end of the month, Father. It's difficult to go back into history and carry the cross of someone's mistakes!"

"That statement negates the foundations of the founding of the Order of the Red Rose. You know the price of incompetence." As he talked he drew a deadly Smith and Wesson revolver. Erikson stepped back knowing the inevitable result. Before he could move, the gun barked. A small red hole appeared in the centre of Erikson's forehead. His eyes stared for a moment and then he collapsed in a heap face first in the wet sand. Reaching into his small case, Salan took out a small bottle of nitric acid. Turning Erikson's body over, he poured a liberal amount of the contents across each hand and fingers. The remaining half bottle he poured across the corpse's still face. Immediately the steam of burning flesh issued upward, marring the flesh completely. He checked the pockets for identification and found there was none. With a snort he kicked the body over on its face. As he did he muttered to himself, "Ad Majoren Dei Gloriam!"

Chapter 21

The president was late. The curtain at Fords Theatre went up at eight o'clock. There was no sign of the president or his party and as usual the play started on time. Finally, the presidential carriage arrived at the Harris residence and picked up Miss Clara Harris, the fiancée of presidential aid Major Rathbone. The evening was cool. A light wind blew from the southwest with temperatures in the mid-fifties. At eight-thirty, the presidential carriage turned onto Tenth Street and the team came to a smart trot as they approached the theatre. Lincoln carried his coat as a protection against the chill. Meanwhile his aid carried the ever-present plaid shawl Lincoln favoured winter and summer.

As the presidential party entered the special box reserved for them, the actors stopped and the audience applauded vigorously. The orchestra immediately broke into their own version of "Hail to the Chief." It was followed by a series of whistles and cheers in response to the unusually enthusiastic crowd.

Lincoln did something he never did before. He stepped forward in front of the lace curtains where the audience could see him. He bowed and spoke loudly. "Thank you, Thank you!" He motioned with his hands for the audience to be seated. The music stopped and the president said to the actors as he leaned slightly over the railing, "Now, Mr. Emerson, please go on!" Then, he vanished from view behind the heavy curtains.

The audience settled down to see the rest of the play. They were an attentive audience and responsive to the actors and their roles. There was no further activity from the presidential box except for the occasional giggle later attributed to the first lady. As she was a sombre person by her basic nature, these were unusual outbursts.

As the evening progressed, no one noticed two plain-looking men sitting in the back row of the main floor. They sat quietly watching the evening's proceedings as the play progressed. They were dressed in nondescript black suits, were both dirty and wrinkled. They were in their middle years and there was nothing to set Fathers Segregson and Verendrye apart from the rest of the audience. Each wore a tiny red-petal rose in their lapels. Partway through the second act, Father Verendrye looked at Father Segregson and nodded his head with a grim look on his face.

On stage, the actor Harry Hawke stood looking after one of the female actors as she left stage on cue. Pausing only the briefest of moments, he shouted, "Society, eh?" He spoke the lines of the play's author, Asa Trendhard, "Well, I guess I know enough to turn you inside out, old woman, you sockdologizing old man trap!"

A giggle echoed in the front row. Then gales of laughter rippled through the house slowly dying away. The audience settled down for the play to continue. A long moment of silence permeated the theatre. Suddenly a sharp crack or report touched the eardrums. This was followed by a longer silence. Sounds of a muffled struggle came from the presidential box. Someone heard a small cry and a loud shout.

A figure leaped over the railing of the presidential box onto the stage itself. Someone yelled, "Freedom!"

Moments later a man fell to the stage yelling the words, "Sic semper tyrannis!"

Moments later another yell as the man picked himself up from the floor of the stage and stumbled across its width.

"The president has been shot!"

Bedlam broke out everywhere. The audience surged to its feet and moved in every direction. An actor called out from the stage floor, "They've killed him!"

The patrons in the theatre sprang to life and pandemonium broke out all over. People swarmed, filled with panic, and began to move in all directions. A crowd of people collected at the base of the presidential box. At the same time many people were thronging to get out of the theatre. As they poured into the street, they shouted the terrible news, "They have shot the president!"

As people milled about, no one was aware of the two men standing across the street watching. One looked at the other and said, "Sic semper tyrannis! Thus always to tyrants!" There was a look of satisfaction on the faces of both men as the throng continued to pour from the theatre.

Chapter 22

Washington was in turmoil! The overpowering euphoria at the end of the war was gone. The word of the assassination spread like an early-morning fog across the countryside. Across from the White House, a small group of black people stood with tears streaming down their faces. They were thunderstruck. As they wept openly and commiserated with each other two women walked merrily past them and called out, "What's so terrible? You'd think we'd lost the war or maybe General Lee was marching into the city!" The short plump woman laughed. There was silence.

"You mean you haven't heard?" a young woman replied.

"We haven't heard what?" the older woman answered.

"President Lincoln was shot last night at Fords Theatre and died earlier this morning," Another black woman responded.

"President Lincoln killed? That's impossible! No one would want to kill such a great man! He's our saviour and has stopped this terrible war! No, I won't believe it!" she said as she started to sob.

"Well, believe it!" an old black woman said. "I knew he was too good a man to live a long life. Remember what they did to our Saviour. He was so good they had to get rid of him, and they did. God help us all now. We're all going to be slaves again!"

Just before eleven, on the morning of April 15, 1865, Mary Surratt's daughter Anna came rushing into her mother's boardinghouse on H Street.

"Mother, Mother, have you heard the news? They've killed President Lincoln!" She called the news out from the centre of the main hall. Mary Surratt was in her kitchen, as usual. As she heard her daughter's voice, a momentary smile crossed her lips and vanished. Then, she went deadly grim-faced to meet Anna.

"Anna, where did you hear this news? I haven't heard a thing. Are you sure?" she asked.

"Yes, Mother!" Anna replied. "The news is all over the city and the streets are full of soldiers! I was stopped three times as I came here. Everyone is so upset. Mother, have you heard any talk about someone trying to kill the president? There is talk he was shot by a man called Booth, an actor. I know you've often talked to him here in this house!" Anna continued.

"I've always liked Wilkes Booth and talked to him but I find it hard to believe he would shoot the president. No, I've never heard of any plans to kill the president from any of my people. Have you heard anything of your brother? I haven't and wish I knew I where he was!"

"No, Mother, I haven't heard a thing from John. I've told you before, I think he's dead! So many were killed in this damned senseless war."

"Are you sure, Anna?"

"Yes, Mother, I'm positive. If I knew anything, I'd tell you," Anna replied impatiently. "Listen, I've got to get back home, there's no telling what's going to be happening next in these crazy times!" With these words, Anna kissed her mother on the cheek and rushed out the front door.

Mary Surratt watched her carriage gallop off down the street. Closing the door, she walked into the front room where so many of the political planning meetings had taken place over the past several months. Reaching for a large family Bible, she drew out the envelope the Brady associate had given her nearly three weeks ago.

"Now, you bastards!" she whispered under her breath. "You think you have forced me into this corner in this whole dirty business! That may be, but I'll leave you a legacy that will outlive us all. I may die as the result of removing the tyrant Lincoln, but my legacy will destroy your descendants!" Another fading smile crossed her lips. As she thought she drew out a small piece of paper and a pen.

Dipping the pen in the bottle of ink she always kept nearby, she began to write:

I, MARY SURRATT HEREBY WRITE ON THIS 15th OF APRIL, 1865. I DECLARE MY INNOCENCE IN THE PLANNING OF THE DEATH OF OUR LATE PRESIDENT ABRAHAM LINCOLN. I WISH TO DECLARE MY LEGACY OF INNOCENCE IN THE PRESENCE OF TWO PRIESTS OF THE JESUIT ORDER. MY LEGACY IS ONE OF ONLY KNOWING AND NOT INVOLVEMENT. THE LEGACY OF THE PRIESTS IS ONE OF BOTH ENCOURAGEMENT AND ACTIVE INVOLVEMENT BOTH PERSONALLY AND OF THE ORDER THEY REPRESENT!

Mary Surratt looked at what she had written and was satisfied. She muttered under her breath, "Now, let's see you and your Church deal with this legacy!"

Chapter 23

It was ten-thirty Tuesday morning when Lynn received the call from Frank Baird. She was so preoccupied with her work and upcoming dinner engagement, she forgot about him. His voice was urgent.

"Lynn, Frank here! Can we get together tomorrow? It's very important!"

"Frank, you sound as if you've discovered the world's crowns jewels! What's the matter?" Lynn asked continuing to sort through various piles of pictures on her desk.

"Lynn, this is no laughing matter. It's that damn picture you left with me! It's a lot more than either of us thought. As a matter of fact, it could be earthshaking."

"I don't follow you, Frank," Lynn said as she raised her eyes to fully listen him.

"Lynn, we may not be looking at rewriting a wee bit of history here, rather you may have unwittingly put your hands on something dangerous!" he said curtly.

"Well, I can be here in my office about ten. I'm officially away on this damn research!" Lynn answered with concern. Frank could get himself worked up and she didn't want to be party to getting him into something over his head.

"Yah, that's fine. I'll see you in the morning at your office!" With these words he slammed the receiver down. Someone who didn't know him would have been hurt. Lynn knew him well and paid little attention to his volatility. She put the phone back in its rack. She wondered what could have gotten him so worked up. She shrugged her shoulders and put it out of her mind.

Finally putting all the stacks of pictures in the complex cataloguing system she had worked out, she piled them in long boxes, which in turn were placed in heavy packing cartons to be returned to the archives. She kept out only those pictures she felt were indicative of a major step forward in the development of the Brady story. She was of the view no one had really settled down to tell the story as it should be presented. She felt this was particularly true of the old daguerreotype method of early photography. Some of the early pictures she saw of this method reflected an immense feeling and character. She worked throughout the day opening vast boxes from the overall Brady material collected by Matthew Brady in his meticulous collecting of everything until his death in 1896. His indeed was the definitive story of the development of photography in America. The more she worked her way into the material the more she felt justified in her original presentation to the Kodak Board for funds for the research.

At five o'clock, Lynn headed into her washroom to tidy up and change for her dinner with Scott Fleming. In her office, she usually wore informal slacks and blouse. Over the past few years because of the demand on her evening time in the city core and with company functions she kept several selections of evening wear at the office. This had been a warm Tuesday, so she decided to wear a simple cocktail dress and carry a light jacket in case the evening air turned cold. Just before four o'clock, Lynn walked past Maggie, who was beginning to close up for the day.

Maggie suddenly stopped what she was doing and exclaimed, "Holy Toledo! I can see Scott made a big impression on you! I've always told you, Lynn, you should wear dresses and suits more often, you've got the best figure in the building."

She looked her up and down carefully until Lynn blushed. She protested, "Come on, Maggie, he's only taking me to dinner, not a wedding or the like!"

"Well, at least you're thinking on the right track, I'll say that much!" she added as she laughed at Lynn's embarrassment.

Lynn was wearing a simple black sleeveless dress with a high neck and cut above her knees. She rarely wore heels but this time she chose a small spike. She set the dress off with a pair of small gold earrings and her dress watch. She combed her hair out and the grey was interspersed with the dark brown.

"I admit I do like to dress up once in a while. I've had too much work of late!" Lynn replied as she put the short jacket over one arm.

"Look, Lynn, I want you to promise me you will have a wonderful time this evening! By the way, where's he taking you?" she asked out of sheer curiosity.

"Maggie, I have no idea! Scott didn't say and I didn't ask. And you know what? That's half the fun of it! I must admit though, I am nervous," she added.

"Nervous? Somebody with your looks. You never cease to amaze me! But I appreciate your honesty. I can think of fifty girls who would kill to be in your position this evening. He's one of the most decent people I've ever met."

"Now you've made me feel even worse. Anyway, I'm going out to wait in the lobby. He insisted he meet me there. See you tomorrow, Maggie," Lynn called out as she walked into the empty elevator and the door closed behind her.

Lynn no sooner walked into the huge foyer of the Department of Commerce, when she heard her name being called.

"Hello, Lynn!"

She turned and came face to face with Scott Fleming. She hardly recognized him. He was dressed in a dark blue three-piece suit and looked every bit the surgeon. He stepped up to her and extended his hand, which she quickly took.

"I guess I'm a little early. I hope you don't mind but I didn't have as much work at the office," he said casually.

"Scott, it's great to see you again! I want to thank you for inviting me to dinner! It was one of the nicest family times I've had in many years." As she talked, Lynn was aware he had taken both her hands and was holding them tightly in his large ones.

"I have to tell you, the girls were angry with me when I told them I was going to have dinner with you this evening. They were determined they were going to came and I hate getting too firm with them," he replied.

"You know, Scott, I'm still thankful I was where I was Saturday morning! I have refused to think of what might have been!" Lynn answered with great feeling.

"Oh, by the way, this is far you!" He reached to a single bundle he had set beside him on a large concrete bench. She took the package and opened it to find three beautiful red roses. Lynn was floored and stood speechless. She felt a swell of emotions welling up inside her she hadn't felt in years.

"Can you help me put them on?" she whispered as she attempted to pin them on the left side of her dress. Scott started to help and suddenly blushed red and stepped back. Lynn was touched by his embarrassment. She worked with the pin for a moment and the roses were in place.

"Thank you so much, they're beautiful! You didn't have to do this, you know," she said in a low voice.

"I know, but I wanted to! I also want to say how pretty you look in that dress and thank you for having dinner with me. It was a difficult thing to get my courage up to ask!" he said nervously.

Lynn noticed how vulnerable and shy he really was. "Scott, thank you for asking me! Someday I'll tell you how much it has meant to me!" she answered. Scott smiled and said nothing.

"Shall we go to dinner or is there somewhere you'd like to go?" Scott asked.

"No, I have to admit I'm starving!" she answered.

Putting his arm about her slim waist they walked down to his bronze BMW which was parked in the short-park zone. As they sat while Scott warmed up the motor, he asked, "Is there somewhere special you'd like to go for dinner, Lynn?"

"Not really, I don't eat out often, except when I'm with someone from the company or officially entertaining. I always prefer somewhere small and intimate if that's all right with you," she replied.

"Sounds fine with me. One of the nicest spots I've found in the past year is the new dining room at the Dupont Plaza Hotel up on Connecticut Avenue. Have you ever been there?" he mentioned quietly.

"No, I've been to the hotel several years ago but never to the dining room."

"This is a new one and much smaller than the large one. Let's go there; I've been there with several people from the hospital and never been disappointed." With these words, he put the car into gear and turned out onto Fifteenth Street.

About fifteen minutes later they were being ushered into a small intimate room on the fourth floor of the hotel. They immediately ordered some pre-dinner drinks and their waiter came and took their orders for dinner. Lynn was rather taken aback as each waiter referred to Scott as Dr. Fleming on sight. Finally she commented, "Scott, you mentioned you had been here several times. It looks as if it might be more than that!"

"Well, I've been here three or four times with a large group of visiting specialists from abroad. I guess they see us as good customers. Don't worry, I've asked them not to pester us this evening," he answered.

As the evening progressed, Scott and Lynn felt themselves relaxing with each other. Lynn had ordered a lobster thermidor and took her time with the unusually large serving she received. Scott ordered a large New York steak and vegetables. Scott ordered two bottles of French wine, white for her and a red for himself. As they finished their main course, Lynn looked at Scott and asked innocently, "How long have you been in neurology, Scott?"

"Let me see," he replied, "I've been at the hospital now for eight years after seven as assistant at Stanford in California. Makes me sound like an old man, Lynn!" he responded.

"Don't feel bad, my marriage broke up eight years ago last month. It doesn't seem possible. I guess we're birds of a feather in a way!" Lynn said with a soft laugh. She noticed Scott's eyes drifting away from her and suddenly felt alone in the small room.

"I'm sorry, what have I said?" As she spoke his eyes suddenly came back to this moment and the two of them.

He said hesitantly, "Lynn, I'm sorry, I didn't hear you there for a moment. Every once in a while my wife's face comes up before me and I'm lost... Will you forgive me?"

"Scott, there's no need to feel bad! You must have had a wonderful marriage. That's not something to forget!" She reached out and took both his hands in hers. "Never feel bad for being part of such a love, Scott! I'm honoured that you've asked me to be your friend."

He looked deep into her dark eyes, never faltering. "You know, Lynn, I think little Francie was so right when she said on Sunday night, 'I like Aunt Lynn so much!' You've made a friend there for life. I hope this won't embarrass you, but if I don't say it I'll always regret it. There's something very special about you, Lynn Pollard, and my little girl saw that right off!" He looked away, his face turning red. For the first time in many years Lynn found she had tears running down her cheeks and couldn't stop them.

Scott was upset and angry with himself. "Damn it, I wanted to take you out and have a wonderful evening and all I've done is make you cry!"

Lynn reached across the small table and shook both of his hands, a fire burning through her tears. "For God's sake, Scott, what are you upset about? You've just paid me the nicest compliment anyone has ever given me. It's been one of the most wonderful evenings I have ever spent!" She snuffled as she talked and then settled back to finish her first glass of white wine.

Just before eleven Scott pulled up in front of Lynn's brownstone. She had been quiet as he drove her home across the city from the hotel. She turned and looked at him. From the look on her face, he knew somewhere in her recent life she had been terribly hurt. He picked up her left hand. "Look, Lynn, I don't know everything that has happened in your life, but I think you've had more than your share of tragedy. I hope you know how much I enjoy being with you. I would like to see you again." He was silent far a long spell.

"I'm afraid I haven't been good company, Scott! You have been so kind to me and I lose it. But if you're sure you want to, I'd like to see you very much," she replied in a low voice and averting his eyes.

"Would you like to come in for a coffee? You've got a bit of a drive to get home," she asked.

"Lynn, there's something more I'd like to do, but I know if I did, I wouldn't want to leave. Would you be offended if I took a rain check?" he asked.

"I don't think you're the type of person to offend someone, Scott."

"Lynn, let me walk you to your door; I'm afraid of these neighbourhoods."

Several moments later they stood inside Lynn's main foyer. She took both his hands and said, "Thank you so much for a wonderful evening! Would you tell the girls for me they've got a pretty nice father!" As she spoke she quickly kissed him on the cheek and whispered, "Good night, Scott. Please drive carefully on the way home!

Chapter 24

Tony was climbing to the top of the long stairs from the beach when he heard his name being called.

"Tony Cassell, we've got to talk!" Tony looked down and saw the smiling face of Father McGuire. "I've got information we've got to talk about!"

"Father, I'm glad you've come, I want to talk to you as well. There's matter we need to clear up." As he reached the top of the steps, Tony felt the priest's arm about him. They walked back to the house and sat by the pool. There was no one else in sight.

"Father, what were you trying to tell April and me yesterday? I've never known you to be confusing. If you've something to say spit it out."

The priest hesitated, then spoke. "Tony, I know you and Gordon are doing research into the Lincoln conspiracy, isn't that correct?"

"Yes, of course it is! What's wrong with that?" Tony replied.

"I suggest you stop for your own health's sake!" the priest replied coldly.

"Alright, I gather you have your reasons, Father. I tell you what, you tell us why and I'll give it some thought, but you'll have to come up with something convincing."

Father McGuire looked at Tony for a long time and stared off to the horizons. Finally, he replied, "Tony, I'm sorry I've been giving you comments without the facts. Are you familiar with the Jesuit Order at all?"

"No more than the usual Catholic layperson, Father, why do you ask?"

"Because what I'm about to tell you could cost us our lives, if we're not careful. At least then, you'll be able to appreciate my confusing answers. Two months ago I was in the Vatican doing research into the history of the Order. Our top officials encourage that sort of thing. As you know, I've been a camera buff for years. My area of research was a small pictorial history of the Order in America. There's nothing wrong here whatsoever. To make a long story short, I got into another part of the archives and came upon material from the Civil War period. Apparently a number of our people were travelling about this country at that time. In this material, I found several pictures taken at the time of Lincoln's death. They showed several Jesuit priests in one of the pictures!" Father was quiet for a spell as he let Tony collect his thoughts.

"Father, are you implying your Order was involved in the assassination of Lincoln?" Tony replied incredulously.

"Tony, this is where the matter gets complicated and dangerous. No, our Order wasn't involved in any way. But when I tried to identify the two priests in the picture, a door was literally slammed in my face. That's when I got curious. After six weeks digging around in this unofficial area, I hit pay dirt. From what I can tell, there has been, on and off over the past four hundred and fifty years, a subdivision within the Order. Its purpose appears to be covert operations and similar situations."

"Good God, are you telling me the Catholic Church has sponsored a terrorist cell, and how in hell could they keep such a thing quiet?" exclaimed a wide-eyed Tony.

"Those were the questions I've been asking myself these several months. From what I can sort out, it was set up after the Reformation, to make sure that never happens again!" the priest said bluntly.

"If what you have found is true, Father, why do you feel there is such a danger to you and I? Is it because of our work into the Lincoln conspiracy?"

"That, my young friend, was my first question. Even if the order was involved in the original plans and known cover-up, what has it to do with today? I think the answer lies in the partial failure of the original cover-up. The last thing this suborder wants is to have the word get out they were involved in the death of America's most beloved president. Imagine the feeling of the American people toward the Vatican, if this were discovered!"

Tony Cassell was stunned. No wonder Father McGuire was upset.

The priest continued, "This small offshoot of the Order has been referred to in several occasions as the Order of the Red Rose. Apparently as Christ's blood was shed for us, there may be times where the blood of others must be shed to protect the Church Herself."

"Father, if this small group is so dedicated to secrecy and the protection of the Holy Church, how did this evidence get into the Jesuit Order's archives?" Tony asked.

"That is the $64,000 question and I wish I had an answer! My only thought from some of the things I dug up was someone got careless and left details. They probably thought no one would ever make the connection. It's a long way from Rome to Washington, especially in the 1860s!" McGuire stated.

"One other question, Father, what about these threats Gordon and Bev have been receiving?"

"I have no easy answer, Tony. It may well be my digging in Rome has touched people I haven't been aware of. There was a case last week of the assassination attempt on the life of Senator Beecham in Iowa. I know for a fact, he, like yourselves, was doing work into the Lincoln business. The difference was he went public with his information and made the whole thing a part of his campaign. Tony, I think this small group is starting to panic, and that makes them dangerous!"

For the first time in their discussions, Tony was speechless. There was a tension in his face.

"Look, Tony, I feel bad over the way I've been treating you and the rest of your staff, but you can see the position in which I find myself," Father McGuire said rather quietly. He looked intently at the young man as he finished speaking, "I don't know what direction you want to take from here, but I would strongly advise exercising a great deal of care. Remember, this group is now exercising cover-ups for past indiscretions as well as present activities. This is where the nastiness may be quick in coming. If they have made an attempt on the life of a public official in this country already, you can rest assured they're on to you and your whole team as well!"

Tony stood up and thought for a moment, then said, "If they're already in this country and as strong as you say, then there's no sense trying to run. If they've been at it for nearly five hundred years, who are we to try and hide? All we can do is try to stop them the best way we can. You know what I am going to recommend? I am going to do my best to expose them. If I succeed, we'll have exorcised a cancer from the world. Excuse me, Father."

"Tony, I wish you and your staff all the best. As a Jesuit by calling and training, this leaves me sick at heart. If you must know, and this is off the record, my life isn't worth much. It may take the deaths of a great number of ordinary priests to bring the Order back to what St. Ignatius envisaged!"

"Father, I feel sick about this whole matter," Tony said thoughtfully.

"Tony, the motto of our Order is 'To the Greater Gloria of God.' Let's hope we can do something to help the spirit of that motto."

"Father, if everything you say is true, why is such an attempt being made to eliminate everyone connected to it? I would think if it were simply ignored, it would fade away," Tony asked.

"If that's what you think, Tony, then you're missing my whole point in our discussion!" the priest said with an edge to his words. "You'd better get the word to your friends in the project to drop it and damned quick. These bastards have been at it as you've said, for four hundred years and don't fool around!" he snapped at Tony, got to his feet and walked down the steps.

Tony told April about the talk with Father McGuire on the drive back to Long Beach on Sunday evening. She was upset by the chat she with Bev the previous day and this only made matters worse. Finally, as they were coming down from the hills, she turned to Tony and said, "Tony, I'm terrified. Don't you think we should drop the research at once?"

"I've thought a great deal about and discussed the matter with Father McGuire as well. He seems to think even if we drop the whole matter here and now, this small group is so paranoid about closing the past, they'll be looking for us anyway!"

"You're saying we're dead no matter which way we turn?" April answered with a quiver in her voice and her face pale.

"Yes, exactly. That's if we want to lie down and do nothing!" Tony snapped in a tone April had never heard before. "April, how long have you been working for me?"

"About three years. Tony, what's your point, I'm not following you?" April asked tensely.

"April, you've known me as a straight shooter all through that period. I'm going to level with you now," he replied as the old Porsche wound its way up another hill. Tony pulled over at a lookout and parked. He turned to April

"I'll tell you what I'm proposing. We need time to plan a strategy in case those damn priests come looking for us. I want to gather as much of the damning evidence as possible and disappear for a week. That way we'll have a breather and plan our next move. What would Art say if you disappeared?"

"Well, he wasn't too pleased when I told him I was coming up here this past weekend."

"April, I'm concerned with the alternative if we sit back and do nothing. Would Art prefer you dead?"

"Now who's becoming paranoid?" April asked not looking at Tony.

"April, I've known Father McGuire for over a decade and he's always been truthful and a loyal friend to me. That's why I take his word as gospel in this case."

"Isn't he worried about his own life?" April asked.

"Strange as it may seem, he referred to himself as a dead man. He says there is nowhere he can hide. I personally feel he's on some of a crusade against them."

"How do we know the whole thing isn't a figment of the good Father's imagination? I'll be candid. I've met the good Father and think you're wearing blinders when you even think about him. Remember, I'm Catholic and I know how the Catholic conscience works. These damned Jesuits are masters in its application. I know, I was almost raped by one of them!" she said.

"Four dead people to start with! How does that grab you?" he snapped. April went pale again, "Three priests have been gunned down and an assassinations attempt last week made on the life of the junior senator from Iowa. He was lucky and was missed, but his wife was killed on the spot."

"You mean Gloria Beecham was killed?"

"Yes, did you know them?"

"I had a long chat with her two weeks ago, when she was here at the university," April said.

"What did you two talk about?" Tony asked.

"Oh my God!" April gasped. "We talked extensively about the views of the senator on the reopening of the Lincoln conspiracy investigation. He was going to make it one of the cornerstones of his campaign for reelection to the Senate in the fall," April answered in an agitated manner.

"That" s what I thought and why we must decide what to do when we get back to Long Beach!" Tony exclaimed.

"Tony, what are you talking about? Didn't you hear anything I said?" April asked urgently.

He sat for the longest time before speaking. Finally he said angrily, "It makes me so damned angry to have to act in this manner, but the nature of who we're up against leaves us no alternative. Look, April, when we get back let's go to the office and gather up as much of the Lincoln material as we can and then go home for an hour."

"Tony, what in the Christ are you talking about?" April said as she shook Tony's arm.

"April, listen to me carefully! Our lives are in danger. When you go to your apartment, get enough clothes to last you a week. We've got to get out of here tonight. It's our only chance. The more I think of your comments about Father McGuire, I think we have little choice. We'll take a night plane to Toronto, so bring your passport. I've got an old Canadian chum there who runs a travel agency and I'll ask him to get us lost for a week."

"But what am I going to say to Art?"

"What did you tell him last Friday?" Tony asked impatiently.

"Oh, I said everyone from the office was going up to a retreat to do our annual staff planning. I don't know what he will say when I'm away for a week!"

"Look, April, mention that I've asked you to come east with me to some emergency research in the National Archives in Washington. My good friend Lynn Pollard is there and I can get her to cover if he calls." Tony spoke to April, taking her by the hand, "I know this whole thing seems as if it's not really happening, but let's get going. We'll go directly to your apartment, and then off to the airport in the morning. What do you think?"

"I would have thought you were off your rocker if I didn't know you as well as I do and also hadn't had that conversation with Bev on Saturday. Alright, I'll see what kind of a story I can leave on Art's message machine. He'll be upset, but he goes out of town for days at a time and tells me it's his own business where he goes." Tony could hardly believe what she was telling him, but said nothing. He started the Porsche again, and roared off into the growing twilight.

Chapter 25

"Well, there we are!" exclaimed Tony. "The Delta girl says we're all booked on their 9:45 flight. We'll have a stopover in Chicago and straight into Toronto. I left a message on Gerry's machine we wanted to go somewhere for a week where no one would find us. I know him well, he'll pick a place where even the good Lord himself would never think of looking." Tony said, a sigh of relief in his voice. They had arrived at April's little apartment about an hour after stopping at the university for a briefcase of material they wanted to take with them.

"Tony, what reason did you give for our absence?" April asked half interested.

"Oh, I said I met this weird girl and we wanted time together."

"You didn't!" she exclaimed.

"Yes, that's exactly what I put on his machine. Besides, I think you and I need to talk in that area."

April didn't answer and walked into her bathroom where she began getting ready to go to bed. She had fixed up the old day couch in her living room for Tony. By the time she came out, Tony was wearing a pair of PJ bottoms and getting things tidied up in his suitcase for the flight in the morning. As he closed it he heard April behind him.

"Tony, can we talk?" she said anxiously. "I'm confused. Why is it necessary for us to disappear for a week? Besides, Art won't be speaking to me when we get back!" He sat down on the day couch alongside April. She had changed from her jeans and shirt to a nightie and bathrobe. Tony saw she was agitated and needed answers immediately. He reached over and held her hands in his own. He saw the fear in her deep brown eyes as she looked his way. There was a slight tremble in her voice.

"Look, April, you might as well know the whole story in a nutshell. You've been involved in a lot of the basic sorting and cross-references in the research but we've deliberately kept you away from some of the hardcore evidence we've dug up. Please believe we didn't do that because we didn't feel that you weren't capable."

"Well, that's how it makes me feel, you know!" April added with a bitter note in her voice, "I had the feeling I saw most of the new material that was coming in regarding the Lincoln conspiracy."

"That's right. But there are certain key areas. Especially this small group of priests of which you aren't even aware. For example, I've seen enough proof this group were involved in pressure tactics at the time of the Battle of Waterloo in 1815. If they hadn't been there, it's possible the result would have been another victory for Napoleon. Then, there was the Italian Revolution in the 1860s. The order wanted the Papal States turned over to Garibaldi and his revolutionaries. Part of the secret Order wanted to save the Church from herself!" As he talked, April sat with her mouth ajar.

"If this is true, they have been tinkering with the development of history itself! No wonder you're scared, it leaves me cold," April said tersely.

"That's right and these facts are, I believe, the tip of the iceberg. It's no wonder they want to shut us up and are willing to pay any price to accomplish this goal! April, the Lincoln business is only a tiny part of the whole mess!"

April looked stunned. Tony continued, "Up to the present time, they have been able to keep all their operations secret. If anyone among their own asked questions, they were eliminated. With the Lincoln affair, we stumbled on something they missed well over a century ago. Right now they're doing their best to close the back door after the horse is gone!" He stopped as he saw April chewing her lower lip.

"Tony, what can we do to stop them or get out of the way?" she asked urgently.

Suddenly Tony was aware he was still holding her hands. "I'm not sure how to answer your question, but we've got to do something. I do know Father McGuire has set his cap to put as much sand in their way as possible! Listen, let's get some sleep and we can talk about this on the plane in the morning!" He looked at his watch and noted it was past ten o'clock.

April got to her feet and said, "Look, Tony, I know I'm a bit of a nut head, but I am grateful, believe me, for all you're doing for us both. I've got to get some sleep. That sun this morning zonked me right out!" She stood up on her tiptoes and kissed him quickly and disappeared into her bedroom. With a slight smile on his face, Tony climbed under the covers and quickly fell asleep.

It was partway through the night when Tony was aware of someone sitting on the couch and shaking him. Rubbing his eyes, he peered at the sleep-tousled face of April.

"I'm sorry to wake you, Tony, but I couldn't sleep! Everything you mentioned kept running through my mind." As she talked, she clasped his free hand tightly. She wore only her light nightie and her breasts were visible through the thin material. He flipped the covers back and she slipped alongside him. Within a few minutes both were sound asleep.

Chapter 26

Maggie pecked away at her computer as Lynn breezed by her Wednesday morning. She was barely in her office when Maggie was at her door.

"Well, how was it?"

"How was what?" Lynn replied innocently.

"Oh, come on, cut the bullshit!" Maggie quipped. Lynn's face lit up in a bright smile.

"Lynn, I'm happy for you! You've cut yourself off the past few years! As I told you yesterday, Scott Fleming is one of the most decent people I know. The only criticism I've ever heard was his treatment of other doctors. He is a perfectionist and demands total commitment from those who work for him. By the way, are you going to see him again?" she asked.

"We haven't made any plans, besides we've only met, you know!" As she talked Lynn took off her raincoat and hung it in her closet

Maggie was surprised to see her wearing a sharply cut suit and skirt. Maggie noticed Lynn's skirt was well above her knees. She often teased her about her good legs. As she left Lynn's office, she said over her shoulder, "Lynn, I'm happy for you. You're long overdue and Scott couldn't have met a nicer person!" Lynn smiled to herself. She hadn't felt as good about her life in a long time.

At ten o'clock, there was a rap at her partially open door. Frank Baird walked in.

"Good morning, Lynn, it's great to see you again. Boy, you look good this morning. You must have had a big night last evening."

"As a matter of fact, a good friend took me to dinner," Lynn answered as he settled down at the other side of Lynn's big desk.

"I don't want to alarm you. But what I have uncovered scares the crap out of me!" He laid on the desk the pictures she had given him. "I know you told me where you got these pictures, but I want to know when and from whom. If what we suspect is true, this will turn this Lincoln affair on its ear!" Scott said.

"Frank, it's like I told you last Friday, I'm doing a thorough study on the

91

Matthew Brady school of photography. One of my contacts at the National Archives found them and showed them to me when I was picking up more Brady pictures. I had no idea the scope of the project when I started. Fortunately for me, the company is backing me all the way." As she talked, Lynn rested both elbows on her desk.

"Lynn, what startled me after I got back to the office on Saturday was this old note that I found crammed in a small pocket on the back of the main picture. You see, Lynn, the first picture included all the people who are in the other picture, and which has been the public domain for all these years. This second picture has these two new faces. That wouldn't have meant much if this small paper wasn't there. Look at this."

He handed her a small piece of yellowed decaying paper. Looking at it she could barely make out the writing:

I, MARY SURRATT HEREBY WRITE ON THIS 15th OF APRIL, 1865. I DECLARE MY INNOCENCE IN THE PLANNING OF THE DEATH OF OUR LATE PRESIDENT ABRAHAM LINCOLN. I WISH TO DECLARE MY LEGACY OF INNOCENCE IN THE PRESENCE OF TWO PRIESTS OF THE JESUIT ORDER. MY LEGACY IS ONE OF ONLY KNOWING AND NOT INVOLVEMENT. THE LEGACY OF THE PRIESTS IS ONE OF BOTH ENCOURAGEMENT AND ACTIVE INVOLVEMENT BOTH PERSONALLY AND OF THE ORDER THEY REPRESENT!

Lynn read the statement through again. She pondered over in her mind what this meant.

"Frank, what does this statement add up to in your mind? It really doesn't mean all that much to me, except there may have been more than the original people involved in the conspiracy," Lynn said to Frank.

"It could mean there was another important player in the assassination. If it is what I think, then we'd better be ready to open a whole new can of worms. Can you imagine how the public might feel if they were to find out the Vatican was behind the Lincoln killing?"

"Come on, Frank, you really don't believe for a minute there is any truth behind this letter, do you?" Lynn, asked, a look of unbelief in her eyes.

"Look, Lynn, with your permission, I'd like to pursue these pictures and this note further. The note was no doubt written by Mary Surratt, and she appears to give credence to the existence of the two men in the picture. As soon as I find anything new, I'll get in touch. Oh yes, I've sent copies of these pictures to half a dozen people I know who might be a help in sorting out the puzzle."

"Frank, do you think there is any danger of anyone getting angry over this matter?" Lynn asked rather casually.

"No, I wouldn't worry about that. Mind you, there could be some red faces in some high circles, if what I suspect is true. Listen, I must go, I had to let you know the importance of this matter!" He quickly got to his feet and headed far the door. Lynn stood at the back of her desk as he headed out. He stopped and added, "By the way, you should wear skirts more often! You've got great legs!"

With these words he turned and ambled out of the office. Lynn Pollard stood shaking her head and a smile on her lips. She wondered why he was getting into such a snit over a change in a historical picture. Who was able to give her an informed answer? Then she remembered the young man from the history department at Cal Tech. He had called her several months ago to see if Kodak was involved with any research in the Civil War period. She remembered him mentioning he and his associates were heavily involved in a reevaluation of the Lincoln conspiracy and investigation. She reminded herself to give him a call later in the morning when he was in his office.

Lynn was getting ready to head out for lunch when Maggie buzzed her office from her outer desk.

"Lynn, there's a call from Dr. Fleming for you! He's on line three."

"Good morning, Lynn!" Scott's friendly voice came over the line. "I hope you survived the Plaza's feed last night!"

"Hi, Scott. It's good to hear your voice. Yes, I'm still stuffed after the meal! Listen, I had a wonderful time and want to thank you very much."

"Lynn, it was my pleasure, believe me! Listen, I've got a problem with the girls, they're up in arms with their dad for not bringing their new friend around. Could you help me out, if I might be so presumptuous?" he asked with a hesitation in his voice. As she listened to him, Lynn started to giggle, something she hadn't done in a long time.

"Scott, how could I refuse your little girls, they're so cute. What can I do?" she answered.

"Well, we often go to Martha's Vineyard around this time of year for a weekend with the whole family. I've got a friend at Walter Reed Army Hospital whose family invites us up there to their spread and we try to go. Mother usually comes along and helps chaperone the kids. There'll be buckets of people and we'd love to have you come with us if you were interested. I wish I could say it was my idea, but it really was the girls'!"

"Scott, are you sure you want a stranger along on a personal weekend?" Lynn asked.

"Lynn Pollard, never think of yourself as a stranger with our family; that you'll never be!" Scott's voice was firm with warmth and affection.

"I'd love to go, Scott! When do you usually go up?" she said.

"We'd probably leave Friday morning if that was all right with you. We could pick you up at nine o'clock. I have a Windstar van I use for these occasions. Lynn, we're all looking forward to seeing you again! Oh yes, one other thing, the AMA is putting on their big Hawaiian bash this Saturday at their resort out on the Chesapeake Bay. Would you like to go?"

"Hey, I've heard about those before, they're quite the bash! Sure, I'd love to if you can still get tickets."

"Oh, I've got the tickets. It should be quite a night. I haven't been there in years. Listen, I've got a big case coming up so I'll give you a ring tomorrow!" he said his voice low.

"I'll look forward to your call, Scott!" she answered. A gentle warmth swept over Lynn as she sat back in her chair.

Getting into her raincoat, Lynn was about to leave the office when the buzzer sounded again.

Chapter 27

The Tel Aviv traffic was terrible. The morning sun was merciless and the streets already crowded. Abram Sharon hurried down the dirty side street lost in the crowd. He turned into a small alley and entered a filthy doorway. Passing through a room crowded with women and children, he was stopped inside the second rusty door by a man with a small Uzi. His eyes spelled business and hands that dealt in death. Abram knew his type, yet he was the breed the Mossad used for years in the security of their little nation. Sharon was slammed up against the wall and searched. When he was finished, a woman entered and approached him at knifepoint. He handed his papers over to her. She examined them and looked at him. Finally she muttered, "This way, Colonel, the general will see you now."

He followed the woman into the next room. There behind a scruffy desk sat one of the most feared soldiers in the country, General Avram Dayal. He clicked his heels together and saluted.

"Never mind the bullshit, Colonel, come over and sit down. I think we have a problem, and have to move quickly if we are to nip it in the bud. Colonel, I know your reputation and won't insult your intelligence."

"I'm with you, General. I know you wouldn't have brought me here without a valid reason. How can I be of assistance?" Sharon added.

"Colonel, as you know there isn't any love lost for our country in some quarters of the Roman Catholic Church. We've had more or less a gentleman's agreement to stay out of each other's way in most parts of the world. Now we may have a problem. There has been a brutal killing of three priests in Dublin. One was a key informant in Britain. We were puzzled at first about the killing. If only our man had been killed, everything would have been pretty clear cut. But that wasn't the case. There were two other Jesuits killed as well. That's the real problem. They were killed in the most professional manner. That was two weeks ago and it appears the killer was another member of the Jesuit Order," the general added bluntly.

"You mean, sir, they were cleaning out their own house?" Sharon inquired. "That seems to be a rare thing, especially for the Jesuits."

"That was our immediate reaction as well. Then we dug up the last package our man in Dublin passed to us before he was killed. It was a revelation. He had met an older American Jesuit, a Father Jim McGuire in the American Jesuit Seminary Library in Rome. McGuire was doing private research and in the midst of it all he came up with evidence to show there may be a shadowy group of Jesuits in existence called the Order of the Red Rose!"

"With what purpose in mind, General?"

"According to the evidence dug up by McGuire, it was founded after the Reformation in the 1550s to insure nothing like it ever happened again," the general added.

"In other words it was set up as a terrorist front for the Vatican! How have they managed to keep this quiet all these centuries? It's quite a feat!" Sharon exclaimed.

"We feel the same, yet there's something fishy about the whole thing. At this point I sent out the call to see you. Since, there have been more developments in the US. A researcher in the National Archives in Washington has evidence there was papal influence in the conspiracy to kill Abraham Lincoln. There has been the occasional outburst of interest over the years about the possibility of a cover-up, but most feel too much time has passed to do anything. Now this new evidence could point the smoking gun directly at Rome.

"Holy shit, General, if this is the case there could be an explosion of anti-Catholicism all over the US, especially in the Bible Belt," replied Colonel Sharon.

"That's where you come in, Colonel. I want you to go to the US and look up some of these contacts and names I have for you. Remember, our basic thrust is the protection and promotion of all things Israeli and Jewish!" snapped General Shalom.

"Are those orders at all costs, General?" Sharon asked directly and officially.

"Yes, Colonel, use whatever means you feel you have to in order to protect and promote our interests!" the general replied with tight lips.

"Yes, General. I'll catch the first flight to New York in the morning!" Sharon snapped.

"I'll give you the names of all our people in the various parts of the US. You can pick them up at that sloppy desk on your way out. May the Spirit of Yahweh go with you, Colonel," he said.

"And with you, General!" replied Sharon walking from the office. In the next office, he stopped in front of the major who had frisked him and said,

"Major, you were thorough, but if I were you, I'd have kicked me in the balls, remember I got by you!" With these words, his left knee slammed the man in the groin as hard as he could snap. The other knee followed in the face shattering the man's nose and scattering teeth all over the floor. "Remember, Major, that's better than being dead. The next time I'm here, I want to see some balls! Remember you're a soldier!" As the man lay on the floor a growing pool grew about his face interwoven with the contents of his stomach.

He was about to leave when he felt a soft hand on his arm. Grasping it so quickly its owner never had a chance, he heard only the girl's words, "Colonel, you had no right to do that! He's a good man, and would give his life anytime and you know it!"

"Good, but not good enough!" the colonel's voice growled as he twisted her arm completely around, hearing her gasp with the searing pain. Snapping the arm over his leg as he brought it up, the bones of both the upper and lower arms shattered. The girl fainted immediately as he dropped her to the floor. The crowd in the outer office stood stunned. He looked about him into the empty faces.

"We were the last line in 1967 and 1973! We didn't faint nor fail. Be like these two, and the state of Israel will be gone in twenty years. If I was in earnest, she wouldn't have a face right now! Remember you are the last line!"

Chapter 28

Lynn awoke with a start on Saturday morning. For a moment, she wondered where she was. Then yesterday's activity came back to her. On the trip up from Washington, Scott's girls treated her like their long-lost friend. Little Francie sat on her lap for most of the trip. By the time they reached the large rambling resort on the shores of Martha's Vineyard, the girls were fast asleep. Scott's friends the Sarnoffs left the place well stocked with food. Even the air conditioning was running.

Lynn saw it was only 7 a.m. yet the sun was streaming in the windows of her room. Climbing out of bed, she wandered barefoot to the patio doors and opened them. The large two-story cottage was built behind a series of large dunes, which levelled out onto a wide sprawling beach. In the distance the ocean was pounding in a never-ending series of breakers. Stepping back into her room, she pulled on a pair of denim shorts and sleeveless shirt and walked down the large rambling steps leading from the deck. There was a gentle breeze whipping the long eelgrass growing over the tops and sides of the dunes. Brushing her hair from her eyes, Lynn kicked off her sandals and waded in the cool waters of the ocean. She gasped at its cold chill. Wading in to her knees, she could feel her legs growing numb with the cold.

"Now you know why the Sarnoffs put in a large pool!" she heard Scott's voice behind her. "Sorry, I didn't mean to startle you."

"Good morning, Scott," she said. "I'm a morning person and was slept out. What a beautiful beach, but you're not going to get me in the ocean!"

"Well, I'm not saying we never swim in the ocean, but I prefer the pool myself. Would you like to come up for coffee and muffins? I put some on, before I saw you walking?" he asked.

"That sounds great, I'm usually in my little office by this hour. This is a real break."

Turning, they walked back over the dunes together to the large deck off the cottage's kitchen. As they sat about the kitchen table, Scott said, "You're probably wondering why we have the use of such a beautiful summer home.

I did some extensive surgery on the Sarnoffs' little grandson about eight years ago. He would have died without it and they've insisted we spend a couple of weeks here every summer as part of their gratitude. I didn't want to at first, but sometimes you have to let folks do something for you!"

Lynn sat and chewed away on a fresh carrot muffin. Suddenly the kitchen exploded with shrieks of girlish laughter. Scott snorted and said, "Here comes the little brigade. There'll be no more peace from now until bedtime."

Turning on the stool, Lynn was immediately pounced on by the two girls in their swimsuits.

"Aunt Lynn, we want you to come swimming with us after breakfast, would you?" asked Angie urgently.

"Of course, I'd love to but you've got to let me finish my breakfast, OK?" she replied.

Francie, who was standing next to Lynn, ran her tiny hand down the length of Lynn's slender thigh and chirped, "Grandma thinks you're too thin! You should be eating more! Don't you think Aunt Lynn is far too thin, Daddy?"

Lynn was beside herself with laughter as she saw Angie's wide-eyed innocence combined with Scott's acute embarrassment. He knew he wasn't going to get off the hook and replied, "Angie, you shouldn't be making personal comments about Lynn like that!"

"But Daddy, you're always telling us we have to tell the truth and say how we feel! I think Aunt Lynn is too thin. We should get her fatter!"

At this stage, Lynn was holding her sides with her giggles over Scott's futile attempts to contain his daughter.

"Angie, that's enough!" There was a tone in her father's voice that caused her to stop. Lynn was still in the midst of her laughter. "Angie, we don't think Lynn is too thin. I think she has a lovely figure and I don't want you to tease her about it!" Scott answered firmly.

"I'm sorry, Aunt Lynn, I shouldn't have said that." Suddenly she started to cry as she put her arms about Lynn's neck. Lynn held her small body tight.

"Don't cry, honey, I know you didn't mean to hurt anyone! Besides, I know I'm a bit on the scrawny side anyhow! Listen, you take your sister out on the deck where I see your grandmother getting your breakfast ready. After I'm finished here, I'll go swimming with you!" With these reassuring words, the two girls bounced out of the small kitchen.

Scott was sitting drinking his coffee and shaking his head. "That Angie will be the death of me yet! She says exactly what's on her mind. I hope she didn't hurt your feelings."

Lynn suddenly reached over and laid a hand on Scott's. "Scott, don't worry about me around the girls. Kids are so honest, it can give adults a jolt when you're not used to them. So for God's sake, don't worry about them." Lynn spoke in soft voice. She was finding herself becoming attracted to Scott in a way she had vowed she never would again.

"Thanks for those words, because I would have been annoyed with them, if you had been. By the way, I meant what I said about your figure, you know. I mean that as a doctor!" He laughed as he said it.

"Scott, you're more than a good doctor, you know, and that's how I took that compliment," Lynn said.

"You're trying to trap me in a corner and I can see it coming and there's nothing I want to do about it!" As she rose to leave she had to squeeze by him. As she did, he took her face in his hands and kissed her. As he did, she put her hands on each shoulder. He stepped back embarrassed and said, "I'm sorry, I shouldn't have done that!

"Scott, if I didn't want you to, I would have said so," Lynn replied. As she stepped past him, she put a hand on his arm and whispered, "I'll see you in the pool, Doc!"

Lynn arrived at the pool in a modest older one-piece. She found everyone there except Scott's mother. As she stepped on the deck the shoulder strap broke.

"Damn! I guess I won't be able to come in the pool, this is the only suit I have with me." Suddenly Martha appeared behind Lynn in the doorway to the deck.

"Don't worry, Lynn, there are several suits the Sarnoffs' granddaughters use when they are here. They should be about your size."

Lynn and Martha disappeared back into the house. Both girls were dressed in tiny two-piece swimsuits and Scott had on an old tattered pair of cutoffs. They were frolicking in the shallow end of the pool when Lynn and Martha returned. Lynn wore a large shirt over whatever Martha had dug up for her. Sitting on a deck chair, Lynn seemed to be upset.

"Look, I'm not accustomed to wearing these two-piece suits. There's a lot of me and not much suit!" Lynn finally stood up taking off her shirt. The suit was a pretty white two-piece. The bottom was modest enough, stopping at her middle and high on the hips. The halter was made from a thin material that fit her well. The suit, while modest, made her figure appear fuller than it was.

"I'm sorry, Scott, your mother had to dig up this suit and it doesn't leave much to the imagination," she said looking away from Scott's face.

"Why you get embarrassed, Lynn, I don't know. These eyes that look at you are the eyes of a doctor you know!" he said with a feigned look of innocence on his face. Lynn rolled her eyes as she walked to the edge of the pool and jumped in. Lynn spent most of the morning in the water playing with the girls. After several hours, the girls tired and went into the cottage to play. Scott and Lynn remained stretched out on deck chairs.

After a quiet spell, Scott laid a hand on Lynn's bare arm and asked, "Lynn, may I ask you a personal question?"

"Is something wrong?" she replied raising her eyes.

"Sometimes I see a great sadness come over you. I hope it's nothing we've said?"

Lynn laid a small hand over his. She didn't answer immediately. Finally she turned and said, "It has nothing to do with you, Scott. Part of me is locked in time seven years ago and I guess I'll never be fully free." As she talked, he could see traces of the deepest loneliness coming over her. "I was coming out of the office one evening when two guys jumped me next to my car. In many ways my life ended there. They beat me almost unconscious and then raped me. I spent a month in the hospital. The physical wounds soon healed, but the emotional ones are still healing." As she talked slowly she was aware tears were starting to flow down her cheeks. Yet she was aware of Scott's hand tight on her arm. She clasped it tight as she could. She stopped, as she could no longer talk.

Scott spoke quietly, "Lynn, I had no idea what you've been suffering. I've had to help a number of women after this sort of thing, but I know little about the emotional trauma you must go through."

Lynn looked at him. A great sadness still dominated her whole countenance.

"Lynn, there are two little girls who already love you. Their father is becoming fond of you as well. Could you let us help you deal with that sad part of your life?"

Lynn looked at him in disbelief but was unable to speak.

"All I am asking is, don't lock us out, you've got so much to give and ahead of you. I hope we can be a part of that life." Scott got up and came around to the edge of her deck lounger. As she looked up into his face, she felt closer to him than anyone since the death of her father. He reached out, drew her toward him and placed his arms around her.

Finally Lynn looked up and said slowly, "Scott, I could never close you out, I hope you know that. You and the girls have done more for me in the past week than anyone else. I know I'm selfish, but I want to be near you, now, I'm not sure what it means."

"I think it means you feel the same as we feel about you. Besides, that bathing suit doesn't exactly help matters, you know! The only thing I'd like better would be you without it at all!" he said, a snicker in his voice.

With these words Lynn finally sat up and snorted. "I think we'd better change this trend of conversation as the girls will be back any minute!" Lynn retorted as she swung her long legs onto the deck. He remained sitting on the lounger. Lynn stopped and looked down at him. She ran a small hand down his rough cheek before leaving the deck.

"Lynn," Scott asked as she started through the kitchen door, "would you like to go for a walk after lunch? It's beautiful down beyond the far end of the dunes."

"Sure, I'd love to!" she answered.

Chapter 29

Tony and April were awakened by her phone at 7:30. She answered with a groggy, "Yes, who are you looking for? Oh. yes, wait a minute!" She handed the phone to Tony, who was still half asleep.

"Tony, it's the girl from Delta Airlines, she says she can offer us a better flight!"

"Yah, what? Why should we wait until noon to leave? Oh... Yes. Oh... sure that's fine. No stop in Chicago! Thanks for calling!" he reached over April's half-sleeping form and put the phone back in its cradle.

"We don't have to go until noon. She found a better flight and there's no stop in Chicago. We won't be so rushed."

By now, sleep was impossible for Tony. Yet, as he turned over on the couch he found April fast asleep again. She lay on her back and she breathed softly. Smiling to himself, he pulled the covers up under her neck. She murmured something in her sleep and rolled over on her side. He hopped out of bed and headed off to the washroom for a shower. April was still asleep when Tony slipped out the front door after leaving her a note that he would be back in an hour. He went over to Gordon's apartment to pick up some material he left there on the Lincoln project. They lived in the same complex as he did, only a twenty-minute drive away.

There was no answer to his raps when he knocked. Finally using the key Gordon gave him, he let himself in.

The apartment was in chaos. Everything was upside down and dumped on the floor. A cold feeling crept through Tony. He called out but there was no answer. He found the small package he had been looking for piled under a cushion in the corner of the bedroom he used when he stayed there. He picked up a rag and dusted his prints off everything he touched. He slipped back to his car and headed back to April's little apartment. Where were Gordon and Bev? In less than twenty-five minutes he arrived back in her apartment. He noted the couch was empty and could hear the shower going. Grabbing his bag he quickly put his few belongings back into it. He heard a shuffle behind him.

"God, Tony, you gave me a scare when I woke and you were gone. Thank God you left the note."

"I went to Gord's apartment for a small box of papers. You should see the mess someone made of his apartment. Completely ransacked!" he said.

"Tony, I'm getting nervous. There's trouble at every turn. I like your idea of getting out of here for a few days," she answered.

"Well, you get yourself dressed and we'll get to the airport. Besides, I want to go to the bank to get some money."

"Give me thirty minutes and I'll be ready to go. Tony, I packed some basic things while you were gone. I threw a lot of sunscreen in case we go somewhere that's hot."

Three hours later they found themselves sitting in a Delta Air Lines Air Bus high over the Rocky Mountains en route to Toronto. The plane was half full and they were receiving more attention from the stewardesses than normal. As they enjoyed a quick lunch as was the custom as soon as the flights were out of LA, April said, "Tony, why didn't you want me to phone Art before we left? He's going to be angry and I'll get hell when we get back!" she asked, a note of concern in her voice.

Tony thought and then said, "Look, You know me well enough to trust me. Or perhaps you don't?"

She looked hurt as he spoke. "Tony, I've worked for you for two years. If I didn't trust you how could I work for you?"

"Look, I'm concerned with your friend Art! I have a bad feeling over what's happening over this Lincoln business. I'm not sure I'd trust your friend's promise to keep silent. That's it in a nutshell."

"Tony, you don't trust Art to keep his mouth shut, is that it?" she asked, a catch in her voice.

"He may be a nice guy but from what you've told me, I'm not sure he can keep a lid on his mouth. And, by the way, this has nothing to do about my other opinion of him," Tony said bluntly. "This is a tedious situation and I don't think Art should know anything about it or where you're going." He looked at her as he talked. There were tears in her eyes.

"I know you think I'm an idiot, Tony, for sticking by him!" she answered angrily.

"No. I don't think that at all and I know your argument, he is always there when you need him!"

"That's right and don't ever forget it!" she said her voice rising.

As they talked, people about them were becoming ill at ease with their evident conflict. As he talked, Tony was finding feelings within himself for this small girl he knew so well. Suddenly the older man sitting across the aisle leaned over and said, "Look, son, I don't know what's the matter with the young woman, but she seems to mean something to you—why not tell her!" He spoke with kindness in his voice.

Tony nodded his head with a smile. Finally he took April's hand and said, "April, didn't it ever occur to you I might care for you a bit as well?"

"No, it didn't, and you never had time for anyone but yourself and your work in the time I've known you. So why should I think otherwise? Now you start picking on Art and expect me to believe you. Give me one good reason why?" she spoke with a note of bitterness in her voice. Tony was quiet for the longest time. Finally Tony turned to April. She had been sitting with a stern angry look on her face.

"April, I've been a real ass about this whole matter. I don't know where to start to say how sorry I am. But there's one thing I know. I don't want anything to happen to you. You're important to me, that much I'm certain about."

As she listened, there was a softening in her eyes.

"Tony, you want to know something? You're starting to discover how I've felt about you for over a year. I'm glad you've found your feelings. Why else do you think I could let you make love to me at Gordon's summer place?"

"April, let's take time over the next few days to get to know each other better?"

"Tony, are you sure that's what you want? I know," she said quietly.

"Yes, this business has me nervous and I don't want to lose you. I think you have a point, we may have to dump it if the danger gets worse." As he talked, he was aware she was holding his arm next to her tightly.

She looked up at him, and said, "Tony, please remember I care, but I don't want to be hurt again."

"Let's think of the next few days as a honeymoon!" Tony said with a laugh.

"I know what you've got in mind," April said with a giggle.

"What do you mean? You came to my room, don't forget, and you didn't exactly walk away!" he answered with a snort. April turned red and looked out the plane's window at the fleecy clouds far below.

Chapter 30

Colonel Abram Wein shifted his feet nervously as he rapped on the door. He looked at his watch: It was one minute past nine, this 30th of May. He flew in last evening with the assurance the Eastern US wing of the international division would have representatives to meet him this morning. He was dressed in a grey suit but looked very much the soldier. Then the door opened.

"Come in, Colonel, it's good to have you in the country. I'm Uwe Volkstien and you know me from our phone and fax messages."

Wein snorted as he walked past the older man. The room was a large suite with a comfortable sitting area. There were eight people waiting for him. As he entered, they all stood. His reputation throughout the Mossad worldwide was legendary. They knew he wouldn't be here unless there was something major afoot here in the States. He signalled for all to be seated. Stepping over to the window, Wein looked at the skyline that always fascinated him. America was still America and New York had a certain charisma for him. He looked down into the street. Nearly forty stories below.

"Ladies and gentlemen, I thank you for coming. The state of Israel has a need of your services. Some of the things I'm going to say will be of classified nature, so please remember the spreading of any of this information could endanger the lives of many people. Have I made myself clear on that matter?" He looked about the room and waited to see if there was any objection. There was no comment. "We may be having a serious political problem world wide with an organization you have probably never heard about. I speak of the Order of the Red Rose." There was no recognition at first. Then a young woman raised a finger.

"Ruth Michelson. Colonel, I know my history; about a century ago there were rumours in Italy that an organization by this name was involved in the Italian Revolution under Guiseppi Garibaldi. I thought they were dead after that."

"I congratulate you, Ruth! As Jews we have to know our history or we'll be destroyed by it. Yes, that's the same organization, except it didn't die out. It was started by the pope after the Council of Trent in the fifteen hundreds to

106

protect the Church from another Reformation assaulting the Church. The pope in 1562 ordered the head of the Jesuit Order to set up this secret order as a type of cutting edge of Vatican policy down over the centuries. That they have been doing. They've been involved in almost every major historical event since. Now you can ask what has this to do with us here in 1997. That's why I'm here and where the Mossad has been called in. There's a small group of people who believe they have evidence this Order was directly involved in the assassination of Lincoln."

"Colonel, you're serious?" an older man sitting on one of the lounge chairs muttered. "I've heard of some strange tales but that takes the cake."

"You're exactly right, and the point is several of the researchers have been getting some nasty threats on the matter. That's where we come into the scene. There've been several rumours floating about Europe they might try to accuse us of getting even with the Vatican, over what we have often felt to be sins of omission in the past. I mean precisely the kid-glove treatment of the Nazis by the Vatican, namely Pope Pius XII, over his treatment of our people in the Holocaust."

"Those bastards," snarled a young rabbi standing by the back window. "If they want a fight, we're the group to give it to them. I've always said the Vatican wouldn't be satisfied until the Holocaust was complete!"

"Now, calm down, Moshe!" exclaimed Uwe as the meeting began to heat up.

"Three of our leading operatives in Europe have been eliminated over the past three weeks. However, the one who was killed in Dublin had sent off a package to us the day before he was killed. This whole Jesuit involvement in the Lincoln conspiracy was linked to a man he met in the American Jesuit Seminary in Rome. Ladies and gentlemen, let me tell you what the overall picture seems to be. There is no doubt there exists a brutal wing of the Jesuit Order, the Red Rose. Why are they becoming so active at this moment in time? That's the question. General Wein's theory is it isn't the Jesuits who are the real culprits here. This year is an election year here in America. If someone could point the smoking gun in the Lincoln killing at the Catholic Church, what better way to get American public opinion to turn against the Church!"

"Holy shit, what a scenario!" muttered the young rabbi again. "But why drag we Jews into the picture?"

"That, Rabbi, was my immediate question as well. And to quote the general, the answer is so obvious it is absolutely ingenious. Whoever is engineering this whole scenario is going to put the blame on us as well. If you spread the blame well around amongst the old scapegoats then there'll be less danger you'll be exposed!"

There was a stunned silence in the room. Finally Ruth asked, "How do we put a handle on this if we don't know who the people are?"

"Yes, Ruth, you're right. I'm afraid to admit, we're not sure who we are dealing with yet, but we do know where the Jesuits' contacts are. We have the names of some people both in Washington and California who are involved in the present research of the Lincoln conspiracy. These people's lives are in danger from the Red Rose and our job is twofold. We must protect these people and prevent the Catholic Church and the Jewish community in America from being the scapegoat at the same time. Your orders will be given to each of you. You are to eliminate these Jesuits quickly and silently. I want emphasis on both of these factors. But remember at the same time to keep one eye over your shoulder for the FBI. They know we're here but they can't act completely blind. If you run up against something or someone you weren't prepared for, remember the silence of death. Death's voice doesn't witness. Finally watch out for a priest, a Father Jim McGuire. He's operating under the guise he knows nothing about this Red Rose and that he's working against them. This story is already being used. Actually he's the most dangerous of them all. He has killed more than two dozen good people worldwide in the past ten years. He is as ruthless an agent as we've ever encountered. The other task we have to solve quickly is who is actually engineering this whole thing and for what reasons. Then we have to eliminate them as quickly as possible. Remember we don't have the luxury of anything except a quick execution, if the need arises. I urge you to do it quickly if need be. You'll get no recognition except the eternal gratitude of the people of Israel." He took a bottle of new Israeli wine from a briefcase and a tube of plastic glasses. He quickly poured a single amount in each glass, stood and raised his glass. Each person present quickly followed.

"Remember our cry from 1967: Tomorrow, in Jerusalem! *Shalom aca!*"

Chapter 31

Toronto was the busiest air terminal they had ever seen. April and Tony came in through the old Terminal One and there was a thirty-minute wait going through the Canadian customs. April was nervous as she had heard horror stories about the Separatist movement. As they were waiting to pick up their baggage at one of the big carousels. Tony heard his name called.

"Tony, Tony Cassell! Over here!" Turning he came face to face with Gerry Lorenzin, the young man he had gone through Fordham University with in St. Louis. He was a big chap, nearly three hundred pounds, and been a star linebacker on the gridiron.

"By God, Tony, how long has it been? I can't remember!"

Tony threw his arms about the big man and slapped him on the back. He turned and said, "Gerry, this is April Savitz! We're up to our eyeballs in this present research together."

"Hi April. I'm Gerry. I see you know my old friend Tony here! I'd watch him—now and then he tends to forget to change his underwear, but overall he's a good friend." He laughed at his own joke and picked April's small form up and swung her around in a huge bear hug. As he set her down, she was winded.

"Gerry, it's my pleasure to meet you. Tony said you were a great friend and that you were tall— boy, he wasn't kidding."

"Yeah. I've tended to grow a bit now and then. Six foot eight the last time I was measured, and I weigh a shade under three hundred. Listen, let's get your bags and we'll get out of this madhouse!"

Forty minutes later they tore along the freeway in Gerry's minivan heading north to the city of Markham, Toronto, before freezing. Tony and April were quiet as the rolling Ontario countryside flashed by. Suddenly Gerry exclaimed, "By the way, I forgot to tell you I got you a room in Salito Domingo in the Dominican Republic. It's called the Hamaca Beach Resort and she's a beauty. I was there two years ago on a promotion by the industry. You'll be flying out tomorrow morning at eleven, but I'll have you at the air terminal by nine so you'll have lots of time to get a good seat. You'll be on a charter called Air Transat. I do a lot of business with them, and they're as good as any in the same league. April, I hope you like the sun, because I was in the Caribbean on my honeymoon three weeks ago and it was beautiful!" Gerry was beside himself with excitement as he mentioned his marriage.

"Gerry, for Christ's sake why didn't you mention it on the phone or let me know?" There was a note of disappointment in his voice that didn't escape April's attention.

"Look, I was afraid you might be hurt remembering how good a friend you were at Fordham but we wanted a completely private wedding. Christa, my wife, was married before and it was a messy divorce. She said it had to be this way or nothing. Mind you, my parents had a huge bash for us when we got back!" Suddenly the big guy was rather shy and turned his attention to his driving.

"Gerry, I hope we'll get a chance to meet Christa either tonight or when we return. If I'd known, I would have picked up something special. I feel so bad about this."

She turned to Tony and asked, "Tony, aren't you sure you couldn't have sensed something special was in the air? I'm sure I would have."

As she finished talking. Gerry interrupted and said, "Here we are at our little home. Tony, you've been here and as you know it isn't much for looks but it's home and we wouldn't have it any other way. In the future we have great plans, but for now..."

As they entered the small condo Tony was stunned at the changes that had occurred since he was here last. As a single guy, Gerry had done his best, but it left a lot to be desired. As they entered April asked Gerry, "Is Christa home or can we get to meet her later this evening?"

"No, it's unfortunate she's down in Boston on business. She's a consulting engineer and couldn't change her schedule at such short notice. But, when you return next week she'll be at the airport to meet you as well as me. Christa feels bad but there's nothing that could be done."

As they set their bags down in the hallway Tony looked at his watch. It was nearly seven with the change in time.

"You folks grab a seat in the living room. I've got a special casserole I threw together yesterday after you called. We love to have friends who think enough of us to want to visit."

Tony took April by the elbow and escorted her to the small living room that was an extension of the dining room. As she was about to sit down, there was a loud "meow" from behind her. She jumped as a huge grey cat bounded on the floor full of protest. It seemed to break some of the tension from weariness filling the air. April sat down where the cat had been lying and giggled to herself. They chatted about the trip and the hectic pace they had been keeping for the past twenty-four hours.

Gerry called from the kitchen, "Food's on. I don't know how good it is, but come and get it."

In the small kitchen in one corner, was a table fully set. There was even a bottle of wine sitting in the middle of the table as well as glasses. Gerry made his own special version of garlic bread using some locally baked sourdough bread. April was amazed.

"Tony, what a lucky girl Christa is. You're a natural born cook!" she said as they sat down, at the table.

"Now you know, April, why we liked having him in the same building with us at Fordham. With Gerry around you didn't eat well, you ate with class and style."

After dinner April took charge of the cleanup detail. She ushered Gerry out of the kitchen to the living room where he started digging out some of his CDs. Tony was put in charge of the dish-drying squad. He started to protest but would hear nothing but that he get to work. A short time later as they were leaving the kitchen, she stopped him with a hand on his chest. "Tony, you have nice friends. Thanks for introducing me!" As she stepped back she stood up on her tiptoes and kissed him firmly on the lips. Before he could say anything she walked into the living room and sat again on the small sofa.

"Gerry, I want to say how much you being here means to Tony and myself. When we get back, we'll tell you some of the reasons why we have to get away for a few days. I don't know if Tony has told you anything, but there is an important part in our research that has to be looked at in solitude. We'll tell you more later."

Tony, who was putting the dishes away in the cupboards, came into the living room and sat alongside April. Gerry said rather slowly, "Look, April, you don't have to explain anything to me. Tony was the best friend I had back in college and whatever you say is fine with me. I don't know you well, but if you're half the person he is then you're one of our gang."

"Gerry, I know I haven't explained our relationship to you, but we'll do that when we get back as well. Right now we have to know what kind of a place you've got us lined up at for the week."

"It's called the Hamaca Beach Resort, about thirty miles from Santa Domingo on the south coast of the Dominican Republic. It's one of our best five-star resorts and a great place. Besides, there is rarely anyone who goes there who ever knows each other unless planned. Remember it's getting hot there at the moment, but there is no bad weather until the middle of October. April, you'll love the place. The beach is completely private. Most of all you don't have to worry about meals, as everything is all inclusive!"

April sighed as she leaned back on, the sofa and replied, "I'm looking forward to getting there. It's too bad we didn't have time to get excited, but I guess that's all we can do this time around."

"Listen, you kids get yourselves organized. I'm going to my little office in the basement to get some business quotes ready for a presentation tomorrow after I drop you off at the airport. I'll get you up at seven in the morning. I'm usually up and ready to get downtown. I do most of my calls in the car or here before I get there. April, come and I'll show you to your room, we'll let Sleeping Beauty get forty winks!" He pointed to Tony, who was asleep with his head falling on the high arm of the soda. April shook her head.

Gerry picked up her small suitcase and showed her to the large bedroom at the back of the upper floor. "There you are, you get some sleep and I'll see you in the morning, April."

As he stepped aside to get past her small figure, she laid a small hand on his arm. "Gerry, I'm not good with words, but thanks for being here. You'll never know how much it's appreciated." He laid one of his huge hands over hers and only smiled as he stepped by her.

Chapter 32

They sat on the beach amidst the quiet warmth of the late tropical afternoon. There were a large number of people in the water but Tony and April found a quiet spot under several swaying palms. She was alone with her thoughts as she dried herself after their plunge into the deep blue waters of the Caribbean. She rubbed some sunscreen on her legs and arms as she seated herself on the beach towel. Tony wandered off to pick up two pina coladas. In a few minutes he was back carrying two unique-looking drinks. Each was poured into a coconut shell and finished off with a large flower and straw. She squealed her delight. He settled himself on the towel. "I've been looking forward to this for days, ever since we decided to get away!" he murmured as he laid his head in his hands.

There was a muffled groan as he drifted into a hazy sleep.

"Tony, could you wake up for a moment please!" April said again.

He rolled over on his side. "What's the problem? You've been preoccupied since we came down here to the beach."

"Tony, who else besides Gerry knows we're here? What's to stop them from coming down here and getting us?"

"The only people who know are Gordon and Bev. I didn't think we should take a chance with anyone else," he answered. "I've been keeping close tabs with Lynn Pollard in Washington but she doesn't know where we are at the moment. By the way, I've brought along those four pictures she sent to me by courier and want to examine them more closely. Lynn is convinced they are authentic, but I want a closer look."

"You mean you brought them here on the trip with you?" she asked with wide eyes.

"Yes, as a matter of fact they're up in the blue safe in our room right now. Besides, they are only copies of the originals Lynn sent. Listen, I wouldn't get too worried about someone finding us down here. Gordon is the best friend I've ever had, and this will give us several days to get our thoughts together."

"What do you think about the whole business, Tony, or have you reached any final conclusions?"

He looked at her for a long moment. "Why do you ask? I thought it was all cut and dried in your mind," he replied.

"To the contrary, I've felt all along there wasn't enough evidence to suggest a change in the Lincoln conspiracy picture," she said.

"April, if for the sake of argument, that were true, who the hell is trying to convince us to the contrary and why?" Tony answered bluntly.

"Well, I don't know about you, but let's leave it until after dinner. My thinking is pretty woozy right now. Tony, would you please rub some of this screen on my back." She handed him the small yellow plastic bottle. As he slowly rubbed the screen on the smooth skin of her back, she laid her head on the towel and closed her eyes. He lay back down on his towel.

After an eternity Tony felt April moving beside him. Turning over he found her sitting up and staring out at the deep blue water. She had removed her halter and was sitting bare breasted in the fading afternoon.

"Come on, Tony, let's go for another swim. I'm getting rid of that damned top. This is far more comfortable." She stood up, brushed the sand off her legs and arms and the both of them plunged into the blue Caribbean.

After an hour on the beach, they returned to their room to change for dinner. Tony showered and was walking across the room when she called out, "Tony, can I show you something?" She was sitting in a chair waiting for him to finish his shower, keeping busy by painting her toenails a bright red.

"What did you say? I couldn't hear everything you said with the water running. By the way, be careful of the shower, the water temperature is erratic."

"Tony, take a look at this letter I received before we left Long Beach." As she spoke she handed him an envelope with her name on the front. It read:

MISS APRIL SAVITZ:
YOU WOULD BE ADVISED TO CEASE ALL YOUR ACTIVITIES INTO THE LINCOLN PROJECT IMMEDIATELY. THIS IS A SENSITIVE AREA AND INVOLVES MATTERS OF WHICH YOU KNOW NOTHING. YOU WOULD BE ALSO ADVISED TO USE YOUR GOOD INFLUENCE ON MR. TONY CASSELL AS WE KNOW THIS MESSAGE WOULD HAVE NO INFLUENCE UPON HIM. WE WARN YOU NOT TO IGNORE THIS MESSAGE AS IT WOULD BE DANGEROUS TO YOUR HEALTH!

Tony cursed under his breath. He slammed his fist down on the coffee table, grabbed the phone and began to chatter to the operator in a soft voice. Momentarily April heard him say Gerry's name. The conversation continued for five minutes then he said a soft goodbye and hung up. He turned to April.

"Well, there's nothing wrong with Gerry. I told him the whole thing and he said someone set a bomb in his car this morning, but, he had loaned it to a neighbour and the neighbour was killed in a huge blast. He says not to worry and he has the Toronto Metro police involved in the whole matter and they have everything tied up tighter than a drum. The only break was the figure of a priest hanging around the area the day before. April, what I suspected is true and we're going to have to steel it out. But there's something else! There was a nasty shooting early this morning in Times Square in New York. Two priests were killed and they were members of the Jesuit Order."

April's face was ashen, and she covered her mouth with the back of her hand.

"Tony, I'm scared. I wish I didn't get such a cold feeling about the whole matter!" she replied. She stood up, about to head to the shower.

"Look, sometimes things happen quickly. No one knows we're here and if they're trying to search the various computer memory banks, by the time they get full access, we'll be back in Toronto. We'll decide what to do and where to go when we get back to Gerry's. I want you to promise me you'll forget everything else in the meantime!" He looked into her deep brown eyes. "We'll have a look at those pictures when we get back here from dinner. Meanwhile YOU go and have your shower and I'll have a shave." She looked at him for a minute and turned and went into the washroom.

After dinner they walked by the water, which was lit up in the moonlight. April was quiet.

"You're not thinking of Art again, are you? Sometimes I wonder about the hold he has over you."

"No, he was the furthest thing from my mind. But now that you mention him, I have to admit a reason I stayed with him was fear. I'm thirty-five you know and not getting any younger. Everyone thinks the world is full of nice guys, but that's a crock."

"Oh, so I'm a louse now—boy, you're full of compliments this evening!" he growled.

"Come on, you know I wasn't talking about you and there's nothing further from the truth," she replied.

"If there's nothing further from the truth why did you laugh when I wanted to take you to dinner last year?" he asked bluntly. "I was serious and you treated me as if I was in junior high."

"I thought you were toying with me and besides I didn't think you were at all interested in a relationship."

"Well, guess what, you were wrong! But listen, let's cut this conversation out. It's going nowhere and what's the point?"

"So, what is the point, Tony? I'd like to know. I know you mentioned things about caring and not wanting to lose me, but with what in mind?" April stopped and faced Tony as they stood ankle deep in the warm water.

She wore a simple cocktail dress for dinner, off her shoulder and stopped at her knees. As she stood in the moonlight Tony realized how pretty she was, when she got away from her closeness to Art. He stepped over to her took her hands and looked deep into her eyes.

"April, I know you haven't taken me seriously and you were right, I didn't take myself seriously. You're right, sometimes you have to bite the bullet and decide what to do."

"Tony, what are you talking about?" she said.

"We came down here to get away from a dangerous situation and also see how we feel about each other."

"So what are you saying?"

He looked at her quietly before answering, "Look, I'm having a rough time figuring out how I feel about you. I know this much. I don't want you around Art anymore!" he responded.

"What do you mean by that? At least he lets me live with him if I want!" she snapped, a bitter tone in her voice. "How about you?"

Tony realized the depths of her bitterness towards him. "You're right. I haven't been strong on relationships. Look, when we get back to Toronto let's do something about us!"

She hung on his every word. "Tony, if you're serious, I'm relieved! Remember don't play cheap with my feelings and emotions. I care for you but I'm not ready to throw my life away for you or any other man!"

He was jolted by her directness and replied, "Look, when we get back to Toronto. I suggest we do something permanent!"

April stood with her mouth open trying to get words out. She looked out over the dark ocean, and then turned back to Tony. "You're serious!"

"What do you say, April?" he spoke with a big grin.

"You don't want to wait until this mess is over back in the States?" she asked.

"Why wait? That's not going to change anything, unless you have some doubts?" he asked as he held her hands again.

"Alright, Tony, you're on! Line it all up and I'm ready to go!" She giggled. "I must be crazy, Tony, but I think it's the right thing to do." As she spoke she slipped her arms around him as he placed his lips to hers. They walked back to the resort with their arms around each other.

Chapter 33

Josie was thrilled. She had met Wray at the airport at three and he told her he had booked at the big Ramada Renaissance Hotel on York Avenue. She had seen the building but had never been in it. She had dropped him off at the hotel and then returned to her job at the National Archives. Josie was a tall girl with a penchant for wearing clothes that overstated her full figure. She changed at the office into a low-cut scarlet cocktail dress that left little to the imagination. Wray was from Denver and if his wife couldn't hold him she figured she'd scoop him up for a fling, if not for anything else. She arrived back at the hotel at six-thirty and headed to the main desk. She was floored when the clerk behind the huge marble counter told her the penthouse suite was rented to a Mr. Wray Potter. The clerk phoned and in turn nodded to Josie and pointed to the elevator. Wray met her at the door and began to embrace her as soon as she entered. When she took her coat off he couldn't take his eyes off her full breasts which were half exposed.

"Come in, my dear. I've been back for about an hour and couldn't wait to see you again."

"How did you manage to get the penthouse suite? I never dreamed I'd ever see such a place!" she exclaimed.

He led her into the huge living room area. This part of the suite covered nearly a thousand square feet. At one end was a small splash pool and a spa. She walked out to the huge terrace. There were small trees everywhere. Walking out to the railing, she could see the White House a few blocks to the south and the Washington Monument in the distance fully lit against the dark night sky. The city spread out in a myriad of shimmering hues in every direction in the night air. She felt Wray's hands sliding around her waist then rising to her breasts. He whispered in her ear, "Come on inside and get in the pool."

There was a warm steam arising from the bubbling water in the whirlpool end of the splash pool. A set of marble steps curved down at the other end with a Greek-type backdrop of curving Ionic pillars on either side of the pool. As she approached the pool, Josie stood at the edge and undid her dress and let it fall to the white marble floor. She stood naked except for a pair of white panties. These she tossed off and stepped into the bubbling water. It was warm and soothing. Wray returned from the washroom dressed only in a towel. In a moment he was in the warm water and they were enjoying it and each other's presence. Soon he began to caress her smooth skin under the water then rising to each other's lips. As their passions began to rise, he muttered under his breath, "It's so good to get away from that bitch I'm married to! She has no sense of adventure and doesn't understand my strong sexual needs."

"MMMMM," Josie moaned as his fingers found the soft flesh of her vagina and began to stroke her clitoris. She began to wrap her long legs about his, forgetting about the warm water that surrounded them in the bubbling spa. Then she felt him slide deep inside her under the water and she gasped with the great passions that were arising inside her.

"God, Wray, do it faster. I've waited all week for this and I've never done it in a tub before!" she moaned as they both surged to peaks of orgasm, one on top another. Finally they found each other gasping for breath and slipping under the foaming water.

Josie was about to reach for Wray again when she heard a deep voice growl in the background, "All right, out of the damned tub!"

Josie looked at Wray. Neither of them had said a word. Then they looked over to the hallway leading to the room they were in. A thin man in a black suit stood there holding a very large revolver with an ugly silencer on the end.

"You heard me—out, both of you, and don't touch anything or you'll never know what happened to you." Slowly they both climbed out of the pool and stood naked before him. He threw a long white cord to Wray.

"Here, tie her hands behind her back and her feet as well and then get out by the railing of that balcony."

In a few moments Wray was standing by the railing as he snapped to the gunman, "Look, mister, just what the shit do you want with us? We weren't harming you or anyone else!"

"Close your mouth and climb up on that stone railing," the gunman ordered, his steel-black eyes never moving from Wray's face.

"You go fuck yourself, asshole!" snapped Wray. The words were hardly out of his mouth when the revolver barked once. He was hit high in the right shoulder and the bullet's impact sent him sprawling back against the stone railing. He screamed in pain and agony.

"Now get up on that wall or the next shot will be through your head!" the man said slowly. Finally with a groan of pain from his shattered shoulder, Wray managed to struggle up on the wall. There he sat and gasped as he looked down twenty-one floors into the busy street below. "Who the hell are you and what the hell do you want?"

"I told you to get up on your feet and face out, now!" the man repeated. Then turning to Josie, who lay on the cold marble, her hands and feet hogtied, "Now, lady, I want some information! If you miss a beat your friend here goes into the street below. You may not care about yourself, but I know you'll not want to see him suffer!" As he jerked her up she spit in his face. He looked at her for a moment.

"Well, lady. I see you'll have to learn to pay the piper." He turned and was about to fire another shot into the standing figure of Wray.

She called out, "Alright! What do you want to know? My life is pretty boring."

"You found several pictures the other day taken over a century ago and you passed them on to another person. Where did you get them and who gave them to you?"

"I don't know what you're talking about. There were several pictures from the Civil War years that I gave to a number of people for examination."

"Lady, don't insult my intelligence! If I didn't know that already, I wouldn't be here. I also know that you gave copies of them to one Lynn Pollard. I don't know if the stupid broad even knows what she has. Where did the pictures come from and who is behind them?" he snapped.

"Abraham Lincoln, you dickhead, who else?" she laughed with a sneer.

He stared at her for a long moment, then said slowly, "As I said before, I guess you need proof. So proof it is!" He got up and walked back the few steps to where Wray was standing on the wall railing.

"Well, Mr. Saleswhiz, your string is done!"

"What do you mean, end of my string?" he asked over his shoulder with a wild look in his eyes. There was another bark of the gunman's gun and the figure of Wray Potter was pushed back over the edge. He seemed to hang there for a long millisecond, then with a great wailing he streaked to his death in a sodden, broken, bleeding heap on the concrete far below. There was silence.

Then he heard a long moaning scream from the bound figure of Josie Keilbowich behind him. "Now, lady, the name of the game, as you see, is cooperation. I hope you agree with me." As he came close, she tried to kick out with her bound feet and hands. It was futile.

"Oh. I see. You'd like to get a crack at me! Well, I'll tell you what I'll do! We all like to know that we have a chance to survive. It's too bad about your friend there, but you wouldn't listen!" He took out a short knife and cut her foot ropes. He then grabbed her by the arm and yanked her over to the side wall.

"Get up there and stand up facing out, like your friend."

She made no move. Slowly he took the knife and with one stroke cut off her left ear. She uttered a scream that could be heard all over the area. She was quickly becoming hysterical as she shivered in the cool night air and as the blood streamed down her neck and chest.

"I'll ask you once again, who gave you those pictures! You still have a chance!" Another scream was his only reply. Then taking his knife in one hand and the smooth flesh of her thigh in the other as she stood on the wall top, he suddenly plunged it into her thigh to the hilt. She gasped and staggered back, fighting for her balance. He stepped back and smiled as she finally plunged after her partner to the street below. A moaning scream following her all the way down. Her body crashed into the top of a taxi, crushing the roof and sides to the floor and showering the area with broken flesh, blood and broken bone tissue. There was a stunned silence on the street below as people looked up to see if there were any more falling bodies.

The lone gunman turned and walked to the door of the suite and muttered under his breath, "Now we head west to find the answers."

About thirty minutes later a huge crowd of people and vehicles milled about the main street in front of the hotel. There seemed to be police everywhere. Then a older priest emerged from one of the side entrances. He stopped and walked up to one of the policemen.

"What's happened, Constable? I was inside giving the last rites to an old woman, when I heard the commotion."

"Oh. I don't know all the details, Father, but apparently several people jumped or were pushed or whatever from one of the top floors. It's one hell of a mess. The bodies are so badly battered, we can't tell whether they are male or female," he said with great feeling.

"Do you think I could be of any help? If they're Catholics they should have the last rites or their immortal souls will be in great danger," the priest replied with great urgency.

"No. I think you'd better stay back, Father, there's far too many people out there now. Besides, there is blood all over the place."

The priest nodded and headed to the corner, heading to Mt. Vernon square. The constable's eyes followed with great feelings of respect and

121

admiration. Suddenly as the priest stepped out to cross the street there was the roar of a car. The priest never saw the vehicle and he was struck at nearly forty miles an hour. He was flung high in the air. His body landed on top of the car, which sped away. The body rolled off the front fender and to the pavement as both front and rear wheels passed over him, crushing out whatever hope for life he might have had. The car sped off into the night and vanished. As it did the driver whispered the word "Shalom!"

The priest's body lay in a broken heap by the curb. In a few minutes the constable arrived at his side. He shook the body even though he knew the man was dead.

"Father. Father, can you hear me!" The constable looked up into the faces of the small crowd that was starting to gather and shouted in a wail, "Why do the good always have to die first!"

Chapter 34

Tony laid the photocopies of the pictures on the kitchenette table. He looked at them through a large magnifying glass. He brought along a large envelope of related photocopied material from their research in Long Beach. As he studied the material, April busied herself in the washroom. He took out the four photographs Lynn Pollard had sent from Washington.

There was something about the pictures that bothered him. Yet he was convinced there were enough unanswered questions in the original material to justify all the in-depth research they had been doing. But why the threats to Gordon and Bev and as he discovered, April too? He remained unconvinced there was enough evidence after all these years to raise the ire of any of the surviving families of the conspirators. He talked to members of the Stanton family and they were fair and honest. They did have the missing eighteen pages from the Booth diary but he couldn't find anything overtly damaging to them. At the time of the assassination, this would have been a concern, especially in light of the activities of Edward Stanton himself. But from the beginning of the investigation, which he was trying to make definitive, his approach to fairness to any surviving members proved to be valid. He found the unique approach had paid off in spades.

"Hi, Tony, what are you doing?" April's voice asked from the washroom. She wore a light dressing gown that came to about her knees. As she neared him, she slipped an arm around his shoulders as he hunched at the table. He was scratching his head.

"I don't know, I keep looking at all this stuff and can't find one reason to give anyone today enough reason to send out threatening letters! I've looked at every angle, but come up dry."

She sat down beside him and looked at the various things in front of them. "I've been through it a thousand times and can only reach the same conclusion, Tony," she replied.

"Which is?"

"Very simple," she responded. "From any piece of evidence I've seen here, in Long Beach or on the three trips to Washington, I have been able to reach only one conclusion. There is no evidence vital enough to stir up feelings resulting in these kind of threats. Tony, there must be other reasons."

"That's my point precisely. However, I needed to get your input as you've spent so much time with all the material and have a good handle on it. Now we must ask about another reason for the threats."

"Are you telling me you have come up with new evidence we haven't seen before?" As she talked she pulled up a chair, put on her reading glasses and settled at the table.

"Yes, but only some pictures my friend in Washington sent to me the day before we left. I told you about them," he admitted.

"Yes, you said something about Lynn Pollard sending out copies of something she had found," April said. "What's so special about these pictures? I've seen them many times over the years and know them by heart! They are the ones taken in the Surratt living room with which we are all familiar," she commented

"That's right! They're as familiar as Lincoln's picture itself! But, now look at these!" As he spoke he laid two other pictures in front of the others. She rose partially out of her chair with curiosity. She looked them over carefully. Then she reached for Tony's magnifying glass and went over each one in detail. Nearly five minutes went by before she settled back in her char and laid the glass down. She looked at Tony with the strangest expression he had ever seen on her small but pretty face.

"Tony, you say Lynn sent these to you?" As she spoke there was tension in her voice.

"Yeah, why? Is there something wrong?"

"Does she have the original copies of these last two pictures?" April's face was ashen. She got up from her chair and walked out on the large balcony.

Tony sat for a few minutes then followed her out. The tropical night was pitch black with a few stars overhead. Below them the beach front of the resort was aglow with the evening's activities. April was sitting in a lounger looking up at the stars. As she heard him coming, she asked, "Tony, what would you say if I told you those pictures may be fake!" she exclaimed.

He was stunned. "What so you mean possibly a fake? Who would try to pull such a stunt?" he exclaimed. He leaned against the railing as she talked.

"I don't know, Tony, unless someone is trying to drag other people into the original conspiracy and link it up with something in the present. What concerns me is the feeling I get about the two pictures."

"What makes you so certain they're not the real thing?" Tony asked.

"That's the hard point. I can't put my finger on any one thing. The first thing you look for in a picture you think has something added is the total similarity of certain parts of the picture. Even here some of the hand positions are different. That alone would throw off most people, even most of the experts. That's what probably fooled Lynn Pollard!"

"Well, for Christ's sake, what makes you so suspicious?" Tony continued to press her.

"Alright, don't get yourself in a flap!" she retorted. "In a modern picture you might be able to pick up a slight difference in focus between the original and any additions made to it. But I don't see where there has been anything of that nature attempted here. These people really know their stuff. However, sometimes the experts will overlook the obvious. If I had some of our gear from my office, I'd probably have been fooled as well," she responded.

"So, what's the point?"

"Tony, look at the pictures again, but from an overall perspective and not the little details," she added.

Tony stepped back and looked from a distance of three feet. Finally he shook his head and looked at April. "OK, I give up, you've got me guessing!"

"Tony, look at the difference in the size of the heads of the two men to the right who are not in the first two pictures. If you look closely, you'll see their heads and shoulders are slightly smaller. Not too much, but enough to convince me the odds of the two men being that much smaller than another six people isn't possible for such a small group. Besides their attempts to give the two the appearance of similarity, they have made them too rigid and I see that fact. This is what gives the whole thing away. They did their job too well trying to adapt to the customs of photography of the 1860s.

"Tony, your guess is as good as mine on that score. But I'll say this: Anyone who has gone to all this trouble is probably one to be reckoned with. That's what worries me about those threats. We'd best be damned careful. But the person I'm worried about is Lynn Pollard and the people who turned up those pictures in the beginning. It's rather obvious they were planted to be found. That's where there's a real danger."

Chapter 35

The sun settled quickly over the trees behind the rambling cottage. It was the most relaxing day Lynn had spent in many years. After dinner, the girls ganged up on her and requested she put them to bed. She suggested Scott go down to the library and wait for her. Martha went off to her night bingo fest and usually was out until after midnight. Spending time with Scott's girls was a revelation to Lynn. They took to her like a duck to water. Finally after an hour of baths and bedtime stories they were asleep. She was still wearing a short robe over her swimsuit and was shocked to find she had forgotten to change.

She wandered back through the living area but there was no sign of Scott. Then she heard his voice talking on the phone from the pool deck. He was standing by the deck railing talking on his cellular. He seemed rather agitated and his voice rose in tempo before he folded the phone and put it back in his robe pocket. He was angry and annoyed.

"Another medical call from the hospital?" she asked in an offhand manner.

"No, I wish it had been. They're annoying but relatively straightforward in most cases. That was an old man most people have forgotten about, Frank Baird. He can be a real pain in the ass at times."

"You know Frank Baird?" Lynn looked at him.

"Yes, we're in the same Civil War studies group at Harvard. Why, do you know him?" he asked in return.

"Oh, he was a personal friend to my dad and our family has known him for over half a century. I wish he would retire, but I don't think it will ever happen," Lynn answered.

"I wish he wouldn't bother me when I go out of town. You know Frank, he's been a workaholic for as long as I can remember. But he's upset because someone planted a bomb in his car!" Scott said.

Lynn came over and sat down on the lounger next to him.

"Somebody put a bomb in Frank's car? What happened and how did it go off?" she inquired.

126

"Well, he's not sure at this stage. Apparently one of his research aides borrowed his car to do an errand at the university and he was killed instantly when the car blew up. Lynn, what's the matter? You look as if you saw a ghost," Scott inquired.

"Frank was in my office this past week. I had some material I wanted him to have a look at! It doesn't seem possible anyone would want to kill him. What would he have that would be so valuable?" she said.

"Lynn, I've learned over the past few years people put the strangest value on the most peculiar things. Oh yes, he said some girl from the National Archives fell to her death form the Ramada Convention Centre. Apparently he knew her well," Scott said.

"Do you recall her name? I know most of the girls who work there through my work with Kodak. I'm always going over to pick up material and return others," she asked.

"Let me see if I can remember what her name was. I believe it was something unusual like Jessica or Josie—like that."

Lynn jumped to her feet. Her face was ashen and there were tears in her eyes. Scott grasped her arms and gave her a slight shake.

"Lynn, what is it? Did you know this girl?" he asked.

She looked up into Scott's face as he inquired. She gulped several times before she answered, "Yes, I've known her for five years! Anytime I've wanted something, I've always contacted her. I know nothing about her private life, but she was always helpful to me. I don't understand, she never struck me as the kind of person to take her own life, especially off the top of a hotel!"

"Well, there's apparently some confusion over that as well. She was up in the penthouse with some man and his body fell to the street as well. It certainly doesn't sound like suicide to me," Scott said quietly. As she stood in the darkening twilight, Scott slipped an arm around her and she leaned against him for moral support.

"Scott, there's something funny going on in this business. Why would someone try to kill two of my friends in a single day?" Lynn said with tension in her voice.

"Lynn, what does this girl, Josie, have in common with Frank that you can think of? And while you're at it, do they have anything in common with you? You appear to have been in contact with both of them over the past few days," Scott said in a clinical manner.

Lynn was stunned. She stood up and wandered over to the edge of the deck but said nothing. She felt she was staring out over a dangerous and unknown sea. Her life since the assault had been peaceful and orderly; now in a matter of hours, everything seemed to be shaking loose.

Scott walked to her side. "What can you think of, Lynn?"

"That's the kicker, aside from a couple of old pictures, I can't think of anything."

"Alright, let's look a the situation of the pictures!" he replied immediately.

"Well, they were two old prints from the Civil War period! I don't see what relation they have with anything today."

"Aside from Josie who actually saw these pictures she gave you?" Scott asked.

"Aside from Josie, only two other people. Frank Baird and anyone he may have told and a research team out in the history department of Cal Tech. Why?"

"Because, I'll suggest it is highly unlikely Josie's death and the bombing of Frank's car were coincidences. I can't accept it," Scott stated firmly. "And if that is the case, and if whoever wants the pictures for whatever reason is willing to use these methods, then not only are you in great danger, so are the rest of us."

"Scott, the only deduction I can reach is the pictures in some manner implicate certain groups who want them out of sight at all costs! Would you agree?" she asked as she looked up into his deep blue eyes.

"I'm not sure," Scott answered. "You're more of the authority in these areas than me and I'm stumped at this juncture."

"I have a feeling there is something in either or both of those pictures I've missed and it has stirred up this whole mess. There has been enough uncertainly about the assassination cover-up after the death of Lincoln to warrant people now and then seeing if they came up with new and different evidence. There is always the chance someone has found something new, although I would want to examine it well at first. Scott, I'm worried about you and your family. I don't want to have you people threatened if matters come down to that."

"Look, you've given me more hope and care than I can remember in a long time. If you think I'm going to walk away now, unless you order me to, you're crazy." As he spoke he placed both hands on either side of her face and placed his lips on hers. Lynn melted against him as if all the strength poured out of her. Never had she felt so close to someone so quickly. Gently he brushed a tuft of dust from one of her dark eyes. As she leaned against him, he could feel her warmth and the firm mounds of her breasts pressing against his chest.

"Let's go for a swim before we go in for the evening."

Chapter 36

"For the first time in all his years of teaching and government involvement, Frank Baird was nervous. It had been just twenty-four hours since young Rick Wisson had asked to borrow his car. The explosion had been immense. Baird was in the small vault in his office at Harvard sorting out some papers when the blast went off. He ran out from his office to the parking lot. There was little left of either his old Caddie or young Wisson. The car had been parked between the arts and chemistry buildings. The damage was horrific. All the windows in both buildings were blown in and rooms facing the lot were demolished. Whoever had set out to eliminate him had set about it in the most serious manner.

He had not slept that night especially after the phone call earlier that day. The male voice snarled on the other end telling him to get off the Lincoln case and destroy the pictures, or the next explosion wouldn't be an accident. The man continued, saying that it would be him scattered all over the lot instead of one of the students. He had spent the rest of Sunday on the phone. His wife was distraught. She had been trying to get him to retire for the past fifteen years and was reaching the end of her patience. As he was talking on the phone for what seemed to be all day, Flo finally stood at the door of his huge cluttered office with her hands on her hips. Fifty-six years of marriage told him when it was time to listen to her without reservation. He hung up the phone and came out of the book-strewn room.

"Frank, I'm not going to bother you with a lecture about what I think you should have done, but this car-bombing bit is scary. Why are they trying to scare you? What have you got yourself involved in now?" As she talked, Frank noted again as he did so often how well she looked for a woman in her early eighties. Flo was a big woman, nearly six feet tall and reasonably heavy. Only over the past year or so had she begun to show her age. She was still involved in a number of charities.

"That's the strange thing, dear," Frank answered, "I'm not involved in any particular thing at the moment. The only think I've been doing aside from getting my lectures ready for the fall semester has been looking for some information for Lynn Pollard, you remember her?"

"Lynn, of course, she's almost like a granddaughter to me. Is she still with Kodak?"

"Yes. She must be there for nearly ten years. She called me the other morning and had some pictures she wanted me to look at. They were rather unusual and may have some very profound historical ramifications, but I fail to see the link with this bomb in my Caddie. I keep thinking of the poor young Rick!"

"Do you think it was the pictures that Lynn gave you that were the reason for the warning?" she asked. "Frank Baird, if you do that to poor Lynn after all she's been to us, I'll put a bomb in your other car myself. You know me well enough after all these years! We've never let the bastard side of society buffalo us and there's no reason we should start now. By the way, what's so important about the pictures to begin with? They must be pretty special for someone to get that excited," she snapped.

"That, dear, is the question that has me stumped. They're pictures taken around the time of the Lincoln killing and are related to the conspiracy," he said.

"And you're telling me someone is angry enough over what happened so long ago that they are willing to kill again?" Flo inquired.

"That's the way it appears at the moment, or at least someone feels they will be implicated by these new pictures that a friend of Lynn's found," Frank responded.

"That's the other scary thing about this case. That girl who worked in the National Archives took a dive off the top of the Ramada Convention Centre last evening along with her boyfriend."

"What?" Flo gasped as Frank mentioned the other two deaths for the first time. "That's a twenty-story building, Frank!"

"That's what I'm telling you, Flo. This affair is getting nasty and I'm wondering if we're getting too old for all this nonsense?"

"Frank Baird, we've been married for all these years. When have we ever run from a fight? You do everything that Lynn asked you to do. If those bastards call again, tell them to put their words where the sun never shines!" Flo was becoming very agitated by the whole discussion and finally said in disgust, "Look, Frank, you get your teeth back in this whole matter and shake the bastards loose! By the way, when you talk to Lynn again, tell her I want to get together with her. I hear she's been very active in the damn women's liberation movement and we need to have a chat!"

With these words and a distinctive snort she walked away from him and back into the main living area of the house. Frank Baird followed her with his eyes as he had often done many times over the years. He was still in awe of Flo's sense of righteous indignation and fury. Chuckling to himself and shaking his head in admiration, he headed back into his cluttered study to take up the cudgels of battle once more.

Chapter 37

Father Jim McGuire sat in the newspaper section of Cal Tech University Library. Folding the Tuesday morning copy of the *LA Times*, he tossed it onto the table in front of him. He was troubled by some of the messages he had received through various Jesuit channels. The killings in Dublin had been a puzzle to everyone. He had received a written message to meet an unknown priest here about half an hour ago, but no one had showed. He would have left except there was a small red rose drawn on the right-hand corner of the notepaper. It was one thing to receive messages of urgency from various Jesuits throughout the country; he was used to that and it was one of the lasting strengths of the worldwide Order. But it was an altogether different matter to receive a note without warning under the mark of the red rose. It had been well over a decade since he had even had a greeting from any member. There were times he had wondered if the secret branch of the Order had vanished. As he looked around him his eyes glanced over the great rack of papers from around the world. Then, a headline on a week-old copy of the *Christian Science Monitor* caught his eye:

ASSASSINATION ATTEMPT ON JUNIOR IOWA SENATOR

He picked up the paper and read of the attempt on the senator's life and how close it had come. The story continued with the details of the killing of the senator's wife.

"You're still a good-looking Irish bastard!" said a voice suddenly over McGuire's shoulder. He jumped to his feet and came face to face with a rough mousy-looking man in his early seventies.

"Do I know you, sir?" McGuire asked bluntly. "Because your face doesn't ring any bells."

"No, you won't know me, but I've been a part of your life for over thirty years! My name officially is Father Guiseppi de Medici and, no, I'm no relation to another of that famous name. I'm glad you got my note and were serious enough to wait even if I was late. By the way, I've been watching you for the past forty-five minutes—you're a very nondistinguished presence!" he said.

"You're from the Brotherhood, Father?" McGuire snapped, "I haven't heard from anyone for a decade. I assumed that was according to plan."

"Yes, I see you've retained your obedience to the call. There hasn't been a need for any activation for many years. That's the very nature of the brotherhood, as you will remember from your initial training. Now, however, we are being called to active duty. There is a threat not so much to the Church but to the very existence of the Brotherhood itself."

The older man seated himself in one of the reading armchairs next to father McGuire before he spoke again.

"Father, we have a problem in the country and it must be dealt with immediately. We thought we could deal with it on an individual basis, but because of the incompetence of half of the head of the Brotherhood in America, the situation had simply got out of hand. You've been our anchor on the west coast for the last ten years since you moved here from St. Louis. We had five operatives here on the coast but we've had to question their competence. They've resorted to threats to try to stop the flow of the problem here at Cal Tech."

Father de Medici was beginning to overwhelm Father McGuire with the story and great details and he finally interrupted, "Look, Father, I can see you have a problem. And I agree that the basis I remained active in the early eighties was only on the basis that the Brotherhood was in jeopardy! Is this the case?" he asked with a note of impatience in his voice.

"Yes, very much so, and that's the point I was coming to," he replied.

"Father McGuire, in April of 1865 in Washington several groups of people felt it was necessary for the future of the country to get rid of Abraham Lincoln. This was also the feeling of the Brotherhood and it was their feeling they should do something about it."

"So, how can that affect the existence of the Brotherhood at the present time?" McGuire asked in an icy tone.

"If proof was uncovered today that the Catholic Church was instrument in the assassination of Lincoln, the fate of the Catholic Church would be mortally damaged in this country and affected all over the world."

Father McGuire was stunned. He leaned back in the chair and stared at the ceiling.

"Are you telling me there is tangible proof that this was the case?"

"Yes, in the form of two photographs taken, we believe, by Matthew Brady, the foremost photographer of his day. Further, we believe if this information gets out, it will be the death knell for the Brotherhood specifically."

"Are you telling me that you have pictures of our members of the Brotherhood in Washington in 1865?" McGuire asked bluntly.

"Not only in Washington, but right in the living room of Mary Surratt, one of the conspirators later hanged by the U.S. government for her part in the plot."

"Holy Mary, Mother of our Lord... when you say we are in a bind, you really come to the point. I have to admit I'm having some difficulty understanding why these pictures haven't turned up until now. Has any credence been given to the possibility that they might just be fakes? I've got some friends in the picture business and there isn't much that can't be done in this area now if given to the right people," McGuire asked.

"We've covered all of that, and besides, we're dealing in the daguerreotype method and there was no such thing as copies. Besides, Father, I'm not sure I like your insinuations. I can assure you that every avenue of the latest technology has been well covered," de Medici replied acidly.

"Well, that may be true in your own minds, but I'm compelled to ask, especially in the light of the troubled situation in the Brotherhood here in America!" he snapped. The Italian priest's face went ashen as he knew that the American had touched on a very sore point. There was a moment of silence between the two men.

"Father McGuire, that's not he reason we've had to call upon you at this time. We have reason to believe there is another espionage group involved in this matter and that we're being shadowed at almost every corner."

"You're telling me another group is on to you and you need help, is that what you're saying?" McGuire asked bluntly.

"Yes, that's right and that is the mystery," de Medici replied.

"I'm afraid you've lost me again in all this cloak-and-dagger stuff," McGuire said.

"Alright, let me give you an example. Last weekend on of our people cornered a girl from the National Archives who had dug up the two pictures I've been talking about. She and her boyfriend wouldn't talk and were disposed of according to plan, but then our man was killed just outside of the hotel.

"This sort of thing has happened three times in the last week: the case I mentioned and twice in Germany."

"If there is another group involved as you think, what are their reasons and who might they be?" McGuire asked impatiently.

"This is where we come to the crunch of the whole matter. If the news gets out that the Vatican was involved in the killing of Lincoln, there will be hell

135

to pay. The influence of the Church will be dead as Patty's Pig in this country. It will turn a great percentage of the population who are already lukewarm on the Church away completely and to the likes of televangelists. This other group doesn't want this to happen either and feel they would be tainted with the same brush!"

"Then, why are they opposed to us?" snapped McGuire.

"Because historically, many Catholics have always referred to them as the Christ killers!" he said.

Father McGuire's mouth opened and closed silently.

"You mean, we're dealing with the Mossad! Jesus Christ, That's suicide," he snarled.

"That's right, Father McGuire, and it will be your responsibility to see that all the people who are involved in the Lincoln research project are eliminated immediately. You simply cannot fail! If you do, the Brotherhood will be finished in the Western world and the name of our Holy Mother the Church, disgraced!"

Chapter 38

Scott sat up in bed. His medical background had ground out of him the ability to sleep soundly. He heard something but wasn't sure what. Then here it was again. Slipping on his PJ top, he walked to the door of his bedroom and listened. Nothing. He crept to the girls' room where they usually slept with their grandmother here at the cottage, but they were asleep. His mother had phoned earlier to say that she was staying over with her friend Earla, and wouldn't be home until morning. He knew his mother's passion for bingo and made no attempt to argue with her.

As he walked past the room where Lynn was sleeping, he thought he heard something. He saw the door ajar. He was about to go back to his room, but on the hunch turned and slowly opened the door. Looking about he saw she wasn't in her bed. The covers were tossed back, but Lynn was nowhere to be seen. The patio doors, which were a part of each bedroom, were open. Finally he saw her; she was standing in the early-morning twilight looking out over the far reaches of the ocean. As she stood with her back to him, he could see she was dressed only in a translucent nightie. The slight glow of the first wisps of the dawn outlined the slimness of her body through her nightie. Then he heard her sob. He hesitated a moment and said in a quiet voice, "Lynn, are you all right?"

She turned swiftly around and faced him across the small patio. There were tear streaks running down her face and her hair was somewhat askew. As she faced him she seemed unaware that her nightie was almost transparent in the early twinkling light. It only seemed to make her seem all the more vulnerable. The slimness of her long legs was accentuated in the pale light broken only by the dark shadows where her thighs met. There seemed to be an air of desperation about her.

"I'm sorry, I didn't mean to wake you, but I just couldn't sleep. Scott, I've no right to involve you in my problems. I feel I'm dragging you and you family down with me." As she talked she raised her hands in a sign of desperation. He walked up to her and took both of her small hands in his and looked deep into her dark eyes.

"Lynn, I know some terrible things have happened in you life in the past few years. I can't erase those but I wish there was something I could do to be a help," he said.

As he spoke Lynn found herself leaning closer to his chest. She had not allowed herself to be this close to any man since that terrible evening nearly seven years ago. Yet there was something about Scott that drew her to him. At one time she vowed she would never get near another man as long as she lived. As she spoke she placed both of her open palms on his chest.

"When you went to the basement last evening to get some more ice, the phone rang and I answered it." She sobbed again as she talked. "I'm sorry, this crying isn't like me," she added.

Scott placed a hand on each of her shoulders and asked, "Who was on the phone, Lynn? It had to be something pretty bad to get you in this state. Come on, let's have it," he asked urgently.

"It was a male voice and they knew who I was. He made some filthy remarks and said if I didn't drop this whole Lincoln thing, you and the girls would have some sort of an accident. Then he asked if I knew Josie Keilbowich. He said she was now at the city morgue if I wanted to see her." Lynn's last words were barely audible as she leaned her head into Scott's firm shoulder. Then she raised her head and looked him in the eyes.

"That's why I've got to get out of here immediately! I've brought enough heartache on you and you family, without this on top of it." She started to pull back from him but he held her tight.

"Scott, please don't, I can't fight you as well," she whispered.

"Lynn, you don't have to! Don't you know the girls and I are now part of your life? You must know now that whatever happens to you happens to us as well," he said in return.

"But it just isn't fair that you should be drawn into this mess!" As she spoke, she stepped back, a fire of anger in her eyes. In that moment, Scott could see the strength of the girl that had gotten her through the terrors of a few years back.

"Lynn, when Rose died, I thought I'd never get through those terrible months afterward. If I hadn't had the girls, I don't know what I would have done. I swore I'd never let myself ever get that close to anyone again, Lynn. Then over the past few weeks, your friendship had changed into something entirely different. Lynn, you've allowed three people to care for you, don't walk out on that. I'm sorry you can't have it both ways!" There was a real note of anger in Scott's voice as he spoke and his eyes hardened. "If you must go, then make it quick, you can take the keys and use my wagon if you must!"

As he turned and walked away, there was a long moment of silence and then Lynn's voice cried in a plea, "Please, Scott, don't leave me now. I couldn't cope with that!"

Scott turned and faced her again about twenty feet away. He walked back to her as she stood facing him. She seemed to have all her protection stripped away and seemed totally vulnerable. There was something about Lynn he had never seen before.

"I'm so sorry, Scott. I've been trusting in myself so long now that it's almost become second nature. There's been so much happiness in my life since I met you and the girls!" As she spoke, she slipped her arms around his waist and laid her head on his chest. As she did, he could feel the warmth of her body as he put his arms around her. She seemed ready to collapse as he held her tightly. As he did he heard her whisper, "Please don't leave me, Scott, I couldn't stand to be alone right now."

"I had no plans to leave, but I think we should get you back to bed. It's pretty cold out here this hour and you wearing that nightie, it would be easy for me to get other ideas. It doesn't leave much to the imagination, you know," he added with a deliberate leer, to lighten the conversation as he stepped back. For the first time, he saw a trace of a smile cross her face and knew from that moment that he would have a great deal of difficulty leaving her.

With a slight smile, she asked, "So, what's wrong with other ideas? I'm only as human as you are, you know, smarty pants!"

He ran his fingers gently through her short hair as she leaned against him and placed her arms around his deep chest. He could feel the soft pressure of her breasts as she pressed against him. He lowered his lips to hers and as they kissed he heard her sigh as a great peace surged through her. After a long moment, Scott stepped back with a concerned look on his face.

"Lynn, I am only a man and if we don't stop now, I'll find it very difficult!"

The soft smile only grew on Lynn's lips as she listened to him.

"I know what you are thinking and I love you for it, but please stay with me. Everything is fine. I've buried most of my demons a long time ago. Just remember, you are not the only one who is human."

As she talked, he slowly slid the straps of her nightie off the smooth flesh of her shoulders. Then it fell to the floor of the deck and she stood naked in the growing morning light. He slowly ran his hands over the soft smooth flesh of her back and around her waist. As he did, she placed both of her arms around his neck and watched his gentleness. He caressed each firm breast as he drew his hands up over her chest. Her nipples hardened with feelings of desire that were beginning to well deep inside her. It was so long since she felt like this, it almost seemed like the first time she was close to a man. As he kissed her, his tongue began to seek out hers and he felt her shiver as she leaned against his chest. She ran her hands over his shoulders and slipped his top off and let it fall to the deck.

"Are you very sure, Lynn?" he whispered.

Her only answer was her lips as her tongue began to seek out his as great waves of passion began to surge over her. He picked her up and carried her back into the bedroom and laid her gently on the bed. He slowly ran his tongue down the centre of her chest and then to each nipple. His fingers skimmed ever so lightly over the softness of her abdomen. He allowed his tongue to follow, barely touching her. She gasped with her passion as her body began to move with great feeling. His fingers touched the small patch of pubic hair and he began to caress her. He probed gently and urgently. Lynn moaned with desire as she could hardly control herself.

As he caressed her, he was careful to be gentle, always keeping the brutality of her experience in his mind. As his fingers began to caress deep between her legs, waves of warmth and desire began to flow through her in all directions. She had forgotten how long it had been since someone had been so gentle with her. As he explored the softness of he body, Lynn found herself beginning to move with motions she had forgotten about. She slowly slid off his bottoms and touched his surging manhood with her fingertips. Lynn urged him to slide between her legs. As he did, ever so lightly, she began to writhe with passion and wrapped her legs tightly around him. Finally she felt his erection begin to penetrate her slowly and firmly. She felt herself moving in the ageless motions of love and passion as he surged deep into her. For a long time it seemed he would surge deeper and deeper until she felt she was about to faint. It seemed the walls of the room were beginning to move as she locked her legs around him and as they moved together in the increasing motions of their passion. She reached peak after peak of passion. Finally the shuddering feelings of orgasm overcame both of them and they fell back on the sheets of her bed exhausted from the effort of their lovemaking. The warmth washed over her in a presence she hadn't known in a long time. Finally she dozed off in Scott's arms with her head resting on his broad chest. Just before slipping into the fuzziness of first sleep, she felt tears again, but this time the tears of joy and peace.

Chapter 39

The black Olds pulled up quietly in the parking lot of the Bayview Hotel in downtown Oakland. The four priests had flown in from Chicago and were dressed in sports clothes. Entering by the main door, they quickly but quietly took the main elevator to the seventeenth floor. Getting off, the four men, all in their late forties, walked along the long hallway until they came to room 1436. They had barely reached the door when it opened and a tall blond-haired man greeted them.

"Welcome to Oakland, gentlemen, I hope you had a good flight. We're just about all ready to commence our meeting." The hotel room was a large one with an adjoining sitting room with a big table and matching chairs. There were several large plates of sandwiches and muffins piled in the centre of the table and a small liquor cabinet off to the side.

"Make yourselves comfortable. There is all kinds of food and if there isn't anything to your liking, I'll call the kitchen and have the cook oblige. He is a faithful member of the local St. Rita's Parish and very accommodating."

For the next forty-five minutes, the five priests helped themselves to the food and liquor. Each of the men mixed well with each other with no one dominating more than anyone else. Finally, their host called their attention to himself.

"I want to welcome each and every one of you here today. My name is Father Jules Rowchuk from Brotherhood Central in Geneva. There was a meeting last week in Marseilles and a special call for action was brought forth. You have been called because of this reason first of all. Secondly there has cropped up some important unfinished business from over a hundred and thirty years ago. Believe it or not, several of the fathers were a bit sloppy back at that time and we have to go out and tidy up. Most important, we have a new foe in the country and aren't sure who it is." There were a few minutes quiet amongst the fathers. Their host continued, "Several of our attempts to close off the old loose ends have been checkmated by forces or people unknown."

"Father Weisse from Pittsburgh. Don't we have to expect this from time

141

to time from the FBI and CIA before our plants there spread the word who we are?"

"Yes, that's true and that's the first thing we did and came up dry. No, it has to be someone whom we haven't dealt with as opponents before. They seem to know what our plans are even before we do! I wouldn't be surprised if they have a plant in this meeting right now!"

"Father Jim Norrie from Boston. I resent your insinuations. Unless you have facts to back up your accusations, I want a total retraction this minute!"

"That, my fine Irish friend, is my very point. Just to stand on the strength of our friendship and faith isn't enough. If we go back to the very reason the Brotherhood was founded after the Reformation, the overall aim was the willingness to use whatever means were at hand to protect the Church. That is still our mandate and we have to be prepared to do what we have to. My point is that someone else is just as committed and equally prepared as we are," Rowchuk replied.

"If that is true then why have we been called in from the outside?" Norrie asked again, sounding still unconvinced.

Father Louis Sandez raised a hand and asked, "Could you point to the washroom, please! I'll be right back, because I have a very important matter to bring up." Rowchuk pointed to a narrow hallway to one side of the room.

Several minutes later as he was standing before the mirror in the bathroom he saw a sudden rustle behind him. He started to turn as a figure stepped from the shower stall. Two brawny arms wrapped quickly around the front and back of his neck simultaneously. There was a sudden squeeze and wrench and violent jerk to the man's right. There was a loud grinding snap as his neck broke and his body went limp. He uttered not a sound as he died. His body was lowered quietly to the floor. The shadowy figure stepped over the corpse and into the small hall. Just as he did, he heard a noise in the small kitchenette. Tiptoeing to the edge of the small doorway, he saw the small figure of Father Jakiwchuk, standing in front of the coffee maker, preparing a fresh pot. The priest also heard something from the hallway. The grey-dressed stranger hesitated only a moment.

"I don't believe you and I have met! I'm Father Briegstein from the city here. I work in a parish about three miles from here and it was hard to get away at the last minute. By the way, what part of the country are you from?"

"I'm Father Jakiwchuk and I work in the philosophy department of Notre Dame University on the east coast. It's good to make your acquaintance. By the way, could you pass me the salt over there, I want to spruce up this damned coffee a bit!" He turned his attention to the coffee maker again. It was a fatal mistake. In a flash the other figure grabbed him from behind and ran a ten-inch steel awl deep into the left side of his back. As he did he jerked it in deeper with three steady penetrating jerks. The last one was calculated to penetrate deep into the heart muscle. His attacker stepped back. The man turned and stared at him with eyes in agony as he felt the pain of the awl as it quickly killed him. He reached out and tried to mouth some words, but never got them out. He then crumbled to the floor with a loud thud.

In the sitting room, there was a sudden silence. The attacker listened for a moment before taking out two small but very lethal grenades from his left pocket. Stepping to the kitchenette doorway, he pulled the pins, tossed them around the doorway and rolled them onto the sitting room floor. There was a stunned silence for a moment in the room, then someone yelled, "Jesus Murphy, they're grenades, get down!"

The stranger dropped to the floor and covered his head. The two blasts were deafening and devastating. The sitting room was demolished and the windows blown out. Part of the kitchenette wall had fallen on top of the stranger. He struggled to his feet, his ears roaring from the blast. When he stepped out into the living room he was stunned by the destruction. The remains of the four men were scattered in bloody heaps in the middle of the room. One was minus legs, and the head of another was missing. There appeared to be no signs of life. Then he heard a moan from behind the upturned sofa. There he found the battered remains of Father Norrie. The priest was still alive although both legs appeared to have been shattered and one arm was missing. He tried to speak when he saw the man standing over him.

"We were just talking about you people!" He gasped the words out. "We were just figuring how to deal with you. Why has the Mossad turned on us? We've never done anything to you and now you've been killing out people everywhere! We should be on the same side!" Norrie's eyes were beginning to cloud as the waves of pain swept over him.

"I don't know what you're talking about. I know nothing about the Mossad. We've never had anything to do with them then or now. You people have dared interfere with American politics it appears too many times and now we have to take matters into our own hands. The American Freedom Party is about to take control of the destiny of this nation and the Catholic Church will interfere no longer!"

As he spoke he pulled out his large awl again and very slowly ran it deep into Norrie's chest. The man attempted to struggle as the sharp point plunged through his heart. His mouth gurgled twice and he was dead. His eyes stared up at the shattered ceiling. The stranger looked about the room, muttered under his breath, "See you all in hell, assholes!" and walked carefully from the scene of shattered plaster, furniture and bodies. Unknown to him, under the sofa was the badly bruised figure of Father George Rowling. As he had listened, there were tears in his eyes as he thought of the attack on his good friend, Father Norrie. He remembered for the rest of his life, the name of the American Freedom Party.

Chapter 40

Colonel Sharon was barely in bed when the phone rang. He had been asleep about an hour since his arrival in Chicago earlier in the evening. He had received the message about the mass killing of the priests in Oakland when he was checking into the hotel. Sleep hadn't come easy. Slowly he shook off the drowsiness and picked up the receiver.

"Yes, who is it?"

"This is the long distance operator from New York, Mr. Smith, I have the Tel Aviv operator on the line with a highly urgent message for you," she chirped in a cheery voice.

"Colonel Sharon, is that you?" a husky male voice asked curtly in Hebrew.

"No, it's actually the third wife of King Solomon, who the shit do you think it is? Who is phoning on an open line?" Sharon growled.

"This is General Josef Zadok, who the hell did you think it was? Listen, there will be a man by the name of George De Chardain phoning you tomorrow morning. You will have lunch with him and he will fill you in on many of the facts that were in that Irishman's last report. Secondly, the third group we chatted about before you left was the American Freedom Party. The threat to our nation is crucial and the people will be relying on you to even the score. Do you have any questions?" he snapped.

"No, General, those were the missing gaps. All I can add is the point that several of our worst suspicions were true and then some."

"Good night, Colonel, and sleep well."

Sharon shook his head, as he was still stunned with the general's use of the open telephone line. Then he remembered his comments "never use the same medium of communication twice.

Sleep was now impossible and he walked into the small sitting room and sat down with the pile of documents he had compiled since his arrival in the U.S. the previous Sunday. Searching through the various reports he had compiled from his slim net of operatives across the U.S., he again looked at the several conclusions he had reached. General Zadok was convinced there was a third group playing off both the Red Rose and themselves, the Mossad. He had not been able to present any proof aside from his own intuition and past experience. With his past track record, his fears were given very serious credence, but Sharon felt he had to have a substantial amount of proof. The killing of the priests in Oakland was both a scary event and an omen. He had been aware of the meeting but was more concerned with protecting the Lincoln research team in Cal Tech at Long Beach. Now that had suddenly become a priority. He was also aware two members of the team had flown to the Caribbean and he had decided to leave them alone there until the end of the week. But there was still the problem of Long Beach. He knew of the reputation of the Irish priest who used to teach at Fordham and also the fact that he had been in California for the past two weeks. He would see the man with the French name tomorrow and then fly to LA for insurance sake. There were at least eight other people there whose lives might be in danger and he wanted to see they were protected. He was about to return to bed, as it was already nearly 2 a.m., when his phone rang again. It was the main desk.

"Mr. Smith, it's the main desk, there's an urgent fax that came in for you about five minutes ago. Do you want me to send it up?"

"No, thanks for calling! Please keep it there! I'll be down for it in a while."

Before getting dressed, he went into the washroom. As he was finishing there, he thought he heard something. Every instinct he knew came into play and warning signals started to buzz in his head. Flicking off the washroom light, he slowly opened the door and cautiously reentered the main room. The lights were the same and there wasn't anything moved that he could see at a glance. Then he saw it. It was just a flicker. But that was all he needed. He again heard the soft rustle, just barely audible to the human ear. It was the soft rustle of a foot on carpet. It was light and he knew it must be a woman.

For ten minutes, all the training he knew came into play, as he moved not a muscle. Finally he saw her. She was a tall woman in her late thirties and was dressed all in black. Slowly, she reached a hand out to pick up some of the documents he had left on the coffee table.

"Help yourself! Read through them and see what you're up against!" he snapped from the shadows. The figure in black jumped back, obviously totally surprised he was there.

"How in the hell did you…?" her high-pitched voice asked anxiously.

"How did I get in here? I didn't, I've been here all along. I heard you come in and wanted to get a good view and see how you operated!"

Slowly she put the papers she had picked up back onto the table. Her head was uncovered and she was a rather plain-looking woman. She noted that he was unarmed and suddenly became very aggressive.

"Well, old man, do you want to take your chances with a woman? I'll bet you can't last ten seconds. Most of your kind fall into the same boat." Sharon moved slowly in her direction.

"Sit in that chair! You want to get out of here alive, I would suggest you do that!" he snapped as he came within striking distance.

"Don't make me laugh!" she snorted. "Your kind are all alike! Always hiding behind coattails of other nations. You think our new party is going to let your kind run us, we've got news for you. The senator has been clear on that point from the beginning!" she ranted.

"Ah, that's what I suspected. The good senator is the new Messiah of the nation. It's too bad you won't be around to see the collapse," he whispered. "Remember what our nation says, the dead have short memories!" The last words came on in the form of a snarl as he circled her black-clad form. Suddenly she lashed out with a vicious-looking knife in her hand, missing his neck by inches. He ducked his head slightly to the right, lashing out with the most vicious right chop he had ever thrown. Curling his fist into a ball, he caught her flush at the base of the sternum between her breasts. She collapsed on the floor and her limbs danced a shuddering jingle on the floor.

He grabbed her by the feet and dragged her to the balcony. He heaved her up on the railing and pushed her inert form over and watched her twenty-two-floor plunge to the darkened street below. There was a sodden smack as her body shattered and split open by the force of the descent and impact. He muttered as he turned, "Rest in peace, bitch!"

Chapter 41

The Tuesday morning after Lynn got back from her long weekend away with Scott and his family was a happy one for her. She arrived back in her office shortly after nine. Maggie as usual was there before her and was smiling like a Cheshire cat. As Lynn came through the outer office and past Maggie's desk, her only comment was, "Well, don't keep me in suspense! How was everything?"

Lynn, who was dressed in a smart blue suit, set down her briefcase and looked at Maggie with a quiet smile on her face.

"You know, Maggie, I think it was the happiest weekend I can recall in ten years. I don't know why a family would treat me so kindly. Those little girls could melt anyone's heart. Their mother must have been quite a lady."

"I didn't know her too well, she was very attractive, in voluntary hospital work and I only met her twice. But she was very well thought of by everyone! By the way, how was their dad, did you get to him at all? If you'd look me straight in the eye, Lynn, perhaps you'd give yourself away!"

Lynn, becoming embarrassed, raised her face, which by this time was a deep pink colour. Maggie, who had stepped around from her desk, took Lynn by the shoulders and put her arms about her. After a few minutes, she stepped back and looked Lynn in the eye.

"You know, Lynn, I can see it in your eyes, you're in love with the man even at this short an acquaintance, aren't you?"

"Yes, Maggie, I never thought it would happen to me, especially at my age, but it has! And the problem is I'm not sure how to handle it," Lynn said somewhat agitated.

"For heaven's sake, girl, what's the matter with you? Why can't you simply accept it for what it is! You've met a fantastic person who obviously feels the same way about you and be happy. Just make sure you don't kill it even before it gets off the ground. You're very lucky, but then so is Scott as well."

"Thanks, Maggie, you've just made this a wonderful day for me. Now I must be getting to work as I've got to get this Brady thing all together for you to edit and get ready to send to the publisher," Lynn replied cheerily.

The rest of the day passed busily and without incident. Then about three-thirty, Lynn heard a commotion in the outer office. There were several loud voices to be heard, then quiet. There was a loud pounding at the door of Lynn's inner office. As a rule, she left it open, but today it was closed as she wanted to remain undisturbed to finish the compilation and cataloguing of all pictures. By this time her office was in shambles. Then suddenly the door flew open. Lynn rose to her feet immediately.

"Maggie, what's the meaning of this intrusion?" she asked with an edge to her voice. Almost as soon as she spoken, Maggie was thrust through the door and sent sprawling on the floor with a cry of pain. Behind her were two grim-faced men dressed in black. The first man, somewhere in his early fifties, carried a deadly-looking machine gun. The other carried a small coil of rope and several large pieces of cloth.

"Are you Lynn Pollard?" he snapped in a vicious voice. Lynn's ire was raised immediately, as it was easily ever since her assault.

"What's it to you, mac?" she retorted immediately. "Besides, what do you mean throwing my assistant on the floor like that? Put that damn gun away and get the hell out of here!" Even as she talked, Lynn could feel her anger surging.

The man with the gun turned and pointed it at Lynn and for a brief moment, she thought he was going to use it on her. He nodded to the other man. "Feisty bitch, isn't she! Gag her and bind her arms tight so she can't move. Also put a blindfold on her."

Just as the other man was about to start tying Lynn's hands, Maggie made a dive for him. He shoved her back against the wall.

"You stupid woman, that move has cost you your life!"

Maggie suddenly knew fear as the small machine pistol rose up and was pointed at her. Lynn watched and cried out, "No, for God's sake, no! She knows nothing!" At that moment the gun roared for only a few seconds. Yet over twenty bullets struck Maggie full in the chest and neck. She was slammed back against the wall. Her blood was spattered all over the beige paint. For a moment her body danced a jig as the bullets passed through her. Then she collapsed in a bloody heap. Dead before she hit the floor, she landed on her back with one leg and arm grotesquely twisted under her. The eyes stared blankly into nothingness.

Lynn winced as her arms were tied behind her at the elbows. Her arms went numb and all feeling vanished. She was quickly gagged and blindfolded. Something hit her on the back of her head and she plunged deep into a sea of blackness.

Several hours later, Lynn Pollard slowly regained consciousness. She could hear muffled voices somewhere in the background. She was still blindfolded but the gag had been removed. She found herself hanging by her bound wrists from an overhead beam. There was something holding her feet though they were swinging clear off the floor.

"Well, I'm glad to see you've finally decided to return to the land of the living. You had us worried!" She recognized the voice of the man with the gun who had shot Maggie. He continued to talk, "Now, we want to get down to some specific questions and don't give me that nonsense that you know nothing. We're not stupid and neither are you, so let's put that to rest from the beginning. You had those photos of the Lincoln conspirators before you disposed or copied them. Where are they and how many copies did you make? Remember the answer you give us could determine whether you get the same fate as that other woman in your office!"

"I suppose you have the same fate in mind for me as you had for poor Josie at the National Archives. You can take your questions and go to hell! I'm a dead woman at this very moment, so you can't scare me!" Lynn could hardly believe the line she was using. "You see, I know a lot about you and more than you think I know. Your Order of the Red Rose is in sick condition! How about your dragged attempts to poison Napoleon? And what about your so-called alliance with Mr. Garibaldi in the 1860s. Wouldn't the Vatican like to get their hands on some of that stuff! So don't try to scare me, asshole, I've been down that route!" The older man turned and walked off in a huff. She could hear some muffled voice in the distance.

Then she heard the two familiar voices close to her again.

"Strip off her clothes and we'll try her toenails first and see what happens! If she doesn't talk then I'll get the soldering iron! That usually makes the most stubborn cooperative!" Lynn tried to squirm but she knew it was to no avail. Then she felt someone cutting off her jacket and sliding her skirt off.

She kicked out with her feet and received a hand across her mouth in return. Then she thought she heard a muffled grunt and the sound of something heavy hitting the floor. Several muffled coughs followed and there was another muffled falling sound. There was a long silence. Finally she heard movement near her.

"Please don't be alarmed, Miss Pollard, they won't hurt you again! You don't know us, but we're on your side. Give me a minute and we'll get you down!"

Suddenly the blindfold was off her eyes and Lynn was dazzled by several bright lights. Then she was gently lowered from the rope where she was hanging and laid on a small cot. Next her hands were freed. She rubbed her wrists and looked about herself. She found she was in a dirty warehouse, her clothes were grimy and she had a terrible headache. Then she saw the bodies. On the floor one of her abductors, a small knife protruding from his back. The other man was sprawled near a door face down in a large pool of blood. Lynn was still stunned by the whole chain of events. She heard the low familiar voice beside her. He was a swarthy dark-haired young man in his early twenties, with black eyes and a distinct Mideastern accent.

"Miss Pollard, I'm sorry you have had to go through this messy business, but I prefer to not to think about what they may have done to you if we hadn't arrived."

"May I ask who you are and where you fit into this growing mess?" she asked.

"Some of us would prefer to be known only as nationals who protect the interest of our country."

"You're saying you're from the Mossad if I understand what you are saying correctly." He grinned and said nothing. "Who are these people and why are they so vicious and fanatical?" she inquired.

"They're members of a fanatical splinter group of the Jesuit Order of Catholic Church. They've been involved in various historical flashpoints now for centuries, ever since the Reformation."

"But what brings them out of the woodwork at this point in time? I have a few ideas of my own, but I need more information," she asked.

"As far as we can comprehend, they had several of their operatives or whatever they called themselves in those days involved in the conspiracy to kill Lincoln in the 1860s. Some proof of this seems to have cropped up now, for example those pictures you were given."

"But what's so bad about that discovery?" she asked again.

"Well, it appears some feel this will deal the Church's reputation a severe blow here among the American people. Look, Miss Pollard, I'm going to make a suggestion that you come and stay in hiding with us for a few days until this whole business has settled. Otherwise, there is a chance they will make another attempt on your life again!" he spoke softly.

"I certainly don't want to, but I know from what I've seen that you're probably right!"

"Alright, come with us and we'll see that you're protected courtesy of the state of Israel!"

Chapter 42

The golden Caribbean sun had quickly settled into the azure-blue sea. As rapidly as the beach had filled in the morning, once the sun started to settle, the beach was vacant. Tony and April had found the sun too strong by two, and returned to the shade of the pool-side bar. April's face was a deep pink from the sun even though she had kept her hat on for most of the day. As they sat on the bar stools, which were just under the water, April sighed and commented, "Tony, I don't know about you, but I don't think I've ever had as much sun as today. How about you?"

"You've had far more of the sunscreen on than me and I'll probably look like a lobster tonight," Tony replied as he signalled to the barman for two more beers. As he talked, April sat on the bar stool with one arm holding up her head.

"Boy, another day in the sun and I'll sleep for a week. I don't know about you, Tony, but I'm going upstairs when I finish this beer and have a snooze. How about you?"

"Nah, I'm going to stay here and put the moves on that cute blonde over there on the other side of the pool, you go ahead." He had no sooner finished when April jumped up and dumped her entire glass over his head.

"Be careful of this guy, you girls!" April announced in a loud voice. "Once he thinks you're an easy mark, you're sunk!" She laughed as she waded over to the other side of the pool with Tony in hot pursuit. Catching her at the edge, he picked her up as she yelled, "Tony, put me down this minute! I'm all dried off and don't have the top of my suit on!" she yelped.

"Well, you should have thought of that before now! Hold your breath as here goes!" She tried to grab him as she felt herself flying into the water. Several minutes later, April climbed sputtering up the pool steps, soaked to the skin and her hair streaming water all over her face. There were gales of laughter from all around the pool area. April waved to them all with a giggle as there was suddenly an applause as she took a bow.

Turning to Tony she quipped, "You realize, Cassell, this means war! From now on, you're dead meat! Besides, if you were a gentleman, at least you'd have the courtesy to look scared!" With these words April bounded out of the area and headed off to their room.

A few minutes later, Tony arrived in their room with his towel over his shoulder and a book in his other hand. He heard the shower in the washroom and knew April was back ahead of him. Going to the small vault, he took out the folder of material he had brought with them from California. He was sitting on a plastic chair on the small balcony when he heard April come out of the washroom.

"Tony Cassell, why didn't you tell me everyone could see right through my shirt when I came out of the water? I'm mortified! I'll never be able to show my face around the pool again!" she said with a degree of remorse in her voice.

"I don't know what you're so uptight about," Tony replied. "You were the hit of the pool area. Don't you realize that?"

"Sure, all you guys had a real eye full as well!" she replied with a grin. "Tony, can I ask you a question? It's been bothering me since we got down here and it's really getting to me!" she asked.

Tony looked up at April and could see the real concern in her eyes. She was obviously very distraught. Gently he drew her over and sat her on his knee. She was wearing a light blue housecoat and still smelled of soap from her shower.

"April, what's bothering you? You seem very disturbed. If it's tossing you in the pool, then I'm sorry, I won't do it again."

"No, Tony, it's not that at all. I have more fun with you in one day than a year with Art. I just hope you're being honest with me. I couldn't stand it if you were leading me on. I have to know!"

"April, surely you know how I feel about you. I know the boss-employee relationship is a bit hard to chuck, but I don't know what else I can say. I have no smart-ass comments to make about that except to say how much you mean to me and I don't want to lose you. I'll admit it now, that's the other reason I brought you way down here. Besides the safety bit." As he stopped talking, he kissed her gently for a long moment.

"I'm sorry, Tony, I just had to know for sure. While I think of it, you said on the beach you had several papers you wanted to show me? I presume they are in the envelope?" As she spoke she slid off his lap and pulled up a chair beside him. He drew out the contents on to the table. First he laid out the two pictures he had shown her before and about which April had been so sure they were fakes.

"These are the same pictures that I saw last time, Tony!" she exclaimed as she raised her eyes to his.

"That's right, April, but there's also this statement which was found behind the second picture. It was fastened there with some kind of a second layer of metal glue. If it was placed there Mrs. Surratt was a smart lady."

> I, MRS. SURRATT, HEREBY WRITE ON THIS FIFTEENTH DAY OF APRIL 1865. I DO DECLARE MY INNOCENCE IN THE PLANNING OF THE DEATH OF OUR LATE PRESIDENT ABRAHAM LINCOLN. I WISH TO DECLARE MY LEGACY OF INNOCENCE IN THE PRESENCE OF TWO PRIESTS OF THE JESUIT ORDER. MY LEGACY IS ONE OF ONLY KNOWING AND NOT OF INVOLVEMENT. THE LEGACY OF THE PRIESTS IS ONE OF BOTH ENCOURAGEMENT AND ACTIVE INVOLVEMENT BOTH PERSONALLY AND OF THE ORDER THEY REPRESENT!

April looked up shocked.

"Tony, do you think there is any chance this could be the real thing?"

"April, I'm not at the point where I really just don't know. What bothers me, however, is the fact that many people will believe it is real and it will end up having the same effect as if we knew for sure that it was real, perhaps even more so. I think it's the same thing with the pictures!"

"I'm afraid I don't follow you, Tony," April stated.

"April, my real concern isn't the threats we've been getting so much as who has stirred this whole thing up in the beginning. It would be nice to believe that it's just a matter of Rome hearing about it and trying to correct history. However, I think not! I think someone is orchestrating this whole business for their own purposes," Tony said.

"Tony, who do you think this might be? If this is the case, then the whole thing is downright scary!"

"April, I don't know, but it's Lynn Pollard I'm worried about. She sent me these pictures via courier I'm convinced to get them away from her. I just hope she's watching over her shoulder."

"Tony, what are we going to do? Now I'm getting really nervous," April whispered.

"When we get back, I'm going straight to the FBI. I've never been a government man, but I think this is a case where they should be involved from our side. Besides, I want you to lay very low when we get back. Listen, I think we should put this stuff away and hash the details out over dinner. What do you say?"

"As a matter of fact, Tony, I'm starving. I'm glad you mentioned it," April replied. "You go ahead in the bathroom and I'm going to change out here."

As they walked across from their part of the resort to the big dining room, Tony caught April's hand and walked at her side. As he did, she looked up, and smiled and slipped her hand about his waist. She had dressed in a loose beach skirt, which hung loose about her hips but reached to her ankles. Her blouse was a sheer white silk that was short above her waist with a single button in the front. He could see her breasts moving under it and it was attracting a lot of male attention. Tony had changed into a matching short-and-shirt set that he hadn't worn before. As thy entered the dining room, he whispered in her ear, "Every second male eye in the room is looking at you, how about that!"

"I love every minute of it," April said with a laugh. As she spoke he could feel her hand holding even tighter on his waist.

Dinner passed slowly and the subject of the Lincoln material never arose between Tony and April. For the first time in his life he had found a person who mattered more than his own life to him. Partway through his dinner, he stopped and simply looked at April's pretty face across from him. She was busy working her way through a large piece of Dominican goat before she realized that she was being watched. She gulped and asked with food in her mouth, "What's the matter? You look troubled?" and continued to chew.

"No, I'm just thinking, April, how often I've been around you and took you for granted. Never again. I want you with me."

"Thanks for telling me, Tony, you'll never know how much that means to me," she whispered.

After dinner, they walked down onto the broad private beach. It was almost deserted, but the air was humid and warm. They could hear several people in the water. The moon was high in the sky and its rays gave an eerie glow all over the beach. April sat on one of the large picnic benches and inhaled deeply.

"I just can't get over this tropical air! It's so beautiful."

Chapter 43

The day's activity at the history research department at Cal Tech in Long Beach was winding down. There was some concern over Tony and April's absence. Gordon Haskett had come back from the weekend conference with a new vigour that they would be soon wrapping up the seemingly endless Lincoln study. The three students and two hired researchers were looking forward to seeing the end of it. Randy Nicholson, one of the two researchers, greeted the news with a sigh of relief.

"Thank God, we'll be able to put that damned business where it should have always been, in the grave." He was sitting in the small coffee room with Luke Pallister and Anna Capling, two of the research coordinators.

"Well, I don't really think Booth ever pulled the trigger, but after all these years I just don't see the point of digging all this up again. I hope Gordon will have something definite when he comes in," Anna commented, a cute black girl in her early twenties. "You know last month when I was doing an interview with a member of the Stanton family, the guy made this very point! Why bother after all this time? What's it going to prove?" she concluded. Luke was the older of the group.

He had been quiet during the discussion, but finally chimed in. "I don't know about the rest of you, but there's something going on that I can't put a finger on. There's more to this Lincoln bit than we've been told! I think it has a lot to do with the conference last weekend up at Gord's father's big spread. I'm also very suspicious about Tony and April. It's too easy to say that they just wanted a quick week in the hay!"

"Get off the pot, Luke," Anna injected. "April just isn't the type. Besides, that prick Art has her wrapped around his little finger. I just wish Tony would pay some attention to her!"

The chatting in the staff room continued until about three-thirty. The other two members of the staff remained at their desks and were buried in their computer screens. The office was apart from the main university history department. There had been a scramble for space until finally they had found the present space at the back of a large health services building. It was a quiet corner that was inaccessible unless one had specific guidelines how to reach it. This had suited Tony Cassell when he had come up with the funding to do the three-year project. He had managed to scrounge the computers and other equipment from Standard Oil through Gordon's dad. The whole project had been a dream setup. As a result he was able to use most of the grant money for staff salaries.

The receptionist was busy with her other job as information collator when she heard a shuffle in the main entrance. She looked up. She saw no one and turned back to her screen. There was another soft rustle. Again, she looked up. As she did she thought she heard someone behind her. It was too late. As she looked up a thin garrote was slipped around her throat and snapped tight. Her breath was immediately cut off. She reached up with her hands to try and remove it, but it only became tighter and tighter. In desperation she began to kick and thrash as she was dragged from her chair behind her computer. She tried to scream but no sound came, no matter how hard she tried. Then she began to realize her life was beginning to slip away as simmering colours began to flash through her head. Finally she lashed out in one final spasmodic kick before slipping into the black vault of oblivion. Her body went limp as she was laid on the floor, her eyes wide open as death quickly overcame her. The shadowy figure behind her silently signalled to his comrade towards the other figure who was working away at her computer and totally unaware of the receptionist's final struggle. Then she moved and turned and came face to face with two tall strangers dressed entirely in black. Her face went ashen as she saw the other girl's corpse on the floor.

"No, please don't!" she whispered in a hoarse voice as the closer man reached out and grabbed her. He pulled her against his chest and masked her face. As he did, he thrust a long thin knife into her chest with awesome force. The blade thrust deep, entering just below her left breast and plunging deep, penetrating in and through her heart. He stepped back. The girl grasped the handle of the knife and looked down at it. Her lips moved, forming words, but no sound came out. Suddenly her knees buckled and she crumpled to the floor in a bloody heap. The two men quickly began to search the various desks and files through the office.

Then one of them heard a sound of laughter from the staff room behind a door at the far end of the office. One attacker waved to the other and pointed to the door. As he did he pulled out of his pocket a small revolver equipped with a silencer. The first intruder moved without a sound and rapped on the door. There was a moment's silence. Momentarily, Luke Pallister opened the door and called out, "Yes, Jayne, what is it now?" As he yelled he moved the door. That cost him his life. The intruder's revolver coughed twice and two dark red holes appeared in Luke's chest. His body was slammed against the wall by the force of the bullets. He collapsed lifeless on the floor. The intruder moved to the entrance of the staff room. Only one other person was in sight. Randy Nicholson slowly stood up by the small table.

"Well, asshole, if you're going to do it, first tell a dead man why he's about to die," he said with a snarl.

The man thought for a moment. "Die you will, mister, and why—now I'll tell you! You've heard of the American Freedom Party? Well, they're the new wave of our nation's scene. This stupid Jesuit Brotherhood have been trying to close some doors over their part in killing Lincoln, but we've put a stop to that. That's where you come in! You're trying to get the true story out and that has to stop. So look at it this way, you're going to die for your country." As he finished he raised his gun toward Randy. Randy's eyes suddenly grew wide as he saw the final moments of his life approach. The gun barked only once and a small hole appeared over Randy's right eye. He stood for a second and then his eyes glazed and he crumpled to the floor. The stranger looked down at him. Randy was already dead with not a move from his body.

In a small cupboard at the end of the staff room, the cramped figure of Anna Capling shuddered. In his last act, Randy had stuffed her in under the sink and slammed the door with his foot, just before the attacker appeared at the entrance of the staff room. Tears of fear and sorrow streamed down Anna's face as she heard the last gunshot and knew Randy had died so she could live. She had heard his taunt and remembered every word and syllable of the attacker's answer. Then she had heard the thump, and knew only too well it what it was.

"I've got some stuff over here in files as well as some hard drive disks. Let's get the shit out of here." The last man out of the office had dumped a number of piles of paper and other material into the middle of the floor. Scooping up the papers and disks, they walked out the door turning as the last man threw down a phosphorus flare that quickly started a small blaze in the centre of the office. Then there was silence.

As she slowly opened the cupboard door and unfolded her cramped legs, Anna was almost suddenly overcome with great clouds of smoke. Jumping to her feet, she grabbed one of the several extinguishers that Tony had so insisted on. She sprayed the dry white powder and within moments had the fire under control. Then she saw the extent of the horror. She knelt by Randy's still body. His eyes were closed and he was unmarked except for the small stream of blood running from the wound that killed him.. He had been so kind to her, and now this. She ran her hand over the side of his young face as tears dripped off her cheeks. Then she felt an anger she had never known. The four people who had given her a reason to live again were suddenly dead. She picked up the phone and called information.

"Operator, could you give me the number for the FBI!"

Chapter 44

Scott Fleming was very worried. He had phoned Lynn's flat several times on Tuesday, but there was no answer. Finally, after his long session in the hospital OR on Wednesday, he called her office. The phone rang over ten times before a strange voice answered. He was informed that Ms. Pollard was unavailable and that no one was in the office. He received the same answer throughout the day. Finally, later in the day, he called home and asked his mother to drive around Lynn's office and see if there was something wrong. Less than an hour later, she called his office in a very agitated state.

"Scott, I've just come down to Lynn's office. There's something wrong, but I've not been able to determine just what. Her office is closed and the place is crawling with police. When I asked about Lynn, they grabbed me and gave me the third degree!"

"Mother, could you find where Lynn is, or even what's happened to her?"

"Scott, all I know is something terrible must have happened or there wouldn't be the security around here that I saw a few minutes ago. I've been around this city too long not to smell the trouble. Scott, I don't know what else to say, though you might get some more answers if you could call any friends you have at the police headquarters! Listen, I've got to get back to the children, I'll see you at dinner." There was a click on the phone as Martha hung up.

Scott sat at his desk and stared at the wall in front of him, with a gnawing at the pit of his stomach. In the back of his mind he could see Lynn's pretty face, this person whom he had only known for a few weeks was suddenly occupying such a pivotal place in his life. What had happened? It was so unlike her! She had promised to call on Tuesday evening and now it was late Wednesday afternoon. He buzzed through to his secretary in the outer office and asked, "Cathy, would you please call the police headquarters and have Det. Dick Schantz give me a call as soon as possible! Also, give the hospital's OR a confirming ring and tell Dr. MacLean I'll be with him at three tomorrow as he requested. Thanks."

Thirty-five minutes later the phone buzzed and Cathy announced, "Dr. Fleming, Det. Schantz is on the line waiting for you."

"Hi, Dick, thanks for being so prompt. Listen, I gather there was some sort of trouble over at the Commerce Building. Can you tell me anything?"

"Scott, it's good to hear your voice. I assume you know someone there or you wouldn't be asking. Someone came into the Kodak Research Office yesterday afternoon and ransacked the office. As far as we can tell, one woman was killed and another is missing."

A cold fear suddenly gripped Scott and his voice was tense as he spoke. "Do you know the name of the woman killed?"

"Well, I'm not supposed to say, but you're a good friend. The woman killed was a Mrs. Maggie Shane. This was a real professional job. She was shot three times through the heart."

"Look, Dick, I appreciate you sharing this information. Do you know anything about a Ms. Lynn Pollard?"

"It's funny you should ask me about her. I had a call a few minutes ago from overseas wanting to get in touch with her. I think the call came from Marseilles. Did you know the woman at all, Scott," the detective asked.

"Yes, she's a very special friend, Dick. That's why I called in the beginning. She spent the weekend up at the cottage with our family and was supposed to call last evening," Scott replied.

"I'm sorry, I wasn't sure but I suspected as much. I'm afraid that's all I can tell you at this stage," Dick Schantz replied.

"Dick, I want to thank you for your information. I guess all I can do is wait and perhaps pray," Scott answered.

"I suggest they obviously took her with them is some sign of hope. At least they didn't kill her on the spot. Remember, there are all the signs that these people are real pros and they would have killed her if there weren't any reason to keep her alive. She obviously knows something they want, and that's her best chance to still be alive."

"I had a feeling this might happen after we talked on Sunday, especially over this Lincoln conspiracy business, Dick," Scott replied.

"That was my next question, Scott. Did either of you know anything about the talk that's going around the city about that very thing? We've been talking to the FBI and said we'd turn any information we have over to them. We were dragged into this business because we were called, and then because of the killing."

"No, they haven't been in touch with me as yet, but I gather they will be. I'll be glad. This business is starting to get scary," Scott said.

"Look, I'm afraid I have to go, Scott, there are two of my lines flashing and I've got a pile of paperwork. Listen, I'll call you just as soon as I hear anything and would appreciate you doing the same. Phone me at home if you have to." Scott placed the phone back on the table.

That evening Scott Fleming sat down with his two daughters for their bedtime stories about eight-thirty. As he was reading to them, they sat snuggled up on either side of him, there came a sound from the front doorbell ringing. Martha called out from the kitchen, "You and the girls stay put, I'll get it!" Scott dropped his eyes back to the copy of Grimm's Fairy Tales as he read to the girls. As he did, he wrapped his arms about them even tighter. In several moments, Martha Fleming appeared at the door.

"Scott, you'd better come out here immediately! There are two gentlemen here who insist they must see you. You go and I'll finish the girls' story and put them to bed."

Little Angie let out a cry but her father gave her a hug and whispered, "Don't worry, sweetie, I'll be back in a minute to tuck you in. Meanwhile, Grandma will get you ready for bed as only she can!" Running his fingers through Francie's hair he stepped out into the hall to come face to face with two men dressed almost entirely in black. They were somewhere in their early thirties and spoke immediately.

"You're Doctor Scott Fleming?" the taller of the two inquired.

"Yes, that's right. Gentlemen, why are you here and how can I help you?"

"Dr. Fleming, I'll come right to the point. I think you're aware of the raid on Ms. Lynn Pollard's office and the killing of her assistant?"

"Yes, that's correct. Do you something about Lynn? If you do, please tell me!" Scott asked urgently.

"Yes, Dr. Fleming, we have her in our protection and aside from being bit shaken, she's fine and asking for you and your family. Listen, she was abducted yesterday, by a group who call themselves the Brotherhood of the Red Rose. They are a strike force, kind of splinter group of the Roman Catholic Church's Order of the Jesuits."

"Where is she right now? Do you have her with you?"

"No, Dr. Fleming, that is what I'm saying. We think there's a real danger to her life and have suggested she stay with us for protection for the moment. I've explained to her we have no connection with this group or anything in this country. We represent the government of another country who have a great deal to lose if this Order achieves what they appear to be trying to do. If you've heard of the Mossad, then you'll know who we represent!"

"What do you want of me and my family, gentlemen?" Scott Fleming asked curtly.

"We think there is a real danger to you and your family in this situation. I'm going to suggest that all of you come with us and we can guarantee you safe hiding until this ordeal is over. I don't want to seem alarmist, but you have small children and there could be danger to them as well. This group was, by the way, planning some examples of some of the most hideous forms of torture I have ever seen, for your friend, Ms. Pollard."

"You want us to go with you this minute?"

"Doctor, the sooner we get you folks settled in hiding, the better I'll feel about everything!"

As he finished a third young man came running up the steps with his gun drawn and shouted, "Moshe, there are two strange cars just down the street. I think we've been discovered. If you're going to get these people out, you'd best do it now, or let's get the hell out of here. If they're coming, I'd try and find a rear entrance!" He panted with the effort of his run up the front lawn from the street.

"You've heard the young man, Doctor. We'll help you if you want, or we leave matters as they are and you can take your chances. What will it be?"

"As a neurologist, I have to live with quick decisions. Let me get my girls and mother and we're with you."

"Doctor, is there any sort of back or underground door out of the house? If they have two cars out there, they are going to be watching both sides of the house," the older man of the three asked.

"Well, the only thing I can think of is the old root cellar that we haven't used in years. The door still comes back through the basement, but I don't know if it is still passable," Scott replied quickly.

"Doctor, you're the answer to a dream! Let's get going!"

Meanwhile, the two remaining Mossad agents came through the front door and one shouted, "There are three very nasty looking types coming up the front walk."

"Avram and Ariel, you two hold the front door, here, we have to get these people out through the back, so hold the barrier at all costs. By the way, did you put one of the cars on the back street?" The other agent plunked a set of keys in his hand and nodded his head.

Scott and Martha, each carrying one of the girls, went into the basement where Scott led them to a dank and dark part which led out to the back garden. He hadn't been there for years, but the door swung open and they were outside and raced across the garden and through the thick hedge. They piled into a fifteen-year-old Ford Crown Victoria. As they were climbing into the car there was a sudden chatter of light-machine-gun fire from the front of the house.

"Shouldn't we wait for those young men?" inquired Scott in shock.

"No, Doctor, those young men as you described them are two of the best agents we've ever put into the field. They're expected to look out for themselves."

The car roared off into the deepening twilight. After dodging traffic for nearly ninety minutes, the agents pulled down shades on all the windows.

"Don't be alarmed, this way no one can get out of you information you don't have. We'll be at the house in about five minutes and there you'll be safe for a few days. Oh, yes, Miss Pollard is there as well."

"Does she know we're coming?"

"No, sir, she does not!" Suddenly the car seemed to be pulling into a large garage and there was the sound of a garage door closing. Suddenly a bright light flashed on. They were helped out of the car and were led from the garage through a kitchen and into a palatial living room.

"Good evening, Dr. Fleming, to you and your family!" Scott was shocked to come fact to face with Mr. Franco Morgenstein, one of the Israeli government's top representatives in America.

"I'm sorry, Doctor, we have to meet under such circumstances, but my government is glad that we can give you some protection against this vicious group of people. We can talk about it tomorrow. I'll leave you to the second apartment upstairs! By the way, here's someone who has been very anxious to see all of you." Scott turned toward the door and there was the tattered figure of Lynn Pollard.

"Scott, is it really you? I thought I'd never see any of you again! Thank God!"

"Auntie Lynn!" cried the voice of little Angie Fleming as she raced into Lynn's arms as she knelt to receive the child. Lynn's clothes were torn and dirty and her face was drawn and weary. In a moment she had her arms about both girls. Scott Fleming would recall the scene for years. Even Martha Fleming came over and put her arms about Lynn and the girls. In a moment, Lynn and Scott came face to face. There were tear streaks on both of her cheeks as she caught his hands. He opened his arms and she came naturally into his embrace. It seemed like an eternity before they stepped back to gaze into each other's eyes.

"I thought I'd never see you again, Scott, I don't think I could have survived that possibility." It seemed there was no pretense left in either of them. Placing hands on either side of her face, he kissed her for the longest time until she began to giggle.

"I think we're embarrassing these good people who are watching us!" As she talked she placed her face against his chest and he let his fingers wander through her short hair. Lynn wished that moment would last forever.

Chapter 45

The phone jangled. Father Jim McGuire had been dozing in his frustration waiting for his instructions for his next move. He had served the Brotherhood well down through the years, but had come to the final conclusion he would not be able to do what would probably be required of him this time. Existing as a mole for over a decade had not diminished his faith but, in retrospect, had demolished his respect for himself. Picking up the phone, he recognized the now familiar voice of Father De Medici.

"Good morning, Father McGuire."

"Good morning, Father."

"Listen, it's crucial that we get together immediately. Right now, I'm across the street from your hotel. Can we meet in the greasy spoon next to the hotel in about fifteen minutes?" he asked.

"Yes, Father, I'll be there in less time than that." He hung up and grabbed his jacket. Within twenty minutes, they were both settled in a quiet booth at the back of the grubby restaurant.

"Father McGuire, there has been a drastic change in plans. Do you know Father George Rowling?"

"Yes, of course, I studied with him at Fordham. Why? Has something happened?" McGuire inquired.

"He was very lucky. You know the meeting that was scheduled for Oakland two days ago?"

"Of course, I would have been there except you gave me orders to lay low. Why? Did the meeting not come off well?"

"Not really! Someone got wind of it and assaulted them. They're all dead except Father Rowling. He was somehow hidden under a sofa and is still alive, though for how long, I'm not sure!"

"Jesus Christ!" snapped McGuire. "Who the hell was it, or do you know?"

"Yes, as a matter of fact we do, although not very much. At first we though it was the Mossad. They've been a re-occurring nightmare for us ever since this operation started. We made a stupid mistake in that Irish killing. One of the priests was a longtime Mossad plant. As a result they have declared war on us. But that's not the problem here!"

"What do you mean?" asked McGuire.

"Very simply, this wasn't the Mossad's style. They're a very disciplined outfit. As much as we are, perhaps even more so!"

"So, if it wasn't done by them, then who?" McGuire asked with a look of deep shock on his face.

"We knew there was someone else on the scene even before this tragedy, but with Father Rowling surviving, we've managed to get a fair picture, at least in generalities. They're part of a movement on the extreme right wing of American politics and call themselves the American Freedom Party. Apparently, they're out to get this Lincoln material as we were, but in their case to discredit the Catholic Church in America. Let me tell you, Father, if they keep on with the success they've had against us, then they just might manage to pull it off."

"But Father, that being the case why would you ever think of pulling our group away from the search after a commitment of so much time and life? I don't see your logic," asked McGuire.

"Very simply, Father McGuire, if we don't back out now, then we're liable to get ourselves in more of a public mess than we were first willing to accept. Remember our philosophy? To thrust and probe only when there is an acceptable risk. That risk is no longer acceptable to the head of the Order. As it is, we're going to have to keep a very low profile for some time after this setback!"

"So, you're telling me we're going to take our chances with this Lincoln thing, is that right?" McGuire asked.

"If it were just this Freedom Party and ourselves, we would be forced to fight it to the end. Now, however, since the Mossad have decided to become a major player, we felt it most prudent to back off."

"You mean you feel with the Mossad willing, we could accord to pull out, lick our wounds and let the Mossad do our dirty work for us!" McGuire snapped. De Medici looked at him for a few silent moments. McGuire said to himself, *He knows that I've changed my mind, I know these guys. They're never happy unless they own you body and soul.*

"What do you want of me, Father, now that we've done a pullback? You didn't come here just to tell me what you have so far," McGuire said.

"That's correct, it's not that simple. We still want to get any or all of the Lincoln material that implicated the Order. You're good friends with most of the key people concerned. Go to them and see what you can dig up and what you can get. Remember there may be a chance we've lost the battle to protect the Order's reputation for a while, but this could mean the reputation of the Catholic Church in North America. That in itself is no mean feat!" De Medici spoke bluntly. "By the way, in case you haven't heard there was also an attack on the history department research office at Cal Tech in Long Beach in California. The office was ransacked and at least four of the staff were brutally killed. We don't know whether anyone escaped or not. There was a fair amount of speculative evidence there, but from what we can tell, not a great deal of hard facts."

"Father, where are the original pictures we've been looking for? That's what I'd like to know."

"We're not sure. You see, Father, there are several places it could be. The director of the research office that was attacked yesterday wasn't there, nor was his assistant. They haven't been seen for days, I've a feeling they've left the country. The girl who works at Kodak was captured by the Freedom bunch and we do not know if she is alive or not. Her assistant was shot on the spot. The final couple we're trying to reach was Gordon Haskett and his girlfriend Bev. They were up with you at his father's but where they are now, we're not sure."

"Look, Father, leave them to me. I think I can find them for you. Don't forget I've known some of these young people for over a decade."

"Alright, Father McGuire, we'll leave it in your hands as of now. Time is of the essence, and we have to be so careful." Drinking the last drop of coffee, De Medici got to his feet and walked briskly from the restaurant. Father McGuire's eyes followed him all the way out.

That bastard thinks he owns me body and soul! We'll see just how much of it they really own. They deserve everything the Mossad can dish out!

169

Chapter 46

A few people from the resort were walking along the short private beach. There was a barrier at both ends to restrict the local population. Tony had left April still sitting in the old wooden chair, and he strolled down by the sea's edge which was lapping quietly. Taking off his sandals, he waded in to his knees as he walked parallel to the beach. Coming to the barrier wall, he pulled himself up and gazed into the moonlight night. Despite the stress of their anticipated return, he was mesmerized by the beauty of the spot. The soft warm air wafted in the from the lazy sea and rustled the semi-visible palm branches over his head. Again Tony pondered the options open to them. There was far more behind the various threats they had heard about. He kept thinking about Father Jim and why he had shown up at the Haskett summer home. Yet there was something about the man's whole approach that bothered him deeply. That, combined with the basic conclusion that there was nothing new to point the finger at in the Lincoln conspiracy, was deeply troubling. Yet, the Surratt note was a bombshell and everything else paled beside it. Was it possible that the whole conspiracy had been engineered from outside the country? Part of him said it was impossible. Another part said he should be realistic and face what appeared to be the facts.

"Tony, what are you doing? I though you'd gone back to your room!" chimed April's cheery voice from behind him, "I've been looking for you for the last ten minutes."

"Oh, I've just been sitting here thinking about this whole business we talked about before supper."

"Tony, what do you think? Should we go back to LA or hole up somewhere else?" she asked.

"April, I need some help in this matter. I find it very hard to be objective. I do think we should agree at least on part of an overall picture. Then we can determine a plan of action."

As he talked, April settled herself on the concrete ridge Tony was sitting on. They were both quiet for a long time, lulled by the sweet aroma coming with wind. Tony sighed and asked, "A penny for your thoughts?"

April turned and looked at him for a moment. "Tony, before I saw that note from Mary Surratt, I was ready to say, 'Chuck the whole research project.' Now, I think we should bring the FBI into it. This matter could easily get out of hand."

"That's a damn good idea, April. I think we should lay low when we get back to Toronto and see if we can get them in Washington. I do know they operate out of Canada quite frequently."

"You mean to say you want to stay in Toronto and wait to see what happens?" April asked.

"Exactly, April. I called Gordon Haskett in Long Beach at his home late this afternoon and there's been a fire at our office."

"What!" exclaimed April. "Why didn't you tell me about this when you first heard about it? Tony, what are we going to do!"

"That's why I am suggesting we stay over in Canada for a while until we hear more about what has happened since we left. Gordon said he and Bev have asked the police for protection and they have someone guarding their house day and night," Tony added.

"Oh, sure, with all the efficiency they used in the OJ Simpson investigation!" April said with a note of bitterness in her voice.

Turning to April, Tony took her left hand and said, "Look, April, I know you're scared. Don't feel bad, you've got lots of company. I'm not sure where to turn at this stage except for our friends in Toronto. Besides, we have to have a base when we get back so we can see where things are happening." As he talked, April rolled her eyes and he held on to her hand.

"Who would have dreamed three years ago when I went to work for you in the research department, it would all lead to this," she said with a grim look of resignation on her face.

Tony reacted with a tightening of the muscles in his face. "Look, April, usually you're the upbeat one of the two of us. We're here to give us a breather and a margin of safety. If we'd stayed in LA, we might have well have been dead at this stage. When we get back, I'm going to phone Gordon and tell him something of the nature of the Surratt note. That way we can keep ourselves relatively safe and see how things develop. I'm making sure we don't get caught up in any sort of squeeze play."

April remained silent before turning to Tony as she wagged her feet back and forth as she sat on the ledge. Then she jumped off and turned to Tony. "Tony, have you ever had the desire to live close to the edge?"

"I have no idea what you're talking about, April. What in the hell do you mean?"

"All my life I've been so conservative! I've never really let everything hang out! This might be the last time you and I ever have the chance to do such a thing. Let's get some drinks and catch the remainder of the show over on the beach stage!" As she talked she grabbed Tony by the hands and pulled him off the ledge where he had been sitting for nearly an hour. As she did, she tried to tickle him and he responded by chasing her. Catching her, they tumbled into a jumble of legs and arms on the cool sand. Tony found himself lying on top of her. As he eased himself off her, he looked into her dark eyes before lowering his lips to hers. In their tumble to the sand, April's blouse was snapped open and he found himself with one hand on her left breast. Afraid of hurting her feelings more, he removed his hand and sat up.

"I'm sorry, April, I shouldn't have done that. It's very easy to get carried away when you're dressed like that."

April made no attempt to cover herself. "Tony, if I didn't want you to caress me, I would have asked you not to. Would you be shocked if I asked you to make love to me right now?" she commented looking directly at him, not moving her eyes. He reached down and pulled April to her feet.

"Let's do as you suggested, get some drinks and let the night take us where it does!" He cracked with a smile.

April reacted instantly. "Let's do it right now! The bar is over this way." She grabbed Tony by the hand and led him in the vicinity of the Beach Bar which was still open. They slipped their arms around each others waists and trundled off to the Beach Bar.

Returning from a trip to the washroom a half an hour later, Tony found his stool next to April was taken by a tall man who had his arm around her shoulders and was obviously heavily intoxicated. He had somehow undone her blouse, which was half off her shoulders, and several of the men about the bar were leering at her exposed breasts. Coming up behind April, he was about to whisper in her ear, when suddenly a strong arm knocked him sprawling on the ground.

"Touch my gal again, asshole, and I'll break your arm!"

As he climbed to his feet, Tony could see the fear in April's eyes.

"Look mister, she's my fiancée and please take your hands off her right now!" Tony said in as non-challenging a tone as he could muster.

The man left April's side and made a grab for Tony. He sidestepped the lunge, grabbed his arm and twisted it behind his back. As he did he whispered in the tall man's ear, "Look, mac, we all have too much to drink occasionally. Go back to your room and sleep it off!" He let the man go. As he did the man made another lunge for Tony. Tony then twisted the man's arm behind his back and marched him to the pool's edge and said in a loud voice, "Like I just said, mister, it's time to cool off!" Tony then released him and shoved him into the pool. He came to the surface sputtering. He climbed out and an older woman went to his side and helped him out of the pool area. Tony felt someone clasp his hand.

"Mister, you're a real class act! If that had been me, I would have broken his arm. Black belt, I gather?"

Tony looked at the man in amazement. "Jesus, you're a perceptive bugger," he muttered. "Yes, I've got a black belt, but I don't like to talk about it. Please don't mention it!" The young man smiled and walked away. Tony looked at April. She had come over to him and was resting her head on him arm.

"Tony, I'm so sorry, I couldn't get rid of that guy! He was a real ass. And too strong for me." As she talked she started to shake, and he put his arm around her.

"Well, I had a bad moment with him, but I managed to get myself under control and not hurt him."

April stopped and asked, "What do you mean, 'not hurt him'?"

"April, that's what the other man was talking about. He spotted my judo training and that's what we try to avoid if possible. If I had strictly reacted on my training, the guy would probably have a broken arm now, no question." April stood with her mouth open.

"In fact, if I had followed my first instinct when I saw him fondling you, he'd now be dead!" April saw a coldness in his eyes she had never seen before. She was surprised it filled her with comfort and not fear. Tony put his arm around her and said, "Let's go up to our room, April. It's been a long day and I just want to be with you." As he looked into her eyes, he saw peace and lack of fear for the first time in over a week.

After a few minutes in the washroom, April had changed into a light pair of silk pajamas that were sleeveless and ended at her knees. Tony had changed into another light pair of shorts as their room was hot despite the air conditioning. When he came out of the washroom, she was nowhere to be seen. Finally, he found her on the wide balcony.

"Tony, I can't thank you enough for what you did for me at the pool. Art would have walked back to the washroom," she said with a note of bitterness in her voice. Suddenly she felt herself being turned to face Tony.

"April, I know you've had a long relationship with Art. That's fine and can't be changed, but I thought we had discovered something special between us. Look, I happen to love you, but I'm beginning to wonder what that means to you. I'm trying to...." He was stopped by April as she suddenly kissed him. Then she stepped back and looked at him, her eyes shining and filled with tears.

"Tony, I didn't mean it that way at all! I mean everything I've said to you! I guess I just mention him out of habit. Forgive me?"

"It's not a matter of forgiveness, but I get tired of hearing his name." She had walked over to the low red-brick wall that formed the edge of the balcony. As she did she slowly removed her top and bottoms, to stand nude by the wall. The slimness of her figure stood out in the moonlight. Tony drew her into his arms as she slid his shorts down his legs. He picked her up and carried her to the first small bed in the room and was quickly lost in the warmth and softness of her arms.

Chapter 47

The big Boeing touched down with hardly a rumble and ran the length of the main runway. Frank Baird had called ahead to Des Moines and requested a meeting of the Freedom Party Council. There was some grumbling about the quickness of the meeting, but Baird's orders were firm. He disliked flying even though he had used the various airlines since before the beginning of the Second World War.

He found the open spaces of the Des Moines Municipal Airport a welcome change from the crowds of Washington. After deplaning at the terminal and waiting for his suitcase, he heard his name being paged over the PA system. It seemed that the announcement and his bag arrived at about the same time. Walking out to the main concourse, he went over to the Delta Airlines desk where the announcement had asked him to report.

"Frank Baird here, someone paged me from here a few moments ago."

"Aw, yes, Mr. Baird!" replied a cheery blond-haired young woman. "There's a Mr. Brian Vaschuk waiting over there in the dining lounge. He asked me to ask you to meet him when you were ready."

Baird nodded his thanks, picked up his suitcase and walked into the restaurant. A young man in the corner table stood and came over to meet him.

"Mr. Baird, I presume? You look very much like your pictures."

Baird grunted his agreement and plunked himself down on the nearest chair at the corner table. When he was settled, the waiter came and asked if they would like something to eat. Baird muttered he would like to see a menu. The waiter nodded and went off to another table to get several. Baird looked at his watch and saw it was five-forty-five.

"Do you have everything ready for our meeting tomorrow?" he asked the young man, who appeared to be very nervous around him.

"Yes, sir, our staff have got everything you wanted," he replied.

"They goddamned better or I'll have their balls for breakfast. Have you got all the material ready I asked you for last week? I'll need them first thing tomorrow morning. I want to get started at 8 a.m. sharp, and then we can be finished by early afternoon!"

"Yes, Mr. Baird, I've been over everything with my people a thousand times and we couldn't be more ready!" Vaschuk answered.

"Well, you'd better go over it one more time! I don't care as long as you haven't made any slips. Now tell me is my room ready at the hotel? And how about the mansion at eight this evening?" Baird asked looking directly at the young man with the coldest eyes Vaschuk had ever seen.

"Like I said, sir, everything is arranged just as you wanted and asked for. If you have any complaints, please call me at the number on this card and I'll have it looked after immediately."

"You're goddamned right that is what I'll do and the first thing I'll ask for is your head on a platter. Remember, punk, you screw up on this project and I'll be taking this personally!" The young man gulped at the unveiled threat.

"Now get the hell out of here and I'll see you in my room tomorrow morning at seven. Remember, be there or you'll wish you'd never been born." Vaschuk nodded in Baird's direction and was gone in a flash.

After supper, Baird took a cab to the local Ramada Inn in the main part of the downtown city core. After settling in his room, he took several files of material out of his briefcase and placed them inside a small leather portfolio and prepared to head out for his evening appointment.

At two minutes past eight, Frank Baird arrived at a large mansion overlooking Lake Easter and the surrounding park. At the door he was met by a tall butler who ushered him into a type of sitting room and library. After a few moments, he heard his name.

"Frank Baird, it's good to see you after all these months!"

"Good evening, Senator Beecham, it's good to see you as well. I'm glad we could have this time before the meeting tomorrow morning."

"Frank, come over here and have a seat. We can talk here and the room is completely soundproofed. Now, please fill me in on the most recent developments. I've been hearing a variety of things in the news."

"Senator, are you still on board? I've been hearing a few things here and there from some of my contacts."

The senator's face went pale. He suddenly became furious and slapped his hand on the coffee table in front of him.

"Jesus Murphy, you have your arrogance! I arrange to have an assassination attempt staged on my own life and you have the unspeakable audacity to question my dedication! I don't know whether to call the police or laugh! I tend to think the latter."

"Look, Senator, you're not the only one involved in this whole thing. I know as well as you that you wanted an excuse to get rid of your wife. Most of all, this has given you a real tap into the sympathy vote come the next election, when we are going to start running our candidates across the nation. I'm just as glad to see your old woman gone; she was the biggest threat we have faced yet."

"I have to admit you're right about the sympathy vote. I just have to remind myself of the fact when I'm out and see a nice piece of ass. That sort of thing could cook my goose right now quicker than anyone else."

"Senator, how many members do you figure we're going to be able to get into Congress in this coming election?" Baird asked directly. There was a moment of silence.

"I would think we would be lucky if we can get more than two dozen the first time around!" he responded. Baird was shocked.

"You mean to tell me that after all our work and effort that is all you think we'll be able to get in? That seems pretty piss poor to me!" he replied.

"My friend, you must remember the tradition in this country of a two-party system. We're not like Canada or most of the European countries, where you can have a dozen. The first thing we have to do here is to shatter the faith of the people in the validity of our present system."

"It sure seems a pretty slow way to go about it!" said the senator. "I thought that was your original plan, to go about as basic a change in the government as took place in the days of Andrew Jackson or after the Civil War. What I want to know is the state of this business with the Lincoln pictures," Beecham stated.

"Senator, all I can say so far is everything is on schedule. The opposition of this brotherhood group isn't nearly as vicious as we were led to believe. That shooting our people did out in Oakland took the heart out of them."

"I saw that in the paper. I thought ours here in Iowa was bad, but nothing like that!"

"Senator, if you're going to play games with these people, you have to play as rough as necessary to get it done. That's what we've been doing. I even got a copy of the pictures from this Pollard girl, an old friend of the family. She gave me copies of them and I think I spooked her sufficient enough. The only problem here was in her abduction. I thought we could scare the rest of the information out of her, but our people were killed before they could get their work done."

"I heard about that incident! Who are these people, Baird?" the senator inquired.

"I'm not sure of that fact yet, Senator, but if my suspicions are right, we've been the victims of a miscue by the Red Rose people in Ireland. It was one of those quirks of history that can upset the whole applecart."

"I'm afraid you've lost me," the senator replied.

"The simple fact of the matter is that one of those priests killed in Dublin by the Red Rose to eliminate informers, was a member of the deadliest antiterrorist group in the world. The Israeli Mossad. Now they're taking some of our people out as they figure in shaming the Catholic Church. The blame will rest on them over their traditional distrust of each other," Baird said.

"How do things stand at the moment?" the senator asked.

"Well, we're keeping the lid on tight, but these people are good, and they've brought a whole contingent of their people into this country."

There was a long silence between them.

"Mr. Baird, how does the boss feel about the whole thing at this point?"

"When I talked to him this morning, just before I left, he used that old naval term, 'Steady as she goes!'"

Chapter 48

Lynn Pollard was devastated by Maggie's killing. For twenty-four hours she seemed to retreat into herself, despite Scott's attempts to reach her after they were together again. It was useless. Finally, the girls came to their father the next morning, asking in Angie's words, "Daddy, what's the matter with Aunt Lynn? She doesn't want to talk with Francie and I? Doesn't she like us anymore?" Scott put his arms about the two distraught little girls.

A short while later Scott found Lynn sitting very quietly by the side of a small sheltered pool in the legation's walled compound. As he approached, she looked up with a glance of detachment and a vague smile. She was dangling her bare legs in the warm blue water. Pulling over a chair, he sat beside her.

"Lynn, can I talk to you?" he asked in a gentle voice. She looked up with a sadness in her dark eyes and reached out and rested her hand on his arm and nodded her head.

"Lynn, I wish I could say something that could atone for Maggie's death. She was a patient of mine for years and I thought the world of her!"

"Why, Scott, why Maggie? She never hurt a person in her life! She didn't deserve that kind of an end!" As she talked, he could see tears welling up in her eyes.

"Lynn, what I wanted to talk to you about is the girls. They seem to think you don't want to be near them and they came to me all upset this morning. They really love you, Lynn. Perhaps you might share with them something of how you feel!" he said quietly.

She looked up at him again and said, "Are you sure, Scott? They're not very old for this kind of thing."

He took both of her hands in his and looked her in the eyes. "Lynn, about a year ago, I almost walked away from my medical career. I was removing a tumour from the brain of a gal younger than you. I made a stupid mistake, there's no denying the fact, and she died. Basically I killed her, Lynn! Don't ever think your life is the only one with long shadows. I'll live with that all my life!"

"Oh God, Scott, how terrible!" Lynn whispered.

"Yes, and it was even worse than that, Lynn. I have to live with that case all the rest of my days, like it or not. Do you know who gave me the most help? My girls! I don't know how they understood, but they did. And most importantly, they gave me life back! I don't think I could have survived if it wasn't for them. Don't you see how important your saving Angie that day was to me!"

Lynn was hanging on his every word. When he finished speaking, she slowly turned her eyes away and said with great emotion, "Scott, do you think the girls will forgive me? Right now I couldn't imagine my life without them...and you!"

"That's where you have to learn about kids, Lynn. They are the most forgiving people I know," he replied.

Lynn's face slowly lit up in a bright smile of relief as she put her other hand over his.

"You know, Scott, I just can't believe what has happened to my life these past few weeks. And you want to know who has become a good friend? Your mom! She's something else again!"

"Oh, Mom's all right. She has her moments, but she's been a wonderful help over the past few years with the girls," he replied.

"Scott, how long are we going to be in this place? I don't like being cooped up, even in a huge estate like this one," Lynn asked as she waved her legs back and forth through the warm water of the pool.

"That's the other thing I want to talk to you about. Some of the information I got from the Israeli people is disturbing. Apparently there is a real conspiracy here in town and on the West Coast over these Lincoln pictures!"

"I knew it! That's what Tony Cassell tried to warn me about just before he left the country!" she exclaimed. "And that's why I sent him those two pictures just before he left."

"That's why there's been so much trouble out West, Lynn. Tony's office was raided yesterday and four of the employees were killed."

Lynn's right hand flew to her mouth and her eyes were large. Scott continued, "The Mossad man who rescued us said they weren't involved in this at all, neither was the Red Rose Brotherhood he was telling me about. Lynn, there is quickly being established in this country an extreme right wing party called the American Freedom Party. They've got involved in this Lincoln thing for all their own reasons. They want to discredit the Catholic

Church and also the Jewish community, if possible. They want to do this by pointing to the proof of the Red Rose Brotherhood's involvement in the Lincoln conspiracy!" Lynn was still in a state of shock over the news of the LA killings. "That's why the Mossad want us to stay here at least for a few days! And to be blunt, I'm very worried over the girls' safety!"

"You know, Scott, if you hadn't met me, you wouldn't be in this predicament now," Lynn said with a certain note of sadness in her voice.

"Yes, that's true, but on the other hand, we wouldn't have known each other as well. Come on, let's go see what the kids are doing," he said as he pulled her to her feet. As he did, he gave her the slightest shove towards the water. Before he could realize what was happening, she gave him a much heftier shove and he toppled in to the water. As he plunged into the warm pool, he managed to grab Lynn's arm and she teetered for a moment before following him into the water. As she came sputtering to the surface beside him, he put his hand on Lynn's head and shoved her under again. From the edge of the pool came the squeal of the girls.

"Daddy, what are you doing to Aunt Lynn?" Angie shouted as she stood at the pool side in her PJs. Francie was on her knees by the water looking for Lynn, who had swum under water and surfaced a few feet from Scott for safety. The girls raced over and tried to help her out.

"Aunt Lynn, are you all right? I saw Daddy shove you into the water! I think he's a big bully!" Lynn tried not to laugh at the little girls' fury with their father. She called out to her father, "Daddy, I'm not going to speak to you until lunch! You shouldn't have pushed Aunt Lynn into the pool and now I'm going to protect her!" The girls helped a dripping Lynn Pollard from the water. She had been wearing only her short nightie and a housecoat and this clung to her like skin. As Scott pulled himself out of the water he came face to face with two cross girls and Lynn who was trying to keep a straight face.

"If I were you I'd wear some clothes next time, Lynn!" he snorted.

"There's nothing wrong with my outfit!" she answered with feigned anger until she looked down at herself. Her outfit clung to her like a second skin, showing her figure almost as if she was nude. Grabbing the girls she hustled them ahead of her as she went into the large house.

"I'll get even with you for this, Scott Fleming, don't you worry!"

As she entered the house with the girls, she could hear him laughing, and felt a warmth inside her she hadn't known in years.

Chapter 49

The phone was ringing with an unusual buzz. Tony and April had just fallen asleep in each other's arms. As he awoke, April murmured and rolled over on her side tossing off the covers. He grabbed his shorts and padded out to the sitting room of their suite and picked up the phone. The voice on the other end was distant and the connection fuzzy.

"Tony, Tony Cassell?"

"Yes, you got me, who is this?" he asked in a low voice so as not to alarm April.

"Tony, it's Gordon Haskett here in California, can you hear me all right?"

"Yes, what's the matter that you're calling at this hour?"

"Listen, Tony, you and April stay away! I'm calling from my dad's place up here in the Big Sur. They raided the offices and killed four of our staff. Only Anna Capling managed to hide and survived. She's called both me and the FBI so all hell has now broken loose.!"

"Gord, you mean both Randy and Luke are dead? I can't believe it," he stammered.

"Yes, Tony, they were both shot and Jayne and Maria were apparently strangled. So I'm calling you to say to lay low. There's a third group in on the whole Lincoln thing now and there have been attacks all over the map!"

"Gord, what about Lynn Pollard in Washington? If I were her, I'd do the same thing we did to get out of danger for a few days," Tony said.

"Tony, Lynn's office was hit as well and her assistant killed. She was captured by this new bunch and we haven't heard anything. She may be dead! Tony, we're not sure who this new group is, but they appear to know everything almost before we do! I'd say someone on the inside has been funnelling information to them in some fashion. With most of our office dead, I tend to think of someone on the East Coast."

"Sweet Jesus!" Tony muttered under his breath. "Gord, what about you and Bev? I'd be goddamned careful if I were you! They'll have you fingered even if you weren't in on the ground floor as April and I were."

"Tony, listen, I've got to run quick. I think I hear some noise downstairs..." There was a sudden click on the phone.

Tony looked at the receiver for a moment and placed it back in its cradle. He was shocked. Now for the second or third time he again felt justified in grabbing April and clearing out before the whole house of cards came tumbling in on them. He felt as if he'd been kicked as he thought of the death of his dear friends. And for what? He had dated Maria a few times but nothing seemed to happen. She was a sweet girl and deserved better than what she appeared to have gotten. It was Randy's death that hurt the most. They were soul mates in many ways. They had shared rooms together in university and travelled overseas for over a year before coming home and going back to school. Now Randy was gone. First he felt a bitter anger and then a great sorrow that felt like a kick in the stomach. Then he felt the tears coming. Before he realized it, there were great sobs racking his muscular body. The word "why" seemed to tear at him.

It was over an hour before he returned to the bed where April was still lying in a deep sleep on her side. He was glad he was able to take the phone call. April had had enough tragedy in her life and she didn't need this right now. He sat on the edge of the bed and watched her breathe in her sleep. Suddenly she shifted and rolled on her back, tossing off the covers. She hadn't bothered to put her PJs back on and lay nude to the waist after the covers were thrown back. Her breasts had settled on her chest but were still in full view. Smiling to himself, Tony slipped back under the covers and snuggled up to her warm sleeping form. As soon as he did, she rolled over and laid her head on his chest and stretched one leg over his. She murmured something. "Tony, who was that on the phone?" she asked.

"Oh, it was Gordon Haskett wondering when we were coming back. I said we would be here until next week and then would be flying home. He also mentioned there were several more of the attacks, so it's good that we are down here."

She raised her head and looked at him. "Are you telling me everything, Tony?"

"Everything you need to know at this time, April." As he talked he pulled her face down to his and began to kiss her again. She murmured for a moment and then pressed against him. He ran his hands down the smooth skin of her side and thighs and back up again. He cupped his hand about her breast and kissed her. She moaned as the fires of passion began to surge through her again. Climbing out of the bed, he slowly eased her onto her stomach and came up behind her. As he stood he began to caress her with his manhood. She seemed puzzled for a moment until he guided his penis and began to enter her from behind. April began to move about as he slowly probed deep into her. Finally he thrust deeply inside her and she suddenly screamed with pleasure as he plunged into the bottom of her very being. They moved back and forth as their passion carried them up to and over the brink of ecstasy.

April collapsed on the bed alongside Tony with a funny smile on her face. Finally she whispered, "If you ever gave me an argument not to go back to Art, you've just done it." As she spoke she laid her head back on his chest and in several minutes was fast asleep again.

Tony lay for a long time wondering what the next few days would bring. He thought about Gordon and the sudden cutoff of the phone line.

Chapter 50

Gordon slowly paced the floor by the bed. He was in the final minutes of his call to Tony in the Dominican Republic when the door opened and a figure entered with his arm around Bev's neck and holding a nasty-looking knife at her throat. He signalled to Gordon to put down the phone. The man was somewhere in his early thirties and thoroughly nasty-looking individual.

"Look, asshole, you do exactly as I tell you or I'll slit your girlfriend's neck from ear to ear."

Slowly, Gordon eased his way from the phone and stood in front of the sofa. "Alright, let her go, I'll do whatever you want, just don't hurt her!" he said slowly. "What do you want from us? We're just a pair of graduate students at Cal Tech. Help yourself to whatever you want," Gordon spoke slowly.

"Look, dickhead, you think we're here to rob you? You're even stupider than I first thought. Don't insult me! We want all the material, especially any pictures you have relating to the Lincoln conspiracy. Now get it and don't give me any more bullshit!" he ordered.

"Alright, I'll get to the point! There is nothing here! All of our matter is down at the office at the university. This place belongs to my father!" Gordon was getting a cold feeling in the pit of his stomach.

"Look, mac, we've been there and could only find a few old papers and the people there wouldn't say a word. I will say that friend of yours, Randy, had guts before I iced him." There was a gasp from Bev, who started to squirm when she heard the news.

"Mister, I'm telling you the truth, we have nothing here and after what you've told us now, I'd never tell you. Even if I did, you're going to kill us anyway."

"You know something, asshole, you're not far wrong! If I had my way, I'd do the job right here, right now, a nice small hole over your right eye, no fuss or mess!" Bev was as pale as a ghost as the words sunk in and the threat she and Gordon were faced with.

"You two are lucky! I've got to take you back to Iowa and you're going to be grilled there. The brass are getting ready to get this country back to the things that founded her, and get rid of social parasites like yourselves. Jake, get in here and tie these two up, I'm going to radio for the chopper!" An older man came in behind the man holding Bev. Gord and Bev had their hands tied and were hustled downstairs. Stiff gags were also placed about their mouths. They were taken outside to the large front lawn where there were two more members of their group, one of whom was talking into some kind of portable radio. The rest of the four were quiet and watching the sky, apparently looking for the expected helicopter.

Then out of nowhere there was a sharp report of a high-powered rifle. The report echoed down over the wide lawns and over the cliffs and out over the blue Pacific. The figure called Jake was suddenly picked up and thrown in a wide sprawl on the closely cropped grass. There was no movement from him as he lay on his face. Within two seconds a second report echoed out and the head of the second man suddenly exploded in a brilliant red mushroom. Where his head had been seconds before, there was nothing. The other two men panicked. They ran for the veranda in an attempt to avoid the deadly gunfire. They almost made it when the man who had held Bev was hit high in the right leg and thrown down on the grass by the force of the bullet. Then there was an eerie silence. The only sound were groans of pain from the man hit in the leg.

Meanwhile, Gord and Bev were unable to move because of their bonds of fear. Finally after struggling for what seemed to be an eternity, Gordon managed to undo his hands. As he rolled over and sat up, he came face to face with the fourth assailant.

"Not so fast, mister, I don't know who your sharpshooting friend is, but you haven't got a chance! There's another half dozen of our people...!" There was a sudden thump and the man straightened up. He gasped in the most ragged fashion and stepped back several feet. He seemed to be trying to reach at something that was biting him in the back. Then a stream of red began to pour from his lips and down over his chin. Slowly he sank to his knees and finally with glazing eyes pitched forward face first onto the grass. Then they saw the source of his final agony. There was a large knife almost as big as a bowie knife buried to its hilt in his upper back.

In the midst of all of this, Bev seemed to be in a state of speechless terror. Again, the only sound to be heard were the moans of the wounded man. Gordon climbed to his feet, numb by the sudden and violent death he had seen. Then he saw a familiar face. It was Father Jim McGuire, standing at the railing of the large deck.

"Gordon, you'd best get Bev over here quick as there are a whole mob of these people out front of the house. Come on, we've got to sneak around the house and see if we can steal a car. If they catch us we're finished!" As he stepped down from the deck, he stopped at the inert form of the wounded assailant. Looking at him for a moment, McGuire pulled out a small revolver and quickly shot the man through the head, ending his moans. As he did he muttered, "That's one thing they always taught us, remember dead messages are harder to hear!" Finally McGuire and Gordon helped Bev, who was totally unable to talk, to her feet and crept around the side of the house. There were three strange cars in the lot and not a soul in sight.

"You two run for that Taurus over there. I think it's one of those new V8 models and should be able to go. If there are keys in the ignition, wave an arm and I'll come over and drive. If not, move to the second car."

"What are you going to do, Father?" Gordon asked quickly.

"I'm going to sneak around the front of the house just to make sure these idiots haven't placed a guard for the cars. If so, I may have to give him a date with St. Peter as well."

Very quickly Gord took Bev by the hand and they ran down to the red Taurus that was at the end of the lot. Sure enough there was a set of keys in the ignition. Meanwhile, Father McGuire found a muscular young man sitting by the back door having a smoke. Sneaking up behind him, he quickly slipped a lethal-looking garrote wire about his neck. For a fleeting second the man sensed something was terribly wrong. With one vicious yank of his right hand, which held a knob like T, the wire tightened quickly and mercilessly. The man's neck was almost severed. He toppled over on the ground with hardly a sound. Then the priest saw Gordon waving his arms. He dropped the guard's corpse and raced for the car. When he reached the car, he leaped behind the wheel and turned the key. The big engine roared to life and he slammed the car into reverse. In a cloud of dust and gravel, the Ford tore out of the lot and down the long driveway. In a moment, five more of the assailant gang tumbled out of the Haskett house where they had been looking for material from the Lincoln research. Meanwhile the expected chopper had loomed over the top of the house and was beginning to settle on the lawn. Two of the figures raced out to meet it. The other three men jumped into the large Lincoln Town Car that had been parked next to the Taurus. They raced down the driveway and onto the main road in pursuit of the Taurus.

Chapter 51

The main highway, California #1, clung close to the edge of the Santa Lucia mountain range, which dropped sharply into the ocean. The road was a picturesque winding ribbon of asphalt that dipsy doodled its way southward. Father McGuire pushed the new V8-powered Ford Taurus to its very limits. As he drove, running the tires on the edges of the rims, everyone was quiet. Could he outrun the other car, which was back several miles but gaining rapidly? As they drove with the car jerking this way and that, Bev finally managed to find her self-control.

"Gord, was that true what I heard about the raid on the office in Long Beach? Are they all dead?" There was a panic in her voice.

Before Gordon was able to answer, Father McGuire spoke up. "You kids might as well face the facts, we're in a race to the death over this whole Lincoln conspiracy business. Up 'til yesterday, there were three groups who were starting to slug it out for control of the Lincoln material."

"That's the funniest thing I ever heard of," muttered Bev as she listened to what the priest was saying as they rocketed along the narrow road.

As he drove, McGuire noted the big Town Car was beginning to gain on them. Finally, even after pushing the smaller car to the limits and the road, he realized they were going to be caught. Suddenly he hit the brakes and pulled off to the side of the road and pulled down a narrow road. As he could see them coming closer to what appeared to be a steep cliff into the ocean, he pulled the Taurus to a halt at the edge of a clump of small trees. Jumping out, the priest grabbed a small long case he seemed intent on carrying with him wherever he went. Stopping at the back of the car he snapped open the trunk.

"Holy shit! Would you look at this!" he exclaimed and waved to Gord and Bev, who had just gotten out of the car to come around the back. There in the small trunk were crammed two large tubular-looking weapons.

"Do you realize what these are?" McGuire asked.

"Father, I haven't a clue. Are they some kind of a missile or the like?"

"Bingo, you take the prize! These are American Stinger missiles and they are the very thing for taking out a chopper should that bastard come after us."

He reached into the back and heaved one of the missile launchers up onto his shoulder. Opening up the front and after removing the caps he stated, "All you have to do is put this thing on your shoulder, aim the crosshairs and slowly squeeze. Then swoosh and bingo—scratch one target. Listen, I've got to try and stop that big Lincoln. If anything happens to me and that chopper comes along, as I think it will, use this missile. Remember one thing if nothing else, try and get the missile off before the chopper arrives! The Stinger is designed to seek out the air intakes on the turbines. That's why they had such a success rate with the Soviet Hind Choppers in Afghanistan. Do as I told you and you can't miss."

"Look, Father, here comes the big car!" Bev called out.

McGuire quickly unzipped the small bag he was carrying and pulled a strange-looking gun.

"This is my favourite, by the way, it's an Austrian Steyr 5.56mm, fully automatic. The handle is also the high-power sight and has interchangeable barrels. This one is fully automatic and I'm using extra-length mags. Get that Stinger over into the trees and stay hidden. If they get me, I see two Kalashnikovs in the trunk. I'd take one for each of you. They're crude but can kill you just as quick. Now get going!" McGuire shouted as he took off running to the edge of the bush for a position to fire down on the car.

In a very few minutes, the big Town Car came to a halt about a hundred yards behind the Taurus. There was a total silence and everyone waited. Finally three men climbed out of the Lincoln. They looked about . Then there was an ominous roar of machine gun fire from a small knoll on the edge of the bush. The driver collapsed in a bloody heap, cut down by the first volley. The passenger from the front seat was hit in the head and rolled down over the front on the Lincoln to fall on the ground dead. The remaining man from the back seat ducked around the back. Then there was a sudden savage round of shells that ripped through the engine area and the driver's seat. There was more silence. Nothing moved. Father McGuire finally stood up. He was about to move when a shot from the Lincoln zipped past his ear with a nasty zing. He dropped to the ground and remained still. Finally, a lone figure slowly inched his way around the back of the Lincoln. He was carrying some kind of rifle with a scope. He stopped and looked about. Then there was a single shot. The man's body stiffened, the single shell struck him just behind the right ear. The entire top of his head was suddenly blown off. The body collapsed over the trunk and rolled lifeless on the ground. For nearly five minutes, nothing was heard or moved.

Again Father McGuire stood up and called out, "I think that's got them all. We'd better get out of here." His words were hardly out when there was the odd-sounding chatter of light-machine-gun fire. Father McGuire's figure stiffened and a funny look came over his face before he fell face first onto the grass. He attempted to move but the pain was so great he was unable. Suddenly there was a tall blond-haired man standing over him with a stubby Uzi machine gun in his hands.

"Who the hell are you, mister?" he asked as he pushed McGuire over onto his back. "That's the best shooting I've ever seen!" McGuire groaned as he was turned over, his eyes glazed with pain and his chest rapidly becoming very bloody. The man heard sound behind him. He turned and fired. Gordon had grabbed one of the machine guns from the car, but couldn't get the thing to fire. The man grinned for a moment as he saw Gord struggling with it.

"Say your prayers, asshole!" as he brought his Uzi up and pointed it at Gordon.

Then he heard a female voice say from over near the bush, "I think you'd better say yours, mister, whoever you are!" The moment she stopped talking, Bev squeezed the trigger on the Kalashnikov she had picked from the Taurus' trunk. There was only a short burst from the distance of nearly sixty yards, but her aim was tried and true. Three of the shells struck the man high in the chest. He was thrown off his feet and laid out on the ground on his back. Bev raced from the shallow hole in the ground from where she had fired. Carrying the machine gun, she slowly approached the fallen gunman. He moaned when he saw her.

"Who are you, mister, and why do you people want to kill us?" she asked as she reached his side.

He grimaced as he looked at her. "Go to hell, bitch. When we change this country we'll have to cleanse it of scum like you!" As he finished, he attempted to spit in her direction. All the anguish of the past few hours welled up inside her and she raised her gun. She pointed it at him and squeezed the trigger. The man's body shuddered as over a dozen bullets crashed through him. He quivered for a moment and then was dead. She threw the gun on top of his body. She ran over to Gordon, who had watched her brutal killing of the gunman with fascination. He got to his feet and put his arms about her as she started to shake with the realization of what she had done. Then they remembered Father McGuire.

Rushing to the priest's side, they were dismayed to find his condition grave. He had been hit twice through the lungs and was sinking fast. Looking up he spoke quickly but clearly, "Look, I'm finished. I want you to do something for me. Put me in the red car, start the car and put it in gear and start it off towards the cliffs. I don't want to be a stiff on a slab. I'd rather go out this way. Besides, if you do that, then you can sneak out of the scene and not be dragged into a police investigation. I know this bunch we're up against and they're a real threat to the stability of this country. If they get you, one of their plans will be sure to see that you never get out of their hands alive!" The effort of talking was almost too much for him as he was draining quickly.

Looking at each other for a moment, Gordon and Bev gently picked him up and placed his bleeding body behind the wheel of the Taurus. He gasped loudly in agony as they did so. Gord started the engine and pointed the nose towards the cliff's edge. Running around to the other side, he placed the shifter in drive and car jerked forward. Gord looked at the priest and his eyes were closed. He seemed to be in prayer. Slowly the Taurus crept towards the edge, teetered and plunged over two hundred feet to the pounding surf below. Partway down the car bounded off a rocky outcropping and spun in the air. Striking the rocks, there was a white flash then a billowing mushroom cloud which rolled up the cliff face. Then there was silence.

Bev turned to Gord, her face ashen with shock. "Gord, what was that big bang? There was only gasoline in the car?"

"There was one other Stinger left in the trunk and that was probably the warhead that went off. The poor guy, though, after all that he did for us, we'd have been dead several times without his ruthless professionalism!"

They were about to start walking back to the highway, when they heard the rumbling thump of a helicopter not too far away. Bev screamed. "Gord, get that missile the good father took out of the trunk. If we're not careful they'll get us for sure this time!"

Gordon ran back to the edge of the little wood lot where he had lugged the missile. Before he could reach it, the chopper roared over the field, two guns chattering. The pilot swung out over the ocean preparing for another approach. As fast as they could get the missile on his shoulder, Bev helped him. He tried to remember what the priest had said. He seemed to remember the words "aim for the engine intakes." He could see the chopper turning about half a mile beyond the cliff side. Bev sprawled herself beside Gord as he looked into the eyepiece. Finding the large trigger, he pointed the launcher with the cross-hairs on the approaching profile of the chopper. Slowly he squeezed the trigger.

There was a deafening swish from behind them, but no recoil whatsoever. In front of them, a small but deadly missile roared out of the pointed tube. Its

191

speed was surprising as it took off running only about twenty degrees above the horizontal as it surged towards the chopper. There was a sudden lurch in the aircraft as the pilot saw what was approaching him. He was good. He attempted to veer away and lure the missile into speeding off into the warm ocean. He almost made it. But then something in the sophisticated guidance system reacted and the missile veered as well. It plunged into the small intake and exploded with a thundering roar. The force of the blast blew off the rotor and the machine's tail. The remainder of the fuselage spun out of control and plummeted into the cliff face where it blew up upon impact. Large pieces of metal and body parts rolled down the jagged rocks into the blue water below.

Gordon and Bev stood as if in a trance as the horror of the chopper's end unfolded. He turned to Bev and said, "Bev, let's get out of here. The priest had a very good point, we have to stay away from the police!"

Chapter 52

The next morning, Frank Baird was up at six and had breakfast in his room. By the time Brian Vaschuk arrived at seven, he was ready for a briefing from the various groups throughout the nation. He noted they were to start arriving at eight in his room. He planned to have the meeting over by one or so. The main meeting could begin at the senator's home at three. This was the day so many of them had worked towards. Brian arrived with a large briefcase full of papers and documents for the first meeting. As Baird let him in after he rapped on the door, he was greeted with the comment, "One minute early, not bad!" Baird cracked as the younger man walked past him.

"Mr. Baird, just how many of these people do you expect to have with us this morning? Any more than six and it's going to get crowded in this room."

"I expect there will certainly be no more than that. When I sent word out we wanted someone to be at this meeting, I emphasized it was to prepare for the pivotal meeting with the senator later this afternoon. Brian, what do you have for me from the action groups? I like to know what a man's going to say before he says it. Fill me in!" Baird ordered.

"Well, there are several breaking problems you certainly should be aware of before we get started. First and most important is the Dominican incident," Brian replied.

"As we found out late in the week, the two pivotal people in the West Coast research team at Cal Tech fled the country and ended up in Santa Domingo. We didn't locate them until late yesterday. Two of our people, not our best types, I might add, broke in and roughed them both up. As far as we know the girl was killed. They were literally heading out the door when a single Mossad operative arrived and shot them both."

"Shit, you mean they went in and got what we wanted and then were killed? What the hell is going on? Can't any one of you do anything these days? You seem to forget that we're playing for pretty high stakes," Baird snarled angrily.

"Look, Mr. Baird, don't take your frustrations out on me! I'm just reporting to you what has been given to me!" Brian responded with a flushed face.

"Well, I'm not one to take excuses lightly! That pair from the office in Long Beach were the key. They must still have the source of the Surratt legacy. Look, we've got to come up with both of those pictures and whatever documents they have in their possession. Under the direction of Lynn Pollard here in the city, they've been doing some very extensive work on many of the sources in the original Lincoln controversy. If we're to dump this blame all over the Catholic Church here in America, we're going to have to have more proof then a couple of possibly doctored pictures. What the Christ do you propose to do about it, Vachuk? Or has the thought even crossed your mind?" There was a flash of anger that crossed his face for a fleeting moment then was gone.

"Mr. Baird, there was a complete takeout of the office in Long Beach. Our people ransacked the office and could find very little. I have the complete report here. Oh, yes, four of the staff were killed in the immediate assault, but none of our people were hurt," Brian replied curtly.

Baird was getting more frustrated by the minute. "I just don't understand the lack of facts. We were led to believe from our man in Europe before he was killed, that there was enough evidence in the actual Surratt legacy to destroy the validity of the Catholic Church's undercover operations in Europe, and with even more details in America with the discovery of the legacy of Mary Surratt. I want to know where the shit is and who has it at the moment!" Baird had risen to his feet and was walking about the room as he talked.

"Mr. Baird, what I've been trying to tell you was a very simple observation but may have a grain of truth in it. You're all upset about the failure of the operation in Santo Domingo. The fact that those two from Cal Tech were there in the beginning tells me they must have the material. If they didn't have it, they wouldn't have gone way down there to hide. We still haven't figured how they got there, but I have a suspicion it was through the Canadian city of Toronto. The key now is to find out where the guy is going to go, if he is still alive. We've just received word that the girl was found dead by police and the death certificate was signed by the doctor."

"I want to see that certificate when you can get a copy of it. I trust no one when it comes to this sort of thing. I saw the kind of governmental bullshit that went on over the Warren Commission Report. That was the biggest scam I ever saw in sixty years on the Hill."

There was a hard rapping on the door. Baird looked at his watch. It was just past eight and the operatives were arriving for the briefing before the main strategy session later in the day.

"Brian, you start off this meeting. I'm going down to the lobby for a few minutes. I have a meeting with the senator's chief aide and our link to the Justice Department. I'll be back in less than thirty minutes. Make sure you find out what's happened about Gordon Haskett and his girlfriend! I haven't heard a thing and I want to know. Find out what you can and put it in the small case under the desk over there. When I get back, I'll pick up the meeting from you." As he talked, the door was being rapped at again as the rest of the sectional representatives arrived. Frank Baird passed through the group of younger men all dressed neatly in conservative suits as he passed out of the suite.

Some twenty minutes later while he was standing in the lobby there was the report of a thundering explosion somewhere else in the building. The very floor of the lobby of the hotel quivered. Baird walked over to the main desk and asked what had happened.

"Sir, if we had any idea we might not be here ourselves. They've been doing a lot of blasting for the new subway line here, it was probably just a bigger blast than normal."

Frank wandered back to the news stand and browsed through a pile of papers from various parts of the world.. Then a young man came over to him.

"Mr. Baird, Mr. Frank Baird?"

"Yes, that's me, what can I do for you?" he replied.

"Would you please come with me?"

"What's the matter? What's happened?"

"Sir, I can't tell you. The manager wants to see you as soon as possible."

Baird followed the young man over to a small private office as various police and fire teams raced back and forth through the lobby of the big hotel. There was an older man behind the large oak desk who stood as Frank entered.

"I'm Neil Samuelson, the manager. You would be Frank Baird?" he asked in a tense voice.

"Yes, that's right. What seems to be the problem?"

"Mr. Baird, there's been a terrific explosion in the suite listed as occupied by you. It was destroyed and as far as we can tell at this point, at least five people were killed!"

Frank Baird muttered in an oath and got to his feet. He turned in anger and said, "Are you sure there wasn't anyone left alive? There are some very important documents there and I have to see if anything was left!" he said bluntly.

"Look, Mr. Baird, the force of the blast was so powerful that it even blew part of the wall out into the street nine floors below. What was left was burned and there are only a few piles of ashes to be found there."

"Look, Samuelson, I was out of the room for only about a half hour to meet several more of our people here in the lobby and was heading back in a very few minutes."

"Well, it you're determined to go up, you'd better get going; once the police start their investigation, no one will be allowed in. All I know is someone really wanted to do some real damage with this blast. There must have been a hundred pounds of TNT to do this kind of damage!"

In a moment of frustration Frank Baird got up and walked from the small manager's office, bidding Samuelson a muttered thanks as he did.

Chapter 53

The tropical night was warm and humid. The air conditioning was broken and Tony and April lay on top of the covers. Tony tossed this way and that, finally getting to his feet and wandering out on the small balcony peering out into the black tropical night. Sitting in one of the white plastic chairs, he looked up into the dark sky overhead. The moon was nowhere to be seen but the stars winked dimly. He thought about Monday and their flight to Toronto. He was still feeling guilty about flying south in the midst of all the trouble. Despite the phone calls from Gordon, he was deeply troubled over the effect of the Surratt Papers. He shook his head. How could one woman, dead nearly a century and a half, have such an effect on the lives of so many people today? People on three continents were scurrying to find ways to kill each other in order to avoid the protracted effect of the papers from touching them. Then Tony knew what he would do! He would get both the pictures and the papers to the media. He knew they would plaster the story all over their pages and the damage would be done no matter what might happen. He was tired of running. He was tired of seeing April suffer as they tried to hide from three different national groups. They were getting scared to enter a strange room for fear who might be waiting for them.

He leaned over the low brick railing as he and April had done so often over the past few days and felt the load gone from his shoulders. He now at least knew what he would do and that felt good. Looking out over the water, he saw light on the small private beach winking in the darkness. He got to his feet, getting ready to return to bed, when he thought he heard something. He stopped. Nothing. Yet a knowing fear dug at his stomach.

There it was. The muffled sound again. A cry! As he ducked behind a curtain, something heavy struck him hard on the back of his head. He saw a shower of sparks and lights before plunging into a bottomless darkness.

Slowly and vaguely, after what seemed to be an eternity, consciousness returned to Tony. His head throbbed as he found himself sitting tightly bound in a chair. He was on a dingy room with only a single light winking far overhead.

He heard a voice behind him. "I think idiot here is finally coming around. How hard did you hit the bastard anyway?" a gruff voice intoned.

"Shit, all I did was give him the back of my gun on his head. Listen, what's the score on the girl? Did you get anything out of her?" another voice added.

"Naw, I used a fag on her belly but she just tried to scream through the gag and then passed out!"

Tony jerked his head around to see if he could find April. She was hanging by the ankles from some sort of an overhead beam and appeared to have passed out. Her arms hung lifeless near the dirty floor. She wore only a pair of panties and the rest of her body was dirty and bruised. Her body slowly rotated from above in the murky light of the single bulb. There were large welts on her back and belly and some sort of liquid appeared to have been dumped over her.

"What have you bastards done to her? Leave her alone; she doesn't know anything!"

One of the men struck Tony on the side of the head with his fist. The force of the blow knocked him over onto his side on the floor. Looking up, he was sick at heart as he watched April's lifeless body as it slowly swung in a circle.

"What's the matter? You wondering if the bitch is still alive?" he snorted. As he spoke, he punched April hard in the ribs. Tony heard an audible grunt from her as she was struck. "Alright, asshole, you've seen what we can do and are prepared to do. Unless you give us the answers we want, your girlfriend will be dead in less than fifteen minutes. It's as simple as that."

"What the hell do you want from me? You haven't even told me that much," Tony gasped.

"We want everything you have and know about the Surratt Papers. We know you both were involved, so don't try to stonewall us. Make it quick and we'll cut your girlfriend down!" the younger of the two shadowy figures snapped. Taking a cigarette out of his mouth, he pressed it against the soft flesh of April's abdomen and laughed as the smell of burning flesh filled the room.

"Alright, alright, you bastards. I'll give you what you want. It's all in the small safe in our room," Tony said from his side on the floor where he remained.

The older man held up the large folder of material in his right hand. "You mean this stuff, eh!" He spoke with a grin on his face.

"You prick!" Tony whispered. "You had it all the time!"

"That's right, dickhead, we just wanted to see how much you'd take before you'd break. Worried about your friend? Well, she scratched and bit me before you came to, and she won't ever do that again." The man pulled a nasty looking knife from his pocket. April's body had stopped swinging and was still. He reached over and cut her panties off, and she started to swing slowly again. The man reached out, grabbed her body and placed the point of the knife against her skin just below her right breast.

"What do you think, asshole? How far will this knife go in?" With these words, he shoved the knife about five inches into April's chest. A shudder went through her. The man smiled and pushed the knife into her to the hilt. Suddenly there was a great moan from April. Her body shook from the pain of the stabbing. Blood started to flow from the base of the knife as well as from her nose and month. Her eyes were open and stared into nothing as warm blood coursed its way over her blank face and dripped unto the floor.

The other man looked at her still bloody body and exclaimed, "Good god, you've killed her. We'd better get her down and buried before the local authorities stumble onto the scene."

"Good riddance to the bitch! She deserved everything she got," he snapped as he butted out a cigarette against April's left thigh. "The hell with her, leave her hanging there. Let's get out of here; I've got a car out behind the building."

With these words, the two were gone in a flash as Tony tried to get back to a sitting position. The room was silent and the only motion was the swinging of April's bloody body as she swung from the overhead beam.

Outside the building, the two men were climbing in the car when they heard a voice calling out to them. "Stop where you are and hand over the material you took from the young couple!"

"Fuck you, asshole," said the man on the far side of the car. The stranger in the shadow of the building fired two shots from a heavy 48 Magnum. The younger attacker was lifted up and thrown back by the force of the heavy rounds. He lay still on the ground. The second attacker froze in his tracks. He was about to speak when a single shot struck him in the middle of his forehead. The entire back of his head was blown away in a sodden red spray. He flopped on the ground without a move. The stranger picked up the brown envelope and headed into the building where Tony and April were held.

Three policemen stood looking at April as she hung from the ceiling. The sergeant was shocked. He pointed to the blisters in her pubic area from the burns. Her body had stopped oozing blood, but a trickle of urine still ran down the front of her body and across her face. The blood on her head was beginning to harden. He was about to remove the knife from her chest when the other officer held up his hand.

"No, Corporal, I wouldn't touch anything on the body, as it has to go to the morgue. Listen, get the body down and off to the morgue immediately! I've got to go over and see the young man who was tied up in the room." He walked over to where Tony was being untied.

"Señor, is this lady over here rooming with you?"

"Yes, Officer, how is she?" he asked with a note of great fear in his voice.

"I'm very sorry, señor, the young señorita has been dead for some time. I would say she died from that terrible knife wound!" Tony covered his bruised and cut face with his hands and began to sob. They tried to talk to him, but there was no consoling him, so they left him in peace. Meanwhile, April's body had been cut down and was lying naked on a stretcher on the floor. Finally two men covered her with a rubber sheet and carried it out and put her in the back of a black van. It roared off into the night with her body. About a half hour later, it arrived at the hospital morgue. The gurney with April's body was taken inside and into the examination area. Immediately, two hospital officials lifted her corpse up unto a slab and removed the sheet. The doctor who emerged from the cramped medical lounge was an American student surgeon on exchange. He gave April's body a quick check and then stopped as his face went pale.

"Señors, get that other doctor in here immediately. We have an emergency here!"

"Doctor, what do you mean an emergency? This is a morgue, not a hospital OR."

"Well, you'd better get ready for a jolt! This girl isn't dead! She's breathing. Someone was smart enough not to remove the knife or she'd have bled to death immediately. Somebody sure tortured her, look at these burns," he commented.

About four hours later, the young American surgeon arrived at the room where Tony had been put when he was discovered to have a mild skull fracture and severe concussion. As he walked into the room, the young doctor asked, "Are you Tony Cassell?"

Tony, whose head was heavily bandaged and was having trouble focussing, turned to face the doctor. "Yes, that's me. Doctor, I can't believe it! April's still alive? After what they did to her?"

"I'm Dr. Alex Cameron. Yes, your fiancée is going to live! As a matter of fact, she is conscious and looking for you!"

"How did she manage to survive, Doctor? I thought she was dead even before they stabbed her!"

"Well, that's the miracle of the whole thing. She has to be the luckiest girl I know. That blade missed every major organ. In fact it missed her aorta by less than half an inch. She's got some nasty burns, but after a week or so in the hospital, I think she'll be all right. Mind you, I'd say she'll need a lot of home care for several months. I hope you're the guy who can do that, as she keeps mentioning your name."

"Doctor, how about her recovery? Will she be able to make a full one?"

"Hell, yes! After what I have seen so far, there's no question. Our only problem has been to keep her in bed. She's determined she's getting up and with several of her burns, I simply can't allow that for a few days. But, I think the best thing for her right now is to see you. Her room is only three doors down the aisle to the right. There's one other thing and that's yourself. I've told April about your condition and I'll say the same for you. Tony, you've had a terrible blow to the head and that could have killed you. You have a slight skull fracture, a very bad concussion. You'll have to be careful for at least three months. Believe it or not, you were just as lucky as April in some ways. Listen, come along with me and I'll take you down to see April. I think you'll find she's pretty perky."

When they wheeled Tony into April's room, he was stunned how well she actually looked. She looked freshly washed and her short hair was all cleaned and curly. When she saw Tony, she tried to pull herself up in her hospital bed, but was unable. Tony tried to speak, but the words wouldn't come. He still couldn't believe she was in front of him. Finally, she could see how emotionally wrought he was. He slowly inched his wheelchair over to the side of her bed. She whispered in a voice that was somewhat difficult to understand, "Tony, please hold my hand if you can! Are you all right? Dr. Cameron told me you've had a skull fracture and a very bad concussion?"

Finally, he managed to get himself under control. "April, they came and told me you were dead!... I just went to pieces, and then the doctor came up and said he'd seen a miracle. You were alive and even conscious!"

"Tony, they've told me apparently I was out most of the time I was hanging there. The only thing I remember is this damn pain in my mouth and this terrible pain in my chest!" She stopped and winced in pain as she tried to move.

"Tony, I wish I knew who those bastards were! I've never thought such evil could exist."

Tony held her hand tightly as he answered, "April, they're both dead! They were killed after they left our room. An agent of the Israeli secret service was in to see me and mentioned he had just arrived outside our room when the two were coming out. He challenged them and in the shootout, they were both killed. If it's any consolation, April, the guy who did those things to you had the back of his head blown off. I only wish I could have got my hands on him!" There was a sob in his voice as he looked into April's dark eyes. They were as clear and firm as he had ever seen them.

As she tried to talk, she whispered, "Tony, you and I have been very lucky. We've another chance to start over, I don't want to miss that chance." Her voice was becoming more blurry with the swelling in her tongue.

Tony picked up the conversation. "April, I don't know about you, but I'm thinking I'd like to try anew somewhere aside from Long Beach. How about you?" he asked.

"Tony, I don't want to have anything to do with the Lincoln thing again! My parents live in Denver and they've been after me to get out of there for several years. Where would you like to go, and what about the job market?" she asked slowly.

"April, when we were in Toronto, Gerry was after me to help him start up a specialty publishing house for some time now. I think I'd like to talk to him some more about it. Most of all, April, Dr. Cameron tells me you're going to have a lot of special care for the next three months. I figure with my savings and the little trust fund account my mom left me, we can live for about a year before we have to worry about money. Thank God for the low Canadian dollar."

April looked at him for the longest time and asked in a very quiet voice, "You want to take three months and nurse me back to health? I can't tell you what Art would say in this case!"

"Look, April, I don't give a shit about what Art thinks or doesn't think. I thought I'd lost you once there yesterday, I'll not chance that again. For better or worse, you're stuck with me. Would you like to go to Toronto?"

"Tony, I think you know my answer to that question! Besides, Mom has two sisters who teach somewhere in the city. Tony, I don't know where I'd be without you. I just can't get over the way you care."

"Look, April, you're looking tired and I'm getting out of here, my head hurts like hell. I'll see you this evening." He leaned forward in his wheelchair and kissed April ever so gently and whispered lightly, "Sleep well. I'll see you after supper."

The second day after her attack, April was looking much better and anxious to get on her feet. She had stood up but her burns were very painful and made her think twice about any further ventures. Even more painful was the deep knife wound in her side. Every once in a while she experienced spasmodic pains under her ribs. She was reading a newspaper when there was a knock and Tony emerged in the doorway, sitting in his wheelchair.

"Hi, Tony, come on in. You're looking so much better this morning." Then she saw a stranger behind him. He was a young man about Tony's age with one of the kindest faces she had ever seen. The door closed behind them.

Tony wheeled over to her bed in his wheelchair, leaned over and kissed April. For a moment he ran his hand down the smoothness of her cheek and whispered, "I missed you, April!" She could see he was still having trouble with the shock of almost losing her.

"April, this is Yigal Hansaez. He was the man who killed those two who assaulted us yesterday."

April's eyes widened as she looked into his deep brown eyes. He extended his hand.

"It's a very great pleasure to meet you. I'm sorry I didn't get there a few minutes sooner. I might have prevented you some unnecessary suffering."

April's mouth opened and she asked from her bed, "You killed those two monsters?" Her voice shook as she spoke.

"Yes, I was forced to eliminate them both. When I found you inside, I wish I had done matters much slower," he replied.

"You found me hanging inside our room?" she asked and lowered her eyes, embarrassed at the discovery.

"Yes, I did, April, and you were left hanging there for over an hour before the local police cut you down. All the official pictures were taken of you right there!" April was becoming very distressed as she listened to the vivid descriptions.

"April, I wouldn't bother you with all this hideous detail if I didn't think it was necessary. You see, there are at least three agents in the city who are trying to make sure the news of your death is true!"

April's mouth opened in shock. "They think I'm dead?" she gasped. Tony thought she was going to jump out of the bed.

"Yes, and that's what I am here to talk to you about. I mentioned the idea to Tony and he said it were crazy. You see, the American Freedom Party thinks you and Tony hold the key document to the Surratt legacy and will do anything to get it."

"Yeah! Tell me about it!" April winced as a stab of pain struck her in the side.

"You wouldn't be here if you weren't helping yourselves as well as us, isn't that right?" she asked, her eyes sharper than Tony had ever seen them. "What do you want of us, Yigal?"

"We think it would be best for all of us if this Freedom bunch went on thinking you were both dead. With Tony, there's no problem. He was registered here under his own name and is now listed as having died from the blow to the head. But, in your case, April, it was very different. You were brought in registered already dead. All the pictures are here as well as all the documentation."

"How are you going to get us out of the country?" she asked.

"That's strictly the point, April. With Tony, there's no problem. He died of his wounds here and that'll be on his death certificate. That keeps the Dominican authorities happy. But with you, we have a problem."

"I don't follow you, Yigal?" Tony asked.

"The police report says since you were killed in the midst of a crime, you have to go to a local funeral parlour and be buried here, April." She looked dumbfounded.

"What we have to do is satisfy the locals so they won't report you either as missing or leaving the country illegally. We have to make you look like you're dead again and ship your body to the local mortician. There we'll pick you up and you'll be officially dead."

"Is there no other way Yigal?" she asked.

"None that would insure you're permanently dead," he said. There was a silence as Tony and April tried to grasp all the details Yigal had talked about.

"How do you pretend to make me look dead again? They're bound to look at a body as it leaves the hospital and goes to the funeral parlour," April asked.

"April, Dr. Cameron, who first saved your life in the morgue, will give you a drug to make you sleep for a few hours. When you wake up you'll be in the funeral parlour. The doctor is coming with you to take care of you. Then we'll place you on board one of our Israeli Defense Forces Hercules. We're in and out of here every day trying to sell some used jets!"

"Well, I guess I don't have much choice, do I?" she replied.

"April, this is the safest way we know. We've done it on varying occasions all over the world," he answered.

"When do you want to get everything going, Yigal?" she asked nervously.

"We would like to fly out on our regular flight tomorrow at noon so as not to cause suspicion. Dr. Cameron would like to start in about five minutes."

Suddenly April became very nervous and reached out with a plea. "Tony, I'm very scared, stay with me for a moment." He reached out and held her.

"I'll see you both on board the plane tomorrow! Don't worry, you'll both be safe and sound."

A few moments later, the familiar face of Dr. Alex Cameron entered the room. "Hi, how's my best patient ever?" April held out her hand and he held it for a moment.

"April, I'm going to give you a little injection to put you to sleep. The next thing you'll know, you'll wake up tomorrow in the funeral parlour and I'll be right there with you."

"Doctor, can I ask you a favour?"

Alex could see the nervousness in her eyes as she spoke. "Of course, April, what is it?" he replied.

"Is there something you can give me, that if I get captured I won't come to?" she said very slowly. "If I'm captured by those animals again, I want to make sure I die! I can't face them again!" she turned and looked directly at Alex Cameron. There was deadly silence in the room.

"April, for God's sake, don't talk like this, it just tears me apart!" Tony said with pain in his voice.

"No, Tony, I'm very definite! Do you understand me, Alex?" she responded. There was a silence as he thought about her request.

"April, we have a new drug which is extremely powerful, basically a systems inhibitor. We have only used it in small amounts to slow or retard overactive body functions, but never by itself. Then an antidote has to be administered within a certain period or you never wake up. Mind you, we've used it in animals with complete success when rigidly controlled. There was only one definite drawback that we noticed with them after they woke up, but it's no big deal."

"What's that, Alex?" Tony asked still very anxious.

"Well, there appears to be a considerable increase in sexual awareness in a number of cases!"

"You mean I'm going to wake up as horny as hell, is that what you're saying, Alex?" He was at a complete loss for words. April started to laugh until the pain in her side caused another spasm.

"I like what Alex is saying too, April, we've got to get on with this injection."

Slowly he pulled over a tall IV bag with a clear liquid in it. He found the vein in her arm and eased the needle into it. She winced at the pinprick. Within a few minutes everything became very blurry for April. Then she gasped and tried to sit up again. She cried out to Tony in a heart-wrenching voice, "Tony, it's burning inside my head! I think it's going to explode! Oh God, Tony, please stop it, it's killing me!" Her eyes became very wild and she fell back on her bed. Her body began to shake and thrash as the drug took effect. Then she went limp. The doctor sat with her for nearly another hour watching as her coma deepened. There was the occasional gasp from April.

"I know the first effects of the drug are alarming, but this quickly passes. The drug basically shuts down all the body's basic systems completely, except the cardiovascular and respiratory systems. Everything else stops."

Finally there was hardly a movement from her body. Meanwhile, Tony slowly wheeled himself out, stopping at the door for one final look at the girl who meant so much. As the doctor waited he removed her clothes until she lay nude on the bed. There was no sign of life in her body. He then walked to the door and called for the nurse.

"Nurse, this girl is dead, please call the morgue staff."

Within five minutes, two Dominicans arrived in the room and began to lift April over to the gurney. They covered her with a sheet and quickly pushed the gurney from the room. When they left, Dr. Cameron muttered to himself, "God go with you, April Savitz." He then walked to Tony's room.

Tony tried to get to his feet as the doctor entered.

"Is everything all right, Doctor?" he asked.

"Yes, Tony. She's now in a very deep coma and anyone looking at her would think she's dead," he replied.

"Doctor, what happens if the drug starts to wear off?" he asked.

"Tony, the drug doesn't wear off. After thirty-six hours it's imperative to give the antidote. If this isn't done death comes within an hour. I'm sorry, Tony, it was the only way. I wanted to save April's life, there was no other way. The authorities know who she is, Tony, and want her dead. If you and April hadn't agreed to this route, there were two men ready to kill April this morning. That's the power of this new American Freedom Party."

Tony was stunned. "Alex, if you were caught doing this, what's in it for you?"

"Oh, probably shot in the back of the head by the Freedom Party, or expulsion by the government here!"

Chapter 54

The next morning, a small van arrived at the back loading area of the hospital. A young Dominican driver jumped out and waltzed into the office.

"I'm here to pick up someone who died yesterday. An American woman, I think."

"Yah, she's up in the morgue. Go get her yourself." The young man was still new to the job and wary of anything connected with death.

Arriving in the morgue, he asked the lone attendant, "I'm after a body of a young American woman who was killed several days ago."

"Oh, yes, the American girl. She's a mess, some prick knifed her!" He walked over to the wall where there were a series of small doors. He looked up and down until he came to drawer twelve. He opened the door and slid the drawer out. Suddenly there was a curse.

"Shit, you've got a messy one! Tell you what, I'll clean her up but I'd suggest you get her in the ground long before noon! The flies will be at her by then!" They rushed and quickly put April's body on the portable gurney, and into the van.

By ten the van arrived at the funeral parlour and soon April's body was lying naked on the embalmer's slab. The young assistant was about to cut into her neck to drain the blood out of her body for embalming, when he heard a voice call out, "Shit, don't bother with that business. Just shove a sheet over her and we'll get her out to the cemetery."

April was lying on the cold porcelain slab with the wooden embalmers block placed under her head. The young mortician closed her eyes and washed her hair. He then washed all the blood off her body and covered the enlarged wound in her side.

"OK, she's ready for burial now!"

About nine-forty-five, the small van arrived at the old graveyard by the sea. There was a shallow grave already dug alongside a tree. It was only about three feet deep, as was the custom for burials of unknown people. They parked the van a few feet from the open grave. The older man turned to the young chap and said, "Alright, let's get her in the ground." Sliding out the gurney, the wheels automatically hit the ground. One chap got on each end of April's body, and lifted her off the gurney and laid her on the ground next to the grave.

"Should we leave the sheet with her? She doesn't have anything else on."

"Yah, let's do it, I want to get out of here." There was no coffin, rather only a cheap, shoddy, rough board box into which they put her. They picked up each end of April's body and got ready to put her in to the box. The sheet slipped off and she lay nude in the morning sunlight.

"You know, Manuel, she was one beautiful-looking girl. But look at that hole in her side! The blood is still pouring from it."

One took her hands and the other her feet and they laid her on the bottom of the box. As they threw the ends of the sheet into the hole as well, the younger man said, "Shit, I'd hate to go in naked like that!" Then they picked up the large wooden slab that formed a box in the ground. The young man looked at April's unconscious form, as the top was shoved in place. Then each took a shovel and began to pile the dirt over the shallow grave. Some ten minutes later, the job was completed. The younger man patted the earth over her grave and said, "I still say that was a hell of a way for a person to end." In the grave, April's body lay still, dangerously close to the edge of her coma. She lay in silence, unaware of the blackness of the grave where she had unknowingly ended up.

On the surface, the two men climbed into their van and sped off. About twenty minutes later an old truck arrived on the scene with old patio stones. In less than fifteen minutes, April's grave was covered over with heavy flat concrete stones. In her grave she was beginning to have difficulty getting air in the pitch darkness.

The small station wagon pulled up at the back door of the small funeral parlour. The driver, Dr. Cameron, casually climbed out with his small bag and walked inside. There was no one in sight. Finally, he found young Manuel in the shabby front office.

"Hi, Doctor, what brings you out this Sunday morning?"

"Oh, I'm here to pick up a body of a girl who was killed and who we are taking back to Israel for burial."

"There's no body here, the only one was picked up, but we buried her earlier this morning!" Cameron rose to his feet.

"You did what?" he demanded.

"We embalmed her and took her out by the old cemetery and buried her in a nice grave by the trees."

Alex grabbed him and said, "You have to get me out there immediately. There's something I must do that hasn't been done." He reached into his rear pocket and placed a hundred-dollar US bill in Manuel's hand.

"Oh, alright. I'll take you there, but only for a minute."

Some fifteen minutes later, Alex was standing by the concrete-covered grave where April lay. He turned to Manuel. "Quick, we have to get her body up! She must have a special service before burial. It's part of her Jewish faith!" Manual shrugged his shoulders and muttered to himself. Alex Cameron looked at his watch. She was in the ground nearly two hours. He knew he had to get to her in less than thirty minutes or she would be dead. Then again, if they embalmed her, she would have died in the funeral parlour.

With great effort they quickly pushed away the patio stones. Then with two shovels that Manuel had thrown in, they began to dig out eighteen inches of rocky earth that was on top the box. Finally they came to the rough wood lid that rested over April's body. They carefully cleaned off the lid itself. Finally, very carefully, Alex lifted it. He said a simple prayer for the girl he had come to like so much. About a quarter of an inch of dust had settled over April's body. Manuel looked in and said, "She's dead! She hasn't moved since we laid her down."

Her body was completely covered by the white sheet, under the dust. Alex pulled back the sheet from her face. She looked at peace. For a terrible moment, Alex was sure she was dead. Then he noticed a slight stirring in the dust that was about her nose. Reaching in he gently lifted her body out and carried her to the back seat of his old car. With his stethoscope he could hear the slow beat of her heart. He turned to Manuel and said, "Drive me to the airport or I'll tell the police you killed her. Now get going."

In a moment they were tearing along the highway towards the Santo Domingo Airport. Alex sat in the back seat and wrapped a heavy blanket about April's slight body. Her dirty face slumped against his chest. Taking a needle from his medical bag, he filled it from a small vial as he held her small form. Finally, he found a vein in her forearm and watched as the fluid passed into her body. After nearly a half hour, a moan uttered from her lips. With the Israeli sticker on the wagon's windscreen, the airport police quickly waved them through. Alex heard April moan again. Looking at her, he could see her eyelids begin to flutter. In another five minutes, the wagon pulled over behind a large Israeli Defense Forces Hercules transport parked on the edge of the tarmac. As he climbed out carrying the semi-conscious form of April, he saw the figure of Yigal waving from the lip of the big rear launching ramp. There was a small army of Israeli guards surrounding the big plane and watching anything that moved in the area. In the back of the plane, there was a small three-bed medical unit set up. In half an hour, April was fully conscious though very weak. Tony lay in the other bed slowly recovering from his concussion. Alex Cameron sat on April's bed beside her as she looked up at him.

"We got through it, April! In about six hours, we'll have you both in Toronto and with the eternal gratitude of the State of Israel and your new life!"

April was only able to whisper in a soft voice, "Doctor, Tony and I will never be able to thank you enough. You've given us our lives back!"

Dr. Alex Cameron turned to Tony, who was trying to see his way through a drug-induced sleep. "Tony, I hope you realize what a gem you have here in April. She's got more courage than anyone I've seen in a long time!"

"I know, Alex, I'm just beginning to understand that. I want to talk to Yigal about that documentation for a new start for April and myself. April, did you know that Alex has put his life on the line to help us get you out alive? The Freedom Party has had many people looking for us."

April struggled to prop herself up on one shoulder and grimaced with a pain as she did so. Alex tried to stop her but she waved him aside. "I just want to say to the both of you I'll never be able to fully say thank you for what you've done for me!" As she spoke, her pain was visible in her eyes. Tony struggled to his feet and moved to her cot. When he sat down, he gingerly eased an arm about her small shoulders. She said nothing but laid her head against his chest. Suddenly there was a loud whining sound as the big rear ramp was winched up and closed. Then came the clear sound of the big engines being started. As they did, Tony looked down at April. She had a look of peace in her face for the first time in days.

Chapter 55

Scott Fleming awoke to a shaking of his bed. He drifted back to sleep. Again he was drawn from his light sleep by a motion on the bed. He stirred and rose up on one elbow. Less than three feet away he found the dark figure of Lynn Pollard.

"Oh, sneaking into strange men's beds again, eh, Pollard?" he said off-handedly. He saw the door of their adjoining rooms was ajar.

"Oh, so you don't like strange women in your bed at all?" she giggled. "You just keep the naked women in your office?"

"Yah, that way if I'm too much for any of them, I can call one of my nurses," he quipped. There was a quietness and a look of trouble surrounding Lynn despite her bravado.

"Scott, can I stay here with you? I'm troubled."

He got up and put on his housecoat. Holding out his hand he took Lynn's small one and sat her down beside him on a large sofa that sat at one side of the bedroom. She looked very troubled. He smiled and asked, "How can a friendly doctor help, Lynn?"

She smiled back and replied, "Scott, do you know a man called Frank Baird?"

"Sure, he's been an institution around this city since the Truman administration, why?" he asked.

"Well, he's been a friend of my family longer than I can remember. Yesterday, Mr. Morgenstein took me aside and said he had called the legation here and wanted to speak to me! What do you think?"

"Lynn, I would be very leery about anyone who calls you here. Did he say how he found out you are here to start with?" he said.

"Yes, Morgenstein said he was contacted by this rebel Freedom bunch and that they've threatened he and his family." She looked at Scott and seemed at a loss.

"Lynn, does he know anything about this Lincoln business or even more the Surratt reference?"

"Scott, I called him over a week ago and asked for his help. I gave him copies of the two pictures, but not the Surratt note I found hidden behind one of them. I've always believed you shouldn't tell everything to one person," she said.

"What did you do with the rest of the material, Lynn? It seems to me that is the important question!"

"I sent it all out to Tony Cassell, the day after giving the copies of the pictures to Frank. Tony and I have worked on this project for the past three years, ever since he approached Kodak for a grant. Why?" she stopped as Scott became very agitated.

"Scott, what is it? I've never seen you this way before."

"Lynn, both Tony and April have been killed! I saw copies of the death certificates this morning but felt you've had enough to carry at this stage."

Lynn's hands flew to her mouth and she turned pale at the news. "Are you sure, Scott? Tony's a pretty resourceful guy. I've never seen a person so focussed on his work. Besides, he's one of the deadliest judo experts around. I can't see him being captured without a fight!"

"Lynn, I've seen both certificates and also the grisly pictures of April's corpse. She was brutally tortured before being stabbed. She had to be dead at least two hours before the pictures I saw were taken. If she wasn't dead, there are only three men in the world who would know how to make her look like that and still be alive!" He looked at her for a while before continuing. "Lynn, I'm getting to know you well enough to know that you've already made up your mind to do something. Let's have it!"

"Scott, I have to go and settle this thing once and for all. I've got Frank into this and he may need my help. So, I'm going back to the office where all this trouble started and settle it with him."

Scott was shocked. Lynn continued, "I know it's in your nature to protect me, but there's another side of me you perhaps don't know as well. I know I have some terrible down days, but I've always managed to claw my way back to the top. Unfortunately some people see me as a wimp. I hope you won't think the less of me for having to do this, Scott?" She looked at him with a softness in her eyes, yet he saw there an iron-ribbed determination he had seen wisps of at other times.

He sighed deeply. "No, Lynn, I know enough to realize there would be no use trying to stop you. I just hope nothing will happen to you. Don't forget, I saw those pictures and saw what those monsters did to April."

"I'm sorry, Scott, but I have to do this! My real fear is that this may affect how you feel about me. You know I just couldn't live without you and the girls." There was a pleading in her eyes as she looked at him.

"I think you know me better than that by now, Lynn! I used to think I owned my wife when I was still married and that's one of my big failures. I would never stop you from doing whatever you wanted, even if the thought of you doing it was painful. I will admit this is like that, but I'm trying not to use the surgeon's weakness of controlling everyone!"

"Thanks for saying that. I'll try and not take too many chances. I wish I didn't have to do this, but I feel I have no choice!"

"Look, Lynn, there's still over four hours 'til breakfast, why don't we get some sleep or we'll be dead tomorrow—you know the girls!" he added. He got to his feet and walked to the bed and asked, "Lynn, would you stay with me? I miss you in the early hours." She smiled as she jumped into his bed and pulled up the covers. He lay down beside her and put his arm about her as she rested her head on his chest. Soon they drifted off into a restless sleep. Lynn's last thoughts were of the difficulties of the day ahead.

Chapter 56

Lynn Pollard's departure from the legation was a difficult one. As she prepared to leave over everyone's objections, she was approaching the door when Franco Morgenstein and Scott Fleming met her.

"Miss Pollard, I want you to take this little package and keep it in your purse at all times. You've made a lot of friends here amongst our staff. Even the property crew say you wear a bikini better then anyone they know!"

Lynn turned beet red and turned very flustered to Scott. He laughed and turned both palms upward in feigned innocence. "I kept telling her she shouldn't run around the pool topless!"

"I did no such thing, I'll have you know. Besides, I don't have the figure for it!" she grumbled.

"That's not what I hear the pool boys saying!" snorted Scott. Lynn had reached the point she was so flustered she was speechless. Then all three of them broke into gales of laughter, breaking the tension.

"Miss Pollard, if you look in that small parcel I gave you, you'll find a nine-millimetre revolver. It's the standard issue for our security forces. We have our own armour-piercing ammunition and there's fifty rounds there as well. I know you know how to use it from security checks. I'll leave you folks alone before Miss Pollard leaves."

Lynn stepped over and put her arms around Morgenstein's neck and said, "God bless you and your people! I'd be dead without you."

There was a quiet moment as Lynn and Scott faced each other. The air was tense with uncertainty and fear. Lynn took Scott by both arms and said quietly, "I know this isn't easy for you, but I want you to know one thing. You saved me and I'm not talking from the surf. I mean my own fears and bitterness. Do you know how much you mean to me, Scott? If I didn't have you and the girls, I don't know what my life would be like!"

He looked deep into her dark eyes and he could see both fear and love. But there was also a fibre of strength there he hadn't seen before. Now, for the first time he knew she would be all right.

"Lynn, I won't even ask about the gun and your use of it, as that isn't important right now. You've given the girls and me a whole new reason for living. Please remember that when you're out there. We all love you very much, even if you do swim naked in the legation pool!"

Lynn shook her head knowing she would never live that one down. She buried her face in his shirt and could smell the fresh clean aroma of his morning shower. He kissed her for a long moment before she turned, stepped through the front door and was gone. There was a sadness and a peace on her face as she strode down the walkway to the street. She was dressed in a pair of form-fitting jeans and matching jacket with a leather coat. She wore it open because of the warm weather. Walking three blocks from the legation, she hailed a taxi and told the driver to take her to the Kodak office.

The building was deserted except for a policeman at the main door. She showed him her official ID on the premise he wouldn't know her name or face. It worked as he waved her through. Her office was in chaos. Everything had been scattered on the floor, files emptied and thrown about. Then there was still the large area of dried blood where Maggie had fallen when she was shot. Lynn stopped for a moment and tears came to her eyes as she looked at the spot. There was an inner ache deep inside her.

Stepping into her own office, she found it was in even worse shape. Lynn shook her head after some fifteen minutes of searching for the basic Lincoln file she had always kept hidden. The she remembered she had broken her pattern that last day and placed it in the wall vault. It was located in the small bathroom, which seemed to have been untouched. She was greatly relieved when she found it with the main file and the basic research file was there as well. She could hardly believe her luck. Picking up her phone, she called Frank Baird's office but there was no answer. Finally on a hunch, she called his home where she had finally located him the previous week. His wife answered the phone.

"Mrs. Baird, it's Lynn Pollard here. How are you this morning?"

"Lynn, for heaven's sake, it's so good to hear from you! Frank and I were just talking about you over breakfast this morning. He's been out in Des Moines for two days for Party meetings! Here he is, he wants to talk to you as well!"

"Lynn, for Christ's sake, it's so good to hear your voice! I need to see you just as soon as possible. Can I pick you up there at the office right now, or at least give me twenty minutes to get there."

As she listened there was a sudden grimness to Lynn's face. "Frank, that's what I was calling you about as well, I want to see you immediately, it's about those pictures. I'll meet you out front of my office here in thirty minutes!"

She quickly hung up. Anger seethed through her. Normally she wouldn't give a second thought to his knowing where she was calling from, but she knew he had a penchant for the old dial phones and there was no phone in the Baird house that could have told him where she was calling from. She took the thick files and placed them in two shabby plastic garbage bags she had in her bottom drawers. Just as she was placing them over by the door and she was starting to walk from the office, she heard something in the outer office. Setting the bag down, she crept tiptoe to the short hallway. It was a move she'd recall for years. As she slowly moved into the outer office, she saw a form of a man rummaging through Maggie's desk. She was about to speak when she sensed something behind her. At that moment, six years of intense judo training came to Lynn's aid. Falling on her hands and knees on the floor, she kicked out with both legs in a vicious snap. Wearing a pair of heavy flats had not been accidental. One vicious thrust caught the man at the base of his rib cage. His sternum shattered along his ribs. Her other heel caught him at the base of his nose. His nose broke and the force of Lynn's kick was so vicious it drove his whole nose bridge back through his forehead into his brain. He was dead before he hit the floor. Lynn looked up. Two other men were cautiously approaching her.

"Holy Jesus, did you see what the bitch did to Charlie!" one of the two men muttered. "No one told us she's one of these judo experts!"

The other man had drawn a revolver and started to laugh.

"I didn't care how smart she is, she can't stop a bullet!" He raised the gun to fire. It was his last move. Lynn had seen the other man's gun on the floor and dove for it. The gunman fired twice at the very spot he had last seen her crouching. Scooping the man's small snub-nosed gun, she remembered her training. Aim and fire and put the person down. She lay on one side and suddenly time appeared to be in slow motion. She aimed from the prone position. Her first shot caught the man full in the chest, throwing him over Maggie's desk and into a still heap on the floor. The other man panicked and rushed for the door.

Lynn's eyes went dead cold and the man saw the change in her. She fired three times. Two shots hit him in the chest and the third blew out the side of his head. She climbed to her feet and walked over to his fallen body and whispered, "That's for Maggie, asshole!" Then she heard a groan behind her. She swung with a speed that even surprised her. The first gunman was still alive and trying to talk. She approached him at arm's length.

"You're out of bullets, bitch, and now you're stuck with me!" He tried to laugh as she approached him. "Empty guns don't scare me, lady!" There was another loud report as she fired, striking him between the eyes, blowing his head apart.

"You should learn how to count, dickhead!" Lynn muttered as she stood over him. Walking over to Maggie's desk she whispered in a loud voice, "Sleep well, Maggie, wherever you are."

Tears coursed down her small face. She wiped off the gun and threw it on the floor. Picking up the bag with the files, Lynn walked quickly from the office. The cop at the building entrance had apparently heard nothing and waved to her as she walked to the street to meet Frank Baird. As she did, her thoughts were with Scott and two very small girls.

Chapter 57

The flight in the Israeli Defense Forces Hercules was noisy and tiring. They flew up the Atlantic seaboard of the US before swinging inland over Baltimore and then straight in to Toronto. There was a constant whine and reverberating drone from the big turbines. Finally Tony struggled to his feet and peeked out one of the few small windows in the side of the big military plane.

"Holy Toledo, we're back over the ocean again!" he chirped as he could see nothing but blue water below as the rays of the setting sun refracted off its surface. April, who had slept most of the flight, was awake and finally starting to feel a bit perkier. Tony was still having trouble moving and keeping his balance. He didn't know why.

"Actually, that's not the ocean, rather Lake Ontario. These Great Lakes are so damned big, you'd think you're over the sea itself!" replied Alex Cameron, who had just roused from several hours of sleep.

"April, how are you feeling, you were sound asleep when I stuck my own feet up on this cot several hours ago." He stifled a huge yawn as he talked.

Then April spoke up. "I think for the first time in days I'm starting to feel human again. Alex, what's the matter with my side? I put my hand down a few minutes ago and it was all covered with blood!"

"April, you had a knife wound there from the assault. I had to drain it and the wound had to be enlarged as a result. The bastard put the knife in very deep, April, and I wanted to make sure there was no infection!"

Suddenly an Israeli officer appeared at the entrance to their little makeshift cabin.

"I thought you folks would like to know that we'll be landing in Toronto in about twenty minutes. As a military plane landing at a civilian airport, the Canadian customs people will be coming out to us. As it is we're going to be here for a day and the plane will be under armed Israeli guard. Listen, hang on, this plane is a bit of a beast to land, but I'll do my best to smooth it out for you!"

218

"Excuse me, can you tell me where Yigal is? I haven't seen him since we took off," Alex Cameron asked the pilot.

"Yes, he's been up with us in the cockpit. He's been on the radio most of the time getting our agenda all set up for you folks at the Israeli Legation in Toronto, and where you will be taken from the airport. He should be down shortly." With these words, he turned and returned to the cockpit.

About five minutes later, Yigal suddenly appeared in their midst. Looking at Tony and April, he broke into a smile. "It's good to see you both looking so much better. You were ready to fall over when we left Santa Domingo. Listen, everything is set for you in Toronto. First you're going to spend some time in one of the city's big hospitals to make certain you're well, then you'll come over and stay with us at the legation until we can get you set up in an alternative life. This may be only for a relatively short time, maybe not. But we feel, for your sakes, we can't take any chances. By the way, you're both going to be Israeli citizens who were injured on overseas duty with our government. You were born in the US and that'll explain the fact that you don't speak Hebrew. By the way, your names are Anthony and April Casselstein. We have an apartment all set for you in the city and you'd be surprised how much of your lives are already in place."

April looked at Tony and tried to laugh, but a stab of pain suddenly gripped her.

"How's my dear husband feeling this afternoon?" As she spoke, April reached out and took Tony's hands as he sat and seemed to be somewhere else.

Alex reached over and looked closely into one of his eyes. Tony seemed to be passing into some sort of coma. Yigal and Alex struggled to place him in the third bed as the plane was quickly descending and banking around to line up with the main Toronto runway. Alex spoke to Tony in a sharp voice. "Tony, can you hear me?"

There was no visible response. April began to panic. "Alex, what's the matter with him? He's been doing that all afternoon! One minute I'd talk to him, then the next minute he'd be somewhere else!"

Alex took April by the hand and replied, "I wouldn't get too alarmed yet, April. That's why you're both going to the hospital in Toronto. I think that crack he took on the head may have been harder than we first thought."

As he spoke, there was a sudden roaring from the four big engines and several bumps as the plane settled onto the runway. The big rows of wheels in the main body of the plane vibrating. Within ten minutes, the Hercules arrived at a small slot in a long row of civilian EL Air 747s.

"April, we're here and for a while you're home. Toronto is a great city and a reasonably civilized place." Alex consoled April as she was uptight with Tony's condition and the pain from her knife wound and burns.

April was sitting up in her hospital bed looking over the *Toronto Star*. Dr. Alex Cameron walked in and she greeted him with a cheery, "Hi, Alex, how's Tony doing?" As she spoke, she laid the paper beside her on the bed.

"He's better, April, but I think he may need some serious surgery to fix the problem permanently." April's big smile vanished in a millisecond.

"Alex, what's wrong with Tony? I've had a bad feeling about his condition for several days."

"April, it goes back to that crack he got on the head. It is more serious than I first thought. I think he has a piece of bone pressing on a lobe of his brain. It's not life threatening, but his condition will only get worse if we don't do anything about it."

April's face went pale and she was very quiet. "Alex, what do you do have to do to fix it?"

Taking April's hand, he replied, "He has to have some surgery to relieve the pressure. They have a world reputation here and in London, Ontario, for this sort of thing, so we should get right to it."

"Alex, is he going to be all right?"

"Look, April, any brain surgery is tricky, but he's in the best hands possible."

April looked very relieved. He stood up as if to leave when she asked, "Alex, how am I doing? I'm still awful sore!" As she spoke, she placed her hand at the bottom of her rib cage to the knife wound.

"April," he answered sitting down again on the bed, "you're doing just fine! In fact, I've told the staff that you can get out of bed and get some exercise. You've got to remember that knife went in you almost ten inches and damaged several ribs. That's why you're so sore over here." He touched her side where she'd been having all the pain. "One thing I want you to promise me, April, is that you'll never touch a cigarette. That knife blade passed through part of the lower lobe of your right lung, and that needs time to heal. Why your lung didn't collapse, I'll never know!"

"Alex, why am I so sore down here?" she asked as she placed her hands over her abdominal and vaginal area. As she asked, he could sense the urgency in her voice.

"April, that's because of the burns. But don't worry, they're only first degree and there's no skin or organ damage whatsoever. You see, that's the nature of those asses who attacked you. Burning you there was supposed to be a prime insult to you as a woman. I've run into several cases in the Caribbean and normally they use something like gasoline before igniting it. In your case they forgot that part or you'd have a terrible problem." As he spoke, he placed an arm about the girl's shoulders. "Tony asked me about you just before I came in here and I said you were fine. He said you were worried since you want to have five kids!"

She pushed him away as her face went pale. "He said that? I'm going to kill him! Just for spite, I might make him a father of triplets and get him to nurse the third! That'll fix him!" Alex Cameron dissolved in laughter before April realized she had been set up to relieve the tension. Her colour turned from pale to slight red.

"You know, Alex, you may be a doctor and we both owe you our own lives, but you're just as much a bugger as Tony can be!" She shook her head in mock anger. There was a moment's silence.

"You know, April, you remind me of my wife Rhetta so much it's scary!"

April looked up, her eyes big as saucers. "Alex, you never told me you were married. Where does Rhetta live?"

"We live right here in Toronto, April. This is my hospital and that's why I have privileges here. I spend a week a month in Santo Domingo working free for a clinic. They need the help and I feel very strongly we in Canada don't do enough. You just happened to hit me on my second-last day there." April looked at him with a new respect. "By the way, we have four kids—here, have a look!" As he was talking he pulled a pocket diary and produced a picture of four smiling youngsters, all under the age of ten. April looked at them for a long five minutes noting the names and ages at the bottom.

"Alex, you're a very lucky guy. Your wife must be kept on the move when they're so young!" she replied.

"That's the fascinating thing about Rhetta, April, she's a part-time lecturer in economics at York University here in the city. Our house out in Mississauga is like a computer centre at times. Then I have a small office there as well. That's Rhetta sitting in the background, keeping the troops in line!" he added with a snicker. April noted a dark-haired pretty lady holding the youngest little girl. "Listen, I don't mean to change the subject, but I want to get you on your feet. It's important that you get regular exercise right now."

As he helped her out of the bed, April winced with the sharp pains in her side. She was surprised how good it felt to be on her feet again.

"One other thing, April, Tony asked me if I would get this package of your research material to this man Moshie at the Israeli Legation in Washington by morning."

She nodded her head in agreement, only too glad to see the last of the whole business.

Chapter 58

Standing in front of the Commerce Building, Lynn flagged down the first taxi she saw coming her way. The car veered over to the curb as he hadn't a passenger all day.

"Yah, lady, where to?" he drawled.

"Would you take this package to the address on this sheet of paper? If you deliver this in the next fifteen minutes and tell the man everything is fine, there'll be another twenty in it for you!" Lynn replied in her most personable manner and with a big smile.

"Shit, lady, I'd have done it for the twenty, don't worry, I'm out of here." He grabbed the bag, the address and the twenty and roared off into the early afternoon. Lynn breathed a sigh of relief and walked back to the bench to wait for Frank Baird to pick her up.

As she sat, her thoughts went to Scott and the girls. She shook her head, as so much had happened during the last three weeks. As long as she lived, she would remember the look in his eyes as she walked out the front door of the Israeli Legation. She remembered her mother. She was always so protective, even when she was in her mid-twenties. She often said her mother had given up on her ever providing her with grandchildren. How would her family react when she broke the news of two instant grandchildren, and a son-in-law, a surgeon. After her attack and rape, her mother was a pillar for her. She was her mother's daughter and that was that. She was jolted back to reality by the honking of a car horn. A battered Ford Crown Victoria pulled to the curb in front of her. The figure of Frank Baird was waving to her from the driver's seat.

"Where were you? I honked and waved and you were nowhere to be seen!" he said in his most friendly manner.

"Oh! I get so busy these days I almost forget people are around me." She ran around to the passenger side and climbed in. He roared down 25th Street and hung a right unto Constitution Avenue.

"Frank, where are you taking us? You didn't mention this on the phone?"

she asked in as matter-of-fact a voice as she could muster.

"I think I mentioned earlier my concerns over those pictures you called me about. I want you to meet someone who will show you the importance of your find. Lynn, you've done the American people a great service and we want to recognize the fact." As he talked, Lynn sensed a great change in the man. He appeared to be reading from a prepared script and she had a strange feeling in the back of her neck. She had never sensed this in him all the years she and her family knew him. What would be coming next? Before she knew exactly where she was, the car pulled up in front of the Baird ancestral home.

"Frank, where's your old Cadillac? It's always in your driveway," she asked, making conversation.

"Oh, I had more trouble with it and it wasn't worth fixing, so I sent it to the wreckers!" Frank added as he exited from the car.

Something was wrong and still Lynn couldn't put her hand on it. Lynn wondered why Frank kept working all these years. He could have retired during the Nixon years and the Vietnam War, but that wasn't Frank. She knew he was the type to slog on until he dropped. He expected everyone else to do the same and was known to question the integrity of anyone who didn't. Lynn hugged Louise and muttered endearments as the older woman's arms went about her.

"Lynn, it's wonderful to see you again. Come in and meet our guests." She led the way while Frank put the car in the garage. She still wondered about the Cadillac. The joke around many circles in the city was he would get rid of Jenny before the car. Louise led Lynn into the large cluttered and rambling family room. There she was met with six strange faces. Then she recognized Senator Beecham from Iowa. Recognizing the tragic death of his wife from the papers, she walked over and clasped his hand offering her condolences. For the next thirty minutes, there was a circulation in the room and various discussions on the Middle East and conditions in Europe. Finally, Frank Baird walked in and called for everyone's attention.

"Ladies and gentlemen, I think most of you have made the acquaintance of Lynn Pollard. She's the gal who found the Lincoln pictures and passed them along to me last week." He nodded in her direction and she was floored to have the attention of a number of relative strangers.

"Well, I stumbled on these two prints and passed them on to you, Frank, since I knew you had various contacts in such matters. Besides, you had been a friend of my family for many years and I trusted your judgement in such matters." Lynn turned and stepped back, hoping to be apart from the rest of the discussion. She was annoyed. Why was she brought here, singled out and introduced to all these people? As she circulated, she was able to pick up pieces of different conversations, which died out as she came near. Finally, she spotted Frank standing at the bar with the traditional single-malt Scotch in his hand.

"Frank, why did you bring me here? I wanted to speak to you on the phone and you dragged me here to your place and still haven't had a chance to talk. What the hell is going on?"

"Come on, Lynn, stop being the dummy! You're here for the same reason I am, to finally meet the man who will lead this country back to her true path of prosperity and glory. I was telling the senator of the great service you've done for the party and he assured me it won't be forgotten. Listen, I've got to circulate and I suggest you do the same. Now get going and remember our special guest will be here any minute."

Lynn was stunned but she remembered Scott expressing his fears about this new Freedom Party. She was entertaining the strange feeling she was being drawn into an eerie web of intrigue and sinister planning. Finally, she slipped off to the washroom. As she passed a bedroom she heard someone crying. Looking past the door, she spotted Louise Baird lying on a bed on her side. Sitting beside, she asked.

"Louise, is there anything I can do?"

Louise rolled over, looked up as she wiped her eyes. "Thank you, Lynn. I should have known of all the people out there you'd be the only one with any compassion. It's far too late to do anything now. Frank has got us so far down this road, I'm afraid there will be no return. Lynn, Frank has himself tied up with a group who are nothing more than a bunch of Fascists. I've heard them talking and they're a ruthless bunch and they're merciless with anyone they suspect. Lynn, for God's sake get out of here before they hurt you. You have no idea some of the plans they have for the future of this country," she wailed.

Lynn looked at her then turned and fled. She searched about until she came to a set of back stairs that all houses of this vintage had when they were built. As she was about to start up, a heavy arm grabbed her from behind. Almost instinctively she lashed out with her right foot on the upper centre of his right foot. There was a grunt of muffled pain. Stiffening the two main fingers of her right hand, she jerked about and drive them into his eyes. There was a sudden scream of pain. He was a small man and in a minisecond, she decided to flip him. She brought him down to the floor back first just as she bent her right knee under him receiving the full weight of his falling body between the third and fourth vertebrae. They snapped with a dull crunch. A moan issued from his lips as he gasped his last word and was immediately dead. She lowered him quietly to the floor looking about as she did so.

She carefully backed away from the stairs and crept silently along a dimly lit hallway. She heard voices ahead. She asked herself what she was doing here. Why had Frank brought her here if he was so committed to this radical new party? What had she said to lead him on? Why would these people be so friendly when they were capable of such hideous acts? The voices ahead became more audible.

"Mr. Justice, I think now's the time for you to come out and show your colours. The American people are right for a person of your stature to came forward and present themselves at this critical time in our nation's history. We haven't had this kind of crisis since the end of the Civil War." Lynn edged forward to see better who was talking. Through a crack in the door she was able to see two people. She gasped and felt sick to her stomach. The younger man was none less than the senator from Iowa, Senator Beecham. Then she saw the other face. As she recognized the figure of Justice Hamilton Sherman Saunders, Chief Justice of the United States, she thought she was going to throw up.

Chapter 59

Clutching her small purse, Lynn slowly backed away from the doorway. Looking behind her, she quietly made her way down the narrow hallway. Finding a small washroom, she sat down on the toilet and pondered the various facts racing through her mind. She was certain Frank Baird was associated with this whole business, but it was the chief justice's involvement that gave her a sick feeling. She wondered, who was really the thrust behind the American Freedom Party? The chief justice was a fine man but never for a moment did he strike her as the type of individual who would be an original thinker. Even Baird or the senator weren't up to that kind of a challenge. She drew a blank. Someone had not only to come up with the idea for the founding of the party but also the direction. Who? As she pulled the nine-millimetre revolver from her purse, she thought of Tony and poor April. They were good people and she had grown fond of them over the past two years. Finally the question that bothered everyone passed through her mind: What was so insidious about the Lincoln research material and most of all the Surratt paper that got people so upset? She determined what she would have to do. She would start with Frank Baird and if this was empty, she would try Senator Beecham. She knew from his reputation his weakness was women. Checking the clip in the revolver, she snapped it back in place. It was a risky game she was determined to play but she had little choice. Placing the revolver back in her purse, she left the washroom and returned downstairs. Entering the living room, she was approached by Frank Baird.

"Lynn, have you seen Louise around?"

"Yes, I saw her upstairs a few minutes ago. I think she was going to the bathroom," she answered.

"Damn it all, I wanted her to meet the senator's chief aid. He's been a good friend of mine for years," he stated. Looking about her, she took him by the arm and guided him over to a small love seat by the front bay window.

"Why, Lynn, trying to get me into a love seat, I thought you gave up on men years ago!" he responded in a bantering tone.

Ignoring his comments, she sat down beside him and asked, "Look, Frank, thanks for bringing me down this afternoon. It's been so sudden, you left me a bit floored." Attempting to sound as convincing as she could, she took his hands in hers and squeezed them in a tight sincerity. "If my dad were alive now, he'd want to be here and he'd be proud of what you're trying to accomplish. You know he felt betrayed by his country when he returned from Vietnam the first time." She lowered her head as she talked about him and her twisting of the truth.

Frank Baird was suddenly overwhelmed. Taking her small hands in his, he looked deep into her eyes. "Lynn, I had no idea your dad felt so passionately about these things. What a sacred memory for our movement. You must share it with us this afternoon," he responded.

She saw her opening. "I wish you'd tell me what's so important about this material? Especially those pictures? I don't see the link with today's world."

There was a long silence before he spoke. "Lynn, in our movement, as in many others, there are some things that are best known to only a few. This way the overall party can't be damaged by any one person. But I think I owe you this much. We believe we have proof that the Catholic Church was directly involved in the planning and killing of our greatest president, Abraham Lincoln." He stopped and looked directly at her in silence, almost testing her patriotism.

She did her best to feign shock and muttered, "Oh, my God. those bastards!"

"That's right, they're a bunch of bastards and are trying to control our nation like the present situation in many other parts of the world. Well, I tell you, we're going to have something to say about that."

She stood up and turned to Baird in mock anger and snarled, "You're right, they're trying to take our nation away from us. Tell me, Frank, what's your new party going to do about it? If you want my support, you're going to have to show some respect for my dead father! He died for this country and don't let any of your people forget that fact." Her voice was becoming strident and she surprised even herself. He pulled her back down to the sofa.

"Alright, you've put us all to shame, I can tell you that much. Lynn, we need all the material you can give us. The more ammunition we have, the more effectively we can present our case to the electorate that Rome is pulling the strings here in Washington. Listen, we've tried to get in contact with a Tony Cassell in California as we understand he has a lot of valuable material related to this subject. Do you know him or even anything about him?"

As he spoke, she felt little bells running up and down her spine. Was she taking her ruse too far with Frank?

"Yes, I've met him at several conferences and have had a number of talks with him on the phone, but nothing about the Lincoln material. Anything we have done has been very formal. One detail, Frank, are you telling me you want all the Lincoln material you can get your hands on to set up the Vatican as a foreign meddler in American history?"

"That's right, and that's why you are a crucial person in the Freedom Party's future. You came up with those pictures and now we need to find the original daguerreotypes and related original material. Without it, the FBI could crucify us if they ever get their hands on what we have in mind." As he spoke, she could feel the passion of an embittered old man who had found something new to hang on to and make all the failures and struggles of the past years seem worth while.

"Frank, who is the real power behind the party? If I get involved, I'd like to know them," she asked.

"Lynn, the person who will speak for the party will be introduced to the public soon. However, he has to have a solid issue around which to make his speech and claims. He holds a high government position and has to wait for the right moment. Remember, in politics, timing is half the battle. That moment will be when we have all the information we have about your revelation in the Surratt material. We need everything you've got to make our charges stick! Until then, I can't tell you more," he replied.

"Frank, I recognized Senator Beecham when I first came in. Is he a vital part of everything?"

"Not nearly as much as his wife was. As you know, she was killed last week in a violent attempt on his life. Since then he has more or less come on board, yet his ultra-bleeding-heart background gives me cause to have doubts. Listen, I think I see Louise and she needs me. Stay around, Lynn, I want to talk to you more."

Carrying her leather purse and jacket in her left hand, she casually walked to the living room where she had first met everyone. She wandered to a corner where there was a large collection of autographed pictures of national public figures and personal awards for public service since the days of the Truman administration. As she stood looking over the awards, she felt a man's hand cupping her bottom. Lynn fought a surge of instant anger inside her.

"Well, Ms. Pollard, I hear you've been quite the help to the party," said the overdressed and pleasant figure of the junior senator from Iowa. She turned, and felt him undressing her with each glance.

"As I said before, Senator, I was sorry to hear about your wife. Please accept my condolences again." His hand caressed her buttocks as she talked and it was with great restraint that she kept from slapping his face. She walked from the room into the long hallway but found he had followed her. In a small study, he caught her with her back to a small desk.

"What's the matter with you? All young broads like to be handled. You've made your little move but it's time to get serious."

As he talked, he placed a hand on her right breast and caressed it. She was jammed against the desk and was unable to move. He wasn't a big man but well developed and solid. Finally, her judo training took over. She placed the fingers of one hand on either side of his Adam's apple and squeezed hard. He gasped and slumped to his knees. She whispered in his ear, "Senator, I don't like to be handled in public. I was beaten badly a few years ago and react violently to anything like it today. Why don't you call me later and we can get to know each other better. Besides, I'd like to apologize more privately."

He grunted and stood up. He looked her up and down for a brief moment. She wondered again if she had overplayed her hand. He seemed to hesitate. She placed his right hand high on the warm inner side of her right thigh and a smile of desire tugged at his lips.

"Meet me at my flat over at 4587 Wisconsin Avenue, near the Washington Cathedral, in two hour's time. We can go wherever you want for dinner and private quietness," she added.

"Alright, I'll pick you up in three hours' time. Wear something besides that damned jacket. I've got a meeting to chair, the damned justice wants to stall and we've got some issues to settle before the week is out."

He tucked in his shirt and left the room. She could hardly believe her luck. He appeared to be a far more important figure in the party than even Frank alluded. If the keystone person was a member of the Supreme Court, the influence of the party was far deeper than anyone suspected. How far and how deep did it really go? She could see storm clouds looming on the national horizon. Walking back to the front door, she again encountered Frank Baird.

"Frank, I have to leave early and go home and tidy up. I'm meeting the senator this evening to talk about the party and I want to see if I can get everything he wants."

He looked like a man for whom a prayer had just been answered. "Lynn, you'll never know how relieved I am. You're making a smart move. He's a real power behind our movement and you'll want to be in his camp."

Chapter 60

Lynn Pollard arrived back at her brownstone at four-thirty. She was still shocked that a man whose wife was dead less than a week would think of asking her out. Looking at her watch, she remembered he would be picking her up in less than an hour. As she was about to phone Scott she recalled the possibility of phone taps. Stepping out next door, she used Gail Longstreet's phone to make the call.

"Scott? It's Lynn here!" As she spoke she felt a warmth spreading through her.

"Lynn, thank God, we've all been worried. Are you all right?"

"I'm fine. I've been home for a few minutes and finishing up everything I've had to do."

"Is it safe to talk?"

"Yes, this is a private line and there's no reason why it would be tapped. I'll be glad when this is all over." He heard a strain in her voice but knew enough not to ask at the present time.

"We're all fine here. The girls keep asking when you're coming home and that tells a big tale in itself. We're staying at the legation until everything is over and I've been taking a taxi to the hospital every day and will be damned glad when it is all over. When do you think you'll be back?" he asked.

"I want everything cleaned up by tomorrow evening and the next day at the latest. There are a number of things I want to get cleared up with Frank Baird and that'll take time. Have you seen him today, Scott?" she inquired.

"Uh-oh, there's my buzzer from the hospital, one of today's cases must have a problem. I'm going to have to go. That's one problem with the surgery thing, my time is never my own. Please take care, Lynn, and I want to see you sometime tomorrow!" The phone clicked as he hung up.

As he hung up, she realized the senator would be picking her in less than thirty minutes. Going back to her apartment, she took a quick shower and did a fast job on her hair. As she dried her hair, she realized to get the information she wanted out of the senator, she would have to dress the part. Pulling out a black cocktail dress given to her by a girlfriend several years back, she held it up in front of her in the mirror. She shrugged and pulled it on. It was knee length, but with a back that plunged to the waist. The front covered her chest and tied behind her neck. Removing her bra, she fastened the ties behind her neck. The neckline dipped low and most of her breasts were exposed. For a moment she was shocked but remembered she was trying to solicit information from the senator and she knew his reputation with women. Making a final check of her short grey-flecked hair, she was ready. She felt an inner glow of confidence in her daring appearance. As she put on her grey London Fog raincoat, there was a beep of a car horn from the curbside. Looking out her window, she noticed a small limo sitting at the curbside with the motor idling. As she approached, the young driver held the door open to the passenger compartment.

"Well, for a moment I thought you'd lost your nerve!" came the senator's voice from the rear seat as the door was opened. As she climbed in beside him, she felt his eyes on her legs as she settled herself. The big car pulled away.

"Where're we going?" she asked in as innocent a voice as she could muster. "I'm looking forward to this evening."

"I have a regular suite and private pool at the Key Bridge Marriott Hotel. I'm out of town so much and this is cheaper than having a full-time residence."

"Are we going out for dinner or will we eat there?" she asked.

"Hell, no, we're going straight to the suite. I have a special dinner cooked there every time I'm in the area," he said as the car wormed its way through the heavy city traffic, finally coming to a stop at the front of the large hotel.

The entrance to the senator's suite was spectacular. There were large marble columns on either side of the entrance with a white statue of a bathing woman in the middle of the foyer. Lynn had a funny feeling in the pit of her stomach but ignored it. The main room was an extension of the entrance with paintings on every wall. The quietness of the room was interspaced by the gurgle of a small fountain. There were two bedrooms on one side of the main room and a kitchenette on the other side. Lynn, feeling nervous and fearful, walked through a fourth door and found herself in a large glass-covered type of solarium with a splash pool in the middle. The beauty of the room took her breath away. The late-afternoon sun streamed through the tinted glass on the sides and overhead. It was the most spectacular hotel suite she had ever seen.

"Nice pad, eh? It's my favourite," Beecham proclaimed as he took off his spring coat. "Here, let me have your coat and I'll fix us some drinks."

As she took off her coat, she felt his eyes cover her from head to toe. In a moment of panic, she walked back to the pool area and felt the water. It was warm and inviting and in other circumstances, she would have jumped in. He returned carrying two martinis and a shaker. He passed her one of them and raised the other.

"To a great evening," he said, dropping his eyes to her chest and across her waist.

She knew a moment of panic, wondering if she had let herself in for more than she bargained for. She knew she could cripple him in an instant but that wasn't why she was here. After several sips from his drink, he took her by the hand and pulled her against his chest. Before she realized what he was about, he lowered his mouth to hers and kissed her roughly. His tongue began to probe her mouth and she felt his huge erection as he pressed against her. She tried to return his kiss so he wouldn't become suspicious. Soon his right hand was exploring the top of her dress. He cupped her right breast in his hand and caressed the large nipple.

She pulled back and whispered in his ear, "Let's not rush things, I'd like another drink."

He disappeared for a few moments. Lynn felt the soothing effect of the alcohol and realized the drinks were stronger than she bargained for. He returned wearing a shiny white robe and carrying another. He handed her the one he was carrying.

"Here's one of these for you, go and change and I'll refresh the drinks."

Lynn was concerned at the speed with which the evening was progressing. She returned and found the senator sprawled on the large white sofa by the pool working on a martini. She sat next to and leaned against his shoulder trying to be obvious. She asked sipping her martini, "Senator, there's one thing I don't understand about this whole Lincoln business. What's so important about a few old pictures?"

He looked at her for a long moment without speaking and she wondered if she had overplayed her hand. Then he commented, "I know! That's what everyone on the council says as well, so you're in good company. We're going to take power in this country in a few years and we need the vital effect those pictures and the Surratt papers will have when they are presented to the public in the right manner by the right person. We have at least 60 million Catholic voters in this country and this material will help us discredit the power of the Vatican once and for all. Furthermore, it will enhance the position of our party if we do it the right way. Remember, so much in the field of politics is a matter of timing and presentation. So you see, my dear, what you've got is crucial for us and you've done our party and country a great service." His eyes looked at her, seething with desire and lust.

"Why was it necessary to kidnap me at first and kill my associate, when you knew I was a sympathizer for your movement?" As she spoke she feigned a seething anger with roots in a sad reality.

He replied, "We didn't know until Baird informed us. Secondly, there was the attack on the other office by that Vatican group. Now, they're gone and there are only two incidents I can't account for."

At that very moment, the thought went through Lynn's mind that he wasn't aware of the presence and role of the Mossad. He continued, "Did you know there was a guard killed earlier today while you were at the Baird residence?"

"Of course I did, I'm not stupid. I stumbled over his body in the back hall and wasn't going to get caught for killing him by anyone. I've seen several people back at Baird's home who are nothing more then a pair of idiots. I'm not getting killed for their stupidity," she snapped in feigned arrogance.

"Pollard, don't get your Irish up. I like you and you don't try to bullshit me. I can smell one a mile away. That guy was a martial arts expert and would have broken your back in a moment." Lynn looked at him as he downed another martini. "Let's have another drink as I have a meeting at ten and have to be out of here."

She pretended to finish hers and he poured her another. He continued, "We had trouble with two people in the Dominican Republic, but we got them out of the way. Our guys there put it to the girl but she wouldn't open her trap. They buried her the next morning in Santo Domingo. We don't know what happened to our guys after they knifed the girl and shot the guy, but someone did them in as well. But, what the hell, they're casualties of war. In this business you have to be prepared to lose a few lives. Pollard, you sure came on at the right time. There's going to be things happening in the next few days that will change the direction and history of our great country. Hell, enough of this, let's get down to more serious stuff." He reached for her as she snuggled up closer to him as he stretched out on the sofa.

"Let's have another drink! You stay here and I'll go mix them."

She bounced back onto the sofa and waited for him to return. She was feeling the effect of the drinks but also the general surroundings. Strange feelings coursed through her and she wondered for a moment how good he would be in bed. She flushed and turned crimson at the direction of her thoughts. As he returned, and sat beside her on the sofa. His hand caressed the smooth skin of her upper thigh and she felt strange urges starting to flow through her. His lips pressed on hers and his tongue searched her mouth and she returned the passion before she realized what was happening. His hand searched her upper thigh until he touched her groin. She wore nothing under the robe and moaned as his finger stroked between her legs.

After several minutes, she jumped up and said, "I don't know about you, Senator, but I'm going for a swim. Come on, don't be an old poop!" She pulled him to his feet and urged him towards the splash pool. At the pool's edge, she stood and removed her robe as he watched. As it fell to the marble deck, she stood naked in the soft twilight. She felt his eyes cover her breasts as they jutted high and firm. Her nipples hardened in the cool air. His eyes slowly ran down across her small waist and flat stomach. Her thighs were slim tapering into full toward her groin. Only tiny traces of pubic hair concealed her most private area.

He pulled her against him and muttered, "You want this as much as I do!" as he crushed his mouth against hers. His robe fell to the floor and their naked bodies pressed hard against each other. His muscular body glistened in the fading light.

Lynn moved as in a trance. Her body and desires were telling two different stories. Great feelings of unbridled passion surged all through her as she dropped to her knees in front of him. Waves of desire swept over her as all control vanished. She felt like an unbridled animal as she grasped his huge manhood and caressed him. Slowly and gently she moved her fingers up and down it as his erection grew more and more. His breath came in rasping gasps. Drawing him towards her mouth, she caressed him with her tongue before finally slipping him into her mouth. A great moan issued from deep within him.

Picking her up, he carried her to the small sofa. As she lay on her back, she thrashed about, her passion overpowering her and sweeping her along. He ran his tongue up her long legs and over her full thighs. He touched deep between her legs, his tongue exploring her clitoris. She moaned loudly and he growled to himself. Her back arched and her head rolled back in full ecstasy. Opening her legs wide, he ran his hands over the mounds of her breasts and drew each to his tongue. As he did, her head swirled and she gasped and drew him closer over her. Her body shook with passion as he lowered himself down. She jerked her back high to receive his thrust. He touched her and probed. She gasped as he thrust deeply into her. Her legs wrapped tightly about his back locking over him. They began to rock in the ageless motion of passion, surge after surge of orgasm flooding over her. Her nails raked his back as he thrust even deeper. She opened her mouth and screamed in passion. He moved faster and faster in a passion she never knew before. Finally, there came the moving surge of his seed thrusting through her as he locked rigid before falling in exhaustion on the couch behind her.

Sitting up, she noticed a stream of blood and fluid running down her legs. She stood up and said in a small bitter voice causing her to sob uncontrollably as she looked down on him, "You bastard, you drugged my drinks!"

He sat up and laughed. "Don't give me that crap, you wanted to get fucked even more than I did, you broads are all alike. You want to be treated like whores in bed and saints elsewhere. If you don't like that, get the hell out of here."

She looked about her. What had started well had fallen apart. Yet she had obtained what she wanted. As he stood up, she made her move. Her small but compact fist caught him at the base of his neck and he collapsed in a heap on the marble floor. She left him and ran back to the bedroom and dressed. Looking about, she eased herself out the front door.

Chapter 61

A distant voice awakened Scott out of a deep sleep. Swinging his legs out of bed, he was shocked to find it was past seven. There was a vision of the attending in the emerg. panicking, then he remembered it was his day off. Looking back at the bed, he saw Lynn was still in a deep sleep. Getting up slowly not to disturb her, he walked around and sat on the edge of the bed. She slept on her right side with one small hand under her cheek. Short tendrils of her grey-streaked hair covered her face. He reached out and ran two fingers down the smooth skin of her cheek. She brushed a hand across her face, mumbled in her sleep and snuggled further under the covers. Smiling, he got up and wandered to the washroom for a shower and shave.

Fifteen minutes later he was standing before the mirror shaving when he heard a rustle behind him. With his chin still covered with shaving foam, he turned to come face to face with Lynn rubbing sleep from her eyes.

"Good morning. I'll step over to the other sink and you can have this part of the washroom." Still half asleep, she muttered something under her breath moved into the toilet and closed the door.

"I can't believe I slept for ten hours," she commented from behind him on a chair as she watched him finish shaving. As they talked, there was a rapid knocking at the bedroom door.

"Lynn, could you get that, I'll bet it's the girls. They knew you were returning after they went to bed, so be prepared." Within minutes, he heard the squeals of two little girls as they raced through the bedroom.

"Aunt Lynn, Grandma said you were back!" came Francie's girlish voice. When he came back to the bedroom, both girls were sitting on the bed with their arms about Lynn. She was in a world she had never been in before and appeared to be relishing it. He was quickly called over to the bed by an insistent Angie.

"Daddy, could Aunt Lynn take Francie and me shopping this morning? I'm getting bored around here and she says we can't." She had her lower lip out as she tried to play Lynn off against Scott.

"Look, sweetie, I know you'd like to, but we have to stay here for several more days. Besides, when Lynn says you can't, I don't want you asking me," he replied formally. Angie looked sullen and turned away from her dad. He looked at Lynn and rolled his eyes.

"You girls go downstairs with your grandmother and I'll be downstairs in a few minutes. I have to talk to your father about this afternoon!" Lynn said in a firm voice that caught their attention.

They looked at their father and raced for the door. Scott looked at Lynn and said in frustration, "You see what I have to contend with. Both girls have minds of their own and fight me all the way. There are times…!" He sat down on the bed and looked at Lynn.

"Are you sure you can cope with an instant family?" he asked.

"I thought we'd settled that. I love the girls as my own but that doesn't mean I'm a pushover. I think Angie has found that out already. She reminds me of me. She'll try to get her way from the word go and if not she'll fall into line with the rules. Francie is more compliant and tends to go along with the family more easily. Listen, you get dressed; I'm going down for breakfast as the girls will be looking for me."

Lynn spent the morning about the large Legation pool with the girls. It was a long time since she had spent as much time with children their age and she revelled in it. After lunch, they were ready for their afternoon nap. Martha, who spent the morning shopping for clothes for the kids, returned with the security guard who had gone along with her. Scott spent the morning on one of the building's computers working on his medical papers when a courier man came to the front door with a parcel for Lynn. Taking it to the library, she noted it was from Toronto. Opening it, she found it was the folder she had sent to Tony Cassell in California. There were other papers with which she wasn't familiar.

Half an hour later, Scott stuck his face in the door and asked, "Is there anything I can do?"

She looked up and replied immediately, "Yes, Scott, it's time for you and I to talk. You need to see the bigger issue and what we're apparently up against!"

"If that's what you feel, I don't know if I can help or not," he said. As he spoke he came into the library and sat on a leather sofa next to her.

"Well, the point is you, Martha and the girls have been placed in great danger because of me and I owe you a full explanation of what's going on. Look, let's go out in the little sun area at the back of the pool and I'll bring everything I have out and you can see for yourself. I want to be sure of the security of all the staff here; we can't afford to take any chances," she added.

"Alright, I'll get Martha to keep an eye on the girls and perhaps she can con them into watching a movie in the theatre."

They got up and he returned to the computer room and finished the paper he was working on. He knew Lynn was greatly troubled about the material in the courier package as well as with what she brought back from downtown There was a great deal about her that was still a mystery, yet there was a bond between them that already defied human reason.

Chapter 62

Around two, wearing an old pair of cutoffs and with a towel over his shoulder, Scott walked through the back kitchen of the legation and out to the sun area at the back corner of the pool area. There he saw Lynn with several white plastic loungers set up and piles of material. She was standing rubbing sunscreen on her long legs. She wore a small red bikini he hadn't seen before which accentuated the fullness of her figure covered well with her dress style. She stood up and waved as she saw him coming. As she turned to meet him, he was surprised at the brevity of her bikini bottom. The front was little more than a triangle covering her groin before disappearing between her legs.

Seeing him looking at her, she quipped, "Yah, I know this suit doesn't leave much to the imagination. I got it from one of the young waitresses here on staff and can't believe she would actually wear it on a public beach. Anyway, thanks for giving me some time to get this material sorted out and now we can see where we may be headed from here," she added.

"Oh yes, as I was coming through the garden area two of the young bucks who saw you walking back here were taking bets whether you would take your top off before going in the pool! I told them I was going to have a rough time concentrating on what you were saying with you dressed like this!" He laughed.

"You heard no such thing, they wouldn't dare!" she whispered, her face turning scarlet. "Although it's flattering to know you thought enough to tease me about it."

"Well, the good news is you look great in the suit and the better news is what I said was actually true, plus the fact the guys thought you have a great rack. Remember, they're from Israel, where bathing customs are far more liberal than in this country."

Totally embarrassed, she shook in laughter and quickly changed the subject.

"You should hear my final conclusions about this Lincoln business. I've got all the evidence here, from the pictures I sent to Tony and April and the ones I copied and gave to Frank Baird before I realized his connection with this new party. Then there's the vital paper Mary Surratt wrote after the priests visited her before the killing of Lincoln." She handed the paper to Scott. He looked at its faded paper and the 19th-century writing style.

"This is what the Freedom Party wants to use to blackmail the Catholic Church?" he asked incredulously

"Apparently this and the pictures themselves!" she answered. He picked up the various old pictures.

"I can't get over how sharp and clear these old pictures are. The details are nothing short of amazing."

"Remember, Scott, most of these people would sit still for perhaps five minutes or more, the process was so slow. That gave the old film time to absorb the images," she replied.

He continued, "These pictures are amazing, but aren't they only circumstantial evidence? I don't see how pictures will hold up long in the court of public opinion," he added.

"Scott, these pictures are only signposts pointing to the real evidence, the papers of Mary Surratt. These are the implicating ones and the original. These have links with the Red Rose Fellowship, not just through the pictures but through the personage of Mary Surratt herself. Sometime, soon after her last meeting with the conspirators in April of 1863, she wrote these words in her own hand. How they were hidden I'm not sure. But, one thing I'm positive about is the effect this material could have in the wrong hands."

"What do you mean?" he asked.

"Scott, in the hands of people who could put a real negative spin on all of this stuff, many people in this country would see this as enough evidence to believe that the killing of Abraham Lincoln was ordered from the pope himself at the time. Now, do you see where the source of my concern lies? My real concern is not what people will conclude themselves about all of this, rather what they will be led to believe by the wrong people. So many people are simply waiting to be led to certain blame-filled conclusions by unscrupulous leaders." She was quiet, quelled by the direction of her own words.

"This is the evidence the Vatican wants to destroy? Do you really believe they will have the effect the Freedom Party thinks they will?"

"Yes! Not only could I believe they could, and I have no reservations, the material must never fall into the hands of this new party. Besides, there are also a variety of other connections between this Red Rose Brotherhood tinkering with various historical events in the Western world as far back as the Reformation and even further," she replied.

"Don't you think you're stretching the evidence somewhat there, Lynn?" he quipped.

"No, I don't, and all sorts of worm cans will crop up if we let this out to the media. I can think of two historical examples: we feel there is ample historical evidence this Red Rose Brotherhood interfered with the battle of Waterloo sufficient to change its course. Again, there is enough circumstantial evidence to point to the Church as a direct agent in the poisoning of Napoleon," she added.

Scott stood up in a state of shock. "How far does this thing go?"

"It deals with the attempted tinkering by the Catholic Church to manipulate and control the history of the Western world."

"Jesus Christ, it's no wonder the priests were desperate to prevent this from leaking out. What about the Mossad? Where do they come into the picture, and thank God they did," he asked.

"In all honesty, I think they had their eyes on the Red Rose Brotherhood for some time. Then when one of their moles was killed by accident, they went into damage control and were inadvertently dragged into the whole mess. Plus, just when it looked as if the priests might do something to implicate Israel, they swung into action. The Freedom Party here in America was a different story and very much a last-minute sort of thing. They don't give a damn about the Catholic Church or Israel and only deal with or use them when it suits their own end. They want to impose their philosophy on this country and will use any means to achieve that end. Hence the Surratt material is merely a vital means to an end for them. They're fanatical but very dangerous and ruthless." She fell silent.

"What are you going to do now? It seems to me you're at a crossroads, like it or not," he said reluctantly.

"This is why I wanted time to think. I've come to a decision. I'm going to destroy everything! Otherwise, the whole affair will pop up again whenever it or new material is brought to light."

"How do you propose to do that?" Scott said.

"I think of a tale my dad told me about his first tour in Vietnam. He said sometimes you had to flush your enemy out before you could really deal with him. That's what I'm convinced we have to do. I know Frank Baird is somehow linked with this new party but how and to what extent, I don't know. So we'll have to flush him out. I do know he has the inside track of what

242

is going on inside the movement, but I know nothing of his direct involvement and role. So I'm going to flush him out," she responded.

"Those are great words but how do you propose to flush him?" he snapped back.

"Simple, when you think of it. I'm going to give him copies of everything except the Surratt paper itself and perhaps one or more of the original pictures. That way I'll still have an ace up my sleeve. I'd like to take them to Baird's house tomorrow morning. Remember, he still thinks I'm a loyal believer in his movement. I have one favour and a big one to ask of you, Scott. Will you come with me? I'll need the moral support to pull it off." She looked at him with pleading in her eyes and he knew he could never refuse her.

"Alright, Lynn, let's do it tomorrow morning and get the damned thing finished. I haven't trusted Baird from the first time I met him years ago. At that time I dismissed him as a shifty-eyed government mandarin," he added.

As he talked, she placed all the related material into a large manila file folder and that in turn into a small compact case she often carried. She got to her feet, gathering up a collection of extra papers and pencils she had scattered about. Even though the air was cool, Scott was sweating profusely.

"I'm going for a swim, how about you?"

"No, I'm staying here and get some sun. Before you go would you please put some sunscreen on my back?" Taking the yellow tube she handed him, he poured some of the milky liquid on her smooth skin. She unfastened her halter top and he spread it from her neck to her waist. She pulled a small cap over her head and buried her face in a towel, her arms stretched out by her sides. Scott walked back to the pool and dove in. Thirty laps later, he climbed out and sprinkled water from his body on her sun-drenched body.

"How was the water?"

"Actually, it was quite cool. I suppose that's because it is early in the summer, but still refreshing."

"Well, in that case, I'll stay here and enjoy the sun. We won't have much time tomorrow!" she quipped.

Scott closed his eyes for a moment. He heard something and sat up in his chair. At that moment something struck him on the back of the head. At that very moment, he heard Lynn cry out before plunging into a sea of darkness.

Chapter 63

Scott Fleming slowly regained consciousness and found himself lying on the floor of a speeding Chevy van. His hands and feet were tightly bound and there was a piece of duct tape across his mouth. Looking about him, he saw Lynn lying next to him tied in the same fashion and on her right side. He heard voices in the front seat but could see a single pair of legs below each seat. He nudged Lynn and she tried to turn from her tight position. She sighed relief when she saw he was coming to. She appeared to be dressed while he still wore his shorts and a shirt.

The van was speeding through heavy traffic and taking a variety of chances with lights and other vehicles. The two men in the front were talking but he was only able to hear and make out a few isolated words. Within fifteen minutes, the van slowed down, pulled into a driveway and lurched with a grinding halt. The back doors of the van opened and two rough-looking men grabbed them. They were carried into a dank basement, seated on two chairs and their ropes checked.

"Their ropes are fine. They're going nowhere soon," the other guy muttered.

"Hell, if had my way, I'd have iced them immediately and have it over with. Baird wanted them tied and left here and he's calling the shots. Why he wants them alive is beyond me!" the younger of the two said, not really expecting an answer. "Let's get out of here. I'm not into killing women anyhow!"

With these words, they left, slamming the door behind them, followed in close order by the snap of a lock. Then there was only the glow of a small lamp in the corner. The room appeared to be a dirty left-over rec room from the fifties. There was filthy panelling on the walls and the smell of dank air everywhere. Scott felt Lynn trying to move near him. Slowly turning, he saw her trying to signal with her eyes towards the ropes on her hands. He was stunned to find she had already untied half of the knots. Suddenly she was free and untying him. The duct tape was still on her mouth and he removed it with great care. When he was finished, she slumped against him and his arm went around her.

"Are you all right? You took a hell of a crack on the head. I thought you'd never come around," she asked.

"Yeah. I feel fine but I think I have a small concussion. My stomach is off and I've got a hell of a headache. How about yourself?" he asked.

"Oh, nothing physical but they're a bunch of bastards. When I get a chance I'm going to have a crack at that young buck. If I get him, he's going to remember it and regret it for a dozen lifetimes!" There was a biting edge on Lynn's voice. "Don't ever ask, now or ever, Scott. I have my ways of dealing with these bastards and they will pay more than you'll want to know."

He sensed the anger in her voice and said nothing as he slipped an arm about her slim shoulders.

"Do you have any idea where we might be?"

"We've been driving for about thirty minutes so I think we're somewhere around the edge of the city. Before you came to, I heard the two oafs who tied us up saying they were going to meet Frank Baird here soon after we arrived. Can you believe that, Scott? He was a devout friend of my family all through my childhood and now he's involved in something like this. My father would personally kill him if he were here at this moment."

"I didn't tell you at the legation, but the chief Mossad operative told me they were very concerned over his deep involvement in the Freedom Party."

"Scott, I thought Senator Beecham was the main person in the party," she replied.

"Ssshh, I think someone is coming outside the door," she continued. She signalled for him to sit in the chair with his arms behind his back. She ducked behind the door. It opened and the younger man entered.

"Well, I've got news for you, asshole, you're going to see Baird. He's interested in you. He wants no part of the girl—come to think of it, where the hell is she?"

"Looking for me, buster?" she whispered as she came up behind him. He turned but she was much quicker and it was the last move he ever made. Her right heel caught him just above his mouth with the full force of her turn. His teeth, nose, left cheek and jaw shattered at the same time. It was a crippling move. He was dying before he hit the floor. A large pool of blood quickly formed around his face. For a moment, Lynn stood on the balls of her feet ready to deliver another crippling blow.

Scott was stunned by the violence of her attack. He quickly grabbed the large revolver from the body and pulled back. Lynn added in a cryptic fashion, "When I was raped I swore I'd kill any man who was ever mean to me again. I'm not sorry for this. I know his kind, good riddance!"

"Listen," he injected, "we'd better get out of here. I've got his gun and you—well, I really don't think you need one."

They slowly crept up the cellar stairs and into a long dingy hall. There were voices in the distance. Scott turned to her and held his hand to his ear. She nodded she heard them. As they neared the top of the stairs, Scott looked up and saw the older of the two men who had tied them up.

"Well, so you got yourselves untied after all." Grabbing Lynn, he pulled her down on the steps and grabbed the gun from his pocket, firing as he did. He missed. The man reached for his own gun as he started down the stairs. Scott with his arm tight around Lynn rolled to his right off the steps and back onto the cellar floor. Upon landing he fired two quick shots in the man's direction. The man staggered back clutching his chest as he did looking down in disbelief where the two shots had passed through him. His mouth worked but nothing came out. Then his knees buckled and he pitched face forward down the cellar steps lifeless.

Lynn grabbed Scott by the arm. "Where did you ever learn to shoot like that? I can't believe how you hit him from your side here on the floor."

"Well, ever since I became interested in the Civil War, I starting collecting the occasional revolver. I figured if I had them around the place, I'd better know how to use them. I never in my wildest dreams thought it would come down to this."

"Thank God you did. I think he was dead before he hit the floor," she added.

"Lynn, let's get out of here, these shots will have the whole house here any minute," he stated. Suddenly a change came over her face.

"No, Scott. We don't have much choice ahead of us. If Frank and these bastards have the material I had when they kidnapped us from the legation, then there will be dire consequences for this country. After they hit you back at the legation, they grabbed both the package of material and myself. I don't think anyone else inside the building ever knew what was happening. They made mention of the fact they came in through the back as well."

With these words, she turned and moved up the stairs. Scott picked up the other man's gun and followed her. As they neared the top, two shots were heard from somewhere else in the house. At the same moment, Lynn stumbled and staggered back against the side wall. He first thought she was hit, but she was quickly back on her feet, apparently having tripped on the top step. They entered into a long dingy hallway cautiously moving forward a step at a time. Two more shots were heard behind the door of one of the bedrooms and then silence. Lynn dove to the floor and rolled through the door of an opposite bedroom. Silence. He saw the door across from her move slightly. Taking careful aim, he fired three quick shots through the dark wood. The noise was deafening. Then he heard several loud gasps from behind the shattered wood followed by a loud thud. More silence. There was a scuffle from the darkness where Lynn had disappeared. Pressing his body against the wall, he waited a moment. Lynn suddenly appeared, one arm twisted behind her by a large male figure. As he shoved her out into the hall, he twisted her arm viciously, the pain registering on her small face.

"I know who you are, Doctor, and why you're here. Put that gun down or I'll kill her here on the spot. Drop it and quick." Scott knew it was no use and slowly let the gun drop to the floor with a thud. Then he recognized the features of Senator Beecham. He also remembered doing surgery on the senator's late wife.

"You get over by the stair railing or she's going to take a dive to the floor below." Turning to Lynn he snorted, "You thought you killed me, didn't you? Well, that's your mistake, my dear, and it'll probably cost you your life. By the way, did you tell your poor friend here how you tried to sucker me?"

Turning to Scott, he said with a laugh, "I wouldn't trust this broad one inch." As he talked she struggled but he only twisted her arm more and she whimpered with pain. "She's a real whore, this one, and I've known a few of them in my time." As he talked, Scott could feel the anger rising within him and moved slowly towards Beecham. In turn, Beecham dragged Lynn closer to the stairwell.

"One more step and she goes down headfirst. She's really got you hooked, eh? You should have seen what she offered me. She's got the best set of tits I've seen in a while. That's how she's laid half the members of the State Department."

At that moment, Scott lost his control, lunged and grabbed Beecham by the collar, knocking him off balance. The senator was a strong man and shoved Scott to the floor with one arm and still hanging on to Lynn. Yet it was all the time she needed. She stomped down hard high on his left foot, causing him to release her neck. Then dropping to her knees and using all the strength of her small frame, she pulled down hard on Beecham's arm that had been around her neck. He rolled over her back and down the long stairs. He hit the railing at one point with a terrible crunch and finally rolled to a heap at the foot of the stairs. One leg was twisted at an unusual angle and a pool of blood was forming around his head. In addition, his neck appeared to be broken.

Scott slowly got to his feet and looked for Lynn. She was nowhere to be seen. He searched every room. Opening the door he had shot through, he found a body of a stranger, dead on the floor where he had fallen. Then he heard a sob and finally found her sitting on the basement steps. She had the manila envelope with the Lincoln material under her arm.

Chapter 64

Lynn Pollard raised her tear-streaked face to him as he lifted her up by her elbows.

"What must you think of me when you hear comments like the senator's? I should get out of your life. Look what I've dragged you and your family through these past few weeks. I don't understand why I can mean so much to all of you!" The words came with great effort and difficulty.

"That's what I've been trying to tell you since that day in the little cove and I phoned Walter Reid and turned them down on their offer. Look, this is perhaps not the best time to say this? You're a vital part of not only my life but the rest of the family. The more you beat yourself up, the more you hurt all of us." As he spoke, the smile that crossed her lips was something he would remember for years.

"I think we'd best go back upstairs and see if Frank Baird is here. I don't know why we have been brought here or what's been going on but it's time we found out."

Upstairs they found what appeared to the remains of a large meeting. Various reports and associated material were scattered on tables and besides chairs. On a large table, Scott found several sheets that looked much like some of the material Lynn had in her folder back at the legation.

"I think you'd better come over here for a moment. This looks a lot like the stuff you showed me and said you passed over to Baird." She looked over everything and in particular the various lists and schematic outlines on the wall boards. On the walls there were also a number of maps of various parts of the country with lists of names and groupings on each of them.

"I'm no expert but it appears from what I can see here someone is making plans for a nationwide organization. There isn't a state or city that isn't mentioned here as well as many areas in other parts of the world."

Lynn said nothing as she continued to peruse through the different parts of what lay scattered about. Finally she sat down and stated, "I think we'd best call the FBI immediately. There's enough material and organizational data here to start a revolution. Look at the files of those computers, they're the best database for a master blackmail campaign as I've ever seen. It's no wonder the Mossad has been concerned about this whole business, especially with the amount of anti-Semitic material I've seen in the last ten minutes."

"That may be true, but there are still great gaps in certain areas here. Both key organizations and figures are notable by their absence. I have the recurring feeling all of this is nothing more than circumstantial evidence in the loosest courtroom. All of this stuff really adds up to nothing if we don't find the master key." As he talked, he moved various documents and memoranda about on one of the table tops. He stopped and looked again.

"Lynn, who is Major General Kenneth Wyssink?"

She raised her head. "Where did you find that name?"

"Here on a memorandum to Chief Justice Hamilton Saunders. And the most interesting thing is a copy of the same thing being sent to the former chairman of the Joint Chiefs, Gerald Bruder."

Lynn rushed to his side. "Scott, could I see that memo?" She took it quickly and scanned the contents. She turned, a grim smile on her lips.

"I've got it, Scott, I know what's taking place. We've got to act fast or we'll be a part of the greatest travesty of justice in the history of this country. Scott, what religious denomination are you affiliated with?"

He was completely puzzled by her seemingly unrelated question. "I was raised Lutheran, but what has that to do with any of this?" he asked.

She was so agitated she could hardly contain herself. "Scott, what would your feelings be if there was proof that the Lutheran Church was instrumental in an attempt to kill a former president and the charge was made in the presence of the head of your church? And that this was a charge which couldn't be answered aside from an unsubstantiated denial!" she pondered.

"Are you saying what I think you're saying?" he asked.

"Yes, I'm talking about the speech by the new Pope tomorrow at the Justice Building in the presence of the chief justice. The day before yesterday, I heard the late senator talking with Saunders about his role in the establishment of the New Freedom Party. I think tomorrow is the key to the whole thing. If they know they have these papers, then the chief justice will go ahead and make his real speech of introduction and expose the role of the Church in the assassination of Lincoln and in so doing destroy any credibility and influence the Catholic Church will ever have in this country. The pope will be standing there like the emperor without any clothes and in his own backyard. Think of the genius of the whole idea. The pope will be exposed as a man without principle or direction. But here's the real ringer, he'd be exposed as an arrogant traitor, as a man willing to condone and sell out his own country and have the arrogance to stand here and see it happen. Even if we destroy all this material, he will be seen and pointed to as a man and a Church under the thumb of the American president. It's a real catch-22 situation." They were both stunned by the ramifications of Lynn's conclusions.

"I'm flabbergasted! And I gather the next step after discrediting the pope and the Church would be shaming him out of the country with his tail between his legs!" Scott quipped and continued, "Finally, there would be the call of the leaders of the Freedom Party for the allegiance of all Catholic Americans away from the Vatican. It's a real classic Fascist move and would show the Freedom Party for who they really are. But you know what, at this stage if the Freedom Party people play their cards right, the rest of America won't care, they will be so wrapped up in their anti-Catholic anger. It's nothing short of a classic move by these people."

"That's right, and then we have a real flashpoint on our hands. This is where the masses come into the picture, thank God!" She paused. "Remember, traditionally when the chips are down, the Catholic Church is viewed by many Jewish people as anti-Semitic. Remember there are more Jewish people living in America than there are in the state of Israel. And if you want to get historical there is the charge that the Catholic Church looked the other way during WWII when the Holocaust was in full swing. They maintain they had nothing to do with it, but the evidence shows the pope at that time, Pius XII, took neither word nor action against it. That's a raw nerve for many Jewish people to this day and isn't too far under the surface. Look at it this way, if a wedge could be driven between American Jews and their view of the Church, that would be a real tear in the American religious mosaic. Scott, that's what this is really all about! Break open these old and very traditional religious and cultural loyalties and you open the door for American fascism to enter and grow rapidly. Besides, and I'm reaching a bit on this part, all the old Southern racists would be clapping their hands and saying, I told you!"

She leaned against a wall shaken by the tightness of her own revelation. "Lynn, how can we stop this thing? Or do you think it's too late?"

She looked at him, her face pale and drawn. "Scott, here's the scary part. Even if we call in the FBI or the CIA there isn't enough time for either to put together our case for them to act. We may be euchred," she responded.

"There is an even scarier proposition. If these people have managed to organize themselves as far as they have to this point, isn't it reasonable to assume they have people in both these organizations?" Lynn was pale as she listened to his words. "Lynn, it seems to me the only place we have to turn to on such short notice is one of their weak areas or where they have overlooked something. I mean precisely the Israeli Mossad."

"Surely you don't think they would get involved in the internal matters of another country, especially here in the US?" she asked.

"Yes, I mean here in America precisely. That's what the Mossad have been most successful at over the years, carrying out their missions in other countries all over the world. If they hadn't mastered this art early, there wouldn't be an Israel today. Remember there wasn't any Jewish homeland for nearly 2,000 years. This is what they do best and could be our ace in the hole for this situation we're in." He added, "I can't think of a situation that involves their self-interest more than this one. Think about it, Lynn, there are overtones of antisemitism all through this material, and for that matter through many parts of US right-wing politics, if the veneer is peeled away. One thing about the Mossad, they have few qualms about others' sensitivities when it comes to their own national interests. I think we should scoop all this material and get it into safe hands before it falls into the wrong hands again," Scott concluded.

"There's someone upstairs. What are we going to do?" There was a note of fear in her voice.

There were excited voices coming from above. He signalled with a finger over his lips and set to work gathering all the material which they placed into a large briefcase she found by a table. Then he remembered the basement entrance where they had been brought into the building. They crept quietly down the hallway to the door at the far end. As they stepped over the body of the man Lynn killed, Scott searched and by luck found a set of keys. The man was clearly dead, his eyes open and staring. Scott looked at the size of the man and the small stature of Lynn and shook his head. Outside they found the old van where it was previously parked. Then they saw the small Honda parked behind the van.

"What are we going to do? There's someone coming down the stairs and they'll be here in a moment," she asked.

Looking about for a second, he said quickly, "Get in the van, quick!"

Throwing the briefcase in the back, they got in and it started immediately with the roar of an old engine with a holey muffler. He shoved it into reverse, slamming the little Honda back, crumpling the front and moving it like snow before a plow. As they backed out into the street, the Honda crashed into a new Buick Lucerne parked at the opposite curb. The van roared off into the dwindling afternoon twilight. Scott pushed the old van to the fifty-mph mark and held it there with one eye for the city police. The traffic was heavy and they were soon swallowed up in the moving mass. Neither said a word as they drove for nearly an hour. Finally they arrived back at the legation and pulled up in the large parking lot next door. He was about to speak to Lynn when two bullets crashed through the windshield, scattering shards of glass over them both. Grabbing her, he covered her with his torso as they crouched down near the floor between the seats.

"There's a gun with some armour-piercing shells under your seat. I heard the driver talking when we were in the van before. It might be still there," she whispered in his ear as he lay on top of her.

He found it and they rolled out the passenger door and lay on the pavement by the curb. For a moment there was only silence. He took the gun and a second clip he'd found and crawled around to the front of the van. Across the street, he saw two cars parked with gun muzzles protruding from the windows. At that moment, firing began with a roar, knocking out the front windows in the van as well as blowing out two front tires. Scott noticed a tree between himself and the first assault car. He whispered to Lynn, who was right behind him and had taken her small revolver from her purse, "You cover me, I'm going to get that lead car."

"For Pete's sake, be careful, they've got automatic weapons in both those cars," she exclaimed.

He nodded and ran across to the tree, bullets chipping at his heels as he ran. Lynn crouched at the van's front fender and laid down a series of covering shots. Scott sprawled behind the tree. He was about twenty feet from the car. One gunman sat in the passenger seat. Peering around the tree, Scott took careful aim and fired three well-placed shots. Three holes were punched in the window and door. There was a sudden commotion inside the car and the sound of more gunfire from the driver's side. Suddenly, the car erupted in a fiery explosion, blowing itself and all in it to pieces. Three men immediately jumped out of the other car and ran towards the legation. Scott had a clammy feeling in his throat. Then there was the unique sound of an Uzi firing. Each of the three running men was cut down as they ran. They slumped to the pavement in motionless mounds soaking it with blood. Two Israeli guards walked over and kicked each body over. One fired another short burst into a still-living attacker. The other came over to Scott and Lynn who were on their feet and said, "Dr. Fleming and Ms. Pollard, please come inside quickly, it's too dangerous and you are needed inside." Holding Lynn close, Scott followed.

Chapter 65

The weather in Toronto was warm and muggy. April was restless looking at the four walls of her hospital room. Tony had his surgery earlier in the morning and she was beside herself waiting for the latest word on his condition. Finally, just after two, Alex walked into the room still dressed in his OR greens. She had fixed her dark hair in a jaunty ponytail and put on a pair of loose slacks and beige blouse Alex had brought her. They were his wife Rhetta's and she had sent them over. As Alex came through the door, April spotted a tiny dark-eyed woman following him. She rushed past Alex and put her arms about April.

"You've probably guessed I'm Rhetta!" she exclaimed in a low voice that sounded much like Lauren Bacall.

"Alex has told me so much about you and everything you've been through, you poor girl. I just had to come over and give you some support. How are you feeling?" As she talked, she pulled two chairs close to the bed and sat down with April on the bed and Alex in the other chair. April found her open and forthright and immediately liked the woman. She imagined her in front of a room full of students and liked her even more.

"Rhetta, I don't know where Tony and I would be without Alex. I know I'd be dead if he hadn't spotted me in the morgue in Santa Domingo. I don't know all the details, but we owe him our lives.

"Alex, how did the surgery go with Tony? I feel bad but I almost forgot to ask," April inquired.

"He's fine. As a matter of fact, he's awake and asking for you. When he gets to the recovery room, I'll take you up to see him," Alex replied. "He came through the surgery with flying colours. When we go up to the recovery, I don't want you to be alarmed by all the apparatus about him. It's all routine. By the way, the surgeon was surprised that there was no brain damage in Tony's case at all. As a matter of fact, the injury was far less severe than we had originally thought. But, as the surgeon said, it is better to err on the side of safety. Besides, he said Tony has the physicality of a horse. The doctor, Pat

Morrison, is one of the best neurologists on the continent. He doesn't mess around. Well, I think they'll have him in recovery by now and we can head down. Just remember, April, you'll see him hooked up to a great variety of exotic equipment. We're a state-of-the-art hospital here and proud of it."

Fifteen minutes later, they arrived in the recovery room and stood by Tony's bedside. He was hooked up to a bank of exotic monitors and assorted gadgetry and tubes. April was filled with the greatest dread. Alex Cameron noted the fear on her face.

"April, please don't worry!" he intoned. "This is all part of the aftermath of neurosurgery. Remember, we were actually working to relieve pressure on his brain. That's serious stuff, no matter how minor. His was the latter but still scary stuff. Go up to the head of the bed; if I know Tony he's been listening to everything we've been saying and wants to talk to you."

Slowly and with great fear, she walked around the bed and to Tony's side. His head was encased in a great swath of bandages but his eyes were open and bright. As soon as he saw her, he reached out a weak hand and clasped hers, drawing her close. She immediately started to sob as she buried her head in his chest. He reached his other arm about her. Only at that moment was April aware how much this big guy had become apart of her life.

"Sorry, April, I didn't think I was hit as hard as I was, but I was always told I had a hard head."

She pulled her head back and looked into his deep blue eyes. They were as bright as ever and she suddenly knew a strange peace as she saw the years of her life spreading out before her with this guy who had come to mean so much.

"April, how are you feeling? You look incredible and I almost want to jump out of bed and tear your clothes off."

She flushed crimson. He turned to Alex and quipped, "Doc, you should see this gal without clothes; I tell you she makes men out of little boys and old men feel half their age!"

April dissolved in a fit of laughter and tears with Alex and Rhetta doubled over in laughter as well. Finally, April collected herself as she realized how with his usual humour Tony had diffused all their tension.

"Tony, you probably overheard April and me talking and you should know. Your surgery went great and it wasn't nearly as serious as we all first thought. You'll be up and about later today and I'll be able to spend time with you this afternoon. We have to go now as the staff want to tidy you up and remember I'll be here at all times."

She kissed him before they left the room.

"I'm sorry, Alex, I usually don't lose it like that but the moment I saw Tony with all that equipment about him, I was finished," April moaned.

"April, for God's sake it was the most natural reaction in the world. He's under the best care possible and besides, with his attitude he'll be up running the halls before the day is out. Wow, what a sense of humour he has; I thought Rhetta was going to pee herself. He just needs to see lots of you. Remember, the both of you are mending and I know what's on the back of his mind. Tony is as about as subtle as a bulldozer. I think you know what I am talking about," he answered.

April flushed crimson again. "Is there something you haven't told me about my condition?" she asked with great apprehension.

"No!" he answered as he stood with April and Rhetta by a window in the hall outside the unit. "Remember, you had a vicious knife wound and while everything is healing fine, I want it to stay that way. It was very serious and you took a hell of a beating. I still can't believe your luck. The knife missed all your major organs except your lung and that is healing beautifully." As he talked, he saw the worry in her eyes.

"Alex, my real concern is about my ability to have children. Will this injury interfere with my ability carrying children?" she asked nervously.

"No, unless you know something we don't know," he answered. "As a matter of fact, you should be able to have a nice set of twin boys by this time next year!" He giggled.

April went pale with anger before she realized he was trying to ease her tension and worry.

"Alex, I think your patients need you." She laughed as she hugged him.

"Please look after Tony, Alex. I don't want to lose him."

"Don't worry, April," Rhetta said in the background. "He cares about the both of you more than you'll ever know!"

Chapter 66

Lynn and Scott were returned to the large apartment at the back of the legation where they'd been staying for the past several days with Martha and the girls. A small man with greying hair and swarthy skin introduced himself to them in the main hallway. They were still visibly shaken by the events in the street outside the legation.

"Let me introduce myself. My name is Josef Safir and I am the head of Israeli security here in America. We must talk, but I think it's important you have some time with your family. I'll be back with my associate in an hour. By the way, here's your briefcase I found in the front seat of the van. One of my men grabbed it after they finished off the attackers." He smiled and left them alone.

Scott and Lynn looked at each other in silence. The trauma of the past few hours and the shock of the attack in the street was overwhelming. Great lines of weariness filled Lynn's pretty face. He pulled her against him and she offered no resistance. As he slipped his arms about her, she buried her face in his chest. As she raised her face to look into his weary eyes, he brushed away strands of her hair and ran a finger down her smooth cheek. They walked back to the apartment, still in silence. She found the warmth of his body both comforting and uplifting. As they entered the apartment, the quietness was broken by a girlish shriek. Little Francie raced in and grabbed them about the knees. She was followed by Angie close at her heels. Scott gathered the girls to them and knew from the look on their faces they knew nothing about the trauma of recent hours nor the events out front. Back in the doorway, Martha stood watching, a great warmth flooding over her.

"There's something Daddy wants to say to both you girls and Grandma, but I think Aunt Lynn wants to have the first words," he said with a certain flush on his face but with a sparkle of happiness in his eyes. Lynn settled Francie on her lap as she talked.

"Your daddy has asked me to be part of your family!"

Immediately little Angie interrupted with great excitement. "I knew it was going to happen! Aunt Lynn is going to become our new mummie." She jumped up and down and chattered away faster than anyone could follow. As Scott watched the little drama play itself out, he felt Lynn's hand clutching his tightly.

Martha came over and put her arms about Lynn and said, "I'm so happy for all of you. Lynn, Scott and the girls have needed someone in their lives for a long time and this is the best news I've ever had. Especially in light of the horrors of the past few days."

Lynn was moved to tears by the outpouring of affection. Holding a lapful of squirming little girls, she tried to speak and did so with great difficulty. "I'm going to have trouble saying this, but it's important I try. All of you have done so much for me and made me happier than I've ever been. Scott, you have that knack of making me feel good about myself again. I want you girls to know how happy you, your daddy and grandma have made me." As she finished talking she started to cry and leaned against Scott's shoulder Martha knelt down and tried to put her arms about the three of them.

There was the sound of an embarrassed shuffle on the apartment doorway. There was the figure of Josef Safir and another man behind him. Martha quickly gathered the girls and ushered them into the back rooms of the apartment over their vehement protests. Then came that moment that caused Lynn to sob joyfully for the next few moments. Little Francie, usually so reticent, called out to Lynn as she was being ushered away by Martha, "Bye, Mummie, I'll see you after you and Daddy talk to that man!"

Lynn fell into Scott's arms with great sobs and her face ashen grey as her control completely broke. It was ten minutes before Lynn regained her composure. She had never been so moved. Scott finally whispered to her, "I've never seen anyone reach that child as you can! You've become the pivotal person in her little life." Lynn only smiled and said nothing. Josef Safir had remained graciously reserved and quiet all through the domestic drama.

"Doctor, I'm sorry to bother you but it's important we get a few things sorted out. You and Ms. Pollard are at the centre of this storm and we need your help."

Scott turned to Lynn and said, "Why don't we share with these gentlemen any information we have and between us we may be able to get a better handle on everything. Besides, it might help you have a better perspective on the whole situation."

Lynn looked at him for a long few minutes and finally responded, "Mr. Safir, I think Dr. Fleming has a good idea. I think we should all sit down and have the discussion he referred to."

The two Israelis looked at each other, smiled and nodded.

"I think that is a very constructive suggestion, Ms. Pollard. It's about three at the moment; we can get together later if you wish in the main lounge and we can get a plan ready for tomorrow. I think we here at the legation are well on top of everything and there are things I want to share with you. One other thing: I can assure you this building is totally free from any bugs and the like. We pride ourselves on having the most secure buildings on earth. In our world situation, we can't afford anything else."

Lynn nodded her approval as she got to her feet as the two Israelis left them alone. She turned to Scott. "Would you mind meeting with them alone? I know that's a lot to ask, but for the first time in years I'm near the end of my string. I want to spend some time with the kids for a few hours and perhaps pull myself together!"

He could see the deep shadows of weariness under her eyes and knew she was dead on in her estimation of how she felt.

Chapter 67

After the two Israelis left, Angie and Francie scampered back into the room and pounced on Lynn seated on a sofa. They settled about her and almost demanded her attention. Scott observed the emerging domestic scene, smiled to himself and started to walk when Lynn called out.

"Scott, the girls have talked me into playing with them in the pool before the sun goes down. Why don't you join us? I think they'd love to have you with us." There was a sparkle in her eyes daunting him to join them.

"Somehow, I get the feeling that I don't have much choice in the matter and I'm sure it's all the girls' doing. I've got a couple of things I want to talk over with the Israeli security men, then I'll join you."

"Whose idea it was to ask you is a secret between the girls and me and we'll never tell, so there," snorted Lynn with a giggle.

"Daddy, since Aunt Lynn is going to become our new mummie, she'll need part of your room to sleep in! Maybe you can sleep in the spare bedroom or the den downstairs."

"Hummmph!" Scott muttered to himself as he realized the futility of countering his daughter's logic. "Why do I get the feeling that I'm being set up?" Shaking and chuckling to himself, he waved as he left the room.

As he did, he heard Lynn's cheery voice call out, "See you later, Daddy," followed by a gale of feminine laughter.

Downstairs, he found Yigal Burgstein in the main office.

"Dr. Fleming, please come in and have a seat. By the look on your face I see you want to talk."

Scott sat across from him at the large coffee table. "I want to thank you for looking after all of us in this time of great danger. I shudder to think what might have happened if your people hadn't come along when they did."

"Doctor, I would like to say the only reason for us to host you and your family here at the legation was for your own safety, but that isn't the truth. At the moment there is a difficult situation between ourselves and these two groups: the Order of the Red Rose and the American Freedom Party. The truth is if we hadn't become involved, Israeli–US relations might have been at the lowest point in our short history." There was an urgency to his words as he spoke.

"I'm afraid I don't follow your reasoning," Scott replied.

"Doctor, I know you're aware of the Lincoln material Ms. Pollard has in her possession. Whether most of that material is authentic isn't the point, especially the Surratt paper. The Red Rose people believed they are real and wanted them eliminated along with anyone who had knowledge of them. That's where we were dragged into the whole mess. Two of our key agents in Europe were killed for reasons we could never sort out. Then we got a message from Dublin from the one double agent we had as a mole in the ranks of the Red Rose Brotherhood. In the middle of other matters, he dug up info on the new American Freedom Party. In turn, it was looking for a way to capture a large percentage of the American electorate in the next American election."

"But what advantage would there be to have you and the Red Rose people at each others' throats?" Scott asked.

"That's where the matter gets messy and complicated. Remember, the Freedom Party wanted to be squeaky clean in the eyes of the general public. How can they do this? Well, one way is to divide your enemies and get them at each others' throats. If they could pit the two of us at each other, they could sit back and watch everything sort itself out. This is what happened almost as if they were calling all the shots on both sides. But there was a fly in the ointment, our man in Dublin. Unfortunately, he had to pay with his life."

"I'm afraid I don't follow you on that point," Scott replied.

"This is where matters became cloudy. Our agent knew what was afoot and sent a message to us that there was more than one group behind the scheme to steal and use the Lincoln material for their own ends. Unfortunately, by the time it reached us, he was dead. The Red Rose people here in America went into action and there was nothing left for us to do but stop them. Simply put, we didn't know how much they knew or what they were going to do, so we had no option but to eliminate them. At the same time there were agents from the Freedom Party on the move so we had to watch our backs. Our main advantage was a simple one, neither group was aware of our involvement until we had achieved much of what we wanted to do."

"What puzzles me was the involvement of the couple in California and then Lynn here in the city," Scott asked.

"That's where matters became very difficult. The graduate research team in California have been working on the subject for many months and felt there was enough evidence to start reaching some general conclusions regarding the involvement of the Catholic Church in the Lincoln conspiracy. They worked in complete openness because of the age of the original crime and the fact for over 150 years people have been digging around in the dust for new clues from the past. No one cared. Even most of their evidence was based on old evidence. It was the perfect cover. They even went to the FBI and were yawned out of the office. Then in one crucial moment everything changed in a flash. your friend Ms. Pollard made that sensational discovery not only of those pictures of the new conspirators but, most crucial of all, the Surratt papers. In less than a week, the word spread to the good Father Maguire who happened to have a contact working on the California team. This person was also a member of the Jesuit Order. Unwittingly he gave the word of the discovery to Maguire and it was passed on to a cell of the Red Rose Brotherhood. There was not too much worry until Ms. Pollard passed copies of all the material on to Frank Baird. That's when everything ignited. Remember it has only been less then two months since she discovered the material. That pretty well brings us to the present. The first trouble came when the Freedom Party team attacked the research office in California and a day later came the attack on the priests in Dublin, where your man was killed . Tony and April's trip to Santo Domingo no doubt saved their lives as well."

"So that was why Lynn was dragged into it so quickly! That's where I was fuzzy on the details," Scott added.

"Simply because Baird knew the bulldog nature of the woman. Don't forget he's known her all her life and figured she'd not stop until she had dug up the whole truth! By the way, we've talked to a lot of people who know your friend well and she's one of the most respected ladies in her field. The only comment I hear is she is a very private person. I would think you will help fill a real gap in her life," Burgstein added.

"I must get down to the pool and talk with her so we'll know each other's mind when we meet you tonight."

"That's wise, Doctor. I'll fill you both in on what we think is going to transpire at the Justice Building with the chief justice and the new pope."

Scott smiled and left the office. Several minutes he arrived at the pool wearing an old pair of shorts with a towel over his shoulders. Lynn was sprawled on a white plastic lounger wearing a modest one-piece someone at the legation had loaned her. The girls were splashing and frolicking in the shallow end of the pool. Lynn smiled but made no attempt to get up.

"Where do they get the energy? I'm exhausted. Besides, I think I've swallowed half the pool!"

"Well, what did I tell you about the girls? They'll tire you out before you realize it, then try to charm you into spending more time with them." He smiled as he talked. "That's why they're so hard on my mother, yet she never complains."

"Well, I wouldn't have it any other way. I'm so happy to have them a part of my life." As she talked, she laid a hand on his arm. "Did you learn anything from Burgstein?"

"As a matter of fact I did. There were connections he put in place that I wasn't even aware of. I'll fill you in after supper and it'll give a different perspective on a few things. Let's enjoy the kids and the pool until then."

"Scott, did you know Francie hates you being a doctor! I'm beginning to realize how much the girls miss you when you're not around," Lynn ventured casually.

"I know, and I keep thinking I've been missing their most formative years," Scott added.

"That brings up something I've been wanting to talk about with you for some time. You know that not having children has been one of the big regrets in my life but something I had made peace with myself about before I met you. Now the whole thing has come thundering back. Now I want to make sure I can spend as much time with the girls as possible!" As she talked he could see her beginning to choke up.

"Well, there's still time to make up for a certain amount of past time. The girls have already come to me and asked me if it would be possible for them to have a baby sister."

She looked up, her face pale and anxious. "You're not serious!" she quipped.

"Why wouldn't I be serious? There is no reason why we shouldn't try!" he replied. The look of wonderment on Lynn's face was one he would never forget.

"No one has ever suggested before that I should even consider having a baby. My ex wanted to have nothing to do with kids or me working. The marriage foundered on the former as much as the latter. That's the other issue I wanted to talk about. I want to spend as much time with the girls as possible and that might mean I cut back on my hours at the office," Lynn pondered.

"I don't see there's much to discuss. Cut back if that is what you wish, or for that matter resign. You've put more than your share of time there anyhow.

I know where the girls will want you to be," Scott mused. "Oh, yes, one other issue: I like you in the other swimsuits more than this one!"

"I should have known some comment would be coming. You'd like to see more of me and less of the suit," she added laughing as he picked her up and walked to the water's edge, calling out as he walked, "Girls, come over and see Aunt Lynn do her fancy dive."

"Scott, remember one thing, if I go in so do you," she said as she grabbed him tight about the neck. Remembering her unique strength, he thought the better and jumped in the pool with her still in his arms. They came to the surface at the feet of two agitated girls at the pool's edge.

"Daddy, I wish you wouldn't do things like that with Aunt Lynn. You might hurt her and you wouldn't want to do that!" Angie said with a great earnestness.

"You're right, sweetheart, I couldn't live with myself if something did indeed happen to her!" As he spoke, he turned to find Lynn looking at him, her eyes shining.

Chapter 68

Everyone sat around a large table in the conference room in the Israeli Legation. Scott and Lynn were the last to arrive and seated themselves on a leather sofa by the side wall not far from the centre of the room.

Yigal Burgstein called for everyone's attention.

"Dr. Fleming, I want to thank you and Ms. Pollard for coming. It is vital we get matters talked over because they are evolving so quickly and we are all involved. This is especially true in light of what we suspect is going to happen tomorrow at the Justice Building and the visit of the new pope. Before that, however, let me introduce our two guests. Dr. Scott Fleming is the chief resident in neurology at the Presbyterian Hospital here in the city. Ms. Lynn pollard is the chief researchist at the Kodak Lab. Both of them have been heavily involved in the situation as it has developed from the beginning and I have kept the rest of you informed as it has come across my desk. The other guest you may already know, James Cleveland of the FBI. Yes, Dr. Fleming, I see you have a question to ask." Burgtein saw Scott raise his hand.

"I'm a newcomer to this world of espionage and counterespionage and I would appreciate some of your insights. What the hell do you think is going to happen and where is it headed?"

"Dr. Fleming, we believe the original intent is to be found in the speech to be given tomorrow by the chief justice honouring the first election of an American to the throne of St. Peter. In that speech, by using the Lincoln material and the Surratt papers, he will attempt to humiliate the new pope on a public podium here in Washington by showing papal duplicity in the assassination of Lincoln. Other examples of their interferences in the historical developments in other countries will be cited."

There was a stunned silence in the big room as the effect of his words sunk in. Finally, James Cleveland spoke in a voice unusually shrill and yet at the same time, calming. "Over at the FBI headquarters, we have been aware of these developments for the past few weeks. However, without proof, there is nothing we could do. This the Freedom Party is very much aware of and as a result have their security lid screwed down tight. Yet, on the other hand with the various unrest and several killings about the country we had to get involved or the general public would be up in arms."

Finally, Lynn Pollard, who had been sitting quietly with her hand tight in Scott's, spoke up. "As I'm sure you all know, I more or less stumbled into the middle of this mess by handing over several pictures of material I had found to Frank Baird. Have these pictures been the catalyst for all these killings?" There was a clear note of pathos and pain in her voice as she spoke, her low voice shaky but vibrant.

"Whatever you do, Ms. Pollard, don't blame yourself, even though I can see how you could reach such a conclusion." The speaker was one of the legation's staff, Nahum Katzir. "Our security service in this country has been aware of the development and growth of this Freedom Party for several years now. They have been carefully watching and waiting for the opportunity to make a legitimate political move for some time now and in their eyes your discovery was a golden moment. As a matter of fact, it was their moment of opportunity. By discovering a way to belittle the Roman Catholic Church in America, they felt they had been handed a gift. Be it far from this group to look a gift horse in the mouth. Now all they needed was some hard evidence to back up their plan. Your discovery of the Lincoln material was their answer to a prayer. The Surratt paper is the cornerstone of their whole case. All you did, Ms. Pollard, was to give them some tangible evidence for their case."

"Mr. Katzir, what is going to happen tomorrow? Why doesn't the FBI simply go out and shut this whole Freedom Party down? Ms. Pollard and I have come under fire and almost been killed as late as this afternoon on the lawn of this legation. Where do we go from here?" Scott asked, a bite to his words.

"Dr. Fleming, I'll tell what we're up against. First of all, we can't turn the FBI loose on the party because they haven't done anything illegal as yet. Close to the edge of the law, but not illegal. They're experts making the law work for their own purposes. We feel the chief justice is going to make his speech even if it is on the basis of the copies some of their members have already seen. He is a gifted orator from the old school, and why he was chosen and not the vice president we're not sure. Off the record, I think there's something in his speech that's some sort of a trigger, but for what I really don't know. By the way, Ms. Pollard, you'll be happy to know that your former worker, Tony Cassell, and his friend April were rescued and flown from Santa Domingo to Toronto where she is recovering in hospital. We have received the material they had and it is safely hidden away. I believe you have the rest yourself, Ms. Pollard."

Lynn was visibly very relieved and broke into a big smile of relief. "Thank God. I was worried sick and then there was the report both of them had been killed."

"Those reports came directly from my office in a direct attempt to protect them. I'm sorry if it was upsetting for you," Yigal Burgstein intoned.

Scott continued the conversation. "Mr. Burgstein, I want to know two things: where do we go from here and what is going to happen tomorrow?" There was an edge to his words that demanded an answer.

There was a murmuring amongst the Israelis and finally, Burgstein turned to the others. "As usual, Doctor, you cut the discussion to the chase! What I'm going to tell you is, for the most part, classified, but since most of you have been on things since the beginning, I feel you should know what the rest of you may know in part. The intent of the American Freedom Party was and is to blackmail and destroy the influence of the Catholic Church here in America. They narrowly escaped with their lives on several occasions and are now willing to testify in court. One of them, a girl, hid in the office in California and heard a party member talk about the whole purpose of the attacks before he shot the person he was telling."

Both Scott and Lynn were shocked by the magnitude of the plan that was afoot. Then Moshe Arnon took up the discussion.

"The FBI has asked us if we would finish this plan of ours off because of our involvement and mainly because the Freedom Party is still basically unaware of that involvement. We plan to issue an ultimatum to the Freedom Party about four hours before the speech at the Justice Building. It will suggest if they go ahead and the chief justice makes the speech, then we will threaten to produce evidence of their violent involvement in various places over the past few days. Finally, we will use the threat that they are first anti-Catholic and most of all as far as we are concerned, anti-Semitic. These witnesses will testify and produce evidence that they have heard and seen enough to implicate both the senator and Frank Baird as well as the chief justice."

Scott Fleming could sit still no longer. He was flabbergasted. Then Lynn spoke quietly. "Not only do you have these witnesses, but you have me!"

The tension was thick in the room.

"The other day when I was over at Baird's home, he was under the impression I was their latest recruit to the Freedom Party. I happened to overhear a conversation between these three men. I think I was so overwhelmed I put the idea of what they were discussing out of my mind. Remember my family and I have known the man and his family all my life. Now I find he was directly responsible for sending my father back to the front lines in Vietnam for the third time. My father was killed three weeks later. Then Frank set me up with an assignment for the party, a date with the good senator. He saw himself as a real lady killer! He seemed thrilled that Frank was able to bring me into the party."

She turned and said to Scott, "Scott, remember I asked you to trust me about the dress I was wearing the other night? I came directly from the hotel where I met him here to the legation. I thought I had killed him but he has more lives than a cat. I went there to see if I could get to the bottom of this mess but learned even more then I bargained for. In a nutshell, he said that his party felt American democracy had become unworkable and they were ready to move to modify or replace it. Apparently this is one of the premises in the party's founding charter and the real thrust against the Catholic Church. He also mentioned they want to cut all Jewish influence in the US as well."

This news was a shock even to the hardened Yigal, whose grandparents had perished in the Nazis' death camps. Before he could speak, James Cleveland spoke up.

"This is precisely why we at the bureau feel it is imperative we let the Mossad run with the ball. In this manner we will be able to approach the whole matter with clean hands when it is over, and can charge members of the Freedom Party with treason. Secondly, much of what transpires will never be made public by the Mossad. The Mossad is covered, as they are a shadowy group to begin with and just following leads that led to death in their ranks of several of their agents in various parts of the world. Having the Mossad do this will save us a lot of loose ends later and you know what the media do with loose ends. We also want to clean up this Red Rose Brotherhood in this country and that's one of the reasons President Henderson is meeting with the new pope after the speech and will not be present the day the chief justice does his thing. The other reason is the most classified of all and I can't go into that here. Suffice to say, there will be a general housecleaning of the government by the president after he meets with the pope. We want to clean up this Red Rose group and to protect the large Catholic population in this country from this inner cancer. The head of the bureau had been in touch with the Vatican and has its full blessing from the new pope down. In a very strange way, your Mossad is working for both the Vatican and the US government. Both the Red Rose Group and the Freedom Party are pariah groups and the president wants them removed. That's the name of that tune. The Mossad has his full blessing to do what they must to get the job done!" As he spoke, he looked about the room at the shocked faces. He continued, "If the senator is out of the way, it remains to be seen how the remainder of the party will be dealt with. The only loose canon is this Frank Baird. We have no idea where he is at the present time!" There was a moment of silence as everyone present absorbed the gravity of the situation. Finally, Yigal Burgstein spoke as the discussion drew to a close.

"We will issue the ultimatum early tomorrow morning and deliver it to Baird's home here in the city. It appears to be the de facto headquarters for the new party. If we get no answer within the hour, we will put into play any action plan to eliminate all these key people. As far as the US public is concerned, they will never know the whole truth of the situation and we feel that is for the best. I would recommend to you that you destroy all the Lincoln material as soon as possible. I think the most dangerous piece would be the Surratt paper you found in the back of the picture of the conspirators. Unless, there are any more questions, let's call it a night,;we've been here for nearly three hours. Tomorrow will be a tense day for all of us. I've set twelve noon as the absolute deadline for the ultimatum, otherwise what's the point of sending it out. Remember, please stay in the grounds of the legation for safety sake. I'll meet all of you here in this room at that time and I'll share the next step in our plans with you." With these words, he turned and left the room.

Within a few minutes everyone except Lynn and Scott had left as well. Scott sat down beside her. Her hands were folded in her lap and she stared out through the side window. Finally, she turned and whispered, "Scott, have I been the cause of all of this? By giving those pictures to Frank Baird, I seem to have set off a horror story." Her words came out with great sadness and effort.

"Lynn, look at me!" he injected. "These people were looking for something to pin their future on and you happened to come along with what you found."

"You're sure?" she responded. "If I thought I was responsible for the deaths of all those people, I don't know what I would do!"

"Look, for Christ's sake, this thing is bigger than all of us, so don't go blaming yourself for it. Come on, let's go for a walk in the back garden, we need the air after being cooped up in here."

Chapter 69

Frank Baird was beside himself. He had given orders that all loose ends were to be tied off and they had come to naught. The second attempt on Lynn Pollard and her doctor friend had ended in disaster. Then there was the case of the couple in the Caribbean. He received reports they were both dead, yet there was no sign of the Lincoln material that was supposed to be retrieved from their room. He saw the photo of the girl's body and the death certificate. There was the case of their two assailants. As they were escaping, they were killed without so much as a reaction. No local Dominican could have done that so efficiently. Now, he had in his person information the Israeli Mossad were involved. There was no reasonable explanation for that to have happened. A knock came at his office door.

"Yes, come in," he snarled.

A short older man walked quickly into the room. Baird looked up from his desk.

"Freeman, it's about time you got here, get over here and sit down. You'd better be able to tell me what the hell is going on. As it is, the shit's going to hit the fan." Taking a seat across from Baird's desk, he got straight to the point.

"We've had a real problem with our operatives. A new group has been breaking in on us and they're a real bunch of professionals." He spoke with a slurring voice, the result of too many years of smoking and heavy drinking. As he spoke, he fished into his pocket for a cigarette and lit up. Baird hated smoking but ignored it this time.

"Yeah, we know all about these people, they're members of the Israeli Mossad, as deadly and efficient as they come. What the hell happened in Santa Domingo? We thought the guy and his girlfriend were both killed," Baird asked.

"That's what we thought. Jake and Sam, the two who did the job were two of our best. They were leaving the grounds of the villa when they were killed, each with one shot." Freeman continued, "I was there and waiting in the car.

271

If I had waited any longer, I would have been killed as well. Several hours later, I bribed the official at the Santa Domingo morgue and got in for a look at the girl . She was deader than patty's pig. She was lying on the slab with Jake's big knife still stuck in her and wasn't even washed for a post mortem. The official said they weren't going to do one as she was such a mess. They buried her the next morning in an unknown grave. The guy's the one I'm not sure about. They couldn't find his body and feel he tried to escape in the water and probably drowned."

"What do you mean you're not sure?" Baird asked bluntly.

"There was an Israeli Hercules that flew out late the next morning but there was a great commotion before it took off," Freeman replied.

"So what's so unusual about that? Israeli planes fly all over the world all the time, big deal!"

"What's so unusual is that the plane made an unscheduled stop in Toronto on the way back to Israel," Freeman replied.

"You'd better have a good explanation for wasting my time with a far fetched story like this one," Baird growled.

"What would you say if I told you there were two wounded patients on board that Israeli plane that landed in Toronto and who were taken to a Toronto hospital upon landing?" Freeman almost glowed as he recounted the story.

"Can you prove all this? Your track record so far stinks and it's a wonder I don't shoot you myself here on the spot!"

"Well, think about this. How many Israeli Hercules aircraft land in Toronto every day with people like April and Tony Casselstein on board and under heavy armed guard. Mr. Baird, I don't know how they did it, but somehow they staged their own deaths, escaped and are now in Toronto recovering in a hospital. Like I said, I saw the girl in the morgue and could have sworn she was dead. Hell, they even buried someone and still she escaped." Freeman fell silent.

Frank Baird was stunned but quickly recovered. "Now, we've got to get to them and make sure they don't say a word to anyone. You don't think there is a chance the Mossad would feed us this information to lure us into the open to finish us off?" Baird asked, still shocked that such a scheme could be pulled off.

"Mr. Baird, I've ordered four of our top people to Toronto and they should be heading to the hospital as we speak to finish the job. It should be done before the hour is up."

"You'd better be goddamned right or you'll be needing a mortician yourself—I've had enough of these blunders!" Baird replied.

"Mr. Baird, what about the other woman, the one in the city here? I think her name is Pollard, I thought we had her in the bag when we found out she wasn't one of our people," Freeman asked.

"She's a horse of a different colour," Baird added. "It has turned out she is one of the deadliest judo people in the country. It's something to do with an attack and rape incident a few years ago. She's already killed several of our people, including the good senator, which in turn saved us from having to do the job. Apparently, he tried to get into her pants and she threw him down a set of stairs and broke his neck. I always thought he was more trouble than he was worth. Any man who would have his own wife iced the way he did is nothing better then an animal."

"Don't you think we should get rid of her since she knows more than anyone else about those pictures and the Surratt papers?" Freeman asked.

"You worry about the chief justice tomorrow and nothing else. I've known this girl since she was a baby and I'm going to take her out myself. Besides we have three of our people getting into the Israeli Legation where they are staying at the moment. I've given orders to kill everyone except the girl and bring her to me. I'm a believer in the old saying 'if you want something important done, do it yourself.' Now get the hell out of here and make sure those people in Toronto are eliminated as soon as possible."

Chapter 70

As April returned from the washroom, the morning sun streamed through her hospital room window. She was dressed and beginning to feel like her old self. The legation people in Toronto had brought her some clothes and she was ready to go down and see Tony. The previous evening, he sat up for the first time since his surgery and she spent an hour with him. Leaving her room, she walked to the elevator and went down to the first floor where Tony was still in the ICU unit. As she entered the unit, she was met at the desk by one of the duty nurses.

"Hi, Mrs. Casselstein. I tried to get your room but there was no answer. I guess you were on the way down. Several people from the Canadian Security Service were here an hour ago and wanted to talk to your husband."

"Where is he? I see his bed is empty," April replied.

"Oh, we took him to a room across the hall. He wanted to get out of the unit and we needed the space here. Mind you we'll probably catch the devil from Dr. Cameron."

April left the unit and went across the busy hall but there was no one there either. A cold chill came over April. What was wrong? She looked up and down the hall but there was only equipment and extra beds to be seen. She knew there was a critical shortage of care people in the Canadian hospitals but this was ridiculous, she thought. Finally, she spotted a nurses' aide cleaning up a bed three rooms from Tony's room.

"Have you seen my husband? He was in room 234, back there?" she asked.

"No, ma'am, he went down to the cafeteria about five minutes ago with two rough-looking men, but he said it was OK and that they were business associates," the aide answered. "Is there something wrong, Mrs. Casselstein?"

"Is there something wrong? Yes, my husband's life is in great danger! Please call the police quickly and pray that we're not too late."

Racing down the hall, April heard a loud crash from a room next to the elevator. Shoving the door open, she came on a scene she would remember the rest of her life. In the corner a young orderly lay on the floor, his head twisted at a weird angle. His eyes were open and stared emptily. Tony was half out of a bed and a man was sprawled across him, his face covered in blood. As April opened the door, a second man was pointing a gun at Tony as he struggled to stay sitting up in the bed. She threw herself at him from behind, knocking him off balance. With his free arm he tried to shove her aside but she tackled him again and he stumbled into the hall. As he got to his feet, he swung and fired to April's direction. As she saw him move, she sprawled herself on the floor and rolled under Tony's bed. Everything was happening so fast he was unable to utter a word. The gunman was about to fire a second bullet in her direction when a bullet caught him in the arm and sent him sprawling on the floor. Climbing to his feet quickly, he fired two shots down the hall. One caught a young nurse high on the right side of her chest and slammed her against the wall. She slowly slid to the floor, leaving a smear of blood on the wall. The gunman turned and ran down the hallway and up a narrow flight of stairs. Struggling against the pain of his shattered arm, he climbed to the top of the stairs and found himself on the roof of the tenth floor.

He heard feet running in the distance. Looking over the roof's edge, he saw nothing but an empty parking lot ten floors below. Sensing a lull, he inserted a new clip in his revolver. Meanwhile the pain in his arm was dulling his senses. Yet all he could do was wait and see.

He heard movement behind him. It reminded him of the many hours he spent on the party's training range in Iowa. As he whirled, he squeezed the trigger, the revolver firing at the moment of seeing. The young police officer had no chance with such speed. The round caught him in the middle of the chest and he immediately collapsed. His partner threw his gun to the roof and raised his arms high in the air.

"Alright, I give up, where the Christ did you learn to shoot like that? No one can aim and fire that quickly!" he gasped with fear in his voice.

Meanwhile in Tony's room, April rolled out from under the bed, her side aching but she gave it no heed. She grabbed Tony and held him tight as she heard him gasping from the effort of moving. He looked her in the eyes and whispered, "Girl, you saved my life! That bastard had me dead centre and he's a real pro. He broke that orderly's neck with one twist. Thank God you came along when you did."

"Tony, for a moment I thought I was too late when I saw him raise his gun!" She sobbed quietly. He put his arms about her as he felt his strength ebbing fast. She helped him lie back on the bed. Only then did she notice the great expanse of blood all over Tony and the bed. He saw her looking about.

"That's his blood, not mine, April," he said pointing to a crumpled body on the opposite side of the bed and which she hadn't seen before. " I don't know where I got the strength to tag him like that but I guess all those hours of judo finally paid off. The guy bled like a stuck pig," Tony quipped.

Back on the roof, the young policeman was forced at gunpoint to stand on the edge facing out over the hospital parking lot.

"Remember all I have to do fire one shot and you're headfirst into the ground down there. Now, who in hell told you we were upstairs!" At this point the gunman made his only mistake. He took his eyes off the stairwell for a moment. The Mossad guard had removed his shoes and crept forward on sock feet. Suddenly the gunman sensed something. He spoke without turning. "You Israelis are pretty slow, I'd have thought you would have been here before now. Drop your gun or the cop goes headfirst into the lot below."

There was no reply from behind him. He heard nothing else. Was he hearing things. Was the pain from the wound in his arm clouding his senses? He faced a decision, should he gamble and turn or should he ignore it? Still there was no sound. Yet he knew the Israeli was there.

He suddenly whirled firing as he came about. The Israeli was less then twenty feet from him. In a millisecond before he stopped and fired, he knew he had lost by the smallest of margins. The Mossad agent's bullet caught him on the left temple as he came about and blew out the right side of his head. He fell in a bloody heap. Meanwhile, the policeman had lost his balance, fallen over the edge and was hanging by one hand to a steel eve trough.

"Hang on and give me your other hand and I'll pull you back over the edge," the Israeli called out as he reached for his right hand. At first it was no use. The cop's grip was slipping and starting to fall away.

He called out, "Tell Alma I love her and wanted to grow old with her! Tell the kids I love them!" he gasped as he felt his grip slipping from the ledge.

"Shut up and grab my hand. Keep talking and you'll not have the strength to hang on. Now grab it, bonehead." The young cop flailed wildly but missed several times. He was weakening and his grip slipping.

"Come on, put your heart into it, I'm not staying here forever!" snapped the agent. The cop gave one final desperate lunge and the agent grabbed his wrist as his grip on the ledge slipped away. The cop swung free at the end of the agent's arm.

"Come on, grab my wrist, you want me to do all the work? For two cents, I'd let you go!" The cop looked up, anger in his eyes. As he did he closed his hand around the agent's wrist and was quickly yanked up and over the ledge to safety. Back on the roof, they both slumped down with the tension of the moment.

"I owe you gratitude and an apology. You were trying to pull me back over the ledge and all I was entertaining was a death wish. That makes me both an ass and a fool," the cop mumbled.

"Look, we never know how any of us will react when we're in such a situation. Several years ago, I had a young woman in the same situation as you and she gave up and fell. Talk about a death wish and there was nothing I could do. Try living with that for a while. I fought the battle inside for two years before I was able to put it behind me. I kept seeing her face at night and when I was alone. Liquor and I became great friends. Thank God you weren't thinking like her, besides you'd have messed up a good parking lot!" The cop slumped back on his elbows and snickered to himself. Meanwhile, the agent knelt by the side of the other cop who lay sprawled on the roof near the top of the stairs.

"I'm afraid your partner is dead. That last gunman was a crack shot and as good as I've seen. That guy used the same technique on me as he did on your partner and that was his fatal mistake. He turned the same way which I thought he would and fired as he did. If I'd missed, I'd be dead. His calibre don't miss."

"Jesus Christ, we were up against a real pro!" the cop muttered as he looked down at the dead gunman sprawled in a huge spreading pool of blood.

"No, this guy wasn't just a pro, he was an international hitman, the best there is. If I hadn't run up against his type before, I'd be the one lying there instead of him. He was a far better shot than me. I gambled and won and he lost and that's the name of that tune," the agent replied.

Back in the main body of the hospital, April watched as Alex Cameron finished examining Tony. She walked beside the gurney as he was wheeled back into the ICU. Alex finally turned and took her hand.

"April, Tony is one tough young man. If I didn't know better, I'd say the trauma of the surgery did him the world of good. He's in such good shape, I'm going to recommend he be put in a private room. The only problem are the knuckles I think he broke when he hit that gunman who tried to smother him. He hit that guy so hard he killed him; I can't figure where he got the strength this soon after surgery. The blow shattered the man's nose and drove it back into his brain. He was dead immediately.

"Tony, you can start walking by yourself immediately from what I can see, but no bending over or quick moves. Besides, you can get lots of help from April here; she's dying to talk to you."

"Alex," Tony inquired, "what about the other guy who came after me?"

"Oh, yes, he was shot by the other man on the roof but not before he killed one of the policeman here to protect you both. This Freedom Party are a ruthless bunch but we're damned lucky the Mossad is protecting us." As he left, he gave April a kiss on the cheek.

"April, take care of our friend here and I'll see you both tomorrow!"

Chapter 71

It was the warmest Friday in the capital in twenty years and a heat haze hung over the trees. Scott, Lynn and the family were packed and ready to go before eight at the legation. They were quickly ushered into a van by Yigal Burgstein and his agents. They were each given revolvers and told to use them if necessary. All five of them were placed in the back of the large extended Ford van which quickly sped off into the heavy morning traffic.

From the front passenger seat Yigal turned. "I'm sorry to be so secretive but we have to be so careful about security about this whole business. We're taking you to a small airport in the country and you'll be told where you're going when you're airborne. That's all I can tell you for the moment." Suddenly there was a loud buzz from a cell phone. Yigal picked it up and talked at length for several minutes, his voice rising and falling in intensity. Finally he turned to Scott and Lynn. Martha and the girls were in the fourth seat back and deeply engrossed in some form of card game.

"That was the legation on the phone. We were right to be careful; there has been a rocket attack on our legation and a third of the staff were killed. The building is presently in flames and there were snipers firing into the building from across the street. They are presently under full siege by a police tactical squad and the Marines have been called in. In a nutshell, all hell has broken loose and we were lucky to have gotten you out when we did."

Scott and Lynn sat stunned as the van sped through the busy city streets and finally out into the country. Scott looked at Lynn and grimaced. "You were right when you said last evening you would be glad when this nightmare is over. Here we go all over again. I hope the killing is finished." His face showed deep lines of weariness as he leaned back in the hard seat of the speeding van. He looked about them as they sped through the countryside but had no idea where they were.

After an hour of steady driving, the van passed through a clump of trees that covered over a hundred acres. Suddenly, the road opened up at the edge of a small airfield. There was only one large hanger and a single paved runway. At the end of the tarmac sat an El Al Boeing 757 sitting with its loading ramp down. Several crew members were working about the landing gear and one was checking a panel on the right turbine. Yigal turned to everyone in the van and stated, "I would like everyone to hurry to get on board as quickly as possible so we can get airborne. Later, the stumpy Boeing was cruising at thirty thousand feet with brilliant sunlight streaming through the small side windows. The girls had settled into seats on either side of their grandmother and were busy with colouring books. Lynn sat with Scott and waited for Yigal to return from the cabin where he had gone as soon as the jet was airborne. Suddenly, Yigal was back in the main cabin and seated himself across from Scott and Lynn.

"Well, I guess this is what you might call show time. I feel bad for all the haste and mystery but the danger around the legation in Washington was simply too great to take any chances. At the present time we're over the Atlantic and heading due eastward . We will refuel in Lisbon and fly on to Rome and the Vatican!"

Lynn Pollard almost fell out of her seat. "The Vatican and Rome!" she gasped. "Mr. Burgstein, what the hell is going on, that's the last place I'd expect to be going. I'm getting weary of all the mystery—one thing always seems to be leading to another!"

"That's right and you have every right to feel as you do!" Yigal added over the dull hum from the plane's turbines.

"Would it be possible for us to have the whole picture of what's going on, for better or worse? I know I speak for everyone here," Scott asked.

"Of course, Doctor, we've kept you poor people in the dark far too long as it is. You're going to Rome and then to a beach-side resort on the west side of Italy about a hundred miles from the capital. This was directly as a suggestion of the new pope."

"The more I see of this whole scenario, the more confusing it becomes. Why for Christ's sake would you be taking us to Rome on an Israeli plane at the suggestion of the pope, an American-born one at that?" Scott said tersely.

"Mr. Burgstein," injected Lynn, "over the past week, I've had my life in danger several times and been forced to kill two people as well. I've have a lot of issues to work through as a result of that and I think you owe us some sort of an explanation if nothing else." As he watched her talk, Scott's face paled at her mention of the killings she was involved in. She noticed the shock in his face and addressed her next comments to him. "Yes, Scott, I killed two people in the past week, for which I have no regret but it is still a shock when you take a human life, especially with your bare hands!" Turning back to

Burgstein, she added, "Besides, there are three other people on this plane who lives are deeply intermeshed with these events as well."

"You'll have no argument on any of that score from me. Up until this very moment, I've been acting on the direct and specific orders of our prime minister. Under no circumstances was I permitted to inform you of the details of the overall situation but I think the time has come to violate that directive!

"One of the first directives of the new pope was to get a handle on this clandestine group, the Red Rose Brotherhood. There have been several top-secret meetings between the pope and our prime minister during the last month to try and do this. The pope wants to rid the Church of this group once and for all. However, no one ever suspected violence would enter the picture. When one of our long-standing moles in the Jesuit Order was killed two weeks ago at a meeting in Dublin, the lid blew off. There was no one in the Catholic Church the pope could turn to, and then he remembered his long-standing friendship with our prime minister. He contacted him in Tel Aviv directly and then matters proceeded and quickly."

"Good God," Scott gasped, "this gets scarier by the minute. How did the Freedom Party get involved in this whole business? This is where it starts to get scary."

"They were the spark that started the whole thing rolling. Their contact was one of the priests who is a fanatic zealot to say the least. As far as we can tell, he was the real founder of the Freedom Party and the one who dreamed up the whole idea to blame the killing of Lincoln on the Red Rose Brotherhood and the Jesuit Order. How he could equate that with the good health of the Church I'm not sure. However, I have a feeling he was nothing more then an embittered zealot. As you know, they can be the most dangerous."

"I can see where most of the pieces fit into the puzzle, but where does our trip to Rome fit into the picture?" Lynn asked.

"That's where the trickiest chapter in the whole story comes into play. Your coming to Rome is at the specific orders of the White House and the Vatican." Burgstein paused with a slight smile on his face, a person knowing he was in total control of the present situation.

"You people were called to be the hatchet boys!" Scott snapped.

"Yes, Doctor, and we have always done what we do very well and charge a still price."

"You're saying there will be a lot of IOUs after this is all over and settled, you intend to call them in."

"Doctor, you should have been in the diplomatic service!" Yigal laughed.

"What I don't understand is the desire of the pope to get rid of this Brotherhood. I've always thought of the Roman Catholic Church as one of the most successful institutions for survival. Why get rid of something like this if they have been relatively successful?" Lynn inquired.

"It's something some of the popes have been trying to do for over a century. As you can well imagine, the Holy See has been embarrassed more than once by the tactics and methods the Brotherhood have used. Finally in today's world with the advances in communication, people all over the world were becoming more and more familiar with some of their tactics. I think also the new pope has sensed a golden opportunity to strike when the Brotherhood have appeared to become rather lax in their security and perhaps over confident. Generally, Ms. Pollard, we think it has been a case of the tail wagging the dog and now the dog has snarled. The pope wants them finished and to stop embarrassing the Church. Listen, I've got to use the radio in the cockpit and then I'll be back to answer any more of your questions," Yigal replied as he got up and walked the long narrow aisle to the cockpit.

"Lynn, who would have thought twenty-four hours ago we would have been in the middle of one of the biggest chess matches of the century?" Scott said.

"Listen, Scott, I'm going back to see the girls and give your mother a break. She's been a real trouper and will need some help. I promised them and when you're their age, a promise means a great deal, especially when it comes from an adult. I hope you don't mind," Lynn added.

"Of course not. As you can see they've really latched onto you and already think of you as their mother. However, I think you should put on a hundred pounds and then you'll look like a big momma!" He laughed as she ran a hand through his sandy-grey hair as she walked back to where the girls and their grandmother were seated.

Chapter 72

Friday morning was dull and rainy in the capital. Excitement buzzed through the Justice Department. Preparations had been accelerating all week with anticipation of the visit of the new pope. Never before had a pope made an official state visit to Washington and the reaction were as expected. Throughout the Bible Belt, there were the expected rumblings of anger and vehement charges of Catholic conspiracies and the like. Because of the size of the response to the visit of the American-born Pontiff's inaugural speech as Pope, the setting for his address in Washington was changed to the front steps of the Justice Building from the famed chambers inside. All week large bleachers were hammered together and placed about the main entrance in a large semi circle. Large numbers of faithful Catholics poured into the city for the occasion of the pope's visit. When the news broke six weeks before of the election of the first North American pope, great excitement had rippled through the Catholic population across the country. In the first major decision of his Pontificate, Julian IV announced he would make his inaugural speech in the heart of the American justice, the Supreme Court Building. While there was great excitement amidst US Catholics, there were ugly undercurrents through the Bible Belt and in many right-wing religious circles.

By eleven in the morning, there were four hundred thousand people gathered around the steps of the Justice Building and sitting in the hastily assembled bleachers. The crowd grew rapidly and spilled over unto the sprawling lawns of the Capitol Building itself and southward over the Library of Congress. A podium stood on the steps of the Justice Building surrounded by rows of chairs for the endless numbers of government and Church dignitaries. All of these were placed under a clear plastic canopy in case of an early spring rain. Across First Street on the soaring flagstaff atop the massive Capitol dome, the papal standard flew snapping in the early morning breeze. A number of people sitting in the stands were pointing to its presence in the distance and whispering to themselves. Finally, a long stream of people began to pour into the vast covered platform from every direction. By eleven, most of the stands were full and a rising murmur filled the air. The tension grew as people pointed to the fluttering papal standard in the distance.

A large motorcade appeared moving slowly eastward on Constitution Avenue. It slowly turned south onto First Street and stopped directly in front of the Supreme Court and the huge welcoming crowd. The left rear door of the large limo opened and a tall lanky figure in white emerged. After he was joined by the chief justice and the vice president, they walked up the steps of the podium. They were surrounded by countless numbers of priests and security people. The great crowd were on their feet and cheering wildly. The pope waved back with the cheery smile for which he had become famous since his elevation to the throne of St. Peter. Again and again, the crowd waved and cheered. Vast numbers were on their knees in prayer and visible devotion. It was a scene the calloused capital hadn't seen in many years. In a city that at times seemed awash in bourbon and false sentimentality, the display was refreshing and different.

Finally, the slim figure of Thurgood Kavanaugh, the vice president, stepped up to the great battery of mikes surrounding the podium. As he stood, there was a sudden surge of enthusiasm as the strains of "The Star-Spangled Banner" was played by the Marine Corps Band wafted over the crowd. When the band finished, a great cheer arose from the crowd lasting nearly five minutes. Finally a hush settled over the crowd. The vice president stepped forward to the mikes and began to speak.

"Ladies and gentlemen, on behalf of the president..." His voice was suddenly drowned out by a wild series of hisses and boos that ushered from many quarters of the huge crowd. The president had refused to come and address the crowd on this occasion, stating he felt it was violating the sacrosanct US belief of the separation of church and state. This statement had stimulated a great deal of ugly talk from various camps across the country the past week.

"On behalf of the president, the Congress and government, I wish to extend our warmest greetings to the His Holiness, the first American-born pope!" Again, wild cheers and boos swept across the crowd. The pope, who was sitting on the right side of the podium, was watching the crowd very carefully, moving his head constantly. For the next ten minutes, the vice president spoke about the evolution of relations between the US and the Vatican.

In a small attic window of the historic Library of Congress, no one noticed a small hole in the corner of a window pane. The glass was one-way reflective to keep out the hot summer sun and hadn't been opened since the last facelifting thirty years ago. The small slim barrel of a rifle jutted out only about an inch and was almost invisible. The platform on the front of the Justice Building was entirely visible and no one there was more than four hundred yards away. Behind the glass a shadowy figure set up a rifle on a tripod with a huge sniper scope perched on top.

"Ladies and gentlemen, to welcome officially His Holiness to the US and the city of Washington, I give you the chief justice of the United States of America, Hamilton Sherman Saunders!" Again a thunderous wave of applause thundered across the great throng. The chief justice was unique in the city. Beloved by many and despised by many more, he had had a well-defined tenure in the office. He polarized public opinion like a lightning rod since his appointment by the previous president five years before. He was barely five foot three in stature and his rotund figure drew many comparisons to the legendary Stephen Douglas, the great opponent of Lincoln. Like Douglas he had become a legend for his oratorical ability and quick thinking on his feet. In full oratorical flight, he reminded many people of Franklin Roosevelt in his prime.

"My fellow Americans, it gives me great pleasure to have this opportunity to be the keynote speaker on this historical occasion. We have come to a turning point in the destiny of our great nation." Far back on the platform, the rotund figure of Frank Baird fidgeted nervously. He shifted this way and that as was his habit. He knew what was to come and he hoped that Saunders didn't get too carried away with his oratory as the minutes ticked by. As he waited, he spoke into a cell phone.

"Not yet, but it will be soon!" he whispered.

"I can hear someone coming up the stairs below!" a gruff voice spoke back into his ear.

Baird whispered back, "Wait for the word, for Christ's sake!"

"My fellow Americans, the future of our great nation is tied inexorably with the great traditions of our past. This great melting pot of religion and culture has been an example to the world. Ours is the nation as envisaged by Washington and Jefferson. It is the nation Lincoln went to war to save and to reforge anew..." He continued to build the historical basis of his speech. Over in the little window of the Library of Congress Building, the shadowy figure waited. Checking his rifle again and again, he twitched nervously, this way and that. Everything was primed and ready.

"And so, my fellow Americans," Saunders continued, now nearly thirty minutes into his speech, "we come to another milestone in our national journey. We have always prided ourselves in the greatness of our belief in the idea of the separation of church and state. Now we come to a historical moment. One of the great historical churches is about to challenge this belief!"

There was a slight murmur. The pope turned his head towards Saunders. What was the man really saying? He was stunned. Suddenly he felt he was walking into a trap! He was a personal friend of Saunders for thirty years and thought he knew him thoroughly, yet the unexpected was a part of the man's complex nature. Meanwhile Frank Baird reached for his cell phone. A distance away, two FBI agents were whispering into each other's ears.

"I tell you, there's someone using a cell phone in these stands near the main podium who's not supposed to be doing so. I've got a feeling about this business." He carried a load of electronic gear on his back. He turned to a scruffy man with a ponytail and droopy mustache and whispered, "What the hell do you think, Ed?"

"I don't know, but I'll get on it right away. We've got a hell of a crowd here and I don't want something to get out of hand!" With these words, he disappeared under the stands and into a control van parked under some trees. The man with the electronic gear sat down and fiddled with various gears and knobs.

Meanwhile, the chief justice continued: "We have always prided ourselves in this country of having a policy of not allowing others to interfere in the affairs of our nation. Now, my fellow citizens, it appears we have reached a point where we will be compelled to draw a line in the sands of history once again..."

As he talked, Baird spoke into his phone in tense tones. "You've got twenty seconds! Do it just as we timed it. No more—no less! Just wait until he gets the whole paragraph out, then do it. But, for Christ's sake, wait for it." He placed the phone back in his pocket, sat back and muttered to himself, "For God and the American people!"

Two agents raced up the small staircase behind the dingy window. On the other side and behind the window, the gunman stood and readied himself. He peered through the scope as he placed his phone on the floor. His hand settled on the trigger and began to squeeze.

"It appears the Church of His Holiness has been involved in the internal history of our nation now for many years!"

The pope turned an ashen grey and squirmed in his seat. Saunders' words rang out and he was forced to pause as an angry roar issued from the crowd.

There was an electric tension in the air. Baird frowned and muttered unheard words to the gunman, "Wait, wait for the words."

"Now we are of the conviction and we have the proof that the Church of His Holiness was directly involved directly in the killing of one of our most beloved presidents!"

There was an angry surge and another roar from the crowd.

"We all know him…"

There was a sharp high-pitched crack of a rifle in the air, immediately followed by a rapid second and a third. Saunders suddenly rose up on his toes and his right hand flew to his chest. There was a loud gasp as his face went blank. He appeared to be trying to speak but was unable. He pitched forward over the platform collapsing on the ground with the podium falling on top of him. Meanwhile, a secret service man was down clasping his right side. The vice president lay on his back grasping at his arm.

For a moment the crowd was silent in the most eerie moment many later would remember all their lives. Then, there were screams and bedlam everywhere. The tall figure of the pope had vanished into a limo at the hands of his security. It roared off away from the crowd.

Chapter 73

The air was tense in the Oval Office. The president had been receiving a lot of flak over the visit this morning of the new pope. He already was being accused of hewing the official Vatican line and jumping to their tune by members of the new American Freedom Party. There was a rustle at the side of the desk. The chief presidential aide, Thomas Maddox, entered.

"Mr. President, His Holiness' car has arrived and he'll be here shortly!"

"That's fine, Tom. Let me know the minute they're in the outer office. By the way do you have any details about the executive meeting of the Freedom Party?" he asked casually.

Tom looked at him, paused and replied, "No, Mr. President, we know little about them except that several key Republicans have joined them. This includes several prominent members of Congress and the government, I might add! If you ask me, sir, we're going to have to start taking them more seriously!"

"Yeah, I know, Tom, and that's what bothers me the most about this matter. I keep wondering if they are anything more then a bunch of misguided patriots."

Tom let himself out of the office quietly. Henderson enjoyed the rare respite form the normal ebb and flow of human traffic and the lack of jangling phones. As he sat behind the huge desk, he wondered what must have gone through the minds of Kennedy, Johnson and even Lincoln at various points in their presidencies. He looked at several bills he had to send back to Congress and wondered at their chances. This week the radical Medicare bill was on the back of his mind when the damned spy business broke. He thought about the new pope's visit. It would be good to see Wilbert Adrianus again. They were both Ohio natives and had met in university. They had remained close even after Will had entered the priesthood. However they had lost track of each other as their lives went in different directions. Then a few days after Will was elevated to the throne of St. Peter by the College of Cardinals in a move that electrified the world, the president received a message from the new pontiff. The new pope wanted a quick meeting with the president at his earliest convenience.

There was a rustle at the door as Tom Maddox reentered. "Mr. President, His Holiness and his party are on their way to the outer office. Do you wish me to escort them in?"

"No, Tom, make them comfortable and I'll call out when to escort them in," Henderson added curtly.

"Is that wise, sir?" Maddox asked.

"Tom, he asked for this meeting and he can wait on my convenience and I think you know the point I'm making," Henderson added casually to Maddox. There was a closeness between the two men who trusted each other implicitly.

After ten minutes, there was a quiet rap at the side door to the office. Henderson looked up annoyed. "Tom?"

"Mr. President, the chief papal aide is outside the door and wants to speak to you before the meeting. He thinks you have insulted the pope by keeping him cooling his heels in the outer lounge." Behind him, the tall figure of the chairman of the Joint Chiefs, General Armstrong, slipped into the Oval Office.

"One of the things you learn about this job, my friend, is the fact of reality. The reality at this moment in time is that I am the president and this pope has come hat in hand and anxious to see me. He can goddamned well wait until hell freezes over if that's my wish, pope or no pope! Now get the hell out of here and do your job," Henderson snarled. Maddox's face was ashen in shock and humiliation as he slipped away.

"Like I've always said, Mr. President, you wear the mantle of office well and use it even better! It's a real pleasure to serve under you! I have nothing against the pope but some of them see themselves as God's special messengers amongst us, Catholics or Protestants!"

"Don't worry, General Armstrong, if Will doesn't realize that already from his aides, he soon will before this meeting is over. He was fine last year in Geneva as Papal Nuncio but I'm wondering about that mantle you've been referring to. Can you imagine all the baggage along with the mantle of St. Peter! Scares even a good Presbyterian like myself Listen, I'm going out to meet the pope and his party and want you to come with me, if you don't mind," Henderson asked the general.

"Yes, Mr. President, I'd like to be present for any meeting you have with him with your permission. I know his aides will be there as well."

Henderson walked to the main Oval Office with the general close at his heels. Known as a man who didn't stand on ceremony, he breezed past his aides in the outer office into the waiting room where the pope and his three aides were seated.

"Will, it's great to see you again!" the ebullient president exclaimed as he strode towards the figure in white seated on the far side near the large window. He extended his right hand.

Before he was less than halfway across the room, a young priest stepped in front of him and blurted, "His Holiness prefers not to be called by his former first name and should be addressed at all times as His Holiness!" His words were dipped in insolence and sarcasm. Before anyone could do anything, an arm was locked about the young priest's neck and his right arm twisted viciously behind him with a revolver rammed into his ribs. The special security man appeared from nowhere and the effect was stunning.

The young priest was yanked and slammed against the wall and heard the words whispered in his ears, "One wrong move and you're dead!"

The president watched and said, "Take him out and find what he knows, one way or another!"

"Yes, Mr. President, immediately!" he snapped. He yanked the pope's aide through the door so violently one of the man's shoes was kicked off.

"My God!" the pope muttered, "you didn't have to be so strong handed, he's only doing his job."

"That's just the point, Will, we're here in the White House and he was doing his job. You may think it's an overreaction but he's only doing his job. He was acting on my specific orders. You're an American, you of all people should understand that point! Anyhow, come into my office and have a chat." As he turned, he nodded to Maddox and General Armstrong to follow. The pope's remaining two followed rather fearfully in the president's wake.

In the Oval Office, the effect on the visitors was awing as usual and as it was intended to be. General Armstrong closed the door behind the small party and gestured to a large coffee table surrounded by a series of comfortable leather chairs. Even the general himself, fully attired in his blue Air Force uniform with a chestful of medals, was intended to intimidate. There was a quiet hum from various electronic equipment in the background and from the rest of the large building. The pope, resplendent in his full white cassock and cap, looked very much in place. There was a fresh pot of coffee on the middle of the coffee table and two plates piled high with fresh fruit. The president extended his hand again to the pope and was met with a timid graciousness from his longtime friend.

"Mr. President, please accept my apology for the ham-handed affront to yourself in the outer office. There was no excuse for that type of behaviour. He has already been removed from the post as we speak but I take full responsibility for his actions." The pope's voice was strong and firm with no priestly tone.

"I feel bad it happened, Will, but there is a dignity to this office and everything about it and for that I make no apology. It's good to see you again and we must look at this Lincoln situation. I don't want to get the Vatican involved but there's a chance it will be dragged in if we aren't careful."

"Gord, if I may now call you that and that really goes back in my mind, this Red Rose Brotherhood is a violent splinter group that goes back for centuries. They were originally a secret wing of the Jesuit Order that were only called upon when there was a dire threat before the Church. Most of us thought they had vanished late in the 1900s and there has been no instance of them appearing at all the twentieth century. Yet, here they show up acting, as it were, in the terms of their old mandate. Fortunately for, and thanks to, the Mossad, we were able to cut them off early before they were able to do any damage."

"You'll never know how relieved I am to hear that news. Our problem here in the US is the Freedom Party. They won't be happy until they achieve a coup d'etat here in Washington. I'm convinced the government is ridden with their supporters and also I'm sure they were behind the assassination of the chief justice yesterday. I do know their plans were to pull off the act and then blame it on the Vatican. That's why they want the Surratt document so desperately. The evidence of a picture of the Lincoln conspirators with two faces, specifically with two priests, included is held by them to show Vatican tinkering with US internal life. If there was any doubt, it vanished when the chief justice was killed and the attempt to blame it on your people. I've given orders they are to be eliminated as quickly and fully as possible," Gord Henderson intoned quietly.

"Gord, how do you plan to do this without causing a violent reaction against Rome and the Catholic Church from spreading across the country? I know how some feel in the deep South towards my Church," the pope asked quietly.

"Very simple! When one of these people killed those priests in Dublin several months ago, one of them was a longtime Mossad mole. That killing was a real blessing in disguise. That brought the Mossad onto the scene in

Europe big time. We were happy to have them do our dirty work. By letting them do the dirty work here in America, we will hopefully prevent a violent backlash against your Church and clean out the Freedom Party as well. We're killing two birds with one stone so to speak." Henderson placed both hands on the table in front of him and stared directly into the pontiff's eyes as he talked. There was a tension in the big office that was almost visible.

"Gord, is this new party here in America a real threat to the government or is it all perceived?" the pope asked.

"After some of the things that have happened, it would be tempting to say yes, and if I wanted to use fear as a tool to whip the population into line I would say yes too, but if the truth were known they're a small noisy group of fanatics. It's their influence on other people I'm worried about. That's why I want the Mossad to do our work. When all this is over, I plan to make a Gettysburg-type speech and draw the nation together. That way I won't be playing into their hands!"

Looking at Armstrong, he saw the general nodding his approval. The president got to his feet and walked to the window looking out over the Potomac. One of the pope's aides was about to ask a question but his boss waved him to silence with snap of his fingers. Henderson stood silent for several long minutes before turning and facing the pontiff.

"Will, I want you to promise me there'll be no more chances for these random priests finding their way to this side of the Atlantic. Otherwise it might be necessary to leak these pictures and documents to the press and I'm sure you wouldn't want to see that happen." As he spoke, he raised one finger and pointed at the pope. "I think we should have a clear understanding about this, Will, and it will avoid misunderstanding and heartache in the future!" His voice was firm but pleasant and his eyes were clear.

The general, who was silent all through the exchange, had rarely seen a man beat another man so quickly. He could see from the Pontiff's eyes, he had been defeated by a better man. His eyes were dead, his face cold and he sat humiliated.

"I understand, Mr. President. I'm sorry we have been unable to take this agreement beyond the formal level from the understanding we once had. And I find it regrettable..."

He was cut off in mid-sentence by the flash of anger on the president's face.

"Will, you were my friend and still are, but as long as I'm the president don't confuse the one with the other. As an American, I find it very regrettable that I have to remind you of that fact. You may have a church to run but I have a nation to run, with worldwide responsibilities. I also have a Congress to deal with and to answer to. Now, if you'll excuse me, I have matters to attend to and a special meeting of the Joint Chiefs to convene."

The papal party were quickly on their feet and escorted from the Oval Office by General Armstrong. The pope extended his hand but Henderson turned away and ignored him. After they left the building, General Armstrong couldn't remember the president being as furious.

"Mr. President, I've never seen a man deflated as quickly as you did with the pope. Don't you think you overreacted somewhat?"

Suddenly Henderson turned on the general, his face livid.

"You don't get it, do you, General! And you're not even a good Catholic. He walks into the Oval Office about to appoint himself as my God director. Well, I'm not going to answer to his insolence now or ever. I'm glad that young priest tried his bullshit outside the office—I had Will on the run from then on. Look, General, would you get the Israeli prime minister on the blower and see what's the latest news from his end!"

"Yes, Mr. president, I'll get right on it!"

Chapter 74

Bedlam broke loose all around the huge podium. The chief justice was sprawled on his face in the middle of a jumble of overturned chairs and scrambling people. There was a large red stain spreading across the middle of his back. He was surrounded by police and Secret Service people. The vice president was on his feet holding his arm but looking otherwise unhurt. The third shot had struck a policeman in the side but he was sitting up and appeared to be aware he had been shot.

High up in the Library of Congress building, the assassin smiled to himself as he packed the rifle away in a large case. He knew from the beginning this was a once-in-a-lifetime job and because of the stature of his victim, he would never work again. That had been the nature of his agreement. Suddenly, the door behind him was kicked open. A man dressed in black stood in the doorway with a second shadowy figure behind him. He stood still for the briefest of moments as if giving the assassin time to wonder what was afoot. His right hand flashed behind his ear, but he wasn't fast enough. The man in the doorway squeezed the trigger on a vicious-looking Uzi. So many shells were fired so fast there was only a continuous roar to be heard. Over a dozen shells struck the gunman in the chest and abdomen. He jerked back against the wall and twitched as the bullets tore through him destroying his spine and major organs. He fell to the floor in a bloody heap. His head lolled to one side and the eyes stared empty. The shooter turned to the other man behind him and quipped, "Tell Baird we got the bastard. He never knew what hit him. Tell him we'll do everything he has asked us to do. No damned bunch of 'doggans' from Rome are going to run this country or anywhere else."

The second man spoke briefly into a cellular phone, hung up and walked over to the bloody corpse. Kicking him over with his foot, he spit on his face and turned away. A large pool of blood was spreading across the floor.

"Let's get out of here and back to Baird on the phone and see what he wants to do from here. All we have to do now is get a copy of the chief justice's speech and the party is well covered. I just hope he got the right words out before this bastard shot him or we're screwed. If he only got part of them out, then we're in trouble. I tried to tell Frank that the window was too small but the bastard wouldn't listen."

They had just turned and were about to leave the room when they were faced with a slightly built man in his early thirties. he spoke softly with a strong Eastern accent. "Get back into the room and be quick about it."

They found themselves staring into the barrel of a small revolver equipped with a large silencer.

"I don't know who the hell you are, but if Baird sent you to see if we did the job, then see for yourself."

The new arrival glanced at the corpse for only a split second. Turning back to the man who had spoken, his gun coughed twice very quickly. The first shooter staggered back with a strange look on his face, suddenly realizing he had been shot. With a great effort, his lips tried to form words.

"Who the Christ...are...you?" His eyes suddenly glazed and he pitched face forward to the floor, his left legs twitching as he did so.

The second man on black stared and muttered, "Don't, for God's sake, please...!" A single shot coughed in the small room and the shell struck him in the centre of the forehead. He stood still for a moment before slumping dead to the floor. The younger man looked down at the two bodies at his feet. He had been in the country only ten hours and already he had killed twice. The flight from Tel Aviv was long and wearisome and he wanted to get to a hotel room. He vanished quickly. The three killings in the Library had taken less than five minutes. When the agent was gone, there was silence everywhere except for the noise of the crowd as it seethed about in shock over the killing of the chief justice.

The scene in front of the Justice Building was sheer chaos. Women were screaming and the police were moving in every direction. Frank Baird wanted desperately to get his hands on the copy of the chief justice's speech from the podium. From where he sat he could see it and amidst the confusion made his way toward it. It proved a difficult task with people pushing this way and that. He felt a hand on his arm amidst all the confusion.

"Frank Baird, is that you?" He found himself looking into the face of the director of the FBI. "What the hell is happening? Do you know where the shots came from?"

"Mr. Director, I really have no idea what's happened. I just want to get over to the dais and see if I can be of any help." With these words, he left the director with his mouth hanging open and not knowing which way to turn. By the time Baird managed to reach the podium area, the chief justice's body was being carried away on a stretcher as policemen struggled to open a pathway through the crowd. At the podium, Baird found nothing. It was gone yet it was there moments before. He muttered to himself, "Jesus Murphy, where did that paper go? If it gets into the wrong hands, it could spell real trouble for the party." He had a photocopy of the speech, but he wanted to know the whereabouts of the original. If some quarters of the government were to get their hands on it, there would be hell to pay all over Washington. Pulling his cell phone out, he punched in the number of the assassin but there was no answer. He smiled and knew the other team had done their work.

Half an hour later Baird was back in his living room with the five members of the steering committee of the American Freedom Party. There was an atmosphere of impending doom.

"What the Christ are we supposed to do from here? " demanded Rep. Andrew P. Hobson from Georgia, as he leaned forward in his chair. "A number of you people demanded we show our true colours a few months ago and stand up for what we believed. Now, what do we find? We've given our trust to a bunch of incompetent asses!"

"I beg to differ and want an apology here and now!" Baird snapped.

"You'll get that the day hell freezes over!" Hobson quipped.

"Well, what do you intend to do? The senator has already paid with his life and it appears the chief justice may have paid the same price!" Senator Harder from Minnesota replied.

"You two idiots know only too well that we've stuck to the same plan since we started down this path together. Now isn't the time to get cold feet. Besides, we're far too far down that route to turn anyway. I don't know what went wrong exactly this morning. The shooter's timing was all off but everything else went like clockwork. Why the vice president was shot I don't know, but he should pull through. I think we should be very careful to stick with the line that some lunatic killed Saunders and hope this won't spoil relations between the Vatican and us. Only Saunders could have stirred up the hatred in the crowd enough for us to make our move today, but I still think we'll be able to pull it off."

There was a lull in the big ornate room. Shock was still rampant from the morning's events and only Baird was pleased with the manner in which their plans had progressed. Finally, he stood up and said, "I think we should dismiss this meeting and wait until the mourning period is over. The one concern I have is the Surratt paper itself. It was still in Lynn Pollard's possession the last time I had contact with our people in the field."

"I suggest we go ahead and make our claim against the Vatican no matter what the risk. This was the name of the game when I first joined the party. We were called to be to be willing to put our necks on the line for a new direction for our country. You and the chief justice both said you felt the time had come for drastic change if we were going to take the country down the same road again that Lincoln trod so long ago. Now, I don't understand what I'm hearing," said Senator George Mumson from Colorado.

"George, I've told you before and now I'm going to tell you again, there's no change in our course. It's as before—'steady as she goes!'" replied Baird.

"Don't bullshit me, Frank. I wasn't born yesterday. Steady as she goes is fine as long as you know where you're going! Tell me—I want to know or I'm off this crusade as of now!" Munson snapped. There was a stunned silence as the seams of the new party were beginning to show strain.

"Alright, if that's the way the rest of you want to go, that's it. We'll issue a statement condemning the Vatican's past interference in the domestic affairs of this country and hope we'll have the benefit of the public's doubt before the image makers in the media and the government get their hands on them. That's what was so important about the chief justice's speech. He was priming the audience to lay this message for our case against the Vatican. At the end he was going to lay the proof of the Surratt paper on them as all the proof that was necessary. In this day of the media it's all how you present something. Unfortunately, Saunders started milking the audience too long and he threw the assassin's timing off by several seconds. Before, I was unwilling to do this without the heard proof of the material that Lynn Pollard found, but now we don't have much choice. I'll feed the material to the media and we'll see what will happen. With the shock of an assassination in the air and the killing of the assassins, there's a good chance that will do the trick. Let's plan a meeting here for Monday morning." Baird stood up and the group of sombre-faced men slowly left the room.

As soon as the others were gone, Frank Baird was about to pick up the phone when it rang in his hand.

"Frank, Julius here at the agency. Did you hear the news?"

"No! And make it quick because I've got things to do!" Frank snarled.

"Well, pardon me, but I thought I was doing you a favour! We just picked up two bodies that are connected to your Freedom Party. I know as I've seen them before!"

297

"What the hell are you talking about, Julius, two bodies from where?"

"Well, it comes down like this: someone was definitely gunning for the chief justice and the vice president. They hit them both but the vice president will live. Trouble is that someone else was gunning for the assassins as well. The two bodies we found in the Library of Congress Building were the ones from your party. The stiff behind the sniper rifle is a stranger, but has the look of a professional assassin about him. Frank, what the hell is going on?"

Chapter 75

The president walked to his desk while General Armstrong watched him without a word. Finally he asked, "Gord, what the hell was that all about? I thought you were going to have a long meeting with him and set up a working relationship. What's this all about?"

"Alex, those were my plans but didn't you notice the change in his manner since Geneva? Someone has got to him or he's had a change in plans over this Red Rose Brotherhood business!" he replied.

"But I thought it was all looked after and dealt a fatal blow by the Mossad?" Armstrong asked.

"Yes, we all thought so until I get some top-secret messages from the Mossad headquarters saying they were still active. Apparently they have evolved the tactic over the centuries of pulling away and going dormant when they lose a few rounds. The Mossad weren't happy with this and asked permission to root them out in this country. Mind you the Israelis are smart enough to realize without US support they would be no where as a nation. As a result, I gave them permission on two conditions. They would clean out the Brotherhood in this country completely and then take care of a number of our citizens who have been involved in this Lincoln thing. Finally, they would clean out this American Freedom Party."

General Armstrong was stunned and looked bewildered. "Jesus, Gord, why is it so necessary for us to get the Mossad to do all our dirty work for us? What's the matter with the FBI, they're supposed to be such a good outfit!"

"Alex, there's nothing wrong with the FBI or any of the rest of our people. Don't forget this is an election year and I want to have all this dirty business done in secret. Besides, if the media ever gets wind there was even some suspected Vatican complicity in the killing of Lincoln, there will be hell to pay. Besides, that's what the Freedom Party wants. I want them eliminated with as little fuss as possible. This way, my hands will be clean and the Israelis will feel we're in their debt for an eternity," the president explained.

"Holy shit!" answered the general. "What a mess. What about this man

Baird? From what you've shown me he's up to his eyeballs in this Freedom Party."

"Right up to his ass! I've known him all my life here on the Hill, and this is the first time he's been involved in something of this nature. I've talked with a Yigal Burgstein from the Israeli Embassy and he says Baird is the one man they're after more then anyone else!"

"Gordon, will we be hearing any more from the Mossad or will they fade away into the night when the job is finished? What about this business of the assassination this morning? The public is going to demand a thorough investigation and will want to see all the facts."

"Alex, we already know basically what happened. The Mossad called me before the pope arrived with all the details. The original shots were fired by a hired assassin and then apparently killed by the same people who hired him to make themselves look like heros to the public. At least that seems to be the rational at the moment. These gunmen were then in turn shot by a Mossad operative. We know this specifically as the Mossad have said so."

"Gord, are you telling me the second gunmen were hired by the Freedom Party and then in turn killed by the Mossad?" Armstrong asked.

"Yes, that's the way it appears to have happened. As I said, don't ask me why as I don't have too many of the answers in this area yet. As soon as I'm briefed, I'll be in touch. However, since you have asked about the FBI, I should tell you I've asked the director to commence with a thorough investigation of both shootings. They will make the inevitable linkup with the Freedom Party, but by then the Mossad will be long gone from the country. In my last conversation with Col. Sharon, I emphasized I wanted their operations to be concluded within two weeks and I couldn't make any guarantees I could hold the FBI at bay for any longer then that."

"Gord, isn't that taking one hell of a gamble?" General Armstrong inquired.

"More then even you realize, Alex. If this kind of personal involvement by the president were leaked, then all our geese will be cooked. Everyone who knows about it knows they will be toast if any word seeps out. That includes you, Alex!" the president snapped.

"Yes, and I damned well know it as well!"

"Alex, have you thought of the alternative? If the Red Rose Brotherhood ever got a further hold in this country, then there will be a hell of a fight to get them rooted out. Most of all, I don't want it to break out into an anti-Catholic fight. That would do no one any good, save fanatics such as Baird, the late chief justice and the rest of their friends."

Chapter 76

The warm Italian sun streamed through the large windows of their bedroom. Scott Fleming stirred a few times and swung his feet to the floor. He could barely see Lynn under the pile of bedcovers. getting up, he walked to the nearest window to see the countryside in the daylight. Looking at his watch, he saw it was nearly noon, Italian time. The two main windows looked over a sweeping lawn and tennis court to a white sandy beach stretching for miles. He remembered the beauty of the countryside from a trip he took with his wife just after they were married. He pulled on a shirt, shorts and a pair of canvas shoes he found in the legation in Washington before they left. Dressing quickly, he went looking for his mother and the girls. They were in the next room fast asleep, exhausted from the long trip. Closing the door, he went downstairs where he heard distant voices. There he found Yigal Burgstein talking to Guieseppi Andrianno. They both turned and spoke.

"Good morning, Dr. Fleming. We hope you were able to get some sleep! You had a long flight," Guiseppi asked in his delightful Italian accent.

"Well, you're right about the flight. It was tiring, especially when we weren't prepared. Give us a day and we'll be up to snuff," Scott replied.

"I should tell you there was a brutal assassination in Washington yesterday. The chief justice was killed and the vice president wounded. I guess the president was right to listen to his suspicions. However, the killers were in turn slain by one of our agents as far as we can tell. There was some secondary shooting but the situation is now well in hand from what we can tell from this distance and from the contacts at our legation," Yigal responded tartly.

"Mr. Burgstein, that doesn't confirm for me how you are to be so sure of the specific facts," Scott continued. There was a long silence between them.

"Dr. Fleming, I was talking to President Henderson, himself, on the phone less than an hour ago, from Air Force One over the Atlantic, and he assured me they have a handle on everything. That's authority enough for me! He is aware you and Ms. Pollard are here and of your roles in this whole situation. You'll be flown back to Washington as soon as possible. The decision was left to him where to take you and this seemed to be the best place short of Israel," Burgstein responded.

"Are we still in danger or do you feel that point is past? I'm thinking in particular of Ms. Pollard," Scott asked.

"I think the danger still exists in Washington and that is why you are here. Our people in Washington raided the headquarters of the Freedom Party and all their key people were killed or wounded. There is only the figure of Frank Baird yet to be accounted for. The general feeling amongst our people is he was the master mind behind this situation. In particular, the killing of the chief justice."

"That can't be possible. The chief justice was a key figure in the party from what I've been able to decipher," Scott asked with great puzzlement.

"That's what we all believed several days ago. Now, it appears he was only window dressing from the onset and a front man overall. The plan was to kill him and blame it on the Catholic Church. After the new pope was on the dais only a few feet away at the time of the shooting," Yigal said.

"You're saying the Catholic Church was being set up as the heavy?" Scott exclaimed.

"Of course! The killing of the chief justice was to be used by the Freedom Party and linked up with the crucial evidence found by Ms. Pollard in Washington and her people in California on the Lincoln assassination. Their hope was to discredit the Catholic Church in the United States and get the Freedom Party support as never before. I think if they had succeeded they might have surpassed their wildest dreams."

"Surely you must have more evidence than this. That's a pretty fantastic tale," Scott replied.

"That's correct! But what if I told you we have the copy of the speech the chief justice was giving at the moment he was killed? This includes several bloodstains and we've authenticated they are his beyond a doubt. The important thing was the nature of the speech. We all knew the man's ability to work up a crowd. This speech was designed to lead the crowd up to a key point because at a specific set of phrases it attacks the Catholic Church as a meddler in American history, including the killing of Lincoln himself. This attack was to have been delivered against the Church in the presence of the pope himself. The aim was to discredit the Catholic Church in America completely. What the chief justice didn't know was he was going to be sacrificed at the end of these key phrases with his assassination. Somehow the killer got his cues screwed up and fired early. In so doing, Saunders was robbed of his golden opportunity and the US possibly saved from a bloodbath," Yigal explained.

"What I don't understand was the presence of the assassin? Why not let Saunders work his magic on the crowd?" Scott inquired.

"You have a good point. It was supposed to be the final blow. The assassin was never supposed to fire in the first place except he didn't know that. The second pair were supposed to kill him and the word would be put out that guards from the Freedom Party saved everyone from an attack. They would have been heroes in everyone's eyes like they had planned. Like I said, the killer screwed up at the last minute, thank God," Yigal concluded.

Scott drained a cup of strong coffee, was silent for a few minutes and then asked, "Why did you go to the time and expense of bringing us to Italy?"

"Because the network of terror and intrigue was and is so interwoven when it was uncovered, the president made the bold decision to let the Freedom Party make their move and to catch them with their hand in the cookie jar. When we were dragged into the mess by accident, he determined to give us free rein to clean it up and deal the Red Rose Brotherhood a fatal blow. Most of all it would be kept quiet and most of the population will never know the difference. Doctor, the discovery of those pictures by Ms. Pollard was the key. When she and her staff started digging around, the network of terror that was uncovered was alarming, both on behalf of the Freedom Party and the Red Rose bunch. The first indication was the brutal attack on the research centre in California. Then came the brutal sacking of her office in Washington and finally the attack on the head couple in California again. Miss Savitz and Mr. Cassell have been relocated in another city in case another attempt is made on their lives. Finally, there is the example of you and your family. You must remember Ms Pollard is the flashpoint in this whole situation," he said.

As he finished talking, one of his young aids came to the door. "Mr. Burgstein, there's a special message that has just come in which I feel you should see."

Scott waved to Yigal as he left and walked out on the broad lawn high above the beach. There was a gentle sweep down the sloping dune to the broad sweep of white sand. But, as always, he was struck by the deep blue of the Mediterranean itself. Neither pictures or memory ever did it justice. Yet, as he stood quietly in the warming morning sun, his mind wandered back to the question he had asked Burgstein. Suddenly there was a voice behind him.

"Boy, you're the early bird this morning!" Lynn said as he turned to face her. She wore faded shorts and a sleeveless shirt and was barefoot. "I rolled over in bed and there was no sign of you. Besides, the kids and your mom are still asleep."

"I know. I looked in when I got up just after dawn," he said.

"Scott, why did they drag us over here to Rome?" she said as they walked down to the water's edge.

"I don't really know. I talked to Burgstein for an hour but his answer doesn't add up. All I can read between the lines is it has something to do with the president's visit here in the next few days," he mused in an attempt to answer her.

"How long will we be here?"

"All I can glean is that the president will be in Rome and there will be a meeting here at the villa early Monday morning. Apparently they want us to stay here until then or later. I gather this meeting was set up by the Israeli prime minister, so it appears that it is something fairly big. I know his concern was the factor of safety and complete secrecy."

She was quiet for the longest time.

"Scott, where does this leave you and I? I'm getting weary of all this hype and running around. As a matter of fact, I'm getting damned sick of Washington and all the bullshit!" She looked up with a deep sigh, her eyes gaunt and weary.

"Would you be interested in moving out of the city completely?" he asked looking her directly in the eye.

"What do you mean? You can't move. You have your practice and reputation to worry about!" she replied.

"To tell you the honest truth, I don't give a damn about that anymore! Oh, I'll stay in my field, but I'd like to get out of a city hospital completely and find a small one somewhere. There we could settle down and have a normal family life!"

"You're serious!"

"I've never been more serious!"

"Are you sure?"

"Never more serious about anything in a long time."

She looked at him, a wistful smile on her lips.

Chapter 77

It was late Saturday afternoon when Yigal Burgstein found Scott in the villa foyer reading the *New York Times*. Lynn and Martha had taken the girls to the sprawling beach and Scott wanted to find out more about what happened in Washington.

"Dr. Fleming, thank goodness you're not down on the beach. I've got word from the Mossad headquarters in Tel Aviv. Col. Sharon want to see you first thing tomorrow morning. Apparently there are details on the US operation they want to cover before meeting with President Henderson on Monday here at the villa."

"I don't know how I can be of much help in that department but I'll help anyway I can," Scott replied with a note of concern in his voice.

"Dr. Fleming, I want to emphasize the importance of the meeting with the president. Would you be so kind to mention it to Ms. Pollard beforehand? The president doesn't know her but is very much aware of the detailed role she has had in the whole operation. He would have come today but it is the Jewish Sabbath and he didn't want to offend the Israelis. For the record, there was a strained meeting late yesterday between the president and the pope. The public record only states they had a series of pleasant talks. That was far from the truth and is basically for the general public's consumption. The president can't afford to be seen, especially in the Southern Bible Belt, as kowtowing to the whims of the Vatican. That could cost him thousands of votes in the next election. Remember that was and is a cornerstone of the policies of the American Freedom Party. That is the line that is being touted in the US papers and it has been well covered. Tomorrow's meeting will be a horse of a different colour. Remember, Henderson and the new pope have been lifetime friends. This present crisis could blow the lid of US–Vatican relations if we aren't careful, for the next thirty years." He stopped and waited to see if Scott was up to speed with all the details he had placed on the table.

"I'll have a talk with Lynn after lunch when the kids are with their grandmother. She's a levelheaded person when push comes to shove and will quickly get a handle on things."

"I'd appreciate anything you can do. Both our governments want to nip this American Freedom Party in the bud before they can get the whole lunatic fringe on their side. There is a real strain of anti-Semitism in their ranks and we want that stamped out immediately. That's why we're so strong against them and the Red Rose Brotherhood. Dr. Fleming, we want to nail this coffin shut, period," he said curtly.

"Leave the whole matter with me, Mr. Burgstein. I think Lynn is as confused as I was before you filled in all the blanks. I'll be talking with her this evening."

With these words, Burgstein graciously dismissed himself and went back out into the villa. Within a few minutes, Martha, and the girls came tearing up the path from the beach.

"Hi, Daddy. We had a great swim with Aunt Lynn," cried little Francie from across the foyer. "We're going to have some lunch and then a snooze. Then we'll go back to the beach." Martha rolled her eyes at the precociousness of the child as she raced by.

"How was the beach, Mom? I was thinking of going down and having a swim," he asked.

"Oh, I'm sure Lynn is already expecting you. Sometimes I think the girls overpower her, but she never complains! You let that girl escape, Scott, and you'll have me to contend with!" She walked off in a pretended huff amidst his low laughter.

Chapter 78

As they walked along the edge of the gently rolling surf, Scott sensed Lynn's inner pain. Stopping by a small crowd of bathers, she took off the long white shirt she was wearing and wandered into the surf. She wore a modest red bikini with a light skirt hung low on her hips. The halter was well covering but the bottom visible through the translucent skirt was brief. The thin ties from the sides disappeared between the firm globes of her buttocks. He saw her hesitate at the water's edge.

"What's the matter?" he called from behind her.

She turned, a strange look on her face. "I'm tired of this suit, the top doesn't go with the bottom and besides, it's too tight," she quipped.

"Yes, I noticed. Why don't you take it off like the rest of the women here?" he answered.

She flushed crimson, looking about. "You're not serious!"

He shrugged, wading past her into the small waves as the warm water splashed against their legs. Turning to let her catch up, he was surprised to find her unfastening her halter. She tucked it into a small pocket in her beach skirt and walked to his side. He was surprised to see her left nipple was pierced with a small silver ring. For half an hour they swam in the azure-blue water of the Mediterranean saying not a word to each other.

As they finally walked from the water and Lynn fastened her beach skirt about her hips, he asked, "Lynn, what's the matter? Is it Baird's treachery that's got you so distraught ?"

She turned, her eyes brimming with tears and seemed on the edge of control. "What's happening to us? I've known this man all my life and now he's doing this. I don't understand," she moaned.

"Lynn, I wish I knew what motivates people to do some of the things they do. I see that in the medical field, constantly," he answered.

"To top it all off, I've dragged you and your family into this—that's the real kicker!" she whispered, a deep hurt in her low voice.

"Lynn, be very clear about this, if we didn't want to be a part of your life, we wouldn't be here. And you don't have to worry about Mother being a difficult in-law. She says she can't wait to have you in the house permanently!" he added.

Lynn looked at him. "She actually said so?"

"You must know Mother by now—she's an unusual woman, especially for her years. She says if I don't propose to you, she'll do it herself." As he talked, her eyes softened as she felt herself relearning the old art of leaning on someone else's strength. Putting her hand on his he could feel her squeezing out of her need.

The crowd on the beach was increasing and the noise was swirling around them.

"Let's walk down the beach where there are less people and have a swim." As they did, she held his hand tightly and watched the glances her lack of swimming apparel was having on the admiring passing men. The water was blue and extremely clear, which surprised Scott because of their closeness to Rome. Lynn removed her skirt and they plunged into the water for a soothing swim.

As they swam about in water to their necks, Scott said, "Lynn, there must be some sense of deep failure in Baird's personality for him to take such an action. Has he ever been involved in any of the fringe groups you can remember?"

She stopped and looked out over the blue Mediterranean in thought. Finally, she turned to face him. "That's the troubling part—for the life of me, I can't recall another incident like this one. Dad knew him during the Vietnam War era and he was a far more devoted supporter of the war effort than Dad ever was. He often said if he was younger and his health better, he would have been down there fighting."

He placed his arm about her bare shoulders as they walked back along the water's edge. She picked up her skirt and walked by his side. "Sometimes when people age, they feel they have missed something in life and take drastic action to make up for what they perceive was their mistake or omission."

"I don't follow you?"

"I knew one colleague who was in his late sixties and was losing some of the motor coordination needed for complicated surgery. He could have had a great general practise and consultation practise for years, but that wasn't for him. He hit the bottle and everything went down the tube. Lynn, none of us ever becomes everything people want us to be when we get older or what we even want for ourselves."

She listened to him quietly as they continued to walk. "You mean he threw it all away?"

"Yes, and that was the great tragedy! He had all those good years left and it was wasted. I knew a thousand things I would like to have asked him!" He was quiet and walked ahead.

"I gather you knew him?" she said.

"Yes, Lynn, he was my father and he broke my mother's heart when he threw his best years away." There was a catch in his voice as he answered her.

She faced him and clasped both his hands. "I'm so sorry, Scott, I didn't know!" she whispered.

Suddenly the whole veneer that was the Scott that faced the world seemed to crumble as she drew him against her. He held her tight and could feel the soft mounds of her bare breasts pressing against his chest. Finally he said a quiet voice, "There's no way you could have known. He was over forty when I was born and I didn't know him as an adult when he wrestled with this and other problems. What he put Mother through is more than I care to think about. How she became the lady she is today is beyond me. So now you see, Lynn, why I fight the profession so much so it doesn't take over my life!" She slipped an arm about his waist as they walked along by the water.

"How about a drink? I'm thirsty," Scott suddenly intoned.

Lynn was about to agree and then hesitated. "I can't go in like this, not the way I'm dressed—I'll be arrested."

"Hell, half the women here on the beach have less on than you do; besides, you have the best rack on the beach. What are you worrying about!" He laughed aloud.

She laughed aloud and finally exclaimed, "My brother always called me 'chesty' and you're just as bad as he is! What the hell, you've made a loose woman of me and I love it!" She wrapped her skirt about her hips, adjusted her hair band, straightened her shoulders and followed Scott into the little beach bar.

Chapter 79

Frank Baird was furious! He called for an emergency meeting of the new American Freedom Party and only two thirds of the total membership showed up. As they gathered in the large office he kept in his home, the meeting rapidly turned ugly. Some of the members were stunned over the killing of the man they thought was their leader and spokesman. Most were never informed he was only a front man. Even the three Southern senators who sat on the committee were unaware of the fact. Baird was so much an institution around the capital, they deferred to his judgement. Now Chief Justice Saunders and his flowing eloquence were gone. Baird tapped his pen on the side of a glass at the end of a large rectangular table as he called the meeting to order.

"Some of you are in the dark with reference to today's events and I want to bring you up to speed. As you know, Chief Justice Saunders was shot this morning." There were several loud gasps near the back of the room. "He was killed on the spot but the assassin was in turn killed by two of our own agents. So we have a case already where our people have rendered the American people an invaluable service. On the other hand our party has been dealt a crippling blow by his death. However, we will survive and be a leading player in the future of this great nation."

He was suddenly interrupted by the soft southern drawl of Senator Caldwell from Georgia. "That may be true, Mr. Baird, but isn't it also true our two agents in turn were shot by an unknown assailant?"

"Yes, Senator, that's correct! They were killed trying to protect law and order before matters got out of hand!"

"What about the contents of the chief justice's speech? Wasn't he trying to lay bare in the presence of the new pope, the Vatican's duplicity in the assassination of Lincoln as well as other events over the past century and a half?" asked Clayton Stillwell, the millionaire rancher from Idaho.

"That's right, we were shunned by the justice's own oratorical ability! The crowds were reacting more than normal and the assassin's schedule was off when he got the go-ahead. As a result, the key part of the speech was never reached. If he had, the whole crowd would have been worked over Saunders and we would have had them in our pocket. As a result of the early shot, our position has been made far more precarious. Saunders could have done in fifteen minutes with that crowd if he had the opportunity what now may take us a year to do otherwise.!" Baird replied with a bitter edge to his voice.

"Well, what was the point in shooting the vice president? I didn't know it was in the plan!" Stillwell asked.

"That's a complete mystery to me! The gunman was hired to fire only enough shots to hit the chief justice and at a very specific time, nothing else. The only conclusion we can arrive at is that he was hit by a flying bullet fragment. His condition is good and apparently he will survive with no ill effects. But that doesn't change the nature of the mystery! If this isn't the case, then I'm at a loss to explain it. However, if you will excuse me for a moment, I'm going to call the agency and see if they have any leads in what happened. My years in the city pay off every day. Senator, would you chair the meeting until I return? We'll tighten things up for a spell until this problem dies down," Baird commented as he got to his feet and left the room.

The other fourteen people remained seated while the senator collected himself and prepared to continue with the discussion. He was about to speak when there was a sudden shuffle behind him as the side door of the room suddenly opened. Two men wearing balaclavas entered. Each carried an ugly Uzi machine gun.

"Who the Christ are you and what are you doing with those guns?" the senator barked as he shoved his chair away from the nearest gunman. There was a raspy grunt from the nearest gun which had a huge silencer on the muzzle. The senator jerked straight up in his chair and gasped, "No! No!" as he pitched face forward unto the table. Blood streamed from his nose and mouth with his eyes becoming glassy and empty.

"Now the rest of you get to your feet or you'll get the same treatment as he did." Slowly the other thirteen people rose to their feet. One older woman muttered to herself as she did, whispering to the man next to her. Everyone seeming to be moving in slow motion as fear permeated the air. The same gun coughed again and she fell back into her chair, a great red stain spreading over her blouse. She clawed at her chest for a moment as if to tear away the thing that was killing her. Then she slumped over the arm of the chair and was still. The air in the room was tense as the effect of the killings sank in.

"Now get back against each wall in rows of six and not a word from anyone!" snapped the taller of the two intruders.

When everyone was in place, the taller of the two men nodded to the other.

"Now, you in the front row!" the same said curtly. "Get over here and sit in that chair. One word and you're dead. We want you to tell all the members of your party what you have seen here this afternoon and what you are about to see. Tell them to remember the Holocaust! You remember the words—never again—never again!"

He turned and nodded to the shorter man. Suddenly, there was a nasty stammer of both small guns. The various people standing along each wall were quickly struck by a hail of bullets and fell to the floor amidst a collection of screams and moans. In less than five seconds, all eleven men and women lay dead or badly wounded, cut down by the withering fire of the two machine guns. Then the taller of the two assassins took out a small but deadly-looking revolver and proceeded to put a bullet through the head of each victim. The woman who was spared was hysterical but remained quiet. He turned the gun in her direction for a long moment and then placed it back in his belt.

There was a noise outside the main door. The taller man fired a long staccato burst through the door. There was a loud gasp and the sound of a body falling in the distance behind the closed door. The gunman opened the door and the lifeless body of Mrs. Baird rolled through into the conference room. He turned to the other gunman and stated, "Let's get the hell out of here!" Turning to the woman whose life they had spared, he snapped, "Tell all your friends what you have seen here. We will never permit another Holocaust to happen again! Remember—Never, never, never!" With these words, the two men vanished without another word through the side door by which they had entered the room.

The woman whose life they had spared stood paralysed in pure terror in the middle of the shattered, blood-soaked room. She tried to scream but no sound would come from her mouth. Finally, after a lapse of what seemed to be hours, Frank Baird returned from the third room office where he was talking on a private line to the FBI. As he stopped at the bottom of the stairs, he viewed the utter carnage as riddled bodies lay in every direction. He knelt at the tattered corpse of his wife sprawled in the doorway. Standing up, he grasped the pale figure of the surviving woman who still stood amidst the scattered bodies.

"Adrianna, get a grip on yourself! Who in Christ's name did this? Where are the murdering bastards?" He shook her violently but she made no response. Finally, he slapped her hard across the face.

"Goddam it, woman, come to your senses! You're the only one I can see who is still alive! Tell me or so help me I'll break your neck!" Finally, she began to stammer and stumble through a jumble of words. Again he slapped her across the face. Her nose and mouth began to bleed.

"Tell me, you bitch, or I'll kill you on the spot like the rest of these people!" Baird roared.

Finally, she began to stammer words that were somewhat coherent. "Jews, they were Jews! They killed everyone!" she blubbered.

"What the hell do you mean, Jews? Who were they?" he demanded again.

"They were Jews and from the state of Israel. They also said if we ever threatened Jewish people, they would kill us all just like they did here. Never again would they ever allow the possibility of another Holocaust occurring. Before that happened, we would all be killed!" she intoned.

Baird was stunned! Never in a thousand years had he ever expected these kind of reprisals. He knew there were many in the party ranks who blamed Israel for all the trouble in the Middle East over the years but he thought there was a tight lid on them. Then he remembered how this last chapter had started. It had all begun with the phone call from Lynn Pollard. She would pay for this. It was all her fault. His anger seethed and boiled.

"Dear, sweet little Lynn! You're as much a bitch as your father was a bastard. He stopped me from getting the director's job and now you've interfered. This time you'll pay with your life!"

Chapter 80

April stood looking at herself in the full-length mirror on the back of the bedroom door. Alex Cameron brought her two outfits his wife Rhetta picked up the previous day. She was wearing beige slacks and a blouse that fitted her to a "T". She heard someone and turned to find Tony standing leaning against the door frame.

"Hey, you look super, where did you get the new outfit?" he inquired as he walked over and took her by the arms.

She felt a warmth flooding over her with his words of appreciation. Tony looked well except for the bandage around the back of his head. April looked up at him and smiled. "Tony, I've been so worried. How are you feeling?" she inquired as she leaned forward and gave him a hug.

"I feel great, considering it's been only three days since I had surgery. The only pain is this damn hand. That bastard had a jaw like stone. The only other problem is this damn headache but Alex said that would be there for a few days."

He had barely finished speaking when Alex Cameron breezed through the door in his surgical greens. "Hi, folks. You all ready to leave the hospital?" He looked at each of them with a questioning look.

"Yes, we're ready!" April replied. "Tony looks amazing, don't you think?"

"The only thing I'm mad about are these knuckles I've broken," muttered Tony as he held up his left hand encased in a short cast.

"Tony, I don't know how you ever managed to hit that guy so hard, especially from a semi-prone position. Besides, your breaks are hairline at that. You've got the bone structure of a dinosaur," added Alex.

"Oh, that's understandable, Alex," April said with a giggle. "He's a little later coming out of the trees than the rest of us!"

"I'm like the late Rodney Dangerfield, I get no respect!" Tony muttered with a half-hearted grumble.

"Look, I was talking to Moshe Arnum and he'll be here in a few minutes to brief you on his legation's plans for you here in Toronto. I'll be back to pick you up in an hour's time. You'll be staying with Rhetta and I for a few days until the other arrangements are finalized."

Five minutes later, Moshe Arnum, a swarthy young Israeli in his late twenties, arrived in April's room. "Good morning. I passed Dr. Cameron in the hall and he said you'd be expecting me. I'm Moshe Arnum and it's our pleasure at the Israeli Legation to help get you settled here in Toronto until the whole business settles down."

"Moshe, what are your plans for April and myself? We're getting concerned and a little antsy!" Tony asked.

"We'd like you to stay here in Toronto for the immediate future. The situation with the Freedom Party in the US is still very volatile. That was evident with the attack on the both of you yesterday in the hospital. We've lined up a nice two-bedroom furnished apartment here in the core of the city near the subway. The rent and all utilities have been looked after for a year."

"Do you feel we should stay here to be safe?" April asked.

"April, Dr. Cameron feels you need three months' complete rest so you can recuperate and where he can keep his eye on you!"

"Well, if that's what he wants, that's fine, but I'm going to question him about it when he picks us up."

"We also have six months' research work for both of you to work at in several of our city synagogues. We've been trying to get to it for over a decade now and you're the first people we've had who are eminently qualified in the field.

"Look, I have your baggage from Santo Domingo down in the doctors' lounge. Dr. Cameron suggested I put it there and he can put it in his car when you leave the hospital and get over to his house. I'll be seeing you from time to time over the next few months to see how your work is progressing and how your health is improving," he added as he turned and walked from the room. He left behind two small boxes of April's personal things on her bed.

April had walked to the window and was silently looking out when she felt Tony's arm about her waist. She looked up at him and said nothing. Taking her by the shoulders, he turned her to face him.

"Are you sure of everything we talked about the other day? I'm not too swift about family things and I'll need your help," he said softly.

She looked up at him for a long moment's silence. "Do you have any doubts about your feelings, Tony?" she asked directly.

"None whatsoever! There's no one else I've ever wanted to spend the rest of my life with! I want you to know I'm far from perfect but I'm willing to try hard!"

She smiled and put her arms about him as he tousled her short blond hair.

"Alright, you two lovebirds, no hanky panky in the hospital, now!" Alex Cameron quipped as he strode through the room door.

Chapter 81

Lynn and Scott got to their feet as Benjamin Netanyahu entered the villa's conference room. They had seen his face on the TV screen many times over the years but weren't prepared for his charm. He immediately came over to Lynn and took both her hands in his and said, "Miss Pollard, it is a privilege to meet you especially under these trying circumstances. I hope the accommodation here is to your liking." Turning to Scott, he took his hand. "Dr. Fleming, I'm glad to meet you under trying circumstances! Your reputation for the work you did in Tel Aviv several years back still lingers!

"Please be seated and I'll get down to business. I apologize for bringing you all the way here to Italy, but these were my specific instructions. As you know there was a serious killing in Washington yesterday and the ramifications were far more serious then expected. You were brought here in part to protect you and your family and also to cover our own flanks. Whether or not you realize it, the state of Israel is very involved in the affair as well. Both the Red Rose Brotherhood as well as the new American Freedom Party are deeply involved. We want to make sure the material you discovered is the same we had drawn to our attention over the last forty-eight hours. There would seem to be some evidence to deduce or cause some people to conclude that some Jewish people were involved as well. We simply couldn't take the risk by not acting. There was some evidence the Brotherhood was going to try to place the blame for the killing of Lincoln on the suspected presence of Jewish people!"

"Mr. Prime Minister," Scott asked, "are you saying if the blackmail of the Catholic Church by the Freedom Party failed, they were going to make Israel the scapegoat?"

One of the Israeli aides was suddenly very uncomfortable with the doctor's question.

"That's correct, Doctor, you and Miss Pollard would have been caught in the middle. As a matter of fact, you were actually there already. We don't know if there is enough of them left alive to do any real damage or even if they are fully aware of the full nature of the material you have dug up, Miss Pollard!"

"Are you saying, sir, it was actually the contingent plan of the Brotherhood to make the state of Israel the scapegoat in the case of failure?" Lynn Pollard asked.

"Have no allusions about it. Their policy is to claim credit if it works but to pass along the blame if it doesn't. I can assure you the Jewish people have taken more then their share of the blame for many things in past centuries. No more! The Vatican has been soft on the matter of anti-Semitism for years. It is my personal commitment this will cease. We will do whatever we must to insure things do not take place again!" The prime minister's voice became more strident as he reached the end of the sentence.

"Sir, Miss Pollard and I have been asked to attend a diplomatic meeting here tomorrow. Is this the subject of discussion? If so we are basically unprepared at this juncture," Scott asked directly. "This matter is beginning to wear on us as we've just came off a long plane flight and we were cloistered in your embassy in Washington for several days."

Netanyahu looked confused and puzzled. He looked at his aides and back to Scott and Lynn.

"I see neither of you have been fully briefed and I'm sorry about that. Tomorrow the pope and President Henderson himself are in Rome to discuss the whole matter. I would like both of you to be there and perhaps we can clear this whole mess up. I want you to look at the various Lincoln documents as well as the Surratt papers and see if they are the same as the ones you saw previously!" The prime minister was sharp, relaxed and fully on top of his game.

"As a matter of reference," he continued, "I would like you to look at them now and you will have a heads up when you meet with the other people."

One of his aides pulled out a large file of pictures and papers and spread them out on a large table in the middle of the small room. For nearly twenty minutes, Lynn looked at and sorted through the various parts of the collection.

"Are these the papers sent by Tony Cassell?" the prime minister asked.

"Yes, as far as I can tell without taking them into a well-equipped lab and doing certain tests. I'm satisfied these are the pictures and papers I showed to Frank Baird in the beginning when they first came to light and which I sent to Tony and April before they fled to the Caribbean," Lynn stated simply and walked back and sat beside Scott.

"I'm glad we're clear on that matter. You see these are the most damning and incriminating of all. They are part of the material the attack in Long Beach didn't find. These pictures and the Surratt paper, the crucial one, were the ones the Brotherhood and the Freedom Party desperately wanted to get their hands on!" Netanyahu stood quietly as he talked, establishing eye contact in turn with everyone in the room.

"Miss Pollard and Dr. Fleming, there are two things we should talk about before I let you get some rest: first there is a formal dinner this evening at our embassy here in Rome and I would like you both to come as my guests. I realize neither of you will have any formal clothing, so I've taken the liberty of placing a car and driver at your disposal. This afternoon he will take you to several of Rome's finest stores and they'll outfit you at our expense. Secondly, the meeting tomorrow is at our embassy at eleven in the morning and we'll keep you posted on any further developments. Meanwhile, you and your family are welcome to stay at the resort as long as you wish.

"Miss Pollard, you are doing the state a great service! We will be eternally in your debt and we have long memories!" As he spoke, he took Lynn's right hand and placed it to his lips. His eyes gazed deeply into hers for a lingering moment. Turning to Scott, he spoke, "Doctor, once again it has been a pleasure to make your acquaintance. I hope the next time will be under less stressful conditions!" He shook Scott's hand, smiled and walked from the room.

For a long time Scott and Lynn sat alone with their thoughts. Finally they returned to the deck where Martha and the girls were playing. Little Angie raced over to Lynn and threw her arms about her skirt. She dropped to her knees, picked the child up and held her tight. Francine followed.

"Aunt Lynn, would you come for a walk with Angie and me?" Francine asked seriously. "We have something serious we want to talk to her about!" Lynn looked up at Scott and Martha, rolled her eyes as she walked unto the vast lawn with the two girls in tow.

"Scott," Martha asked seriously, "I hope your intentions with Lynn are serious. Those girls of yours are crazy about her. And I think she is a real gem. For a while I was puzzled by the great sadness and loneliness I saw in her eyes. I asked her about it straight out and she told me, no holds barred. So I hope you'll be kind to her, she'll need it!" Martha concluded.

"Daddy, we've had a talk with Aunt Lynn about when she becomes our new Mummy!" Angie talked with all the seriousness she could muster. As she talked, Scott stole a look at Lynn's face. Many years later, they would look back on this moment as one of great joy. Lynn's eyes were brimming with happy tears and she was smiling softly. Angie continued, "Daddy, since she is going to become our new Mummy, Francie and I think we would like her to get us a new baby sister! Martha says Lynn agrees and she thinks it is a wonderful idea. We think Daddy and Aunt Lynn should do it soon!"

Scott was speechless and finally broke out laughing.

"I've been scuppered! I guess I really don't have much choice in the matter." He walked over and sat down beside Lynn and placed an arm about her slim shoulders.

She leaned over and whispered, "Hi, Pops. How're you doing?"

Chapter 82

The Israeli Embassy in Rome was ablaze with lights. Limos were coming from all directions. Scott and Lynn were taken from the villa where they were staying to the various clothiers in the fanciest district in the city. Late in the afternoon they went directly to the embassy where they were to get ready for dinner. About four o'clock, the ambassador informed them there was a change of plans. They would be apart of a formal dinner at the US Embassy since the president himself was in town. As Scott adjusted his bow tie in the tux he was wearing, he called out to Lynn in the suite they had been given on the top floor of the Israeli Embassy. There was no response. Walking into her adjoining bedroom, he found her fully dressed before a full length mirror adjusting her ear rings. Her black dress stunned him.

"What's the matter with me? You don't like this dress?" There was a note of concern in her voice. "I won't tell you what it cost except I'd have to take a mortgage at home to pay for it. However, this was what they wanted me to wear!" Her dress was a shinny floor-length sheath, stunning in its simplicity. Her arms were bare and the front extended from her neck to the floor. Her back was completely bare almost to her buttocks and the paleness of her skin was in stark contrast to the black of the dress. It clung to her like a second skin molding her figure and shimmering as she moved. As he looked her up and down, she flushed.

"That's the prettiest dress I've ever seen. What you do to it should be against the law. Every woman at the embassy will be jealous and the men will be watching you all evening. Besides, the young bucks will be visually undressing you with every glance!" He responded with a soft smile.

She looked at Scott for a long moment before quipping, "Now you have me really self-conscious. I begin to think the dress is too much and then you say something like that! Did you know the guy at the clothiers tried to tell me that I shouldn't wear anything under the dress! Can you believe that! I finally settled for next to nothing and don't ask!" She stepped over and kissed him for a long moment. as she did his hands rested on the warm flesh of her back.

"We'd better get going. I don't know what this dinner is all about but I don't want us to be late!" He took her by the elbow and guided her to the elevator to the main floor.

"I was wondering the same thing, especially since we're going to the US Embassy. Unless it has to do with this whole protracted Surratt business," she said.

"Lynn, I really am at a loss. On the other hand I think it's rather obvious we're there in some capacity to help relations between our two governments. Otherwise, why would they go to all this trouble? I have the feeling we are an ace in the hole for the Israeli government and worth every cent they're investing in us. Many of my medical Jewish friends are always telling me the Israeli government never does anything that isn't to its own advantage!" Scott added.

In a matter of minutes they were escorted to a large limo which in turn took them to the sprawling embassy. They were led up the wide front steps with a number of other couples dressed in the peak of formal attire. As they walked, Scott whispered in Lynn's ear, "I like what you do to that dress as you walk." There was a sparkle in his smile that penetrated her innermost feelings. There was something about this man that appealed to her. As they reached the top of the steps, he whispered in her ear, "I'd like to ravage you right here on these steps in front of everyone. Boy, would that ever make the headlines back home!"

Despite herself, she gasped out loud and her hand flew to her lips to stifle a giggle. "Scott, please, how can I keep a straight face if you keep saying things like that in public!" There was a considerable lack of conviction in her voice. Giving him a yank, she stepped up ahead of him as she reached the top of the steps and entered the main foyer of the embassy.

Suddenly they heard their names being announced and they were lead forward and presented to the US ambassador, Gerald and his wife Valerie. They shook hands and were escorted down the line as more and more people entered the building behind them. They were barely inside the building when they were approached by a young man in full evening dress.

"Dr. Fleming? Ms. Pollard? Would you please follow me? There is someone who has asked to see you." Before Scott was able to answer, the young man turned and they were being led into the centre of the building. He stopped in front of a large set of double doors and then vanished. The large doors opened and a good-looking man with dark hair in his mid-thirties greeted them with scarcely a break in pace.

"Ah! Dr. Fleming! You don't remember but you saved my daughter's life a few years ago! My name is Michael Turner, the assistant secretary of state. Come in and have a seat. President Henderson will be with you in a moment."

Scott looked at Lynn. She was slightly flushed and speechless with all the pomp and VIP treatment. The assistant secretary pointed to several chairs.

"No thanks, Mr. Secretary, we'd rather stand and wait for the president. By the way, I do remember your daughter. She was a very lucky young lady. That aneurysm could have blown at any time and there was no way she could have lived through it," Scott added.

"Doctor, my wife and I will always be eternally grateful. She was our only child. Since then she has presented us with three grandchildren and we owe so much to you." Scott felt Lynn squeezing his hand. "By the way, Doctor, I've heard wonderful things about your lady here!" He turned and picked up Lynn's right hand. "But I owe her an apology! I had no idea she was the 'looker' I see before me! Ms. Pollard, please forgive my directness! My wife says it will be the death of me yet!" he added with a slight stammer in his voice.

Lynn flushed a beet red and was almost beside herself. Before she could answer, there was a rustle and movement behind them. Scott and Lynn turned to come face to face with President Henderson.

"Good evening, folks. I'm glad you were able to spare me a few moments in your busy day." He quickly shook Scott's hand with a crushing grip and turned to pick up Lynn's free one.

"It's so good to meet you, Ms. Pollard. I have been aware of your work for some time now! Doctor, your work among many people I know has become legendary! I'm sorry we have to meet under these circumstances. Ms. Pollard, I wasn't aware you knew Dr. Fleming. He is well known amongst people I know and is highly respected. I sense you are close to him—your eyes give you away! I wish you all the happiness! Look, I want to talk to the both of you when this greeting line is finished. My aide will come and get you and we can talk in private." With these words the tall gaunt figure of the president moved down the line of guests.

Within a few minutes after the greeting line was finished, a young marine came looking for them and led them to a small private office near the back of the building. By the time they were settled in a large sofa, the president was back and waved them back to their seats when they got to their feet as he entered the room.

"Please remain seated. We must get down to the issue at hand as I've got a busy schedule tomorrow and want to get some sleep. That damned plane was all over the sky on the long haul from Washington," he added.

"What is so important that you had to fit us into such a tight schedule, Mr. President?" Lynn asked.

"I see you're a person who gets right to the point, Ms. Pollard," Henderson replied. He was an unusually tall man, in the vicinity of six feet five inches, with a gangly build that reminded many people of Lincoln. Yet he was void of the awkwardness many people saw in Lincoln. He was in his late forties and looked younger, projecting an image of youthfulness and vigour. For many he was a throwback to the days of John Kennedy.

"I think you know I have a meeting tomorrow with the pope and the Israeli prime minister at the Vatican. It will be a confidential meeting as we will be addressing issues that have been plaguing us since the end of the Second World War. The new pope and I have known each other since college days, so it will be interesting. Ms. Pollard, I have seen those documents you have turned over to the Mossad. Do you feel they are authentic?" He looked at her intently as he talked.

As he finished, Lynn smoother out her skirt as she sat and prepared to respond. "Mr. President, I feel there is a good chance the pictures are the real thing. As for the Surratt paper, I have no way of knowing. My expertise lies in the area of photography, not here. As you know, I sent copies of this material to a research team in California. A close friend, Tom Cassell, feels they are probably authentic. My personal feeling is, despite all the conclusive evidence, there is still no final proof that the Vatican ordered the killing of Lincoln. From our vantage point in time it may seem to be very plausible, but you must remember, Mr. President, that was back in the 1860s, and it just doesn't ring with me."

Scott Fleming hung on her every word. He hadn't heard her full presentation on the subject before. Scott injected, "I still have great trouble seeing how the Mossad got involved in the middle of everything."

"It's straightforward, Doctor. One of their agents was accidentally killed by an operative of the Freedom Party in Europe. They investigated and then contacted our foreign office. I could see the recipe for disaster if the Freedom Party got hold of any of this material and so I flew to see the Israeli prime minister for a private meeting on the matter. We agreed on what later transpired. It was a perfect solution to have them clean up the mess. I was in a 'catch-22' situation insofar as the Freedom Party was concerned. The prime minister suggested it would be expeditious for them to tidy everything up in the US as well as here while they were at it. Their point was simply that the American Freedom Party knew nothing about the Mossad involvement and by the time they figured it out, we would be long gone."

"It seems far too neat and tidy to me," Scott said.

"That has a lot of truth to it but at the present it's the only option we have on the table at the moment. Finally, the Mossad has a real handle on the situation on the ground and is dealing with the people involved." With these words, President Henderson stood up and added, "I'm going to suggest tomorrow we destroy all the Lincoln-related material. What do you think, Ms. Pollard?"

"Mr. President, I don't really care if I ever see any of it again. I think if any is kept whether we ever fully know if it is the real McCoy or not, there will always be the possibility."

"Precisely, that's why I want it all destroyed. I may have trouble trying to convince the prime minister of that necessity. It gives him some real leverage in various places, especially with the Vatican, but I'm convinced more than ever they have to be destroyed." As he talked, the president slowly walked to the door.

As soon as he opened the door, his aide standing at the door asked, "Yes, Mr. President?"

"We're getting ready for dinner. Would you please escort Dr. Fleming and Ms. Pollard into the dining room. Doctor, the embassy staff put a great deal of stock in formality and the like. I'm the unexpected guest and I won't come into the room until the last moment."

"Thank you, Mr. President, for explaining the affair to Scott and myself. I was greatly confused with the course of events and now will be able to go home and have some idea why things happened the way they did." As she spoke, the president held her hand and held it warmly. She felt a warmth and affinity for the man. Then he was gone.

The young aide spoke, "This way, please. The president will follow you to the banquet hall shortly!"

Outside the main door, Scott clasped Lynn by the elbow and drew her aside by a tall marble column. As he did, she placed both hands on his chest as he spoke, "It's over, now we can go home and get our family together in peace!"

She sighed as he spoke. "I certainly hope you're right!" She smiled and took his hand as they walked to the banquet hall.

Chapter 83

Four days had passed since Lynn returned to Washington from the sudden trip to Italy. At first she went to her apartment to try and get everything back in order. Finally on Monday morning, she returned to her office for the first time in three weeks. Walking through the main door was difficult. She half expected to find Maggie there to greet her. Instead there was a new face behind the receptionist desk. She was an attractive dark-haired girl in her early thirties. As Lynn strode past her into her office, she said, "Good morning. I don't believe we've met?"

The girl muttered something under her breath and continued with her face buried in the computer. She said nothing in response to Lynn's cheery greeting. Lynn shrugged her shoulders and walked towards her office. As she did, the new girl called out, "Excuse me, ma'am, you can't go in that office— it's private and I don't know when Ms. Pollard will be back!"

Lynn walked slowly back to Maggie's old desk, a certain frostiness settling about her. As she approached the desk, she asked, "And who might I ask are you?" as she rested both hands on the edge of Maggie's old desk.

The girl looked at Lynn with daggers in her eyes, first at her hands and back to Lynn's face again "Ma'am, this is a private office and you can't go in there! Now, please leave this office before I call security and have you removed!" she snapped.

Lynn looked at her for a moment and said curtly, "Call them if you must but have your best explanation ready for your rudeness and stupidity!" Lynn was furious. She was weary from the long grinding plane trip to Italy and back and her impatience was not far beneath the surface. Digging out her office key, she let herself into her private office and settled down to going through the huge backlog of mail.

Twenty minutes later, two of the building's security guards arrived at her door. She recognized them and welcomed them with a cheery response to their big smiles. The younger chap, George Ranksan, had tried to date her in vain a few years before, but she wasn't interested. He called out a cheery, "Hi,

Lynn. We've not seen you for a week or so. Where've you been keeping yourself?"

"Hi, guys. It's good to see you both! I was out of the country for a few days on business but it's good to be back. Listen, I know you're here for more than to tell me how great I am—what's up, guys?" She laughed as she talked.

"Oh, we had a strange call from the new receptionist up front. Apparently some strange woman was trying to get into your office and we'd best get down here if we valued our jobs! Lynn, what the hell is coming down?"

"Yeah! And she's a real bitch to say the very least!" snapped Joe, the other guard, who was usually quiet but seemed to be agitated over the whole business.

"Oh, that's me she's all pissed off about. I spoke to her when I came and she nearly bit my head off. I gave her a chewing out but never did tell her who I really was. It's been a hell of a week and she just set me off and especially when I saw her behind Maggie's desk," Lynn injected.

"Boy, she's going to be plenty frosted when she finds out who you really are!" replied Joe.

"That may be true, but she caught me as I was thinking about Maggie and I blew off. I still don't know why they had to shoot Maggie; she never hurt a soul in her life. This job was her whole life," wailed Lynn.

"Alright, Lynn, don't worry about the bitch out front. We'll tell her we've thrown you out and that Ms. Pollard will be back anytime now. And that she should be on her best behaviour." George chuckled as he waved goodbye to Lynn slumped behind her desk.

"Thanks, guys, I appreciate it. I'm in no mood for her kind of bullshit right now."

About a half hour after the guards left, the new receptionist arrived in Lynn's doorway and asked in a loud voice, "What the hell did those bastards mean when they said you were in your office? I don't understand the whole pattern of procedure and protocol in this office!" There was a flush of anger about her as she spoke.

Lynn raised her face to the girl from the pile of papers she was attempting to work through. A pall of weariness had fallen over Lynn as the real effect of Maggie's death seemed to be everywhere in the building. Even the new receptionist appeared to sense something was drastically wrong.

"Look, I think you and I have got off to a poor start. I'm Lynn Pollard and we're going to be working together, so let's try and make a fresh start!"

"Like hell! My job is to reorganize this whole office and the steps are already in motion. My predecessor was an incompetent fool from what I can tell and from what I see you won't be around this office for long!" she snapped.

"Lady, I don't know where the hell you sprang up from. However, I'll try to keep this simple so even you can understand me. I run this office and am responsible to the CEO of Kodak and you have no place in that picture. How you got here I have no idea nor do I care. Now move your ass out of here before I throw you through the door myself!" Lynn added wearily. The woman's face turned ashen and she turned on her heels and left in a huff.

As she worked through the morning, Lynn found her thoughts drifting again and again to Scott and the kids. This was very unusual for her as she had said on occasions she felt she was prepared to leave marriage and motherhood to others. At thirty-eight she felt her best childbearing years were behind her. Now the whole scene was completely changed. She found herself embracing the ideas of being a wife again and mother with an enthusiasm that overwhelmed her. When Scott's girls approached her with their plans for a baby sister, she was flabbergasted. Even thinking about it in her office brightened her day.

At one-thirty, she picked up her phone and called Sam Crosby, her boss, on his private line at Kodak World Headquarters in Rochester. He was on the phone in a flash.

"Lynn, for Chrissake, how've you been? I had a call from a friend in our embassy in Rome and he said you and your doctor friend had a meeting with the president! Holy shit, girl, you get around!" His deep resonant voice was as cheery as always.

"Thanks for being patient with me, Sam. I'm afraid I haven't been much of an asset to the company these past few months but I've tried to keep you posted on the nature and direction of the research!"

"Lynn, for God's sake don't worry about it! That project you wrapped up last year has probably saved the company over fifty million dollars, not to mention the tax write-offs for all your work with the Eastman Foundation! You know the board, you're their girl in shining armour. But listen, we heard all about the shooting in your office! What's going on?"

As usual it was difficult to get a word in with the effusive Crosby. She always knew he was a genius in the field of people skills and this was visible in her loyalty to the man.

"Sam, thanks for the morale booster! We've had a problem with some pictures a friend dug up over at the National Archives. I don't want to say too much at this juncture except to mention there have been over a dozen deaths already involved in the problem!" she said casually.

"Christ, girl, what have you got yourself into?" he asked urgently.

"Oh, it's nothing I can't handle and as a matter of fact it's pretty well over as we speak!"

"Lynn, just on a hunch, does this have anything to do with the assassination of the chief justice?

"Yes, Sam, and I will have a story for you when this is all over!" she quipped.

"Lynn, for Christ's sake don't take any unnecessary chances. I know you when you get on a roll!" he added.

She rolled her eyes in response and smiled to herself as he talked. If only he knew what she'd been through the past week.

"Look, Sam, I'm going to take a couple of weeks' holidays and when I come back I'll give you a call," she said.

"Thank God, girl. The board have been on my back to order you to take some time off. Tell me honestly, girl, do you love the guy?" he asked the tone of his voice changing completely. Strange feelings welled up in her throat as his words caught her flat footed. She was speechless. "Lynn, did you hear me?"

Finally she was able to manage a whisper for an answer. "Yes, Sam, I do. I never thought it would happen to me again."

"Then go for it, girl! You know how we all feel about you. I knew from the tone of your voice, there was a sense of joy there I haven't heard in a long time. I also knew there was something afoot from the report I got from my friend in Rome regarding your dress at the dinner for Henderson. He said it was enough to make the new pope throw out his vows of celibacy. Lynn, we're all rooting for you here!" There was a happy tone to his voice as he hung up.

Walking from her office, she picked up a few papers and placed them in her small briefcase and closed it up. Putting on her denim jacket, she walked from her office and past the receptionist. As soon as she saw Lynn, she turned her head the other way and ignored her. Lynn laughed to herself, walked past the desk and out of the building.

Sitting in the driver's seat of her old Honda Accord, she threw her briefcase on the floor and reached for her seatbelt. She thought she heard something. As she turned her head, a large piece of white cloth was slapped over her face. She struggled violently but to no avail. The arm about her neck clamped tighter and tighter. She quickly smelled the pungent aroma of chloroform. The more she struggled, the tighter the arm grew. Slowly she started to drift into a pit of blackness. She heard voices in the background but was unable to understand anything. She failed to see the form of the second man climbing into the passenger seat. Then she plunged into a black pit of nothingness.

"The bitch is out cold and will be for an hour or so. I didn't want to give her any more in case she didn't come out of it. I don't give a shit but Baird would have my balls for breakfast if something was to happen to her."

"What the hell are we going to do with her now? We've got to get her out of here before someone comes along," the man in the passenger seat replied.

"Quick, get the trunk open and I'll dump her in there," the man in the back said. Lynn was quickly picked up and dumped roughly into the trunk which was in turn slammed shut.

"Now, let's get the hell out of here and over to that house Baird has been using on the far side of the city," the man in the front seat replied as the car roared away into the busy afternoon traffic.

Chapter 84

Lynn Pollard slowly regained consciousness, her head aching and the smell of chloroform lingering in her nostrils. Before opening her eyes, she heard voices in the background.

"The bitch is coming to, I saw her stir a few minutes ago. Make sure her hands are tied, if she gets loose, she can kill you." The voice was a strange one.

"Don't worry, I checked her ropes and they're tight. Baird said to leave her on the cot. He's known her all her life, so it's going to be hard for him to do what has to be done when he's finished with her." Someone grabbed her by the sleeves of her sweater and jerked her to a sitting position. She slowly opened her eyes and looked about. She was sitting on what appeared to be an old couch or sofa in some sort of a hotel or motel room. On the other side of the room sat the man whose voice she recognized and next to him a total stranger. Somehow she thought she had seen him before but she wasn't sure.

"Where am I and what do you want from me?" she snapped as she struggled to make herself more comfortable.

"Lady, where you are doesn't matter and you're to see an old family friend, Frank Baird! He'll be along any minute, although I'm not sure he'll be very pleased to see you. He's pretty pissed off at you and the way you double-crossed him," her kidnapper blurted out.

"I don't know what the hell you're talking about," Lynn replied as she struggled to loosen the ropes binding her wrists.

"Look, you bitch, if I had my way, I'd have put a bullet in you long before now. Thank your lucky stars you're still alive." The other man sat reading an old copy of *Newsweek*.

Looking about, she noticed two windows with dirty panes of glass. Through them she could see the blurry outlines of tree branches moving in the summer air. She knew then she was somewhere in the city plus the constant whirr of traffic in the distance. From her small Timex, she calculated she had been in their hands for about three hours. She heard a noise at the side door.

Turning her head, she saw the hunched figure of Frank Baird entering the room.

"Well, I never thought I'd see you in a situation like this, Lynn. Neither did I expect you to turn out to be a traitor!" he snapped as he pulled up a chair.

"You know, Frank, you were a good friend of my family, in fact I grew up thinking you were a part of the family's inner circle, with one exception—my dad!" She sneered at him as she talked.

"What the hell do you mean, your dad? You yourself said he was sold out by his country when he returned from Nam!" Baird responded.

"No, Frank, the last time I ever saw my dad before he went back to Vietnam, he said he thought you would end up like this someday! He said he thought you would throw your sanity to the wind and sell out your country for some stupid idea. Looks like he wasn't wrong, Frank! You proved to be the lowlife he thought you'd become. Yes, he was treated poorly when he returned from Nam the first time but he never wavered in his belief in his country and went back again when he was asked. Tell me, Frank, how does it feel to a scum bag at your age?" There was a bitter rancour in her voice. "No matter what you do to me, and I have no illusions about your intentions on that score, my feelings towards you are a bitter disappointment to everything I believe in except this country and what she stands for! I believe in this country as my father did, but in her great spirit and great heart as my father did! I don't believe in traitors, Frank, only those who don't give to this country what she has given to us—greatness of heart and openness of spirit. Nothing can change that!"

The nastiness and completeness of her attack overpowered Frank Baird. He seemed to physically wither under the intensity of her verbal assault. He turned to the other two men and asked, "Did you get the material or find out where it is?"

"No, Mr. Baird, she says she hasn't got it and hasn't been the best example of cooperation," the younger man replied.

"Alright, you guys go outside and wait with the rest of our people. I have my friend coming through the back door in ten minutes' time and I don't want anyone else here." The two men left by the back door.

"Lynn, I'm disappointed you haven't seen fit to come over to join our new movement. We've had several setbacks over the past few days, but there's no stopping us now. You'll see why when you meet my friend who will be here in a few minutes. He is the real silent strength behind everything we have been doing these past six months. As a matter of fact, it was his idea that we set up the assassination of the chief justice a few days ago. Then when you did in the senator, that was a blessing in disguise, as if you had planned it all beforehand."

"You're telling me you had planned that I might do him in?" she asked.

"Yes, we sent out one of our men to follow you, do the job and then blame it all on you. That way, he would be out of the picture and so would you. We didn't realize how adept you were with your martial arts."

"So you were getting rid of all these high-profile people as soon as they outlived their usefulness to you and your party?" she asked.

"Lynn, you're your dad's daughter, a great patriot but unwilling to bend with the winds of reality," Frank muttered.

"Frank, who's behind you and the brains of the outfit? It certainly isn't you!" she snapped realizing she was starting to irritate him.

"What the hell do you mean by that crack? The last time I saw your father, he was such a prick. I had to get him out of my sight and you'd be surprised what a few words on Bob Haldimand's ear could do!" He sneered at her.

"Frank Baird, you goddamned bastard, you sent my father back to Vietnam for the third time and to the centre of the worst fighting! I should have known! You made sure he wouldn't come back!"

He could see the fury in her eyes. Before he could answer, there was a soft rap on the side door. Lynn Pollard looked up and it was a moment she would never forget. There stood the distinguished figure of Thurgood Kavanaugh, the vice president. She never personally liked him but had a grudging respect for the man and his outspokenness. As he entered the room, she noticed his right arm was in a sling.

"So this is the dangerous lady you've been telling me about," he said in a cold emotionless voice looking at Frank Baird. He reached for a chair with his damaged arm and sat down. Then he slipped the sling off his arm.

"I see you're one of those people who heal quickly, Mr. Vice President," Lynn said in a sarcastic voice. His eyes looked at her with a cold chill that sent shivers down her spine. At that moment, she realized who the main thrust behind the Freedom Party really was.

"Madam, you find yourself in a very difficult position. You have made life difficult for all of us these past few days by your refusal to cooperate with Mr. Baird. You don't seem to get it through your head that we're dealing with the seeds of the next American revolution. Lincoln used to talk about a new rebirth of American democracy. We're talking about something even more important, a rebirth of Americanism. You've had you're chance to get on board and missed it. Now you've got yourself in a bind."

"Mr. Vice President, you can go screw yourself. When I hear you talk, I don't know whether to laugh or throw up, except you are so goddamned dangerous! I don't have your damned Lincoln pictures and even if I did, I'd never give them to the likes of you. Tell me, how'd you get that information on the Vatican to begin with, let alone getting the Red Rose Brotherhood on your side?"

"What do you mean getting the Red Rose bunch on our side? Woman, what the hell are you talking about? We've followed our agenda from the very beginning and have been trying to figure out what's been happening to some of our agents from time to time. We know the Israeli Mossad have been there like a dirty shirt, but that's what they do anyway. Some of our people want to cozy up to them but we don' t want any Jews or blacks in our party. Remember what I said about the rebirth of a new kind of Americanism!" Kavanaugh became so angry he rose to his feet and walked back and forth across the room. Her words had struck a nerve as his temper continued to fuel his words.

"I was under the impression they were doing what we wanted them to do from the beginning and nothing more. Baird, you bastard, isn't that what you told me from the beginning? You guaranteed they would stay under our control and you'd deliver the votes of some sixty million Catholics to our cause without the information. Then that damned Saunders screwed up his speech. Thank God we planned the fake hit on myself. Now, I'm the martyr who survived the attack and will pick up millions of sympathy votes."

His outburst was more than Lynn Pollard had ever bargained for. Suddenly she saw the deep abiding and sinister side of the whole plan. As she listened she wondered where the meeting was going and what would be her plan in it. She was sure that she now knew more than anyone had planned and feared greatly for her life. She remembered the attack on April and Tony and they were only after the documents themselves. At this very moment, she knew she was in the middle of a power struggle between Kavanaugh and Frank Baird. There was panic in her chest when she began to realize how precarious her situation was. Then she thought of Scott and her life ahead of her and she knew what she had to. Turning to the vice president, she quipped, "Sir, I gather you've had the conviction for some time that this country was adrift and in need of a new hand at the helm. You've put your trust in other hands aside from your own, and they've stumbled. Now, the whole thing is in your lap."

"Don't believe a word the bitch is saying!" snapped Baird. "She's on the endangered list and is using all her wits to escape. She's no better than her old man!" Baird growled.

"What the hell has her old man to do with this discussion?" Kavanaugh injected angrily.

"My father was a patriot, Mr. Vice President, and went to the wire for this country in Vietnam, but this bastard you call a partner didn't like some of his questions and had a friend send him off to Nam for a third tour! He was killed in action three weeks after he landed. He's even quoted the name of Bob Haldimand to me. I'm telling you he's using you like he used my father thirty-five years ago. You've been had, Mr. Vice President. The only honour you'll get now is a prison cell for treason!"

The air was taut with tension. Lynn struggled to remain sitting as the two men faced each other. Baird backed away with cold fear in his eyes. He appeared to Lynn as a man whose reckless past had finally caught up with him.

Kavanaugh spoke slowly as he drew a small revolver from his pocket. "We should have finished you a long ways back but you're a legend around this town. Now it's too bad but you've outlived your usefulness!" As he raised the gun he muttered, "You're old, Baird, you should have died a long time ago! I'm doing you a favour, this way you go out quick! His revolver barked three times an rapid succession. The heavy form of Frank Baird was thrown back to the side wall of the small room, three small holes appearing high on the left side of his chest. He gasped, his mouth trying to form words as the bullets tore through his body. One more gunshot echoed and a dark hole appeared in the middle of the old man's forehead. His arms dropped and he pitched forward face first to the floor, dead before the body struck the floor. Kavanaugh stared at the still form for a long moment, then turned to Lynn Pollard, her face pale as she saw the man she had known all her life dead before her eyes. There was a grim look on the vice president's face as he raised the revolver in her direction.

"How does it feel to witness the death of a legend? Unfortunately, there is no way I can let you live after what you've been a part of and now after what you've seen!"

Chapter 85

Lynn Pollard looked down at the bullet-riddled body of Frank Baird. While she felt no remorse, it was still a shock to see a man she knew all her life lying dead at her feet. His wife and family had supported him all their lives and now it had come to this! Kavanaugh held his gun on her.

"If you have anything to add to this mess, don't, it can't make matters any worse than they are at the moment! I've known for some time what Baird was up to, but hoped he'd pull it all together. But after Saunders blew the punch line in his speech, I knew we'd have to get rid of Baird eventually as well. Now, we have the problem of you," he added cryptically.

"You don't have to get yourself all worked up about me," she added in a bitter voice. "In your eyes I'm a dead woman and you know it. There's no way you can leave me alive with all the details I know on every side of the issue."

"Is that how you think I view you and everything you've been involved in this past week or so? You are missing the point that what you people think has been happening by chance was planned that way. For example, the whole scheme to drag in the Jesuit Brotherhood and their roles in the various killings. We immediately set them up as the fall guys. We knew they couldn't resist the opportunity to get their hands on that material you sent out to the research office in Long Beach. The problem started when the Savitz dame got her hands on the pictures. She's too goddamned smart for her own good."

"Are you telling me all the material I sent out there was a fake? That everything was a clever contrivance to fool everyone?" Lynn asked with her mouth open.

"That's right—except, as I said, for the Savitz broad. She smelled a rat, especially in those pictures you sent out to the coast. The only thing that wasn't a fake was the Surratt paper. It gave us the whole idea to start the thing in the first place."

"Well, whose bright idea was it? It has to take someone to start things?" Lynn asked as she squirmed in the chair she was sitting in.

"Bright girl, you go to the front of the class. The original came from that priest, Father McGuire," he answered.

Lynn was stunned. She had had some suspicions about the priest from various comments Tony had made on the phone and in his e-mails.

"That's right, old Father Smoothie himself. He was the one who did the original sales job on me at the outset. He even set up the meeting to assassinate the priests in Dublin to get the Brotherhood stirred up. You see, Ms. Pollard, this Brotherhood is a bona fide group historically, but the good father baited them because of his conviction that something had to happen to start a new American revolution. However, he made one tragic and fatal mistake that we are now desperately trying to correct. This was to misjudge the presence and power of the Mossad. Once their agent was killed by accident in that meeting in Dublin, and two more on the continent, there was no turning back. Basically, matters were out of our control from then on. We came so close and yet so far, and that's the real tragedy." He gazed out the window for a long moment.

"All these killings and suffering because some of you refuse to put your faith in the American legal processes," Lynn answered as she stood and listened to his litany of events that had led to this moment.

"Again, I'm telling you you're missing the point. We've done what we've done because someone has to take the bull by the horns and change the nation's direction. You don't seem to understand that point!" he argued.

"Mr. Kavanaugh, I understand what you're saying but what makes you and your people so scared to share your concerns publicly and so sensitive to criticisms?" she inquired.

"Sometimes there are certain people who have a clearer eye for such things like those we have been talking about. Father McGuire was such a person and he was willing to put his life and reputation on the line to do something about it!" he said curtly.

"And that includes killings, murder and the like? Look, Mr. Kavanaugh, I know there are many things wrong with American society and our system of government, but I fail to see any merit in what you're saying! In fact, unless I'm mistaken, a lot of it sounds like the old dusty Fascistic ideal from the thirties, give me a break!"

"Well, no matter, you've just signed your death warrant! There is no way we can let you live as it now stands. It's a shame, you and your doctor friend could have been a great help in the direction we feel this nation must go to achieve the greatness the founding fathers intended."

There was a sound at the door. Kavanaugh walked over and opened it.

"What the hell's going on out here?" He walked out leaving Lynn by herself. The door closed behind him. There were several short bursts of rapid gunfire followed by a long silence.

Struggling to her feet for the first time in several hours, Lynn raced to the small doorway, kicking it open and raced out unto a shaky old deck. A voice called out close by the door, "Hold it right there or you'll be dead on the spot."

Kavanaugh's guard came around the building where he had been standing. He was about to grab her when Lynn fell to the side and grabbed the railing with her bound hands. Kicking out with her flat shoes and mustering all the strength she could in her slim legs, she caught him front and centre. Her left foot struck him in the groin and the right one just under his chin. There was a sickening crunch as his head snapped back viciously breaking his neck at the third and fourth vertabrae. He fell backwards on the old deck and never moved. One glance told her he was dead. She was shocked at the violence of her judo training. She heard several voices nearby and was gripped by a gnawing fear.

"We'd better get inside and finish that broad off. Kavanaugh says she'll be able to finger us and then the FBI will grab us. Listen, I heard a commotion up front a moment ago and I don't want to take any chances. Kavanaugh says there are a number of those Israeli agents farting about and they're a bunch of bastards." The voice was deep and resonant and echoed as Lynn hurried back inside the grungy building.

Inside there were moments of eerie silence. Then a voice called out, "Christ , George, look out behind you!" A new voice called out behind the wall and a distance away. Lynn looked about the room where she was crouching in a dark corner. Several shots rang outside. Then there was a grunt followed by a loud gasp, followed by the sound of a falling body. She looked about the room. Between her and the door lay the bloody corpse of Frank Baird. His dead eyes were open and stared open at the dirty ceiling.

Chapter 86

Lynn stood by the shattered corpse of Frank Baird in a state of shock. She heard a rustle behind her and a gentle hand at her elbow. Turning she came face to face with the comforting presence of Yigal Burgstein. He took her small hands in his large gnarled one and led her to the old sofa at the side of the room.

"Ms. Pollard, I know it's a shock to see someone you've known all your life lying dead before you. I know, it's happened to me many times! That's been the story of our nation. But you can find the strength within to continue, if you reach deep enough. Where would we be as a people if that wasn't true? Besides, I know how much you mean to Dr. Fleming and his family. In addition, you now have the eternal gratitude of the state of Israel for what you've done. We are a people who remember our friends and stand by their side in times of need." He patted her hands gently as he talked.

She leaned her head against his shoulder and sobbed. Finally after gathering her composure, she asked, "Yigal, can you help me with some of the details of this whole mess?"

"I don't know all that much, but what I do know, I'll gladly share with you," he replied.

She sat up straight and continued. "Yigal, how did this whole matter get started? Every time I think about it, the more complicated it becomes. For example, those pictures I found and then the document signed by Mary Surratt…"

"Everything you found was a fake. It was planted so you would find it and take the appropriate action, which you predictably did. You ran true to your training and did what certain members of the Freedom Party were planning on you to do. These people were Frank Baird and of course, Thurgood Kavanaugh himself. The whole scheme was to drag the Red Rose Brotherhood into the centre for the proposed killings and the like. They performed as it was suspected they would and so found themselves in the middle of a messy international incident, the details they were in the dark about."

Lynn stopped him. "This all sounds logical but was it possible for the Freedom Party to set this whole matter up from the outside?"

"You're right, there is much more to it than that. The plan was to drag the Brotherhood in and set them up as the fall guys and it nearly worked. To a point it did. Baird and Kavanaugh have been friends for decades and much of the planning began with them. They were the source of the materials planted in your office. The pictures were so well doctored that everyone else bought the logical explanation. Everything was in place until two things happened. April Savitz spotted the changes made to the pictures and the discovery of the Surratt paper. Off the record we are convinced the latter is authentic. That in itself is scary and the finger deliberately pointing to the Jesuits as directly involved in the killing of Abraham Lincoln boggles the mind." Yigal paused in his explanation.

"If what you say is true, then how could the contrived plans of the American Freedom Party coincide with this new reality? I just can't get my mind around this point! There has to some sort of a connection that no one has yet to sort out!" Lynn injected.

"You're right, Ms. Pollard, and it gets even scarier when you realize who it was. It only underscores the necessity for vigilance in a democracy. The original idea and plan came from the fertile mind of none other than Father McGuire himself."

Lynn was stunned. Yet she had had her suspicions about the priest from the very beginning.

"That's right. He set us up with the original sales job when in reality he was orchestrating the opposite. You see, Lynn, as you may now well know, this Red Rose Brotherhood is a real historical group of which he was a long-standing member. McGuire's design was to bait them and set up himself as the innocent pawn in the whole process. That worked beautifully."

"I don't understand what he had in mind, or was he just another right-wing fanatic?" she asked.

"That's the interesting thing. It was strictly an oversight that dragged us into the middle of everything. No one realized that one of the priests killed in Dublin was one of our key operatives in Europe. Once he was killed there was no turning back. Our government assumed the Jewish would be hung out to dry and used as a historical scapegoat by the Vatican. There was no way we would ever permit this to happen. The Freedom Party tried to tie matters again and again on the old basis but to no avail!"

As she listened to the soft-spoken soldier, a great weariness swept over

Lynn Pollard. She whispered, "Is it finally over? I don't know if I can cope with any more!"

He placed an arm about her shoulders. "Ms. Pollard, you've carried a load few have had to carry, both in weight and length of time. I can tell you this much. With Baird dead and Kavanaugh out of the way, the Freedom Party will be in disarray and disgraced. Come with me and I'll take you to your family."

As she heard his words, a warmth spread over Lynn.

Chapter 87

Yigal Burgstein and Ariel Feiglin sat in the front seat of the old Ford Taurus a block from Scott Fleming's house where they dropped off Lynn Pollard several hours before.

"You didn't tell her the vice president was still alive?" Feiglin exclaimed shaking his head. "I can't believe you would do such a thing!"

Yigal, an intense dark man in his early forties, sat quietly for a spell before answering. "Have you any idea what the poor woman has been through these past few months?"

Feiglin raised his hands palms upward and fingers in a sign of utter frustration. There was an ugly silence as both men smoked and searched for a solution to a situation growing more desperate by the minute.

"Do you really think Kavanaugh will give up without a fight even now as he sees the final handwriting on the wall for the Freedom Party?" Feiglin quipped sardonically. "If you want my honest opinion, he'll give it one final college try! When I played football at Notre Dame, we always had a Hail Mary play stashed away just whenever we found ourselves in this kind of a desperate situation. Yigal, never forget who these damned Freedom Party types are like. They're only one step away from the goddamned Nazis and the Holocaust. I suggest we move and take him out right now. Besides, he's supposed to be recovering from his wounds from the assassination of the chief justice. We'll simply give him a nudge on his journey and he'll be buried like an American hero. These bastards all have that dream. Let's give him his dream."

Yigal Burgstein drew deeply on his cigarette, shocked by the proposal of one of his country's leading operatives. "Do you realize what you're implying?"

"Yigal, you've known me for the last eleven years. We've never failed to be completely honest with each other! Why are you getting cold feet with someone of Kavanaugh's type? I simply fail to understand. Like I was saying, most of the population of this country will be expecting him to die of his wounds anyhow! And have you noticed one unusual thing in this whole scenario? President Henderson's name never comes up. Here we have a man who has been a part of this clandestine party all behind his chief's back. This is especially nasty when you figure Henderson is the most beloved president in a generation."

Yigal grumbled to himself as he saw the direction of the conversation and the irrefutable logic. Finally, Ariel Fueglin added, "Well, I guess we'll have to turn him loose on the US population as we don't have a clue where he is anyway."

Yigal perked up. "That's not true! Moshe's crew cornered him in his back garage where he still is with his three most devoted guards. That's what I've been upset about. We have no way to attack the garage without taking heavy losses. All our men have are their Uzis!"

Ariel grumped again as he started the old Taurus and roared out into heavy traffic.

Thirty minutes later, they were back in front of the rambly house and garage where Lynn Pollard had been held and Baird shot and killed. Two cars were parked in the driveway.

Ariel jumped from the Taurus and ran over to the outer car. The driver, recognizing his fellow countryman, got out to meet him.

"There's no change, Colonel. They're still inside the garage and accusing us of meddling in US affairs. We've also been accused of a variety of racial matters I'd rather not get into." His voice was cryptic and weary. "We've had them holed up in there for the past twenty-four hours and had to deal with the city police as well."

Ariel took him by the arm and moved him back against the house. "Look, if anyone comes out, put them down and make sure there are no survivors! This could be very dangerous for our nation; these guys are candidates for dead heroes." Reaching into his pocket, he took out three concussion grenades and tossed two through a broken window in the side of the garage. There was a thundering roar followed by a cloud of black smoke. Three men staggered through a broken side door, their arms in the air, coughing and sputtering as they came through. A single volley of shots rang out and all three men collapsed on the dirty lawn.

Ariel, waving the black smoke away so he could see, stepped inside the old garage. A single shot rang out catching him in the right arm. He fell back against the wall.

"You damned Jews never quit, do you!" snapped the raspy voice of a grungy Kavanaugh as he approached through the murky light and swirling smoke, a small but deadly revolver in his right hand. "You think you've won but we've got news for you!" he said with a sneer on his lips.

Suddenly two cracks were heard through the dust and smoke around the garage. Kavanaugh gasped and stepped back. Two red spots appeared on his shirt. He looked down as if not believing he had been shot. Yigal stood a short distance, the revolver in his hand trailing a wisp of smoke. Kavanaugh's revolver rose to shoot despite the glaze in his eyes. Yigal's gun barked again and a large red hole appeared over Kavanaugh's right eye. He stood still for a moment before falling face first to the floor, dead before he hit. There was a deadly silence as the two agents stood overpowered by what they had been a part of and what they had just done.

Chapter 88

Lynn sat quiet and picked at her dinner. Martha looked across at Scott but he held up his finger to his mouth and shook his head. Only the girls seemed to pierce her wall of silence. Little Francie moved her chair as close to Lynn as she could get and laid her head on her lap. She looked up and asked, "Aunt Lynn, why are you mad at us? Are you going to go away as our mummie did a long time ago?" There was a stunned silence about the table as her words cut deep into Lynn and she started to sob into her hands.

"No, sweetie, I'm never going to leave you! I met some nasty people this afternoon and they scared me. And you know what? Your daddy came and picked me up and I've never even thanked him!" As she spoke, she lifted her tear-streaked eyes and looked across the table at Scott with a pleading glance.

There was a long silence. Finally, Scott said quietly, "I want you girls to know that Aunt Lynn has had a very difficult day and we want her to know how much she means to each of us. Someday she may tell us all about it if she wants to but that's up to her. And you girls don't have to worry, she'll never leave us unless we make her very unhappy and we're not going to do that!"

By this time, Angie had joined her sister and pulled her chair up close to Lynn. Scott was about to make a move to stop her but decided they would be the best medicine at such a difficult moment. Martha watched all this without a word and nodded her head towards Scott as she saw the bonding between Lynn and the girls. Martha knew an inner peace she hadn't felt since the girls' mother died.

After dinner, Lynn and the girls disappeared into the library and closed the door behind them. Martha saw the strange look on Scott's face.

"Son, don't be concerned about it! They have serious talking to do and I know Lynn needed the girls as much as they need her. Come out to the kitchen and help me with the dishes. By the time we're finished you'll want time with Lynn and I'll get the girls to bed."

It was over an hour before Lynn and the girls emerged and came out to the kitchen.

"Martha, I'm sorry I wasn't here to give you a hand with the dishes, but the kids and I had some talking to do. Someday I'll tell some of the questions they asked," Lynn commented as she stepped over to the sink to see if there was anything she could do for Martha.

"Look, dear, don't you worry about the dishes. You go and spend some time with Scott. He's in the living room and is feeling pretty down about everything you've been through." As she finished talking, Martha heard a rustle behind her. She turned coming face to face with her son.

Before she could speak, Lynn added, "I want you both to know I can't envision myself not a part of your family. I hope I'm going to be up to the task. That's why I'm seriously thinking of cutting back on my job or quitting altogether—I don't know at this juncture."

"Well, I hope I'll be fitting into this picture somewhere as well!" Scott laughed as he stepped forward and slipped an arm about Lynn's shoulders.

"Well, would you listen to him now? He feels he's going to be left out in the cold," Martha added in a tone only a mother could have gotten away with.

"Oh, come in and sit down, we'll give you all the time you want!" she continued. Scott pulled up a chair and sat across the table from Lynn. Sensing there was a desire for them to be alone, Martha added, "Well, I can take a hint when I see one. You have no time for an old lady! I'll just drift off into the TV room and fall asleep." She laughed as she left the kitchen.

"Come on, Mother, you know you can't wait until you get the TV going and watch it for the rest of the evening!" Scott laughed.

When she had left, Scott and Lynn looked at each other for a long moment in silence. It was the first time they were alone since Lynn got out of the embassy car in front of the house. He reached across the table and held her small hand.

"Lynn, are you all right? I was worried there at the table a while back," he asked

"Scott, I want to apologize for my behaviour at dinner. I'm not usually that quiet. I felt as if I was moving in a trance. Thank God the girls were there to bring me out of it. Kids can be so therapeutic without even being aware of what they're doing. I had to forget myself and think of them. Do you know what they wanted to know? What had they done wrong to make me want to leave!" She started to sob as the words came out.

"Lynn, I'm not very good with words. Give me a scalpel any day! You're not by yourself anymore. Any decision you make from now on involves not only me but two little girls as well! That may be scary, but that's the reality of the situation. You're pivotal person in three other lives, whether you like it or not. I get the impression you're a person who has been on your own for a very long time. Now that's no longer true. And, you know the shocker for you? It's not so much that we need your daily presence but something else— you've found you can't get along without us. That's family, Lynn!"

She was listening to his every word. Suddenly in a few months her life had changed so much.

"Scott, you and your family have given me so much in such a short time. I hope I can give something in return!" As she talked, she saw a smile starting around the edges of his mouth and found herself turning crimson. She giggled and buried her head against his chest as an inner joy and peace swept over her.

Printed in the United States
70594LV00007B/37